A COLD WHISPER

Also by Casey Dunn

Novels

SILENCE ON COLD RIVER

A COLD WHISPER

Casey Dunn

SEVERN HOUSE

First world edition published in Great Britain and the USA in 2025
by Severn House, an imprint of Canongate Books Ltd,
14 High Street, Edinburgh EH1 1TE.

Paperback edition first published in Great Britain and the USA in 2025
by Severn House, an imprint of Canongate Books Ltd.

severnhouse.com

Copyright © Casey Dunn, 2025

Cover and jacket design by Piers Tilbury

All rights reserved including the right of reproduction in whole or in part in any
form. The right of Casey Dunn to be identified as the author of this work has been
asserted in accordance with the Copyright, Designs & Patents Act 1988.

British Library Cataloguing-in-Publication Data
A CIP catalogue record for this title is available from the British Library.

ISBN-13: 978-1-4483-1597-0 (cased)
ISBN-13: 978-1-4483-1808-7 (paper)
ISBN-13: 978-1-4483-1661-8 (e-book)

This is a work of fiction. Names, characters, places and incidents are either the
product of the author's imagination or are used fictitiously. Except where actual
historical events and characters are being described for the storyline of this novel,
all situations in this publication are fictitious and any resemblance to actual persons,
living or dead, business establishments, events or locales is purely coincidental.

No part of this book may be used or reproduced in any manner for the purpose of
training artificial intelligence technologies or systems. This work is reserved from
text and data mining (Article 4(3) Directive (EU) 2019/790).

All Severn House titles are printed on acid-free paper.

Typeset by Palimpsest Book Production
Ltd., Falkirk, Stirlingshire, Scotland.
Printed and bound in Great Britain by
CPI Group (UK) Ltd, Croydon CR0 4YY

The manufacturer's authorised representative in the EU for product safety is
Authorised Rep Compliance Ltd, 71 Lower Baggot Street, Dublin D02 P593
Ireland (arccompliance.com)

Praise for Casey Dunn

"Something far more dangerous than a big, bad wolf inhabits the north Georgia woods. For fans of dark obsession in the tradition of *The Silence of the Lambs*"
Booklist on *Silence on Cold River*

"Dunn makes good use of the perspectives of multiple characters throughout her clever thriller debut. Fans of Lisa Unger will be pleased"
Publishers Weekly on *Silence on Cold River*

"A harrowing, beautifully written journey of dark obsession and redemption that will have you double checking that you locked all your doors"
Julie McElwain, author of the Kendra Donovan mystery series on *Silence on Cold River*

"A melodic and gritty debut thriller that gives readers an unnerving glimpse into the mind of a demented killer"
Christina Kaye, award-winning author of *Like, Father, Like Daughter*, on *Silence on Cold River*

About the author

Casey Dunn was born and raised in Atlanta, Georgia. She is
the author of *Silence on Cold River*, a standalone thriller, and
The Hightower Trilogy, published under pen name Jadie Jones.
The first book in the series won the Best Equine Fiction award
at the 2018 Equus Film Festival in NYC, and was a finalist for
the 2015 Frank Yerby Fiction award. She now lives on a farm
in Southern Oregon with her husband and three children.

www.caseydunnbooks.com

For Sarah,
In case you don't know this yet, I only kept going because you
thought I could, and I was determined not to let you down.

Acknowledgments

The journeys of the characters in this story still make me feel a lot of mixed things. Grief and joy. Love and loneliness. Hope and despair. Rage and relief. Pairs of opposites, yes, but one can't exist quite as vividly without the acknowledgment of the other. Rose, fictional though she may be, taught me a lot about the truth in that, and I am grateful for her. As I am writing this, I realize she's one of the only characters whose last name is never revealed, and while it was unintentional, it suits her and the story in ways that both give and take, and if she was real, I'd like to think that she approves.

There are also many real people to whom I extend my deepest gratitude.

To Shauna, my dearest friend, who literally changed the entire third act of this book with one simple what-if over sushi.

To James, my extraordinary agent, who makes me better and who makes me believe.

To my editors, Sara and Laura, whose brilliance helped elevate and tighten this story in ways I never could've accomplished on my own. And to the entire team at Severn House, who reaffirmed with every step that this story of my heart had found its home.

To Sarah, Heather, Kate, and my momma, who'd never let a girl or a book venture into this world without looking her best. To my children, who celebrate this pursuit of mine so wholeheartedly and joyfully. And to my dad and my husband, two men whose faith in me never wavers.

To Nana, who instilled in me a love of voice, and to Papa, who helped me understand the power of storytelling. It is probably for the best that you two are not earthbound to read the crass language and scandal bespeckling Rose's pages, but I hope you'd forgive me for this just like you forgave that tattoo.

To Katelyn, who answered every awful question at all hours across thousands of miles, and, more importantly, for doing real work to help children heal and thrive. I hope this version is as good as you remember. If so, apologize to Nathan for me.

Thank you all. This would not exist without you.

ONE

Lily – Winter, 1993

Rose had promised snow would fall tonight, which would make the ground glow and hide their tracks when they ran away from this house for good. But an hour had passed since her older sister had slipped through the door of their bedroom to follow Everett down the creaky hall. The world beyond their window was still nothing but a black hole. Lily had never felt so alone.

Wind threw a fistful of frozen rain against the pane in a shock of percussion. She jumped back and stared at the glass. The weather, it would seem, was waging war on Rose's behalf.

Lily held her breath and listened for any hint of what was happening beyond their closed door. Rose often reminded Lily of a ghost more than a living, breathing, fourteen-year-old. Her sister could move without making a sound, could vanish from a room without drawing an eye.

Girls need to be good at disappearing.

That's what their mother had told them the morning she'd left this man for an older one, this town for a better one, this house for a bigger one. *A house so big, you girls will each have a room all your own,* her mother had said. Then she'd spoken to each of them one at a time. She'd looked Lily in the eyes and explained how she just needed to get the rooms ready, their new daddy ready, how those things took time. Then she would come back to fetch them, and they would all live in the new house together.

Lily couldn't fathom how long that might take. In her seven years of living, she'd never had a bed to herself, much less a room of her own. And as for a father, those came and went.

'Time to go.' Rose's raspy whisper filled the room.

Lily whipped round, barely catching a glimpse of her sister

before she closed the door, which snuffed out the glow from the hallway light.

'What if Everett catches us?' Lily asked.

Rose kneeled so they were face to face. The corners of her puffy lips curled up. 'Everett is mean as a snake, but he's not smart and he's not fast. What am I?'

'Tougher than a mule, smart as a fox,' Lily answered quickly.

'What are you?'

'Quicker than a rabbit, quiet as a mouse.'

'That's all we need to get where we're going.' Rose stood and crossed their room to the window.

'Where *are* we going?'

'Tula. I got a car. I hid it on that road on the other side of the woods. It's not that long of a drive to town, and there are back-roads all the way.'

'But you can't drive! You're not old enough!'

'Keep your voice down,' Rose growled. Her bared teeth reminded Lily of the big-headed guard dogs chained to the side of the house.

'What about Everett's dogs?' Lily asked, suddenly hating this plan to run all over again.

'I've been feeding them my dinner all week. They don't bark when they see me now.'

Lily nodded, but she didn't feel any better. What were those dogs going to do when they saw her?

'Get your bag,' Rose said as she scooped hers up from beneath their bed and slung it across one shoulder.

Lily pointed at the window. 'We can't leave yet. There's no snow.'

'I'm going now, with or without you. If I stay here one more night, I swear to God, it's me or him. One of us won't make it to morning.' Rose's fingertips searched beneath the window until she unlocked it, then she pushed it up just wide enough for them to slide through.

Even though the walls of Everett's house hadn't heeded Lily's silent prayers to fall in on him after he'd beaten Rose with the buckle end of a belt last week, she wasn't sure she wanted to trade them for the wet and the cold beyond. But there was nothing she'd trade for Rose, and her sister was squeezing out through the gap.

Lily snatched her backpack and flung herself over the sill, then scrabbled down the siding. Both feet landed in a puddle. Frigid water seeped through her sneakers in an instant. Between the wind and the rain and her feet already courting the sting of numbness, the night itself felt alive and furious. She glanced back up at the window, and an ache of yearning spread a second chill through her small frame.

'Come on.' Rose grabbed her elbow and towed her across the yard.

Lily forced her gaze in front of her and hoped her sister could discern a path through the dark ahead. She knew the dog pen on the side of the house was close. Lily gulped air and held it, determined not to let them hear or smell her breathing. But for all her concentration, she tripped on flat ground, stomping on Rose's heel as she caught herself.

Rose yelped, and a single warning bark was quick to answer.

'It's OK, boys. It's just me,' Rose whispered fiercely. 'I brought something for you.'

Lily clutched at Rose's wrist with her free hand. There was no food in Rose's bag. If they had come to expect sustenance at the sight of her, would they just as soon devour whatever or whoever they could reach? The thought drove her breaths from her lungs too fast, making her light-headed as she waited for Rose to work her alleged magic with Everett's monsters.

Without warning, Rose squeezed Lily's elbow hard enough to hurt, then she bolted forward. Her burst of momentum nearly dragged Lily off her feet and triggered an eruption of barking, which echoed against the house, swelled in the dark, and sent them sprinting into the neighbor's hayfield.

Windblown sleet and the fear of discovery chased them across the soaked earth to the distant road, where frozen rain fell harder in a silver curtain, obscuring what little vision they had. They scrambled down the bank on the other side and darted into a scattering of tall pines, branches sawing and cracking above their heads. Rose glanced back once, twice, and Lily wondered if her sister was about to shake her loose and run.

'Don't leave me,' Lily pleaded.

Rose stopped in her tracks and tightened her grip on Lily's arm. 'Listen to me. If something happens to me, or if we get split up and somebody else finds you first, don't say a word about me. You'll be OK. They can find a better home for one seven-year-old girl. Plenty of people want girls like you.'

'But I want you.'

'I'm just saying *if*.'

Wind and sleet slapped at them from all sides.

'Let's go back. It's scary out here,' Lily whimpered.

Rose stared at her for a long second. She pulled her backpack around to her front and searched through it, then offered Lily a metal thermos. 'Drink this. It'll warm you up.'

'What about your flashlight?'

'No flashlight. We don't want anyone seeing where we are. Just drink up. You'll feel better.'

'Is it . . . magic?'

Rose barked a laugh. 'I guess you could call it that. Helps you do things you wouldn't be able to do without it.'

Headlights illuminated the night. Rose swore, then yanked Lily down to take cover behind a tree. From their hiding place, they watched a car crawl down the middle of the road. When it came close enough, Lily recognized the familiar outline of Everett's hatchback. He must've come looking for Rose again and realized they'd left. She sank deeper, wishing the ground would give way and make a hidey-hole for her for just a little while.

Rose offered her the thermos once more and nodded encouragement. Lily took a swallow. It tasted sweet, sour, and bitter at the same time, like drinking fruit punch after brushing her teeth. Even if it made Rose feel brave, *Rose* was Lily's magic. Her sister was the only reason she felt brave enough to be out here tonight.

As soon as the car rolled out of sight, Rose grabbed Lily's hand, and they sprinted away from the road, veering deeper into the woods. Lily gasped in air through her mouth as they ran. Tiny blades of ice littered every inhale, which bit into her tongue and stung the back of her throat. A roar of wind rolled across them; threatened to tumble her like a wave. It was as if everything in the whole world was determined to tear her and Rose apart.

'We should be right next to the car by now. It has to be so close,' Rose said between breaths. The fear in her voice gave her words wings, thrumming and shivering and quick, and it nested deep within Lily's pounding heart.

'Maybe Mom has the car. Maybe she's ready to get us now and she's out here looking for us,' Lily said, desperate to chase her sister's worry away from them both.

Rose's grip clamped down on Lily's arm, her nails digging in like the jaws of a dog, and she yanked her to a stop.

'She's not, Lily,' she growled at her. 'She is never going to come get us. No one good is looking for us. That's the rule from here on out. Do you remember what I told you before? What to do if we get split up?'

Lily dropped her gaze. 'Not to come look for you.'

'That's right.' Rose traded her grip on Lily's wrist for a gentler hold on both her shoulders. 'Promise me.'

Lily raised her head to glare at the darker place in front of her where her sister had to be. 'But I don't, Rose. I don't!'

'Yes, you do. If we get separated, I will come find you, I promise. Now promise me.' Rose's voice hissed through the dark; moved like a snake.

Lily swallowed hard, fear still coursing through her where blood should be. A gust of icy wind lifted her wet hair from her face, then slapped it back down. She flinched and squeezed her eyelids shut. There was no way out of these woods, this dark, without her sister. She would do everything Rose asked. No matter what it took, she would not be left behind.

'I promise,' she whispered.

'Good. That's good,' Rose said, her voice steadying. 'We're going to have to wait out the storm. There are big trees all around us. We just need to find one with a lot of branches. If we sit right up against the trunk, it'll be like an umbrella. We'll wait there and keep each other warm until morning. When the sun rises, I'll know where we are. I'll know where to go.'

Lily grabbed blindly in front of her. Her fingertips lit upon the back of Rose's wet jacket. She trapped the fabric in a pinch, then allowed Rose to tow her forward. She lost all sense of balance and direction, up and down, forward and backward, left and right all feeling the same. Wind howled in a chorus, deafening and otherworldly, and she imagined each roar of air unhinging an invisible jaw, revealing clear, razor-sharp teeth.

Maybe she'd been wrong back in their room when she believed this storm had come to help Rose. It felt like they were under attack, the night lashing at them, punishing them for leaving. Lily would fight back against the night, if she could. Be fierce and tough like Rose, yet there was only darkness in front of them. She wondered if they had gone so far that they'd not just left Coyote Creek, Tennessee, but crossed into a different world all together.

'I think I see a good tree,' Rose called over her shoulder as she turned hard to the left before jumping forward. Lily's feet crossed, and she nearly stumbled again, every step weighed down by helplessness and fatigue. Tears left hot trails down her stinging face. She clamped her lips together. She would not let Rose hear her cry again.

Without warning, Rose stopped and crouched, pulling Lily nearly on top of her. Above them, swaying, shifting branches sent crackling notes skyward, reminding her of the sounds of a fire.

'Here,' Rose said on an exhale. 'We'll be safe here.' Her hand found Lily's arm once more. Between the dizziness and the blur of tears, Lily could barely make out Rose's face, but she was close enough to feel the warmth of her breath.

'You have to let me go,' Rose said.

'No,' Lily blurted.

'Yes, Lily. I need to duck to fit here. I don't want to hit you with a branch. There will be plenty of space for both of us closer to the trunk. I'll sit right up against the tree, then you can sit in my lap.'

Hesitation swelled in Lily's chest, leaving no room for breath.

'Let me go,' Rose said, firmer this time. 'Just give me a little room, then follow me under.'

Lily opened her hand, and her sister slipped from her grasp. She let one full second pass, then tiptoed behind her, her stare tracking Rose's form, a solid black in a sea of dark. Lily's heart thundered, her pulse like a second storm, until she heard the nylon scratch of Rose sinking to the ground with her back pressed to the bark.

'OK. I found a good spot to sit. I'm reaching up. Follow my voice and hold your hands out. You'll find me,' Rose said.

Lily's trembling, searching fingers met Rose's. She grabbed hold of them and lowered herself into her sister's wet, crisscrossed lap, then curled in a tight ball to keep herself from shaking. Freezing rain and gale-force winds thrashed the canopy of branches overhead, multiplying the sounds, but she felt them both less.

'See, it's better under here. Drink a little more. It'll help, too,' Rose said, and Lily felt the hard metal of Rose's thermos as her sister bumped it against her front.

'I don't want any more. It doesn't taste good.'

'That's not the point. It'll warm you up and help you sleep.'

Lily sat up and took another dutiful sip of Rose's magic drink. She could only hope her sister was more right about its effects than she'd been about Everett's dogs or the location of the car.

'More, Lily. The faster you fall asleep, the faster morning will come,' Rose insisted.

Lily felt the added pressure of Rose's touch on the thermos, and a slug of juice flooded her mouth, nearly choking her. Lily dutifully forced it down. Her mind began to swim, and her head became too heavy. She pushed the thermos away and curled sideways between Rose's knees, using her thigh as a pillow.

'Will you sing the sister song to me?' Lily asked.

'I don't feel like singing. It's a stupid song. I don't even remember the words.'

'You have to remember it. You made it up for me.' Lily begged. 'Please. Sing it one more time. Just the whisper sister part. I promise I'll be quiet all night.'

Rose slid her hands under Lily's armpits. Then she pulled her up and held her against her chest. Lily pressed her ear to her sister, listened to her steady heartbeat, and waited.

At last, Rose began to sing, her tone solid and soft, the sound of it barely there and everywhere all at once. 'Whisper, sister, no matter how far. Whisper, sister, no matter how dark. Just whisper, sister, that's all you have to do. I'll come running home to you.'

Lily clung to the familiar refrain as the rest of the world dissolved all around her, black cotton candy in the rain. Rose shifted beneath her, then draped her own jacket across Lily's back, and when Rose began the song again, Lily's mind climbed aboard Rose's voice and sailed away.

TWO

Lily – February 6, 2018

L ily steered her car into the turn lane and approached the green traffic light in front of the Walmart at the south end of Tula. This light was notoriously short, and she was going to make it.

Her focus caught on a girl standing in the middle of the concrete median dividing directions of traffic at the intersection. Lily watched her lean a skateboard against the ripped knees of her gray jeans, then mash the button for the pedestrian signal.

Look up, Lily mentally called out to her.

The girl let her skateboard drop to its wheels on the pedestrian ramp leading to the crosswalk and adjusted her earbuds. She cast her gaze down the traffic coming straight on, which was still stopped for people turning from the opposite side, but she didn't yet have the light. Without looking back the other way, she stepped both feet on to her board and rolled into the road right in front of Lily.

Lily stomped her brakes and braced herself against her seat. She knew she had enough room to stop, but the driver behind her had been riding the bumper of her Honda Civic in his super duty truck for a couple blocks. All she could do was hope he was paying attention.

The driver behind her laid on his horn, his truck tires screeching as they slid across the asphalt, still wet with overnight rain. At the blare of the horn, the girl jumped off her board, scooped it up in one hand, and dashed across the street. Lily glanced at the traffic light in time to watch it turn red, then stared up at her mirror to the reflection of the truck stopped on an angle behind her.

Relief pricked her everywhere at once, making her hot and cold at the same time. In the mirror, she met the gaze of the other driver and wondered if he felt the same. He caught her looking and threw his hands up. Then he opened his mouth in the shape of a shout, like a grown man's temper tantrum could make Lily and her car disappear. She rolled her eyes. He wasn't the first person to consider her presence the last thing standing between where he was and where he wanted to be.

Lily plucked her phone off the dashboard mount, thumbed open two weather apps, then toggled between the predictive radar forecasts, comparing the patterns. The temperature had declined steadily over the past four days, and a storm system was marching toward Tennessee's border, leaving a white trail.

Her fellow social workers at Tula's Department of Child and Family Services would see a blizzard in the forecast and expect a lull. Lily knew better, and it wasn't just because of Rose. Ten years on the job had shown her how easy other kids thought it was to run away under a cover of white. Someone always went missing, and no one else in her department seemed willing to notice the trend. Pattern recognition was a blessing and a curse, something her childhood therapist had suggested was a product of hypervigilance. Of trauma. Of Rose.

Heading into college, Lily had originally wanted to become a psychiatrist, double majoring in psychology and chemistry in hopes of better understanding the why-factor behind people's decisions and how they become patterned behaviors, then how all those behaviors connect and collide. She knew what she was really looking for: the pattern that could explain why people she loved left her and never came back. She would do anything to understand what circumstances would have left Rose with no choice but to leave.

Along the way, she couldn't help but notice historical patterns for whom doctors were more likely to recommend surgical procedures for psychological symptoms (women), the threshold that had to be met for performing them at all (low), and how many complications could occur while still considering the operation a success (extensive). That combination had never been truer than when lobotomies were used to address disorders from insomnia to schizophrenia and everything in between.

Even though treatment options had become less extreme, Lily couldn't ignore that as a psychiatrist, her ability to reach people would be limited to those who were already suffering to the point that it affected their lives and had decided they needed help or had the good fortune of someone else who could see that they needed it. She'd wrestled with this gap, held it down, turned it over, searching for an answer she wasn't sure existed. Then, in her junior year, she'd finally recognized what she'd been desperate to figure out how to do: become someone who could have talked Rose out of leaving. To be the reason someone stayed.

At last, the light turned green again. Lily pulled into the shopping center parking lot and found a spot on the back row. It was one of the few open spaces, the giant lot nearly full of people preparing for the coming snow. The truck blasted by her, honking a few times for good measure, then accelerated down another row. She stared after him, chasing him with her thoughts. She hoped he got home without causing an accident. She hoped he didn't have children. Men like that either wrecked them or made them run.

She wasn't yet sure what had made Andrew Cross run. The fourteen-year-old had been recently declared a ward of the state, his case overseen by Lily's coworker, Katelyn Boyce. As of that morning, he'd also officially been declared a missing person. When Katelyn had asked for help finding him before the snow hit, Lily had jumped at the chance.

The driver's seat of Lily's car had become a well-worn second office. She turned up the heat on the dashboard, then reviewed the list she'd compiled of last known addresses and places he was known to frequent, which were all close to Walmart, making it a good place to get her plan organized and her mind right. After mapping her route, she retrieved her phone and scrolled through the pictures Katelyn had sent her of Andrew, hunting details.

Every time he'd been photographed in the past few months, he was wearing a silver puffer jacket that swallowed his lanky frame. She searched back farther on his social media pages. That past July, he'd worn the same coat slung open over a sleeveless undershirt and gym shorts. It obviously meant something to him beyond his favorite way to keep out the cold, and Lily would bet it had been handed down to him by an older sibling.

Old grief pricked her in the heart. She breathed in and out, counting slowly until she regained control of what she felt and what she didn't. Then she met her gaze in the rearview mirror once more, squaring with herself. She'd decided years ago that this pain was a gift, and she reminded herself of it now. It was the last thing Rose ever gave her, and it had made her very good at locating older children who did not want to be found.

Ten minutes later, she pulled into the housing complex Andrew still listed as his primary address even though what remained of his biological family no longer lived there. The two-story brick building was built in a horseshoe shape around a courtyard, which was decorated with empty folding chairs, a brown corduroy couch, and a patio umbrella, its pole held upright in a bucket. Several older boys leaned against an exterior wall.

She parked her car along the curb and climbed out. Tension swelled in the air the moment they spotted her arrival. One boy shifted from foot to foot. Another rustled his hands in pockets. The third slid his gaze, feigning indifference like she wasn't even worth noticing. Andrew was not among them.

Lily continued her approach anyway and caught sight of a familiar face: Josh Marsden, a fifteen-year-old ward of the state who'd been dubbed Houdini by her office before he'd turned nine.

'Shouldn't y'all be in school?' she called out.

The two boys she didn't know looked everywhere but in her direction.

Josh grinned straight at her and pointed to the bright gray sky. 'They canceled it.'

'Yeah, no.' Lily stuck her hand inside her coat pocket. 'I can call you a ride. You'll at least make a couple classes.'

Josh sucked his teeth. 'Come on, Miss Lily. Don't do me like that.'

'Katelyn's already called a BOLO in for you.' Lily didn't know this with certainty, but Katelyn, Josh's case worker, still played strictly by the rules even after two years on the job, so the chance was good.

'Nobody's going to find me,' he retorted.

'I did.'

'You don't count.'

'I don't know how to take that.'

'Take it how you want to.'

'I'm looking for somebody else. You tell me where to find him, and I'm going to be too busy to tell anyone where you are. But if you don't, well, this is the last stop on my list, and I'd have nothing else to do but make your day hard,' she lied.

'Who are you looking for?'

'Andrew Cross.'

'I haven't seen that kid in a minute,' Josh replied.

Lily held his gaze and flapped her hand in her pocket.

'I'm not lying to you, Miss Lily.'

'I saw him,' an older boy to Josh's left said.

'When?'

'Yesterday. He was at the mall. He came out that door they use when the mall is closed but the movie theater is still open. Some other boys came out behind him. He started running, and they chased him behind the building. I didn't see him after that.'

'You didn't go see if he was OK?' Lily asked.

'Wasn't my deal,' he said. 'He's always rubbing people the wrong way anyhow, running his mouth, flashing that jacket around like he's legit. That fool can't even dance. You ever seen him?' The boy put his hands up in two fists at ear level, then bounced his knees. The other boy broke into a grin, but Josh's expression became serious.

'There are paths back there, Miss Lily. They go just about anywhere you need to get to. The corner store, Brecken Park, school. If he went that way, no telling where he went from there. But if he got caught, I'd bet they took his jacket. Maybe pawned it,' Josh offered. 'Does that count?'

'Yeah, thanks.' Lily turned to leave.

'What about for me?' the older boy called at her back.

Lily glanced at him over her shoulder. Frost gathered on her heart for this boy who could not be bothered to help another in need. 'You're not my deal,' she said.

It was a ten-minute drive from the apartment complex to the mall, and Lily arrived to find a nearly empty parking lot. Calling the row of stores a mall was a stretch. There was a place for wigs and fake eyelashes, a video-game shop, a dollar store, a discount-shoe store, a shop selling sports-themed jackets and hats, a car rental dealership, and an Applebee's, all kept afloat in part by the movie theater that capped one end of the sagging plaza.

Dumpsters lined the back of the building. Broken-down card-board boxes and empty pallets rested against the concrete walls. Save a few birds ransacking the Applebee's dumpster, the back of the mall was just as quiet. A flash of silver winked from the shadows beneath the big metal bin. It was the sleeve of a jacket, the stitching in tatters where it should connect to the shoulder. Lily draped it over one arm and held it close. Then she peered into the trees until she spotted the mouth of a skinny footpath. In her mind, the tall pines on either side yawned closer, and the shadows between them thickened into a palpable darkness.

'You're OK,' she whispered to herself. Then she cast her gaze skyward and held it there until the seven-year-old child within her was convinced no snow would soon fall. More importantly, someone might be in there that needed her, and she would not leave without him. She dropped her stare to the path, ignored her pounding heart, and walked into the woods.

Memories of Rose and the night they ran knocked against the door of her mind and nipped at her heels. Lily shut her out and strode faster, swinging her gaze in every direction. She would not look for the sun, would not remember how it had set that snow-covered forest aglow when it broke through the morning fog and found her alone at the base of a tree.

A high, abandoned trestle was visible through the naked branches, the landmark of a clearing on the north edge of Brecken Park that local kids called No Man's Land. What the area under the old train bridge lacked in vegetation, it made up for in junk, withering and wasting all the same.

'Andrew?' she called out. 'Mars sent me to check on you,' she added, using Josh's nickname in case Andrew was within earshot.

No one answered, but she felt the sensation of someone watching, prickles rising on the base of her neck. It was probably in her head, she reasoned, a product of how badly she wanted to find this child before the snow hit.

'Andrew, if you can hear me, I have part of your jacket. Just the sleeve. I'm sorry I don't have the whole thing.'

The boy from Katelyn's pictures emerged from the shadow of a pillar, hugging the silver coat to his front. One eye was swollen and deep purple. He wore a different jacket, olive green and canvas, something a person might buy out of a farming or hunting catalog.

'Who are you?'

'My name is Lily. I'm a social worker.'

He backed away from her, returning to the cover of the dark.

'I can fix your jacket,' Lily continued without physically moving forward. 'I like to sew. I can fix it tonight and bring it back to you tomorrow, if you don't want to leave here.'

'I just don't want to go back where I was.'

'OK.'

'OK?'

'Yeah. If you don't want to be somewhere, I hear that. We can look at options. It's not limited to whatever house you were assigned to or the bridge.'

'Like a detention center,' he countered, bitterness lacing his voice.

'You've only been in one home, right? The first placement is hard as hell. I know. I ran from mine, too,' she lied.

The truth was the opposite. She'd been placed with a young couple on the outskirts of Tula. She had refused to leave her first foster home, a tidy, if not spartan, manufactured home on a tiny lot just outside town, for weeks. When at last she did, it was because she was being carried to the car by her social worker after those foster parents had decided she'd needed more psychological support than they knew how to give.

'Everything is different there,' he murmured.

'Honestly, it's never going to be the same,' Lily replied. 'Maybe it'll be better, maybe not. But the *same* – that's all gone now. You have control here, though. Not much. But a little. You can tell me one thing that will make it feel the slightest bit familiar, and I will do everything I can to find a home with at least that piece.'

'I don't have any idea what that would be.'

'You don't have to know right now. But when you think of it, will you let me know?'

'I guess.'

'I'll leave you be, then. Do you want me to take your jacket with me?'

He stepped back into the light, then hesitated. 'You're not going to make me come with you?'

'I'm not your case worker. I'm not your mom. I'm not a cop. I can't make you do anything. Honest to goodness, I don't even have my phone on me.'

He inhaled long and slow, then handed Lily his most prized possession. She could feel the utter shift between them as he leaned into the space she'd made.

'Y'all soccer moms be out here like fairy godmothers.' The corner of his mouth pulled back in amusement. 'I got this redneck jacket from another lady yesterday. I guess she saw what happened at the mall.' He raised his fingertips to his darkened eye. 'She showed up just like you did, brought me a jacket and some food from Applebee's. Told me to hang tight, that she'd be back in the morning, but she didn't come.'

The wind picked up, blowing trash across the clammy earth and leaving a slick of moisture on her face. Lily was running out of time.

'You know what, you should probably keep both jackets if you're going to stay here. It's supposed to get really cold tonight, worse than last night. You can use this one as a blanket or a pillow at least. I'll come back tomorrow and bring my sewing kit. I'll sit right here and fix it.' She offered him back his silver jacket, but it was as if she'd raised a blade instead, and he put both his hands in the air.

'You said you would fix it tonight.'

'I want to, and I will fix it. But I can't take it from you tonight. The weather that's coming . . . I know what that kind of cold feels like. Trust me.'

For one moment, Lily stared unabashedly at him and let this boy she did not know peer through her eyes to the seven-year-old girl who still lived inside her, mother unfit and in the wind, birth father unknown. The seven-year-old girl who was found wandering alone in the snow by a woman walking her dog the morning after she and Rose had escaped with nothing but a frozen pink coat and a blood alcohol score high enough to down a grown man. Rose was never found at all.

'That house Miss Katelyn took me to is full of cats,' Andrew blurted, a child's quiver in his voice. 'The whole house smells like their litter box, and it's like I can't breathe. They leave hair everywhere, and it sticks to my clothes. The kids talk shit about it at school, call me dirty, and I swear to you I'm not. I'm not dirty.'

'I had no idea that you're allergic to cats.' Lily frowned. 'That was nowhere in your file, and I read it cover to cover this morning before I started looking for you.'

He stared at her for a beat, his lips gapped. 'I'm not allergic to cats,' he finally said.

'You can be. All I have to do is make a note of it. And with your jacket and your eye, we can come up with a story about why you weren't able to make it home. Let me sort this out for you.'

'Why are you doing this?'

'Why wouldn't I?' Lily replied. What she wanted to tell him was that she treated every runaway like she hoped someone had treated her sister, that here and now she imagined, for just a moment, that Rose had been chased through the woods, had hid somewhere like this old bridge, and was found by someone who meant her well. That she was driven far from Coyote Creek, Tennessee, that she had started over, and maybe now she was a soccer mom who brought meals to homeless kids and had spare coats in her minivan. That she was happy. That she had yet to figure out how to walk up to Lily and tell her that she'd chosen helping other people over coming back to her, whatever her reason. That the ache Lily felt in her absence was somehow the cost of Rose's good life.

Obviously, it hurt. And if she was being honest, it drove her nearly insane. But if somehow she could be sure it was true, Lily could live with that.

THREE

Daniel – February 6, 2018

When Daniel was growing up, his mother swore crime rates rose in the summer. Muttered Spanish prayers would fill their kitchen as she made dinner, pausing every few minutes to peer out of the street-facing window, watching for Daniel's older half-brother to come home.

Statistically speaking, she was right. Summer, bright with color and high with passion, was almost an invitation to do something rash, something regrettable. Summer flings, summer jobs, summer trips. They were meant to be fleeting, to change, to end.

Winter seemed to have the opposite effect, giving people every reason to stay home and reconsider. If someone went outside to kill another person, they'd meant it. They'd thought about it at least long enough to put on a coat and shoes before starting out their door.

What was done in winter was meant to last.

'Any available units near the top end of Tula proper?' an operator's voice came through the scanner on the cruiser dashboard. Daniel, the newest homicide detective with the Tula PD, leaned forward. He was currently in the passenger seat of a squad car on the opposite end of Tula, a city of 200,000 northeast of Nashville that had grown rapidly in recent years.

Daniel stole a glimpse at the driver, Senior Detective Hunter Kepp, wondering if he'd seen him nearly grab the radio. If he did, he didn't say anything. It was a fifty-fifty shot as to whether Hunter either hadn't noticed or was doing his best to pretend he was alone in the car. Hunter wasn't just Daniel's temporary partner and department trainer. He was also his half-brother.

While Daniel, at forty years old, was just beginning his career in homicide, Hunter was within three months of retiring at fifty;

silver hair, tired eyes, and a tremor in his hands all parting gifts of over two decades served in narcotics and homicide. One scarred wrist draped over the steering wheel. His other hand guided a cigarette from between his lips.

'I've got an incoming call from Sirens with reports of an alleged theft leading to a physical altercation; caller is a customer requesting police support,' the operator continued.

Humor hooked a corner of Daniel's mouth. 'Fist fight at a strip club at ten a.m. on a Tuesday. Classy.'

Hunter snatched the radio. 'Unit nine-two-four responding. I'm close,' he lied.

'Do you want back-up?' another voice came through the radio.

'No. I got it,' Hunter replied, then resettled.

Daniel glanced at his brother's face, his own expression a question mark.

'Sorry,' Hunter muttered. 'It's been more than twenty years since I had a partner.'

'What's at Sirens?'

Hunter gripped the wheel with both hands, weaving in and out of traffic. 'A friend.'

Sirens, a two-story gentleman's club, had recently undergone an extensive remodel. Its new exterior was framed with huge, raw wooden beams. Piles of quartz boulders were stacked against the corners of the building. Palm trees grew in oversized glass displays, bathing in the glow of copper lights above. It was a far cry from the crumbling, apologetic building Daniel remembered from the week he'd spent camped in the parking lot two years ago, logging the moves of a suspect in a drug ring. A month later, ownership transferred and demolition promptly began, and the narcotics operation had become little more than a box on a shelf.

Now, the new interior of Sirens was a dearth of strip club stereotypes. The main area was brilliantly lit, and the glow from dozens of crystal chandeliers and spotlights refracted off a white marble floor. To the right, several women swayed on an elevated walkway, which looped around a large oval water tank. More topless girls swam inside. A clear stage floated at its center with a microphone and a bejeweled throne, where a half-naked woman crooned a haunting song to the audience. The human aquarium was ringed with tables and men. It was a quiet group, no hooting and calling. Mouths nursed drinks. Stares latched on rolling curves and gliding limbs.

On the opposite side of the main area, the white floor gave way to actual sand, which stretched into the far corner and was topped with several lines of canvas cabanas, their flapped doors tied shut. A large tiki-hut-style bar claimed the center of the room. The counter, bar stools, shelving, roof, and the bartender's bikini top were all white. The seats were mostly empty, the real crowd gathered near the water tank. Neither scene presented like the stage for a recent battery.

The bartender saw them walking her way and lifted her chin in greeting. A second woman leaned over the corner of the bar. Ink-black curls spilled down her back, and her feet arched unnaturally inside clear high heels. The woman swung her head and pursed her scarlet lips, her expression shifting in a thousand micro movements like the world's most subtle kaleidoscope. She settled on a look somehow both pleased and pissed, then batted her dark eyes at Hunter.

This must be the friend, Daniel decided.

'What brings you here this morning, Detective?' she asked.

'Cut the shit,' Hunter said, then lowered his voice. 'Aren't you a little old for this?'

'That's quite a welcome, Kepp. It's been, what, twenty years? Is that really all you have to say to me?' She leaned closer to Hunter, neck disappearing between her bare shoulders, big eyes looming up. 'Time has been good to you, too, by the way,' she practically purred. Everything about her reminded Daniel of a cat on a hunt, crouched and ready to spring.

A door in the back slammed open, drawing every eye.

'Are you the cops?' a man shouted across the space as he emerged. He was a sweating, flushed bear of a man. He wiped beneath his nose as he advanced toward them. Another man hurried to follow behind him. He was half the size of the first guy and, with his crisp button-down and moussed hair, too pretty for a recent fist fight.

'We are,' Daniel answered, glancing briefly at his brother.

The smaller guy raised a hand and walked faster, nearly breaking into a jog. 'I'm Easton Grimes, the new manager here.

It seems we have a—' he started, but the bigger man stepped in front of him and blocked him with an outstretched arm.

'That bitch went through my wallet,' he interjected and raised a shaking finger at Hunter's friend. 'She robbed me, and everybody in this toilet bowl is in on it.'

'Is there somewhere we can sit for a formal statement?' Daniel asked Easton.

'We're not there yet,' Hunter announced, waving him off, then refocused on the man. 'Do you have proof?'

'She left this in there.' He pulled a card out of his pants pocket and handed it to Hunter. It was a business card for a Baptist church down the road.

Now that the man was within an arm's reach of them, Daniel could see that what he'd wiped from beneath his nose was a smear of blood. A fresh red dribble was gathering on his upper lip.

'Should we show them what you left on me?' The woman held up her wrist, where someone's grip had made a hand-shaped red place. There were scars there, too. Thin, straight lines striped the fleshy place of her forearm.

Daniel looked from her to Hunter. His gaze caught on his brother's upper arms, veiled beneath a sweater, where similar pale scars made a roadmap through his darkest hours.

'That's no way to treat a lady,' she added.

'You think you can be a lady and work somewhere like this? You're just a—'

'Probably need to stop that train of thought right where it sits or this is not going to go how you're hoping,' Hunter spoke over him, a cold calm frosting his voice.

Daniel tensed, then eased his focus to his brother's face, taking stock of Hunter's stony expression. The protective reaction this woman evoked from his brother was so out of character it was as if he'd been replaced by a stranger.

Hunter caught him looking.

Daniel cleared his throat and diverted his gaze to the man with the bloody nose. 'What's your name, sir?' he asked, trying to regain control of something. Anything.

'Do I have to give you that?'

'Yes.'

'Todd Camps,' the woman interjected. 'That's his name.' Then she smiled.

Hunter snorted.

Easton looked at the ceiling as if he was seeking the chandeliers for counsel in the same way one might cast a prayer among stars.

'How is she going to know my name if she hasn't looked in my wallet?' Todd asked, waving emphatically.

'It's no more illegal for me to look at your wallet than it is for you to fall asleep on a stripper,' she sniped at him. 'You paid for a half hour. You fell asleep. I got bored. You paid for my time and expertise, and I gave you what I think you really need. Jesus.'

Daniel let out a hard breath. He had barely slept last night, his mind a storm of hopes and fears for what his first official day on homicide might bring. But he hadn't seen this shitshow coming.

'You spiked my drink!' Todd snarled at the woman.

New interest hooked Hunter's features. 'Now that *would* be a serious crime. Let's take you down to the hospital, get some blood pulled before it's too late to detect anything. Do you have someone we can call to meet you there? Your boss? A friend? Your wife?' He nodded at Todd's wedding band.

Todd made two loose fists and pressed his knuckles against his slacks, hiding the ring from view. 'You're treating me like the criminal here. She punched me in the face. Doesn't that matter?'

'Of course it matters. It looks like she broke your nose. The doctors will set it for you right after they pull blood. Do you want to press charges? We can go file straight after you're done at the hospital,' Hunter offered. 'If you need to be anywhere else today, you should probably call and let them know you won't be coming. This will take a few hours. Maybe all day.'

'I just want you to arrest her. I don't want my name anywhere near this.'

'I can't do that right now unless you want to press charges. This could turn into a big deal, a big case, especially if she's been doing this a lot, like you insinuated when we first arrived. You'd be a key witness.'

Todd became still, his face turning redder by the second. 'This isn't over,' he finally said, then stalked away from the bar and out of the door to the jeers of the men gathered nearby.

'What was that?' Daniel asked Hunter once the spectators had dispersed, trading the impromptu show for what they'd come to see.

'Just saving our department some paperwork and our taxpayers some hard-earned money,' Hunter countered.

Daniel stole a glimpse at Hunter's so-called friend. She was staring at the ceiling, ruby lips gapped apart, the end of her tongue pressed against her crooked teeth.

'So, you run this place now, Easton?' Hunter asked.

'He *owns* the place,' the woman corrected him. 'Fixed it up all nice and classy for his ladies.'

'I fixed it up all nice and classy for customers and their money,' Easton replied curtly. 'I know Todd Camps can be difficult, but he is also a well-paying regular. Whatever that was all about, it never happens again.'

'I'll keep my religion to myself from now on, no matter how hard the boys beg,' she replied with a wink.

'Call me directly if you need something handled in the future,' Hunter said and handed Easton his card.

'I appreciate that.' Easton managed a tight smile as he slipped the card in his pocket. 'Officers, can I interest you in a round of drinks on the house?'

'All due respect, Mr Grimes, but we're on the clock. That's not something we can do,' Daniel said with an uneasy laugh, then cast a glance at his brother.

'I'll take a raincheck. I've had the coffee here before, and it's too early for anything else,' Hunter replied.

Daniel stared at him for a solid second before he realized his mouth had fallen open. He didn't know what surprised him more – that his brother had refused the drink because of time of day and not commitment to duty, or because Hunter had basically insinuated that he would be coming back.

'Fair enough,' Easton replied. 'If there's nothing else that you need from me or that I can do for you, please excuse me. And, Betty, you're supposed to be off the floor and my clock,' Easton said, directing his attention to Hunter's friend, then he hustled to the door at the back of the room.

Betty placed both hands on the counter. Her shoulders sagged with a sudden crush of invisible weight. Daniel didn't hear her sigh, but a puff of warm vapor appeared in the space between her thumbs.

'You OK . . . Betty?' Hunter asked her.

Daniel couldn't stop himself from peering at his brother. This was his first call on homicide and his first shift training alongside him, learning from the best in Tula's homicide department. This day should have belonged to them. Today could be the cornerstone for the foundation of the rest of his career. It should mean something. But the only firsts that seemed to matter now were between his brother and this stripper, who Hunter had both stood up for and comforted. Maybe he should be grateful that Betty had revealed that his brother could care for someone besides himself, but he damn sure didn't feel that way.

'Yeah,' she said, then let out a bitter laugh. 'Every surface in this place is brand spanking new, but I swear it's old times in here all over again.'

'I've heard as much,' Hunter mumbled.

Daniel leaned in, his gaze toggling between them. What the hell were they talking about? He drew a breath, determined to assert himself, to ask the question out loud, but the words wouldn't leave him.

'Did you take anything out of Todd's wallet?' Hunter asked.

'I didn't *take* anything. Just looked around. Read a few numbers.' She shot Daniel a smirk.

'Talk about old times,' Hunter replied, and a grin animated one side of his face.

Daniel could only stare, dumbfounded. Of all the moods he'd ever seen settle on his brother, playful had never been one of them until now. Neither had apathy. If anything, his brother had been accused of caring too much about each investigation for his entire career. Now, this woman was dangling pieces of a confession in front of Hunter, begging him to bite, and he was *smiling*.

'Betty, I'm Detective Daniel Wilder. I'm with homicide now,' Daniel interjected and felt a subconscious swell in his chest, as if he was trying to convince himself that he was big enough to fit the title. He'd thought today would make him feel like he'd arrived, like an equal to the brother he'd been chasing his whole life. But so far all he felt was unnecessary.

Betty arched a brow. 'Really, now?'

'Leave it alone.' Hunter's voice came from a tired place, and Daniel shrank.

'Are you glad to see me, H?' Betty asked and finally loosed the grip of her stare on Daniel to bat her lashes at Hunter.

'I don't know yet.' Hunter rested a fingertip on the back of her hand. 'How long do you plan to stick around?'

'I don't know yet,' she echoed.

Then Hunter turned away and walked to the exit without another word for her or so much as a glance back for Daniel.

FOUR

Betty – February 6, 2018

There's a difference between keeping things to yourself and telling a lie, and you can't tell me otherwise. I'm a lot of things, but I'm not a liar. Not when it really counts, anyway. I can't say the same for Detective Hunter Kepp, and as far as I'm concerned, the jury's still out on the scruples of his pint-sized half-brother. I'd only ever heard of him before meeting him this morning, a name in a handful of stories Hunter told me about his childhood back when we were all younger, a face I'd made up in my head to suit the part. I couldn't help noticing how he barely said a word to anyone. It's unsettling. Quiet cats are on the hunt.

For better or for worse, Hunter says what he needs to say when he needs to say it to get done what he needs doing, plain and simple. He's better at it than he used to be, not that it matters. When you have a badge, you don't have to lie well. You just have to commit to the story. I may not have a badge, but when I'm in dire need of a story, I'm committed as they come. I've been calling myself Betty for about a month now.

I picked this newest name while crossing Kansas, the flattest fucking place I've ever seen. It was like driving in a photograph. I'd started to wonder how real everything really was. If maybe I was just pretending to exist. Or maybe someone else's imagination had put me together for a little while and here I was. Hour after hour, mile after mile, every moment exactly the same as the one before it.

Believe it or not, strip clubs are a lot like that. In the twenty years since I first left Tula, I've traded town for town, name for name, bar for bar, coast to coast, lasting a season at a stop at the most. Different stages, different themes, different dress codes, all of them set to the same whomping two-count beat like the speaker is thrusting its invisible hips in your ear. And every town, every bar, every time, it still amazes me how eager people are to step aboard a show of money like it's a magic carpet, never considering the cost of making something fly that has no business in the air.

Coming back here will cost me, no doubt about it, and staying here might very well bleed me dry. But not returning to Tula came with a bigger price. I owe a debt to a dead girl who doesn't even know she handed me the bill.

Six days ago, she and I were slipping out of a hotel bed at a casino in St Louis, Missouri, creeping quiet as mice even though the big-screen TV was blaring on the wall across the room. The man who'd paid us to climb in it with him was out cold, lying flat on his back, mouth hanging open and arms flung wide. Of all the privileges he had on me, the ability to sleep like that – exposed, vulnerable, and dead to the world – was what I'd envied most.

He'd found us standing on either side of him at the blackjack table downstairs an hour earlier. The other girl was half my age and twice as pretty, and I had already started scouting a new mark to target when I felt his sweaty hand latch around my bare waist. He was grinning at the other girl, too, his opposite arm draped around her shoulders. I guess he was already so far gone he didn't care much about the details, just satisfied by the fact that we were both within reach.

She and I were gathering our clothes off the floor when a commercial for Sirens popped up on the pay-per-view porn channel he'd been watching. The other girl nodded at the screen while she wriggled into a swath of grape-colored spandex masquerading as a dress.

Do you know anything about that place? I heard the money is crazy good there, she asked me like we might have known each other outside of that room, shared more than sweat, skin, spit, and sheets.

I knew she had a tattoo of a dove on the inside of her thigh.

I knew she waxed off every stitch of body hair.

I knew her tits had yet to nurse a baby.

I knew she had so many bruises on her back that an astronomer might be tempted to name new constellations upon sight.

But I couldn't tell you her name.

Why would I know about it? I kept my eyes on the front of my corset while I laced it up in case my face told on me. I'd seen the contact information and the Tula address flashing at the bottom of the screen, a city whose streets I knew more intimately than the man unconscious in the bed.

You sound southern, and it looks like you've been around a while, she said with a wink as we snuck out of the room and headed for the elevator. *My little sister works there. She said they were treating her good, and the owner is nice. Buys her stuff,* she added.

Sounds like she landed soft, I gave her, if only because it would've felt crueler to not say anything at all. And the truth – that a commercial for a strip club hundreds of miles away advertising VIP packages, special member perks, exclusive dancers, and invitations to yacht parties was some Epstein shit on a corporate level if ever I'd seen it – was just too damn hard to say.

She said they were talking about transferring her to another bar the guy owns in Miami, a place called Palm Tree Express. He thinks her look will bank big down there.

Worse places to winter.

She hasn't answered her phone or called me back in a couple weeks. We used to talk every day. Her dark eyes flicked up at me then, two black pits of knowing.

I had to look away.

The address provided for Sirens on the commercial had once been The Alibi, the kind of grimy, sticky, sad topless bar you absolutely did not want to see with the lights on. But I damn near called it home for two years. I'd walked into The Alibi at seventeen after a particularly unfriendly week on the streets, hungry, wet, cold, and tired of being all three. They'd hired me on the spot, never asking for my ID, which was good because I didn't have one. Working there was the first time I'd made a real living. It was also the first place that ever really, truly tried to kill me. I wasn't the first. And apparently, I might not be the last, either.

Same address. New name. Same shit.

Some things never change.

No, that's not true. Good things never last. But bad things – the worst of things – they don't go anywhere.

You could go check on her. It's not a bad drive, I'd said. Hell, it could be a day trip there and back if you had a reliable car, a bladder of steel, 60mg of Adderall, and no respect for tomorrow.

I'm going to head that way as soon as I can. Just stacking paper for the road. She'd winked at me again, then pressed the button for the elevator.

When the door opened, a man in an Armani suit and crocodile shoes stepped out. The girl arched her neck and batted her eyes; ran manicured nails through her elbow-length hair. Her stare lingered on each piece of evidence that he enjoyed spending too much money on pretty things.

I was looking at his hands, his scraped knuckles, how the skin on either side of them was bruised. I grabbed her arm without even thinking about it, every hair on my body standing on end. He took notice of my hand around her wrist, smirked, and latched on to her other forearm.

We're supposed to be downstairs now. We don't want to be late, I'd said, hoping he'd think we had a handler waiting on us, maybe a short-tempered pimp who might not want their girls marked up so early in the day.

She'd giggled, waving me off. *I don't even know her. But I'd like to get to know you.*

He'd tugged her close, and she threw a glance my way, her expression a silent plea for me to shut up, to trust that she knew what she was doing.

I let her go.

I stepped into the elevator. Through the closing doors, I watched them walk away. When the doors were an inch from meeting, I threw my hand into the tiny space, and they sprang back open. I slunk out of the elevator and to the closest corner, where most of the hall was visible, then waited to see what room he took her to.

I don't know why I cared. I'd known this girl for an hour, tops. Maybe it was because she made me think of who I could've been if my worst crimes were selling my body and other people's identities. I could call my sister. I could drive straight to Tula and knock on her door. But none of that is true for me.

After they'd disappeared inside a room, I tiptoed to the door, ready to knock. A playful squeal of her laughter came through the wall between us. I backed away, unsure, then bolted for the noise and chaos of the casino where I could drown out the roar of my memories while deciding how committed I was to my second week of sobriety.

As I passed through the lobby, I made a phone call to the only person I knew in Tula who knew how to mine information from darker places without leaving a trace to see if I could have an answer for the other girl about her sister, save her the trip, lessen her need to make more money faster. But Hunter Kepp didn't answer, and I didn't leave a message. Hunter had also been the one person I'd trusted the last time I lived in Tula, and it damn near got me killed. What can I say? Better the devil you know.

Twenty-year-old memories chased me to the nearest bar, and the next thing I knew, I was sitting on a stool with a gin and tonic sweating between my hands. I watched beads roll down the glass like raindrops on a windowpane, and my heart ran a limping race in my chest.

A man's hand found my bare shoulder. I painted on a pout before turning around, every curve of me arching on instinct, Pavlov's dog to a bell, submission damn near as necessary for survival in this line of work as food in a bowl for anybody else. The guy was puppy-dog-young, hair cut like he'd just come off a military tour, and in a suit that looked like it had just come off the showroom hanger.

Buy you a drink? he asked.

I have one.

I don't think you like it. I've been watching you for a minute, and you haven't drunk a drop.

Then how would I know if I like it or not? I volleyed, toying with him.

He blushed. I looked away, removing the pressure of my gaze so I didn't scare him off completely. Across the casino floor, the door to the lobby stood empty. Then the man from the elevator filled it, smoothing out the front of his Armani jacket as he strode in alone.

I checked the time on my phone. It was just after ten a.m. Then I opened my call history. It had been twelve minutes since I'd dialed Hunter.

No one was that fast.

I stood up from the bar stool.

Hey, where are you going? The guy touched the inside of my elbow.

Get lost, I snarled at him, then swung my gaze until I found the man who'd taken the other girl to a room. He was looking right back at me.

I raised my phone to take a picture, and he bolted toward the service door on the other side of the space. I got two blurry shots of his side and back, then raced for the elevator. It couldn't climb fast enough.

When the doors dinged open on the floor where I'd left them, a woman's scream echoed down the hall and into the elevator. I ran around the corner to the room. The door stood ajar, blocked open by a cleaning lady's cart, which she was trying to shove back into the hall, but a tire was caught on the frame.

Beyond her, I saw the girl. Her long hair spilled over the foot of the bed. Blood-tinged saliva had leaked out of the corner of her mouth, the trail still fresh enough to glisten. Her eyes, half-hooded by slack lids, stared right at me.

Oh my God. Oh my God, the cleaning lady kept repeating to herself. Then she caught sight of me. *Is this your room? I just opened the door. I found her like this. I knocked. I . . . I'm just here to freshen the room. Oh my God. Do you . . . do you know her?* she asked.

I should've shaken my head, not said a word, but my own

name came out of my mouth. My real name. It was the first time I'd said it in twenty years.

Rose. The woman echoed me, said it again, then she burst into tears. *I . . . I need to call . . . She needs help. I can't go in there. The phone is in there. I'll go get help. Stay here with her.*

She raced down the hall, still pushing the cart like she didn't know how to let it go. As soon as she was out of sight, I got the hell out of there.

It took five minutes for me to walk to my car, six hours to get to Tula, and about ten minutes to convince Easton Grimes that I was worth hiring. Since then, I've spent every spare minute asking around about that girl's sister. So far, no one will even admit she might exist.

The irony is not lost on me.

My sister has come close to tracking me down a handful of times. Once in a truck-stop strip joint on a stretch of road in unincorporated Wyoming about ten years after I left town, then seven years ago in New Orleans, and, most recently, four years ago about an hour outside of Seattle. She calls around before she makes the trip, asks too many questions of people who'd rather give a stranger a kidney than a straight answer about one of their own. Shoots her search efforts in the proverbial foot every time. There's a litany of unspoken ethics among colleagues in the skin business, and I get a heads-up while she gets the runaround. If ever she actually got in her car and came looking, I was already long gone.

I can only hope the last place she'll look for me now is right under her nose. Above all else, I cannot let her catch me here. I can't face her, and I sure as hell can't let her see what I've become.

Someone who trades up every chance she gets, who will sacrifice anything, no matter how permanent, at the altar of relief, no matter how temporary. I can admit that I am a collector of names, histories, friendships, and promises in the same way that a gambling man amasses poker chips. We're both just waiting to cash them in.

Our mother. That's what I've become.

Somewhere along the way, I've also become begrudgingly sympathetic toward her demons. How loud and fast the inside of a person's head can be. How a few pills or drinks can make it so quiet; can make you forget. How a man's attention can make for a stepping stone. How fast the sweet relief of a new start can go sour. How addictive it is to believe the next do-over will be the last. How, above all else, you have to do whatever it takes to survive the day, over and over, because no one is coming to save you. Maybe worst of all, how easy it is to leave.

God, you're just like me, she'd said to me the last morning I saw her leave for work. She had been gathering up her things, her movements twitchy and grabby and fast. Then she'd whipped round; stared right at me. *We ruin things, girls like us. We don't mean to. It's just our nature. You ruined things between Everett and me. How am I supposed to compete for a man's attention with you in the house? You don't mean it, though. You can't help who you are. If you love something, stay away from it. That's what you do when you care about someone and you're no good for them.* Those are the last words she said to me, then she walked out of Everett's front door.

In the twenty-five years since that moment, I've learned that while my mother was wrong about a lot of things, there was some truth to that. Staying gone can be an act of love. Then again, that's probably just a lie people like me tell ourselves so we can feel better about the shitty things we do to the ones closest to us.

And the things we keep from them. Nobody, not even Lily, knows about my worst crime, and I intend it to stay that way.

Maybe that's why I really came back. Not to check on a dead girl's little sister, but to see if, in being willing to do so, I could finally feel like I've proved my mother wrong. That sounds just fucking like me.

Sirens has had a facelift akin to identity theft since I last set foot in it nearly twenty years ago. From what I've gathered in the five days since I started working here again, the lion's share of the changes happened after Easton Grimes took over. Customers see the fresh paint, the gleaming marble floor, and the sugar-white sand, and they think the cleansing must be mirrored in the blood and guts of this place. But it's fucking septic. I haven't seen it yet, but I can smell it with every breath.

As for the girl's little sister, she's not here. At least not that I can tell. Without a face or a name, I don't have much to go on, and I'm not going to make many friends by asking if anyone has an older sister who turns tricks in Missouri that they haven't felt like calling back. I'm in a hurry, but I'm not desperate, which is for the best. Desperate me is prone to do some really dumb shit.

If I can't find her or a shred of hard proof soon, I'll ask for a transfer to Miami and see what happens, snoop around down there if they let me go. Hell, maybe I'm wrong, and that dead girl's sister really was happily relocated to a swanky bar down there and is on a beach right now, laying in the sun on a pile of money while I stand here and fret over nothing. But I doubt it.

Easton's creation of Siren's VIP club is, hands down, the most suspicious renovation of what was once The Alibi. VIP members don't pay door fees. They drink top shelf for the price of house liquor. They enjoy a roped-off section with hand-picked attendants, their own entrance and exit, a guarded, underground parking lot, and are invited on exclusive trips to Easton's other properties and party boats, which are literal dots marked on privately held islands and offshore yachts that anyone with a moral compass and a badge could draw a line between as clear and straight as the trafficking pipeline I suspect runs out of this place. So, yes, when Todd Camps came in all hot and bothered about being invited to interview for VIP, I had to try my luck.

I lean against the bar in the center of Sirens and finish totaling my receipts before balancing them against the cash tucked in my belt. While the automatic calculator in my head runs the numbers without much deliberate thought, another part of my brain stares at the pearl-white sand, mesmerized by the way the lights from the hanging chandeliers make single grains wink back. In the last moments that I saw the dead girl alive, she'd reminded me of a piece of glass – breakable, transparent, and light. As she and I had stood there in front of that elevator, surrounded by ways out on all sides, I knew what he was. I knew she would come out shattered. And I let her go with him anyway.

I left her.

I hope Lily has learned that people can be more dangerous to be left with than darkness and snow, but I hope she got to learn it the easy way, if there is such a thing.

I hope one day I become someone who doesn't leave people behind. That one day I'll look in the mirror and not see our mother staring right back at me. Returning to Tula for more than a day is like taking the first step, and something I would bet my mother never did. But that's the thing. Lily can't know I'm here unless this town becomes somewhere I can stay. And I can't stay until Sirens' doors are nailed shut for good.

The first time I stumbled through the front door at The Alibi, it had been three years since I'd left Everett's. It was the first room I'd walked into in my life where everyone in the place looked at me like I was something good, like I'd done something right just by showing up. They treated me like family – my definition of which, I realize now, meant little more than a loyalty to a pattern of reliable transactions and a keen awareness that only one side held the leverage, and that it was never me.

Still, working at The Alibi seemed safer than being homeless. I had a bed, food, access to the bar as long as I promised not to get sloppy, cash in my pocket, and a steady supply of any drug I wanted. I knew of a few other teenage girls who'd been roaming the streets on their own for years same as me, sleeping on a pile of mildewed blankets in a back corner of vacant buildings same as me, turning tricks and stealing shit and scavenging through trash piles like dogs same as me. So I told them to come work there, too. Told them it was their best chance. That our luck had changed. That it was a way out.

They listened. They came. And for a while, we had the world on a string. Extra favors started, extra shifts, extra places. We were kept so busy, so high, I wouldn't see a few of them for days or weeks at a time. Before long I stopped seeing them at all.

Then I found the basement.

It was the only door I hadn't been allowed through in the building. It was the only place I had left to look. And on a Monday morning in the dead of winter, someone had forgotten to shut it all the way. Behind it was a staircase to a hall that was more like a tunnel, checkered on both sides with closet-sized rooms only big enough for a mattress and a bucket, and the doors only locked from the outside. I recognized one girl as someone who'd followed me there. She was gaunt, hollowed out, and the kind of pale from shit nutrition and lack of sunlight that turns a person gray. When I called out to her, she looked at me like she had no idea who I was.

I'd tried to do something about it.

I'd believed I was grown enough.

I'd believed that when I helped expose what they were doing, Hunter would do whatever it took to back me up and shut them down.

I was wrong. Dead fucking wrong.

Now, I feel pretty damn sure something is still going on at Sirens, whether or not it has anything to do with a dead girl's lost little sister. Even with all the glitz, glam, and bright lighting, this place has the same dank, desperate feel as the basement of The Alibi. Hell, the commercial I'd seen in Missouri practically spelled it out. But there's no trace of it inside these walls that I can find. It's rooted here though. I'm going to find it. When I do, I won't give it to Hunter or another badge. I'll find a way to send the story and the proof to every news station and paper in town, let the court of public opinion burn it all down if the legal system won't. I'll be free to go, and maybe then this place and those girls won't haunt me. Maybe I'll even be free to stay and face the living.

This time, I'm acutely aware of how alone I am and how much better it is to work that way. How smart it is to be scared shitless from the start. At almost forty years old, I'm beyond the average expiration date for marketability in both my line of work and my lot in life. I'm on borrowed time and I know it, and I'm not leaving this hellhole of a world without taking a few fellow demons with me.

I bundle my receipts, sort my cash, and head to the employee door at the back of the business. As open as the main floor is, the back of the building is a labyrinth of crowded, small rooms with coded doors between most of them. This is where money is stored, employee belongings are stowed, cameras are monitored, and Easton's office is located, tucked in a small room at the center of it all like a rotten heart. The basement is totally cleared out now, converted to a private parking garage for VIP guests. What other business hides the customers it's most proud to have?

I slow my pace when I move through a cluttered storage room, one of the only rooms you don't need a code to pass through. Its corners are stacked with boxes and plastic bins from what was here before the renovation. When I have time to kill, I rifle through them looking for a clue or a commodity like a kid on a treasure hunt. Just yesterday, I found a waterproof Carhartt jacket that came in handy for somebody who had to spend the night somewhere even shittier than the motel I've paid to suffer the likes of for the month, and that's saying something.

My first shift here, I spotted a white hooded cashmere trench coat stuffed into the top of a trash bag headed for the dumpster. The fit is a little snug, the belt is missing, the liner is an egregious shade of purple, and there's a frayed spot in one corner of the right-hand pocket. But I couldn't give two shits. I'm a little worse for wear myself.

After I stamp my timecard, I make my way to Easton's office door, then pause with my hand poised to knock, and listen. He's not alone. I hover an ear where the door meets the frame, but the voices are too muffled to distinguish anything useful.

Without warning, the knob turns, and the door pulls in, revealing Easton's shoulder and the side of his face.

'Hey, boss,' I announce, my voice so bright and loud that I hate myself. 'Here's my close-out.'

He takes it from me, then steps through the door and moves to shut it behind him. Toward the bottom of the closing gap, I spy a purple backpack and the toes of a pair of Converse sneakers, which are decorated with what appears to be Sharpie doodles. My belly turns to stone.

'Thank you for how you handled the police this morning,' Easton says quietly. 'You're clearly a pro, but that's not all good. I run a tight ship. Either get on board or move on. Plenty of girls want your spot. And whatever the reason Todd Camps fell asleep in your presence this morning, it never happens again.'

I force a smile. I didn't steal shit from Todd Camps. Maybe ten years ago I would've been after his credit-card numbers, identity information, or money, but this morning, I used his sleeping face to open his iPhone, then scoured every text message, email, and item in his search history for any private correspondence with Sirens. Anything that will give me the right words to use, the right questions to ask, a place to start, a foot to jam open the proverbial door to the VIP club and whatever world lies beneath it. I only opened his wallet long enough to stick in one of the business cards for the Baptist church I'd grabbed off the front desk at the motel.

Once upon a time, I used a similar system to let Hunter know who I was working on. Now, I just wanted a way to make sure Todd Camps and others like him knew I'd been there. That I'd gotten the best of them. That someone was watching. With any luck or logic, he'd be too paranoid to come back here. Best-case scenario, he tells all his like-minded friends not to come back, too.

'I'll be good. I promise. No more naps for customers. Anything you need, you just ask.' I throw in a wink.

'Thank you. Go home. Now.'

'I don't have one of those, but I have a room at the extended-stay motel on the south end of town and a king size bed.' I bite my lip. 'Room nine. Just in case you're curious,' I add.

Then I stride for the exit like I don't have a care in the world. As the daylight hits me, I become nothing but a silhouette, and for that one fleeting moment, my insides and my outsides feel like they match.

FIVE

Daniel – February 6, 2018

Hunter's car smelled like an ashtray. Daniel cracked a window despite the cold. His brother glanced briefly at him, brought his cigarette to his lips, and pulled another drag.

From his peripheral vision, Daniel took stock of his brother's profile and wondered what he was thinking. They were as different as two siblings could be. They shared neither last names nor the boxes they checked when asked for their ethnicities. Daniel had spent most of his childhood trying to convince his classmates that he and Hunter were related at all. Hunter had been no help there, offering only a smirk and a single raised eyebrow whenever

Daniel had begged him to confirm their bond to disbelieving friends.

They had been raised within the same walls but in different worlds – Hunter yearning for a father he didn't know and missing a mother who worked double shifts six days a week to keep the rent paid and the fridge full. By the time Daniel was born, their mother had married Daniel's father, who had insisted she stay at home and raise her boys. Finally, Hunter had nearly everything he'd craved, and it became the last thing he wanted. He'd found reasons to stay out more, studying at friends, dates with girls, extra shifts at work, coming home less and less, later and later.

Maybe they were alike in that sense, though. Daniel's father had been attentive nearly to a fault. He coached his Little League teams, volunteered to help in his classrooms, taught him how to tie his shoes and his ties. And all Daniel had wanted was Hunter.

A voice crackled on the radio. 'All units, be advised to be on the lookout for Josh Marsden. Black male, age fifteen. Five feet, eight inches tall, medium build, dark skin, brown eyes, short black hair, last seen yesterday wearing a Brooklyn Nets jacket and Nike track pants. Lives in a group home at fifteen Berkley Road. Last seen yesterday morning. Criminal history. No warrants.'

'He's wearing a Nets jacket. We should check the basketball court at Brecken Park,' Daniel said.

'You wore that Pippin jersey nonstop for like a month when you were in fourth grade, and you couldn't even dribble.'

Daniel swallowed a response and kept the truth to himself. He had practiced for hours after school every day that year, waiting for Hunter to come home. He'd been desperate for his brother to see how he could stand at the edge of the driveway with his back to the goal, then spin and shoot and mostly make it, a trick shot his father had taught him in secret so he could surprise Hunter. With every shot, he would daydream that his big brother would materialize behind him somewhere, linger at the edge of visibility, and watch Daniel without him ever knowing, silent and proud. It was only now that Daniel realized he had still held on to the hope that Hunter had seen him from afar, even just once. Now he knew otherwise.

Hunter made a U-turn at the light and sped north, away from Brecken Park.

'Look, homicide is a different animal. We don't drop everything we're doing to chase runaway kids with a sheet unless they have something to do with a body in the morgue with our names on it. The rest of the police department is here for the living. There are a dozen units on patrol in this city. Let them go check the park. We're the only ones who put the dead at the top of our list. Keep them there.'

'You dropped everything for a reunion with a stripper who allegedly drugged a man and basically admitted to stealing his credit-card information. Do you call that keeping the dead at the top of the list? How do you even know her? Who is she?' Daniel argued.

'She's an old friend, OK? She got a pass this morning. That's true. But that's all it was. The point is, unless Todd Camps shows up dead, those kinds of crimes have nothing to do with us, Danny. Sometimes there's bigger shit at play, and you have to leave well enough alone.'

'What does that even mean?' Daniel's voice rose. He hated how quickly he could be made to feel like a child in his brother's presence.

Hunter wheeled the car into the station parking lot, then came to a stop alongside the main door.

'You're done for the day,' he said.

Daniel stared straight ahead. 'No, I'm not.'

'You're making this about you, and it's not. That line of thinking will hurt your cases. It'll tank your career. This isn't a punishment, Danny. It's a favor.'

'I didn't ask for one,' Danny volleyed.

'First days of anything are hard. They're never what you expect them to be,' Hunter continued as if he hadn't heard him. 'Go home. Get your head straight. Next body is yours, so be ready.'

'That's a morbid thing to anticipate.'

'It's not the body we wake up for. It's the ghost. See you tomorrow,' Hunter said.

Daniel had no idea how to respond to that sentiment. To the day. To any of it. Without a word, he climbed out, shut the door, and watched Hunter drive away.

SIX

Rose – February 6, 2018

I sit in the back seat of my car at Sirens and watch the employee exit for Converse sneakers and a purple backpack. There's no way Easton is going to let them walk right out the front door. I've parked myself in the one spot in the right-hand corner of the lot where I can see the back door through the metal web of a chain-link fence, and where Easton's new security cameras won't catch me in their frames.

During my quick-and-dirty interview in his office six days ago, he caught me squinting at the security screens as I memorized where the frames began and ended. He'd assumed I was high, a presumption I helped along with a quick swipe to my nose, a sharp, messy inhale, and yo-yoing eyelids. You've got to be subtle with that shit or you might look like you're either faking it, or that you're too fried and too far gone for people to pay much to use the rest of you up. It's an art, really. Chew on that as long as it takes to become something you can swallow.

The door opens. I sink lower and peer at what's visible of the employee area between the two front seats and over the top of my dashboard. A girl and a boy emerge, both in jeans and dark hoodies, each with a backpack slung over a single shoulder. They tilt their heads together and share a whisper. The girl is wearing the Converse sneakers I saw in Easton's office, and the boy is wearing a pair of black-and-white Nikes. If they're old enough to drive, I'd be stunned. They're smiling as if they can't believe their luck, and they bump their fists together. If I was a betting girl, I'd say Easton made them an offer or gave them the best kind of news.

I make bets every chance I get.

Still, there's more to whatever's going on here. Trafficking happens in plain sight all the time, but Easton seemed distracted and uneasy when he came out of his office. Something about this very wrong situation doesn't feel quite right.

They walk in hurried steps across the parking lot, hoods pulled over their heads as if that's all the disguise they need to not look like they're somewhere they don't belong. I wiggle into the front seat, start my car, and roll toward the road, tracking their path to see where they go next. I have no idea how to handle this, what I might say to them if given the chance. What I do know is how they're feeling right now if they believe they've just been handed a golden ticket. I also know how they'll feel if a stranger pulls up and says it's a one-way pass to hell.

The two kids reach the sidewalk and turn right. The road ahead of them slopes down in a long, slow hill, broken up by traffic lights at damn near every block. I hang back, regaining a sense of patience. I'll be able to watch them for a solid quarter mile from this vantage point.

Before the first intersection, they duck beneath a bus shelter and drop their bags on an empty silver bench. Sirens is the only open business on this face of the block. Back when it was The Alibi, people raised a stink about a titty bar so close to middle-class living, which had grown up around the bar as an upper-crust flight out of Memphis decided they would 'fix' the top end of Tula to their liking. The sudden growth priced everyone who'd been there for generations out of their homes and opportunities for employment. It's hard to work a line at a factory when the big, metal, chilly building where you make your living is bought and turned into an 'industrial chic' mixed-use high-end apartment complex.

No one seems to complain about Sirens. The outside doesn't disclose the purpose of what happens inside the walls, and I would bet a lot of the wealthy men who live nearby aren't genuinely sad about the proximity, especially with the solid fencing shielding the view of the customer parking lot from the road, and an exit alley that puts them out between two shopping centers on another street.

Still, regardless of the reason these two kids wound up inside the bar, Easton wouldn't want them plunked down just outside of it. I pull into traffic and accelerate to the bus loading area, then stop and roll down my passenger window.

'Hey,' I call out, leaning over the console so they can see me plain as day. But they pretend they don't hear or see me. It's the first smart thing I've seen them do.

'I work for Easton Grimes,' I say, raising my voice. 'You're important to him. He doesn't want God and everyone else to see you get picked up on a bus right in front of a strip club. Or maybe you don't know how that might look, what might happen if the wrong people see you sitting here. Get in. I'll take you where you need to go.' My own words make me feel sick because I know they'll work.

'Oh yeah, what's my name then?' the boy asks, narrowing his eyes. It's cute. Nearly admirable.

'No names, Nike,' I say. 'But I'm going to give you code names, OK? You know yours. And you, you're Lyric,' I say, spying a couple patches on her backpack for Stevie Nicks and Dave Matthews Band. 'Easton figured if you came to a strip club on a school day, you probably didn't ask permission from whoever you answer to first. These buses are all outfitted with cameras, and he doesn't want to make any trouble for you or him.'

I'm making it up as I go. This is how most fortune tellers do it, taking a tiny piece of possible evidence or an unwittingly exposed detail and running with it. It's what I did for a season when I tried to trade the skin business for a tarot deck and a crystal ball. Believe it or not, there are more similarities than differences in the two industries. But fortune telling felt a hell of a lot more intimate than dancing topless for a crowd or riding the laps of strangers, and I only lasted three months before exchanging a velvet-covered card table for another silver pole.

'What's your name?' Lyric asks. She fidgets with the purple-tipped ends of her hair.

'Today, Betty. Tomorrow, who knows?'

They exchange a glance.

'I can call Easton if you want me to.' I present them with my newest burner phone. I don't know the new number for the club by heart, and if they call my bluff, I'm going to have to dial the traffic channel or something.

'Bus isn't going to be here for a half hour anyway, and it's freezing out here,' the girl says to Nike.

'Where would you take us?' Nike asks, standing.

'Wherever you need to go.'

They look at each other again.

'Brecken Park?' Lyric suggests, then gives him a sly smile like she's guaranteed them safety by naming somewhere public, and Nike nods along.

A few hours from now, the park wouldn't be the worst choice, the basketball courts filled with kids. But at this time of day, the only kids that would be there shouldn't be. They'd have to give themselves up to make themselves known, jump in and help, were it needed. So many of us want to believe we'd sacrifice ourselves for the sake of someone else. I have to wonder if that sentiment is not only to prop up our own altruism but to feel safer among strangers. Of course I'd help you. Of course you'd help me. It's a lie more times than it's not, but it's beautiful.

'I can do that,' I say. I want to take her by the shoulders and shake her, tell her that the moment she gets inside my limping four-door, I could lock the doors and take them wherever I want. But I need them in the car right now more than I need her to stand a chance of surviving the next time someone offers her a ride.

Sometimes the truth is the ugliest thing in the world.

They climb in the car and sit side by side with the boy in the middle, the girl on the passenger side, and I wonder if he's anchored himself between us as a physical barrier. I hope his stalwart nature survives as long as he does, but survival itself is a greedy, thieving bitch.

It will take about twenty minutes to get to the park in this traffic, plenty of time to bait a hook and do a little fishing. Any decent fisherman will tell you that the first thing to do once you pick a spot is to sit by the shore and let the fish get used to your presence before you ever cast a line. I have never once hooked a worm and tossed it into water to meet a fate of either drowning or being eaten alive, but I have slept with two competitive fishermen, who fuck completely different but fish exactly the same.

So, I wait.

SEVEN

Lily – February 6, 2018

The walk back to Lily's car was quiet. She let Andrew lead. This was his choice, his path, and if he made a break for it, she wouldn't give chase.

She'd learned a long time ago that it was better to let people go their own way. Forcing someone's hand or mind or feet was just another way to lie to yourself, and above everything else, Lily preferred the truth.

When someone shows you their true colors, don't repaint them. That's what her long-term foster mother had told her when she discovered pictures Lily had drawn of her mother and Rose, happy and healthy and together. *You can want this with every dream and every beat of your heart, but you can't want it enough to make them want it too.*

Lily never drew them again.

But her foster mother's words had resonated deeply in other ways, and she began painting in earnest – capturing moments in time she couldn't stand the possibility of one day forgetting.

Here and now, she stole a mental snapshot of Andrew walking ahead of her, light winking through the canopy of branches overhead and landing on him with every step. Maybe tonight she'd paint this moment for him, a reminder that he chose to walk out of a winter wood that gladly would have kept him.

They reached Lily's car. As she unlocked the door, she looked up to catch Andrew backing a few steps away from the other side, clutching the jacket to his front, head bowed.

'Are you OK?' she asked.

'Where are you going to take me?' His helplessness was palpable.

She hesitated. She could take him home with her, which would give her more time to find a good fit for a better chance of a long-term placement. But she was still holding out hope of making it out of town to her cabin for a night away, and it was the one place she wasn't yet willing to share with anyone.

'As far as where you'll stay, I'm going to make some calls. For now, I can bring you back to DFACS or we can call Katelyn,' she offered.

Andrew hung his head. His twiggy frame shook with cold.

Lily felt herself soften, thaw. 'Or you can stay with me for the day, and we'll figure out the rest later. I have some errands to run. My car isn't fancy, but the heater works well.'

'I'll hang with you, if that's OK.'

'Yep.' Lily stole a glimpse at his face. She had never met this boy before, and she knew she should probably exercise more caution about letting perfect strangers into her car, but Andrew was taking just as big a risk as she was. Plus, she had a can of wasp spray within easy reach of the driver's seat – all the burn to the eyes of pepper spray with none of the noxious cloud filling the car – just in case.

'Where do you want me to sit?' Andrew asked.

'Wherever you'll be more comfortable. I have a blanket and a pillow in the back. There should be a couple flavors of Gatorade, too.'

'Seems like you knew I'd come with you.' Andrew's voice was barely a whisper, and his brow crushed down over his eyes.

'That stuff is in my car all the time. You aren't the first kid to think running away was your best way to stay safe, and to be fair, you aren't necessarily wrong. Sometimes alone is the safest option. I didn't know what you would choose, but I hoped you would come with me. You can tell me to pull over and get out of my car whenever you want.'

Andrew studied her for several seconds, then opened the back door and gathered the supplies she'd tossed into the seat this morning. He glanced at her again as he shut the back and opened the front, then situated himself in the passenger seat. Lily hid a smile. Whenever a kid chose to come with her, it felt like a win. But when they opted for closer proximity, she knew she was truly doing her job.

They wound their way out of the mall parking lot, Andrew

already fighting sleep. With every passing moment, his blinks became longer, and he swayed back and forth in his seat.

'You can take a nap,' Lily said.

'I'm not tired.'

'OK.'

The boy fell asleep before he'd even warmed up enough to stop shaking.

At the next traffic light, Lily sneaked another glimpse at him. The blanket he'd pulled up to his chest had slipped to his lap. Carefully, she retrieved a corner and drew it across his front, tucking it in where his arm was pressed to the chairback.

Rose had done the exact same thing the night she left. Lily had woken up that morning with Rose's jacket tucked tightly around her legs and waist, sealing out the snow. Her sister had cared enough to forfeit her own jacket and cover Lily up, a paradox to a sister who could also walk away and not come back. A sister who, only hours before, had made her promise to never come look.

Lily had kept her word for years, believing that Rose would one day keep hers. As a child, sometimes she would think she'd spotted her face in a crowd at the mall or the park, and she'd squeeze her eyes shut, hold her breath, her whole body vibrating with the thrill of knowing that Rose had at last come back for her. She would count down from ten, anticipating the feel of Rose's arms, how she would squeal and laugh as her big sister swung her in the air. *See, I never looked!* she would say. But each time, she would reach zero without the feel of Rose's hands or the too-sweet scent of her cherry lip balm or her gravelly whisper warming her ear, no matter how slow she'd counted. Lily would flutter her eyes open, and the face she'd thought she'd seen would be gone.

As she got older, she would sometimes spot a face through a windshield and her heart would leap in her chest, an unbidden knowing pulsing through her veins. She'd tailed more cars than she cared to admit, followed more brunette heads through crowds than any sane person should, and she'd finally admitted it to her therapist.

Is there any commonality between the sightings? her therapist had asked. *Maybe where you're seeing her, a color, a time of day . . . a time of year.*

When it snows, Lily had whispered. *I see her when it snows.*

Together, they'd decided it was more likely that she was imagining Rose than spotting her in the flesh. Then, ten years ago, a timid, barely there knock on Lily's door one winter night sent her dashing across her apartment. *Rose,* she thought. *Rose, Rose, Rose.* But it was their mother. Lily had stared at her, blinking, unbreathing, and squaring with two painful truths: how she would rather Rose had been the one standing in front of her, and how easy her home address must have been to find for anyone interested in looking.

Her mother had offered to take her out to dinner and answer any questions Lily had. They'd gone for Italian, a place with white tablecloths and a crackling fireplace in the center of the floor. As they waited for the main course to arrive, her mother said that she was sorry, that she was sober, that she was here to stay.

Have you ever seen her? Lily had finally asked.

Who?

Rose. She'd had to choke it out. She hadn't said her name out loud in years.

Once. She didn't want anything to do with me, though. She has a hard heart, that one. Can't forgive. Not like you. She'd smiled, then pushed the dessert menu toward Lily.

She'd dutifully taken it in trembling hands.

When? she'd asked. *Where?*

Here, her mother had said. *I don't remember when. Not all that long ago, I don't think. Last year or the year before. There was snow on the ground. I admit it took me a second to recognize her, but she wouldn't even acknowledge me. Do you two not see much of each other?*

No, she'd whispered. For the rest of the meal, Lily couldn't speak, couldn't eat. Despite the fireplace and her coat and the thermostat no doubt set to an ideal temperature, Lily couldn't stop shaking. She had never been so cold.

Everything changed that night. Her mother, with a little help, had started a new life, just as she'd promised. Lily unequivocally and immediately broke hers, beginning an internet search for her sister the moment she dropped off her mother and filing a new missing person's report at the police station first thing the next morning.

Cold crept up on Lily from the inside out. She blinked the haze of the past away and glanced up at her light. It was still red. She craned her neck to see the traffic light hanging over the cross street. Immediately, it turned yellow as if prompted by her attention. Had Rose been the one to do it, she would've winked at Lily and whispered: *Magic*. But Lily had stopped believing in magic twenty-five years ago.

As the cross light flipped to red Lily lightened her foot on the brake and looked left, where the gas station and Kwik-e-mart stocked pre-paid phones. Wherever he went, Andrew might feel more comfortable if he had access to the world outside his new home. Lily's light turned green, and she rolled into the intersection. From the cross street, a gray four-door sailed through their red light and nearly clipped Lily's front end.

Lily punched her brakes, swearing under her breath, and glared at the driver. The woman behind the wheel turned her head in Lily's direction just a little, as if she too had been prompted by the same false magic that could change a traffic light.

Rose.

Her sister's name shot through her, igniting every cell in her body. She strangled the steering wheel and leaned hard against the seatbelt as her stare chased the woman the rest of the way through the intersection. She'd only managed a glimpse, a half second at the most. But the driver's face was seared into her mind's eye, and when she blinked, she could still see her plain as day.

For the second time that morning, a car honked behind her. She floored the gas, turned the wheel the wrong way, and sliced a right-turn path between cars making a left turn from the opposite side. Tires squealed, and more drivers laid on their horns. Lily barely heard them, her mind and heart and every sense converging on the gray car somewhere up ahead.

'What's wrong?' Andrew's sleepy voice broke apart her storm of thoughts like a stubborn ray of sun through a blanket of clouds.

Lily glanced at him, wide-eyed. She'd forgotten he was there. 'Nothing. Sorry.'

'You're not driving like it's nothing.'

Out the corner of her eye, Lily saw Andrew move his hand from beneath the blanket to the door, his fingers resting on the handle.

'Someone ran a red light and almost hit us, then sped off. I'm trying to get a plate number so I can report it,' she said, her racing pulse driving her words from her mouth at a manic clip.

'OK, Jason Bourne.' Andrew yawned, then leaned against the window.

Lily's focus toggled between him and the gray sedan, which was still a couple cars ahead as it approached the next intersection. She weaved through traffic, desperate to catch up and prove herself wrong enough to let go of this furious, consuming want. Ahead, the road continued straight as far as she could see. Traffic lights were strung across every other block. If the gray car turned or got through a light without her, she might not be able to catch up.

The next light turned yellow. She accelerated through the intersection, then changed lanes for a better vantage point of the left lane as she raced toward a pair of close lights. The gray sedan was just a few cars ahead of her in the left lane, and finally she could get a better look at the vehicle. There were two people sitting in the back. Two kids. One of them familiar, a profile she would swear she knew from helping guide her through nearly a lifetime in the system. But if Rose was the driver, what in the world was Maya Summit doing in the back seat?

Uncertainty struck her square in the chest. She lifted her foot off the gas, every bit of her suspended in indecision. Her focus raced after the gray car even as her own vehicle lost momentum.

'Stop!' Andrew screamed. A van directly in front of them was at a standstill, and Lily was roaring toward their back bumper. She slammed on the brakes and pushed back into her seat, throttling the steering wheel. Her tires locked up and screamed in protest as they slid across the asphalt, and at last came to a stop at an angle across the lane, Andrew's door just inches from the back of the van.

Lily heaved breaths in the driver's seat, then hung her head between her outstretched arms.

'I'm sorry, Andrew. I'm so sorry,' she said between gasps as she hurried to right her vehicle inside the lane.

'Can you let me out?' he asked, his knuckles pulled white where he was squeezing the blanket.

'I don't know what came over me. I was so upset that they nearly hit us. I lost my mind there for a second. Why don't I grab us some lunch and we can take it to Brecken Park? I'll call Katelyn from the parking lot and get placement calls going, and you can stay with me, or I can have Katelyn come get you. Whatever you want. I'm so sorry,' she repeated.

'It's OK.' Fear made his voice brittle.

She picked her head up and looked at him. 'It's not OK. I should never have put you at risk.'

Andrew nodded. His nostrils flared. Lily knew if she could hear his heart, it would be pounding. Still, she could not stop herself from swinging her gaze from the boy to the road in time to watch the gray car disappear.

EIGHT

Rose – February 6, 2018

The first mile of starts and stops passes in silence, save a nervous giggle from Lyric when I run a red light, then shrug and call it pink.

At the red light near the Walmart, I peek at her in the rearview mirror. She's hugging her backpack to her front. It's covered in music patches for nineties bands and older hippie shit. I flip stations on the radio until I find one that I think she'll like. Then I keep my eyes on the road and sing along, pretending there's no one in this car but me.

At the bridge, Lyric joins in, and her voice flat out puts mine to shame. I'd fall silent just to listen to her better, but something tells me she'll stop singing if I do. Instead, I sing louder, daring her to take up more space. She answers, sailing up the register to find the harmony notes. I glance at them again in the rearview mirror. Nike is grinning.

The song ends, and a commercial comes on. The air in the car is charged, and I've got half a mind to turn the station again just to keep this feeling from disappearing like everything good always seems to do.

'You're talented,' I say instead.

'Easton's going to help me get a development deal with a record label his friend owns in Nashville. It's a start-up, but they're legit. He bought me some new headphones, and he said he's going to take me to get headshots. He's taking me to meet them soon, too.' She smiles, blushing a little, and my heart plummets.

The fuck he is. I open and close my hands on the steering wheel, trying to decide how bad I already regret getting these kids in my car. I took them because it felt worse not to, but I'm going to use them, too. They might be a roadmap to how Easton works his game and to where a dead girl's sister might've gone. The more I can find out about him, how he dupes people, and how he moves them, the better chance I have of finding her.

'How did you meet Easton?' I ask, leaping from the train of runaway thoughts and straight into the fire.

'He saw me singing for tips at a coffee shop a few weeks back. He asked me how much I was hoping to make for the day. I said a hundred dollars, just saying something crazy, and he handed me the money. I think he thought I was homeless.'

'Are you? I mean, no judgement here if you are. My car has been my only roof more times than I care to count.'

'No. I mean, I have a house I stay in, but it's not mine. Foster care. Call it what you want to,' she says.

'I raised myself,' I offer.

'That's what we're doing. Raising ourselves.' She perks up and peers at Nike. 'I want him in on the deal, too.'

'I wouldn't recommend mixing boyfriends and business, but you do you. No offense, Nike,' I pry, using the rearview mirror to study the boy in the back seat. Worry passes over his face, then his gaze and hands meet in his lap. Either he doesn't like this plan at all, or he doesn't want in, and she doesn't seem to know it yet.

'No. It's not like that.' Lyric squirms, making a face. 'Easton already asked. He got nosy about boys in general.'

'That was probably awkward,' I venture, doing my best to strain all hints of suspicion from my voice.

'Yeah. He said if he's managing me, he manages everything. I guess I'll have to get used to it.'

Red flags don't lead to a carnival, baby girl. I keep the thought to myself and steal another glimpse of Nike. 'You sing, too?'

'No. I like to draw, and I write poetry.' His eyes look to Lyric. 'She turns the good ones into songs.'

'He doesn't know how talented he is. It took me a week to convince him to talk to Easton,' Lyric says. 'That's what the meeting today was about. We skipped school and just showed up before he could change his mind. Easton freaked out at first, but when he cooled off, he said we'd showed initiative, and he'd think about it. I'm supposed to go with Easton to Nashville to meet the producer for a demo this weekend,' Lyric says. 'He said if we can show we're better together, Christian's in.' She freezes, and I realize she's just told me his name.

'My guess is your foster parents don't know anything about this trip any more than they know about Easton, or the deal, or the *initiative* you took today,' I reply quickly, hoping they'll think I didn't catch it. I have about six minutes to save these kids from themselves, but I need to play this carefully. Anything I say has the potential to get back to Easton, and they're not worth that risk just yet, so the point-blank truth is off limits and, once again, ugly.

'Look, Easton sent me to make sure you got home and to make sure that you understand that until a deal is signed, you can't tell anybody where you've been or that you've ever heard of him, and you can't come back to Sirens uninvited again. But I'm guessing you know that already. If your foster parents or teachers get wind of this kind of thing, they'll start sounding the alarm, making crazy accusations, and whatever deal you might have will go up in smoke. Anyone you tell will think it sounds too good to be true. Best-case scenario, they'll think *you're* lying about it. I mean, to hear it, it sounds *way* too good to be true,' I finish with a laugh.

If I was the praying kind, I'd be begging to whatever watches this world spin to help these kids read between the lines. I am a lot of things. I am not that kind of girl.

'No, I get you,' Lyric says, suddenly serious. 'So, what do we do?'

Shit.

Maybe these two kids are going to be the ruin of Easton
Grimes. The thought, unlikely and full of fantasy, warms my
heart all the same. But then I think of what it would mean for
them, how far I'll have to let them fall to have proof of injury
enough to matter to anybody else.

The decision is impossible to make.

The only thing I can do is to make sure they think I'm the
one and only person to contact from now on, not Easton. I can
figure the rest out if I just have a little more time, and Easton
doesn't strike me as one to chase. He'd rather they come to him
– just not to his club in broad daylight. What I need to establish
right now is a speed bump between them.

'I've known all about you since Easton saw you. I knew about
your meeting, and I know your names,' I say, building the lie
and the skeleton of a plan as I go, marveling that maybe my
short-lived career as a bogus clairvoyant somehow prepared me
for this. 'Easton wanted to know how you'd handle yourselves
in a random situation like this, if you're good at reading people
and following instructions.'

'How'd we do?' Lyric asks, leaning forward, her hunger plain
to see. All at once, I see her whole future as if I can see the
universe in a glass sphere with a light under it. These streets do
one thing a thousand different ways to a kid whose very soul is
starving. I'll spare you a walk down memory lane and let you
decide on the details.

'Perfect,' I lie again as Brecken Park comes into view. My
mind races, splits in half, and takes off at a dead sprint in two
directions at once.

Lyric can't go with Easton to Nashville this weekend or she
won't come back the same, if at all. There's no way Easton's
going to let Christian tag along unless he's got a job for him in
mind, too, and I'm not so sure the kid really wants to go. There's
no move to make right now. Easton hasn't hurt these kids, hasn't
damaged them, hasn't broken the law. Yet. That one word is the
new ugly truth. It's fishing all over again, sitting here and waiting
until they've all forgotten I'm hovering overhead to watch the
big fish hunt the little ones.

I'm halfway tempted to keep them in the car, take them
through a drive-through for a fast-food meal, and find a way to

split the last roofie I have on hand between the two of them. Then I could drop them off somewhere safe and let them wake up the kind of terrified that makes them second-guess everything about this devil's playground we call Earth. But I can't think of a place safe enough to take them. We aren't all going to make it to the end of whatever this becomes. That's just all there is to it. I don't need a spread of tarot cards or a crystal ball to tell me that.

I pull into the upper lot at Brecken Park and park where I can see the woods below. Lyric and Christian give me their numbers. Then I take all the money I made overnight and divide it equally between them, $200 each.

'I'm going to be the one driving you to Nashville for the meeting. Easton's managing some logistics on the front end, but all communication runs through me from here on out. I'll be in touch soon to tell you where and when I'll pick you up from, and I'm going to bring you work phones ASAP that will have my number in them and just be used for business. Nothing else. You'll be able to write it off on your taxes when you're rolling in money. Speaking of money, there's one last test. None of this is going to be easy, and I want you to know that going in. If you want to come, bring this money back to me the day that we leave. All of it. The numbers on these bills are recorded, and you have to bring the exact same bills back. If you change your mind, keep the money as payment for your time so far, but you won't be welcome around Easton or the club again. That door will be closed until you're of legal age to walk through as a paying customer. Understood?'

They nod, both silent, faces solemn . . . determined. They've bought it. Damn it.

'I won't lie to you – this is a big risk,' I add. 'A lot can go sideways. There won't be any hard feelings if either of you changes your mind – you have my word. I'll call you both tomorrow first thing in the morning. Missouri area code 314. If you still want in, answer. If you want out, just don't pick up the phone. Simple as that. The money is still yours, free and clear. You can even tell me now if you want out. No hard feelings, for real,' I repeat.

'No. We're in,' Lyric says.

I should be thrilled – I'll either keep these kids from Easton, or they'll give me what I need to catch him. But all I feel is sick.

They climb out and close their doors. Then they just stand there and stare at me through the glass as I start to pull away. They look eight and 108 at the same time.

Dear sweet baby Jesus, I hope I never see them again.

NINE

Lily – February 6, 2018

By the time Lily found a good placement fit for Andrew and convinced him to let her be the one to drive him there, sleet and snow had begun to fall. With any new foster arrangement, she usually made a point to stay until everyone involved seemed to take that first step toward settling in each other's presence, but not tonight. Her nerves were frayed, her patience shot, and Andrew seemed more comfortable with her at arm's length, now. He'd ridden in the back seat to the new house.

She hustled to her car and jumped inside, slamming the door to shut out the weather as quickly as she could. Rose, though, was not so easy to escape. Lily had seen her everywhere she looked today. She cranked the engine to check the temperature on the dashboard. Thirty-three degrees. It would likely sink below freezing within the hour. She needed to get to her cabin as fast as possible.

As she put the car in reverse, her phone chirped with an incoming call. It was the number for Bright View Rehabilitation Center, the county's state-funded long-term care facility. Lily checked the clock before answering. It was nearly six p.m., an unusual time for a routine call.

'Is everything OK with Anne?' Lily asked as she answered. Anne was the only reason she'd be receiving a call from the adult facility at all.

Fresh out of college, Lily had begun her career in social services in the adult division. On her first shift, she met Anne as a Jane Doe at a long-term adult care facility; she'd been discharged from hospital with a severe brain injury. Lily had begun calling her Anne, just to call her something, and in the two years she spent working with adults, no one had ever come forward to claim her.

When she made the switch to CPS, Anne was still alone, unknown, and largely nonverbal. While Lily could not stay on as her case worker, she became her advocate instead, unable to leave the woman mute and helpless in a place from which she could not extract herself.

'Anne fell out of her chair and hit her head on the table on the way down. She's making a lot of noise. We can't tell if she's upset or if she needs to go to the hospital,' an unfamiliar orderly explained.

'Shouldn't this be a call for a doctor?'

'You're listed as her emergency contact, and she's documented as a comfort care patient. We thought we'd call you first.'

'Right.' Lily pressed her fingertips against her tear ducts. 'I'll be there as soon as I can.' There would be no time to make the trip to her cabin tonight. She'd have to improvise. At least she'd restocked her oil paint supply on the way home from work last Friday.

Between the weather and the traffic, the drive to Bright View took nearly twice as long as usual. Lily's frustration, although unbidden, rooted deeper with every passing minute. There was little to be done for the decaying old woman, but the self-imposed obligation to try remained. As she walked through the main doors, she tucked her nose behind the collar of her coat and breathed lightly, strangely grateful for something to avoid besides her memory and the cold. She'd been to Bright View a thousand times in the last decade, but the smell, medicinal and filthy at the same time, was the one thing she could never fully acclimate to.

She hoped she would find Anne alone. She could tell her the truth about how she'd panicked and obsessed, and Anne couldn't say a word. Over the years, since discovering Anne, she'd whispered all kinds of regrets and mistakes in her ear. Truth be told, Anne now knew her better than anyone. Lily knew it was selfish to use her this way, but mostly she didn't care. She didn't have to be the one they called for Anne every time the woman fell or had a concerning flag pop up on her medical tests. This was an exchange. Some days she liked to think Anne couldn't hear her, anyway. It took the pressure off. But today, she wanted someone who would just listen without trying to fix it, to fix *her*, and those people were hard to come by.

Lily pushed Anne's door open, stunned by the prick of tears that grew stronger as the woman came into view. Anne was not alone. Gretchen, a nurse at Bright View, was wiping Anne's gaunt, gaping face with a towel.

'Oh, Lily. How good of you to come,' Gretchen said, giving Lily the credit of having come of her own volition and not just because they'd called.

'How can I help?'

'She's been agitated all day. We were hoping you might be able to help figure out what's bothering her.'

'Well, I can try.' Lily stared down at Anne. The old woman's jaw was pushed open too far. Her tongue, filmy with dryness, wagged up and down at odd intervals, and Lily wondered if the movements were deliberate. Anne couldn't manage many of those anymore. The effort must've been extraordinary.

Lily couldn't help but think of 'comfort care' as a cruel turn of phrase for keeping someone like Anne alive. The woman was a prisoner in her own body. That was never going to change. Death would have been kinder.

'What are you trying to say?' Lily murmured, leaning closer.

Anne's gaze limped from its fixation point to Lily's face, and for a split second, their eyes met. Then the pupils in Anne's eyes dropped to the bottom of her sockets like her brain had flipped a switch, and she went rigid in her chair, her fingers curling unnaturally into elongated fists.

'A seizure's coming on,' Lily said, and helped Anne find the corner of her wheelchair before adjusting her straps to hold her harder in place.

'I'll get her meds.'

'I'll stay with her.'

Gretchen paused by the door. 'Thank you, Lily. I don't know what we'd do without you.'

*

By the time Anne was resting in bed and Lily was able to leave Bright View, snow was falling straight down through still air and had already formed a thin crust on treetops and bushes. Lily dashed to her car and hopped inside, then gripped the steering wheel in both hands, summoning the courage to drive through the pouring snow. But she couldn't bring herself to turn the key.

Rage and frustration burst to bloom inside her, and she let out a scream, basic and carnal and pitiful. She met her gaze in the rearview mirror. Anger would not release the grip of the past. It only fed it. She'd spent years and thousands of dollars in therapy to learn this one truth as well as how to cope with it. The action plan began with acknowledging Rose's absence instead of pretending her abandonment had never happened. But tonight, she would need to take a step further and confront her last memory of her sister. To admit that she'd been left. To face the fact that she was still looking, still hoping Rose would come back into her life, despite her betrayal, and that those two things were OK.

The best way – and the worst way – to accomplish that was to face a winter forest at night. The first time she'd tried alone, she'd made it less than a minute before sprinting back out, breathless and shaking. It had taken years and at least a dozen attempts to withstand the sound of wind whistling through naked branches, the prick of a snowflake on exposed skin, and the vacuum of darkness long enough to feel in control of herself and her ability to walk back out. She had a system now. Tonight, she caught herself wishing Rose could somehow bear witness.

She only passed a handful of cars on her way to Brecken Park; most rational people had already holed up indoors. Only those running to or from something would still be out in this. She parked the car in the corner of a concrete lot at the base of a hill and climbed out. Overhead, the cloud cover had briefly thinned enough for moonlight to break through in a meager patch. The world was gray beneath the canopy of trees, but Rose's plan would have been OK twenty-five years ago: the snow reflected what little light was available, and while it was still dark, Lily could see everything.

She slipped between two trees and found herself staring down at a skinny footpath. Whether she was running to something or from something when she did this, she could never be sure. Tonight, the layer of snow painting the trail had been made imperfect by recent footprints. She started walking. The path forked twice before she realized she'd been following whoever came this way before. She had no way of knowing how long she'd been out here, her phone left in the car out of habit and her mind bouncing between decades in its own vortex of time.

Heavier clouds crossed over the moon, and the woods tumbled into darkness. Wet snow and freezing rain made a new assault on the forest, laying waste to the earlier quiet and nipping her exposed skin wherever it could find it. The strange spell the moonlit snow had cast upon her vanished. Fear billowed in her chest. She whipped around, then hurried back over her footprints headed into the woods, which were already filling in with fresh snow and ice. A hush fell with a heavy, resolute suddenness, and she began to run. Thick snow poured in silent earnest, as if the woods longed to close white doors on her from all sides, keep her there forever if given half a chance. At last, she burst from the trees. She didn't stop running until she'd reached her car and touched the snow-covered hood, anchoring herself to the present as she leaned over with heaving breaths.

Hushed voices tucked themselves inside a gust of winter air. The back of her neck prickled, and she swung round to face the woods. Two teenagers were walking toward the same path she'd taken. Her heart ached with the weight of every emotion all at once, and she wanted to laugh and cry and scream. Those two kids probably felt invincible, so long as they were together. Lily wanted to tell them that there was no such thing as safety in numbers, that you never knew the limit of your worth to another. There was almost always a price someone would take in exchange for leaving you behind.

TEN

Rose – February 6, 2018

swing into the parking place in front of my room at the extended-stay motel. My headlights spotlight Easton standing in front of my door, one foot propped on the old brick wall that acts as both decorative accent and a barrier for any cars that might otherwise hop the curb and consequently park inside a room.

I slide my revolver – a twenty-year-old gift from none other than Hunter Kepp – out from beneath my seat and into the main compartment of my oversized purse. On any night, my bag comes equipped with hand sanitizer, a pack of baby wipes, migraine pills, a couple roofies, brass knuckles, a pack of cigarettes, injectable Narcan, a lighter, lipstick, a bottle of mouthwash, a fresh pair of panties, chewing gum, an EPT from the dollar store, and, for the moment, a snub-nose Smith & Wesson .38 special.

I would put the revolver on my hip, but I think I can name at least one reason Easton's here, and if he gets handsy and finds me armed, the mood and the game will change. It isn't unusual for the higher-ups in a strip club to have working knowledge of what their girls are capable of behind closed doors. I angle my face toward the rearview mirror and pretend to touch up my hair and makeup, even though I sure as shit can't see myself in the dark. Then I climb out.

'To what do I owe the pleasure?' I ask, sauntering up to him.

'Just came to check on you.' He doesn't move an inch. 'Today was not a typical day at the office.'

I kiss him on the cheek like a spouse coming home for dinner. 'Do you want to come inside?'

'Sure,' he says, and we step through the door of my room.

Immediately, I drop my purse on the floor beside the bed and use my foot to scoot it just underneath. The bedframe is low, and I should be able to reach it if need be. Half-veiled by the bed skirt, I'm hoping he'll forget it's even there. Then I shrug out of my coat and hang it on the back of a wooden chair that sits awkwardly in the corner like a freshman boy at homecoming.

'I hate every piece of furniture in this place,' I think out loud.

'Then why stay here?'

'I can afford it.'

'You should be able to afford more than this.'

'Not and still put some away.'

'What are you saving up for?' For the first time, he looks at me with real interest.

I tilt my head. 'Why do you care?'

'I'd like to get to know the new girl a little better, learn what makes her tick, why she's chosen this line of work.' He smirks. 'I take care of the girls who work for me, especially the new ones. People treat it like a game, but it's not easy.'

I let out a tired laugh. 'Do I look new to this game?' Immediately, I regret asking the question. It's an invitation to walk down memory lane for us both, a place I have no interest in revisiting.

He studies me hard. I filled out my employment application and paperwork with someone else's identity, but under the microscope of his attention, I'm terrified he saw right through it. That he knows all about my stint at The Alibi. How it started. How it ended. It takes every ounce of resistance in me to not look away.

'You're new to me,' he finally says. 'And you seemed to think today was typical, but that's not what I want to call normal at my club.' He squares his stance to me, stubby fingers cupping his own narrow hips, and I realize he hasn't yet taken off his jacket.

Maybe he doesn't plan to stay long after all. Or maybe he has something literal up his sleeve – more like tucked into his belt. He wouldn't be the first bar owner that's tried to use force to break in the new girl. Either way, the real point of Easton's visit feels like it's getting ready to make itself known.

'We all have a game face we keep on at work,' I start. 'I don't know how many customers would pay to see you in tighty-whities on a dance pole, but you know how it is in there. We all put on a mask the second we walk through that door.'

'I know.' He steps closer. One hand inches along the waist of his pants.

'If I'm being honest with you, I was a little shaken up today.' I force my feet to stay planted where they are on this soiled, smashed-flat carpet, deny my eyes their desire to seek the way out. 'That's why I didn't want to leave. I was scared someone might be waiting for me in the parking lot or would have found out where I'm staying and come knock on my door. It wouldn't be the first time.'

Easton frowns. 'That's not something I would tolerate, personally or professionally. From a business standpoint, I'm not interested in putting bruised and battered women on display.'

Why don't we talk about what your business interests are? I press the tip of my tongue to the place where the backs of my front teeth meet the roof of my mouth like it's a button for keeping a thought to myself. It's probably my subconscious tell. Thankfully, most people wouldn't think to look at my mouth with my tits so often on display. This is a game, after all, and I wonder if I should take the offensive and ask him about the kids in his office. It might look suspect if I do. But it might look even more conspicuous if I don't.

'There was a pair of Converse sneakers in your office today,' I venture as I cross the room and sit on the end of the bed, where my purse is next to my feet.

He eases down next to me on the bed. He rakes his fingers through his hair, which seems to be his tell, if he has one. Then he leans back far enough to need to prop himself up with his hands. I do not like that they are behind me.

He clears his throat before he speaks. 'A couple students from the high school want to write an article for the school paper about Sirens. They even wanted to interview the dancers. I think they think they're being avant-garde. Real, cutting-edge journalism.'

'Are you going to let them?'

'Hell, I don't know. Damned if I do, damned if I don't.'

Jesus, he's good. The excuse is both simple and solid, the lie natural and easy. I could see how Lyric, desperate and young and tragically hopeful as she still is, would've had little reason to doubt what he was saying for long.

He studies my face a moment, then his eyes travel down my front, where a threadbare T-shirt does a shitty job of covering much of anything. He moves an arm closer to me, and on instinct I sit straighter, moving away from the threat of nearness like we're two magnets both pointing south, maintaining the space between us like a law of nature.

It's a mistake, one I'm too seasoned to make.

'I can talk to them,' I say and immediately regret that, too. Easton would want to be present for the conversation. 'Maybe over the phone, keep them out of the club.'

'They know not to come by unannounced again.'

'That's good.' I lean back on my elbows and watch his gaze travel behind me. 'What are you really doing here, Easton Grimes?'

'Like I told you, I just want to get to know you better.'

'What do you want to know?' I tilt my chin, exposing my throat. I hope it says: *I'm not afraid of you, Easton,* even though I'm fucking terrified.

'Honestly?'

'Always.'

'I want to know why that detective seemed to know you when you say you're new in town, and why he played Todd Camps like a fiddle for your benefit,' he states point-blank.

Fuck. This isn't about Todd Camps. It's about Hunter fucking Kepp. Easton isn't here to break me in. He's trying to see if I'm an informant. Every time he's tried to look me over since walking in the door makes more sense. He's searching for a wire.

I lick my lips, buying a split second to think. 'Let's just say he'd be very sad if I had to close up shop for any length of time.'

'You've only been around what, a week?'

'Not my first time in Tula,' I admit, even though it's a colossal risk.

'But he remembers. You must be really something.' He's studying me again.

Nervous prickles of sweat bloom on my scalp. 'I like to think of it as a team sport.' I imagine he's had a working girl brag to him about a special skill a time or twenty, but I would bet he doesn't let down his guard around a girl who treats him like he's got something to learn.

'Are you asking me to play?' He arcs a brow.

'Are you waiting for a written invitation? Or should I just start undressing?' I move to lift my shirt.

'Stay dressed. I want to take your clothes off myself.' He pulls his wallet from his pocket, then he plucks out two little plastic bags, one with white powder and another with a rainbow assortment of pills. 'I brought enough to share.'

'What's your poison?' I lie on my back, wanting to forget the sight of his stash. But it's no use. Childlike anticipation fills me like the thrill of a roller coaster climbing that first big hill. *Clack . . . clack . . . clack clack clackclackclack.*

'My own special mix. I thought you might want to forget today. I do.'

I press my tongue against my teeth again. I've been sober for nineteen days, and clean about a hundred different times. I know all there is to know about getting sober and then fucking it all up. I know those pills and powder don't love me back. But misery loves company, and even with this devil of a man stealing half the air and most of the space in this tiny hotel room, I still feel so unbelievably alone.

The simple, present truth is this: if I say no, Easton's only going to let me in so far. Then again, who the hell knows what he plans on giving me, and if I die tonight, it won't much matter how far I get inside his brain while he plays inside my body.

'I don't know. I'm no good on that stuff,' I say, mostly as a reminder to myself.

'How so?'

'I tend to . . . lose control.'

'That doesn't sound too bad.'

'But what if tonight is worth remembering?' I crane my neck to look at him.

'You don't trust me, do you?' He digs his finger in the bag and deposits the powder beneath his tongue.

'I don't trust anybody.'

'I don't either.'

He plucks a pill out and swallows it, then pulls his belt from his pants before moving to the bed and climbing on top of me. His weight and his breath become part of the environment, two more pieces of furniture in this stale, damp room. I peek over his shoulder at the clock beneath the ancient television set. I can't afford the time this might take, but I also can't afford not to spend it.

Twenty-five years ago, it had taken me weeks to scrounge together the two hundred dollars I had the night we ran from home. But I'd been planning to leave for months. It had snowed that past December, four inches in a single evening. My mother was at work. I was lying next to Lily in the bed we shared, ice cold and waiting. The room lightened a shade like the door had swung open, and I held my breath and made two fists. But no footsteps came. Then the darkness brightened still more, and before my eyes, the air itself glowed blue, like the neon sign at the nightclub where Mom was a dancer had somehow followed her home.

I'd slipped out of bed, walked to the window, and looked out. The earlier snow had turned the ground white, having fallen thick enough to stick, and when the clouds vanished, they'd left a clear sky for a full moon. It was like an untouched, perfect world lay waiting for me beyond that glass.

Before I knew what I was doing, I had the window unlocked and cracked open, when behind me, Lily stirred. In her sleep, she rolled over and murmured my name. Then I heard Everett's boots in the hall. With snow on the ground, Mom working a late shift, and Everett not hiding his steps, I quickly understood that my mother probably wasn't coming back until morning.

I looked at Lily one more time.

Everett was a lot of things, but he wasn't picky.

I closed and locked the window and climbed back in bed, and I told myself that the next time it snowed, I'd be ready, and we'd be gone.

My mind returns to the motel room. Easton is inside of me, and my eyes are on the snow-blanketed parking lot visible through a gap in the long, tacky curtains bordering the one window in this musty space. A little girl in a tattered pink coat runs across my field of vision, there and gone in an instant.

She's not real, I tell myself.

But on the snow, there are footprints.

'Wait,' I say with a gasp, my body balking, my mind in freefall.

'What's wrong?' Easton lifts his weight away from me.

I sit up and stare hard through the window. The parking lot is empty.

'Hey, are you OK?' he asks.

No. God, no. I have never been OK.

'Are you still willing to share what you brought?' I nod at his wallet lying next to the television.

He grins at me. 'Do you have a preference? And don't be shy. I've got more.'

Want seizes me by the throat, reaches deep within my chest, and clutches my beating heart.

'All of it,' I say.

There's going to be collateral damage at the end of this, and all along the way. It might as well start with me.

ELEVEN

Lily – February 7, 2018

Lily slid into her cubicle at DFACS with a cup of to-go coffee between her hands. As soon as she settled into her chair, she brought up the weather forecast. Another dusting of snow was expected overnight, and their region was unlikely to see temperatures above freezing for the next forty-eight hours. Even though their office was kept at sixty-eight degrees year-round, Lily pulled her coat closer to her body and shivered.

'Morning!' Katelyn's voice preceded her face as she appeared above the piling gray divider between their desks.

'Morning.' Lily offered the word without meeting Katelyn's stare. But she could feel it – picturing the way it lasered out of her coworker's blue eyes, slid down her ski-jump nose, and gained momentum as it plummeted the drop from Katelyn's standing height to where Lily sat in her tired swivel chair. The young woman was kind to a fault, a characteristic that, combined with her unwavering commitment to follow the rules, would either make her career go the distance or crash and burn in the first few years. For now, she still leaned heavily on Lily's guidance, at least in part, Lily believed, to share that very weight. The cubicle could become a cage in an instant – one of the many reasons Lily purposely spent so much time out of it.

'What are you doing here?' Katelyn asked. 'I thought you were going out of town,'

'Work went late last night,' Lily summarized without reminding Katelyn exactly why.

'Yes,' Katelyn responded on an exhale. 'Thank you for that. I'm going to check on Andrew today. I'm hopeful it's a better placement. I'm sorry to have wrecked your plans.'

Lily forced a smile. 'You didn't.'

'Why the heck did you still come in? If I was scheduled off

today, I'd be spending the morning with Netflix, especially with all the overtime you work.'

'I don't have a television.'

Katelyn's mouth fell open. 'Seriously?'

'Seriously.'

'Is it by choice or . . .' Katelyn trailed off, and discomfort made a home on her face. Watching her squirm was more entertaining than it should've been. Lily couldn't help but smile in earnest now.

'Real life has enough drama. I don't need to pay monthly fees to watch stress and trauma that other people have made up.' In truth, it was the happy endings that bothered Lily most, the way things always seemed to twist and turn just enough to work out for the better. Life wasn't like that. There was no sense in pretending for the sake of entertainment.

Katelyn grimaced. 'Now I just feel like a lemming.'

'I'm a lemming to other things. I can't drive by a Michael's without buying new paint or a brush.'

'That just makes you crafty.'

Lily shrugged. Her childhood therapist probably would have used a different word. Compulsive and obsessive had seemed to be a couple of her favorites. It wasn't drugs, alcohol, gambling, or unprotected sex, so really, what was the harm? The only casualty had been the cabinet space in her kitchen, where her collection of art supplies had forced her dishes to consolidate into half the allotted room. Why she'd installed security cameras in her apartment, she had no idea. Unless the thief had a penchant for floral décor or crafting, there was nothing worth taking. Then again, maybe she'd installed the entire system to not feel so crazy about pointing the one camera through the window to the street outside her building.

'Maybe I can bring dinner over, and you can teach me how to paint something easy? We could do our own sip and paint kind of deal. I'll pay you in sushi and wine.'

Lily's gaze flicked back to the computer screen where the tab for the National Weather Service flashed with a new notification. 'Not tonight.'

'Do you have a date?' Katelyn wagged her eyebrows.

'No.'

'Sure.'

Tension snaked through Lily. It would be so much easier to lie and say she had a date, start an office rumor, be known as the girl who goes to her cabin to cozy up to a secret lover instead of the foster care success story who could track missing kids like a bloodhound but still fled to a cabin in the middle of nowhere whenever her sanity was on the brink.

The whole truth – that she hadn't been on a date since her high school senior prom, that she had no interest in anyone getting close, that when someone touched her skin, she felt colder wherever they made contact, that she didn't let anyone in her heart or her home – was as cliché as it was sad. Every time she told someone, she would have to watch pity and surprise color their expressions like smears of paint on canvas. Without fail, they would look at her not as the thirty-two-year-old survivor but the seven-year-old left in the snow.

Lily shrugged. 'I like to keep my private life private.'

'I knew it.' Katelyn pushed back from the wall. Lily heard her gather her keys and lock her cabinet, then she reappeared. 'Josh Marsden didn't show up at school again. They're going to charge him with truancy if he doesn't make it in. I'm going to Brecken Park to see if anyone has seen him.'

'Take doughnuts. Whoever you find will be more willing to stick around, maybe say a little more than they would otherwise.'

Victory quirked the corner of Katelyn's mouth. 'So that's your secret to finding them. Baked goods. I've learned more about you in a morning than I have in the last year.'

'Well, don't tell anyone.'

'Your secrets are safe with me,' she said with a wave, then moved toward the exit, a bounce in her step.

Lily shook her head. It was barely ten a.m. and she was already exhausted. But she couldn't blame Katelyn and the assault of her enthusiasm for all of it. Last night, the past and the present had played tag through the layers of her consciousness, pushing her from the edge of sleep each time she neared that dark, quiet place.

Her gaze found its way back to her computer screen. She prompted the page for the National Weather Service and opened a second weather website to compare the five-day models.

'Stop it,' she whispered to herself. Fixating on the forecast would not stop another child from making Rose's mistakes before they made them.

'Lily?' a voice prompted from behind.

Lily quickly closed out both tabs then swiveled in her seat to face her supervisor, Lartesha Cheney.

'I had you out for today,' Lartesha said.

Everything about the woman was warm and soft. She gazed at Lily now with the kind of concern that felt like a blanket. In general, Lily didn't wish many of the mothers she'd met on children, but Lartesha was an exception. Her rare altruism also made her much more difficult to lie to when it was absolutely necessary to do so. Thankfully, today wasn't one of those times.

'I got called to Bright View for Anne late yesterday. I didn't make it out of town before the snow,' Lily answered.

'Let's go ahead and get your annual evaluation done, since you're here,' Lartesha offered.

Lily hesitated. As much as she liked her, listening to another person dissect her every move was the last thing she wanted to do right now. Then again, Lartesha had a point. With more snow coming, the best medicine was a long weekend away, made all the more true if the evaluation didn't go the way she hoped.

Lartesha's opinions and approval had always been important to her. She wasn't just Lily's boss; she was a mentor, a friend who knew her whole story, a touchstone for her to check back with when she began to lose faith in humanity. Their line of work was sometimes a showcase for the very worst. Still, as they settled in Lartesha's office and began her performance review, Lily struggled to keep her mind on the conversation, only managing to dial in on buzzwords as they popped up.

Paperwork.

She thought back to Josh and the boy he was with yesterday, the deal he had wanted to make, the gleam she hadn't liked in his eye. She should've told Katelyn about it, but then she'd know that Lily had found Josh out of school yesterday and hadn't made him go back.

Asking for help.

What if something had happened to him? She had left Josh to deal with whatever came next.

Going through proper channels.

What if, for the first time in his life, Josh wanted to be found by anyone willing to look.

Winter.

The word was a missile, striking her train of thought, and Lily's mind crashed back into Lartesha's office.

'I've been studying your cases. You bend the rules to the point of breaking, and we let you because of your success rates with establishing long-term placements, but sometimes you go too far. People are noticing. It's becoming problematic for office morale.'

'Maybe it's the rules that are problematic,' Lily countered and shifted in her chair. This wasn't the first time she'd been reprimanded for her unorthodox approaches, but until she wasn't who her coworkers called first in emergency situations, she took the lectures with a grain of salt.

'It isn't just the rules, here. You don't seem to operate by the book in court, either. In a placement hearing where it's an option, you are almost four times as likely to recommend a child be placed in a detention center instead of private arrangements during the winter months as you are the rest of the year. That number becomes off-the-charts more likely if that child is also an oldest sibling,' Lartesha noted.

'It's a dangerous time of year to take a chance on one running away or slipping through the cracks, which are both more likely in private settings, and younger siblings often follow in the footsteps of their big brother or sister. I know that to be true, both practically and academically. I won't apologize for it.'

'Your reasoning holds water, absolutely. But I'm also not sure it's that superficial. Make sure it isn't about *you* . . . that it isn't about Rose.'

'None of this is about *Rose*.' Lily nearly choked on her name. 'It's all in how you frame it. Why can't we talk about the rate for kids in my care who go missing and are never recovered? Because that would be zero.'

'Lily, we have an emotional job, but we can't make emotional decisions. That's all I'm saying.'

What about Katelyn? Lily wanted to ask. *First Andrew, now Josh. Natasha disappeared months ago, and I don't think*

Katelyn's even looking for her anymore. Lily bit down on the inside of her cheek instead.

'You are valuable to this department, and I want you to hear that, too.'

'Is that all, then?' Lily replied curtly.

'We need to go over your strengths. That list is a lot longer.'

'I know what I'm good at.' Lily stood and moved for the door. 'Please excuse me.'

'Lily!' Lartesha called after her, but she didn't stop.

On weak legs, she hurried across the department floor to the restroom. She made sure she was alone, then splashed warm water on her face and blotted it dry. Everything inside of her vibrated with adrenaline. She gripped the sink, staring at herself in the mirror, and for one split second, Rose stared out at her.

Lily jumped away from the counter, then hurled her gaze back to the glass, but her sister was gone.

Her phone rang. She fished it from her pocket with trembling hands. It was Katelyn.

'Any news on Josh?' Lily blurted. If Katelyn asked her how she was doing first, she might not be able to hold herself together.

'I found him. It's bad, Lily.' Katelyn's voice shook. 'Can you meet me at Brecken Park where the old gravel road goes to the basketball court?'

'What's wrong?' Lingering adrenaline begged her limbs for movement. She shouldered through the restroom door and hustled down the hallway.

'Just . . . please hurry.'

'I'm leaving now.'

Lily ran out of the building's main entrance and darted between the rows of cars like a hare between trees. Her sister's voice whispered in her mind, soared on a gust of frigid wind, and Lily swore the asphalt under her shoes began to feel spongy, like fresh snow atop a blanket of dead leaves.

TWELVE

Rose – February 7, 2018

I wake up naked behind that goddamn chair, tangled in a ball of blankets and a world of hurt. My bones ache, my skin throbs, and my hair is too heavy on my scalp. Sunlight makes a valiant attempt to come through the grimy window. I'd give it an A for effort if I didn't want to shoot it out of the sky.

What happened last night?

I moan and roll over. The room comes into focus. Every stitch of linens has been pulled from the bed and is wadded up around me. Flimsy, thin pillows line the wall where I'd had my head, which swells with pressure as I sit upright. A couple of my nails are chipped, and my thumbnail is torn to the quick. Scratches cover the tops of my hands. Deeper ones have left wounds across the skin on my forearms.

I push myself up and stumble to the bathroom, ignoring the protests from my feet. My face is unmarked, but I've aged a decade overnight. My hair hangs in knots. I reach up to touch it. Bits of leaves and little broken pieces of sticks are tangled in the strands.

'What the hell?' I mumble.

I cast my gaze down my front. My toes are red and swollen, and there's mud dried between them.

'Betty?' Easton calls from the front of the room.

Easton. He's what happened last night.

I lean out of the bathroom in time to watch him come through the door and close it behind him with his hip, a coffee in each hand. I grab a towel off the shower bar. It's damp to the touch. I wrap it around my body anyway, hard pressed for any other option.

'What the hell happened last night?' I ask as I emerge.

'I was going to ask you the same thing.' He sets one to-go cup on the bedside table. 'It was fun, at first. *Really* fun. Then things got a little carried away for both of us. Maybe there was something extra in that stuff you scored at the park.'

'We went to the park?'

'Do you not remember any of it?' He slugs back some of his coffee. His arms are a mirror of mine, striped with scratches and bloodied half-moons where fingernails had dug into his skin.

'Did I do that to you? Did you . . . did you do this to me?' I hold up my forearms.

His expression sobers. 'We used everything I had, and you wanted one last hit.'

'Sounds like me.' I shuffle across the room, eyeing the coffee even though my blood screams for something stronger.

'You said you knew where to get it, so we went to Brecken Park. Once we got there, you wanted to take a walk in the trees. I figured why not; it was like a winter wonderland. But it wasn't a nice walk. It was like you were being chased.'

I take a sip, barely tasting it beyond the sensation of heat, and wait for a memory to flare in the dark of my brain. But there's nothing. 'Was I saying anything?'

'You were talking out of your head, but none of it made sense. You would bolt off, then sit down and start singing, then you'd jump up and do it all over again.'

Singing. Why was I singing? What was I singing? My gut twists so hard I nearly spit the coffee back out. 'Maybe I was auditioning for a new musical number for Sirens.'

'It was a showstopper – but not in a good way.'

'Sorry to be a killjoy. I tried to warn you.'

'You scared me, Betty. I had to drag you back. You fought me every step of the way. I put you in the shower to warm you up, and it seemed to calm you down, so I put you in bed and took a turn in the shower, and when I got out, the air was freezing. You were gone, so were my coat and my boots, and the door was wide open.'

I stare at him, dumbfounded. I can't recall any of it. Not a moment. Not a sound. The wounds are my only proof.

'Where did I go?' I ask.

'I have no idea. I drove around and looked for you for a while, but I couldn't find you and the roads were terrible. I went back to my place and grabbed a couple hours of sleep and some dry clothes, then picked up two coffees in hopes you'd have turned back up, and here I am.'

'Ever the gentleman.'

'It was twenty degrees last night, and you had my coat and my boots. I wasn't going to chase you through a snowstorm barefoot in an undershirt, and I didn't think you'd want me calling the cops for you. Honestly, high as I was, I shouldn't have been driving at all. I don't think either of us were making solid decisions.'

'That's fair.' My headache crackles against my skull like the swell of a summer thunderstorm.

'Do you feel as bad as you look?'

'Yep.' I look at him through half-opened eyes. Why doesn't Easton feel just as bad? Is it just a matter of tolerance, or did he pull back and let me fly higher on my own, hoping I'd answer any question he had once I'd soared well past sanity?

'Are you scheduled to work today?' he asks.

'I start at six p.m.' Yesterday's promises come filtering back. I have so much to do. Whatever I did last night, I also wasted time I don't have. *No more*, I tell myself. But my veins are already writhing beneath my skin. My blood is no longer enough to satisfy them.

'Take today off. Sleep, drink some water. I'll check on you later, OK?'

I nod again, which is a terrible idea, my head feeling entirely too heavy for my neck.

After Easton leaves, I grab my purse and sit on the floor on the far side of the bed, then pull out my phone. The first call I make is to Christian, but he doesn't answer. I breathe out a sigh of relief. He could be asleep or at school, unable to answer even if he wanted to, but I hope to God it means he's changed his mind.

I call Lyric next.

'Hello?' she answers on the first ring.

'It's Betty,' I say. 'Are you still in?'

'Yes.'

Shit. I close my eyes; think a beat. My brain riots against my demand for effort while it's sinking to the trough of a crash. I don't have to solve anything just yet. All I need to do is create more distance between these kids and Easton, then hold it for as long as I can. I'll have to let Easton make his move at some point. Just not with Lyric. I've learned my lesson. No more pets. From here on out, I'm not naming anyone but myself.

'Don't answer this phone anymore for now, OK? Not for anyone. We want to make sure you can get to Nashville without any problems.'

'What kind of problems?'

'None you need to worry about.' I sound like an asshole. 'Your voice is the only thing you need to worry about right now. Drink warm water with some lemon juice in it if you can. Every morning and every night,' I say, relaying a tip I'd seen on some dumb Hallmark movie a man paid me to watch with him. 'I'll handle the rest. I'm going to bring you a new phone you can use in the meantime. Can you still get by the park this afternoon?'

'Yeah. I'll be by the wall.'

'The wall?'

'The basketball court. There's a wall we can paint stuff on or whatever. It's like . . . a spot. We just call it the wall. It's dumb.'

'No, yeah. A spot. I get it. That's cool,' I say. 'I know where it is. I'll see you there.'

I hang up the phone and press the heel of my hand against my eyes. I wonder if I looked right at that wall last night and didn't even know it. Brecken Park is a hundred acres at least. I don't know what section we went to, but it wouldn't matter – I have no memory of being there at all.

Then again, maybe Easton was lying about all of it. Maybe he tried to kill me and bury me behind the motel, and I clawed back up from the grave after hell wouldn't have me.

I laugh a bitter laugh to myself because it's less scary than crying, and because all of it might possibly be the truth. Then I force myself to my feet.

THIRTEEN

Daniel – February 7, 2018

'Congratulations, Danny,' Hunter called to Daniel from his desk across the room as he put his phone back in its cradle and stood. 'You've got your first body. Let's go.'

Daniel snatched his jacket off the back of his desk chair and followed Hunter to his car. His heart pounded, beating harder now for someone else's who'd gone cold and still. The sensation made him feel a little sick.

As they drove to the scene, Hunter relayed what details had been phoned in: two teenage boys had been found at Brecken Park, one dead, one denying injury. There were no obvious signs of struggle or foul play, but the survivor wasn't talking.

They bypassed the main parking lot and drove up an access road to the most remote section of the park. An ambulance, two squad cars, and two older model sedans crowded the end of the road. In the distance, crime-scene tape was strung across the edge of the woods, a yellow scar against the white snow. Officers milled around on both sides of the tape. A pair of medics stood by the open doors of an ambulance, its lights off. A pair of skinny legs hung over the back bumper.

'Unit nine-two-four, we have a ten-seventy-one on Glen Avenue, officer requesting homicide and CSI,' an operator's voice prompted them through the radio as Hunter parked along the curb.

'Unit nine-two-four currently engaged at Brecken Park. Will check in shortly,' Hunter answered before turning off the car and opening his door.

Daniel pulled his door handle, then hesitated. He longed to ask Hunter what his first case had been like in hopes Hunter would remember how unprepared he may have felt as he had walked up to his first stretch of tape. Hunter would see through the question, though. Daniel knew everything about his brother's infamous first case, as did everyone in the department. His brother's reputation was the only reason the department had quietly decided to let Hunter partner with Daniel even though they were related; the fine print listing the pairing as a temporary training arrangement on paper.

They walked past the ambulance, where a teenage boy sat with a blue blanket draped around his shoulders and the telltale gaze of shock in his eyes. Two women stood with him.

'Should we talk to them first?' Daniel asked Hunter.

'No. Kid's not going anywhere. Scene first. You don't want someone else's story coloring your lens when you evaluate a scene the first time.'

Daniel kept his brother's advice close and trailed him to the tape. An officer held it up for them to duck under, then escorted them into the woods.

'What do we know?' Hunter asked him.

'Kid in the bus is Josh Marsden. They put a BOLO out for him yesterday. Ran away from a group home a couple days ago. Truancy seems to be a personal hobby.'

Daniel stole a glimpse of Hunter, but his brother didn't acknowledge him or the familiarity of the information.

'Before he stopped talking all together, Josh says he found the body and didn't know what to do. Didn't want to call the cops. Damn near froze to death. He's lucky his case worker came looking for him here this morning,' the officer continued.

Daniel cleared his throat, which drew looks from Hunter and the officer. 'Any information on the deceased?' he asked.

'Male. Probably fourteen, fifteen years old. Looks to have been dead for hours, but it's hard to tell if he's stiff from rigor mortis or from being frozen. No one has moved him or touched him other than the kid. I am fairly sure he knew him, but he won't say,' the officer answered.

Daniel frowned. 'What makes you think that?'

'If you find a stranger's body in the woods, are you going to sit by it all night?' Hunter interjected.

Daniel had no idea how to answer, and he immediately felt every bit of the rookie homicide detective that he was.

They'd traveled back about a hundred yards. Ahead of them,

more tape looped around a group of tall pines. The boy's body came into view. He was curled into a tree, knees drawn up nearly to his chin. His temple rested on a tree trunk. Snow marbled his hair, crystalized in his lashes, and dusted his nose and cheeks. It was not Daniel's first time seeing a body, but his heart sought refuge in the base of his throat. The kid looked peaceful, content, like he'd been waiting for Daniel to show up and just fell asleep in the snow.

'You know what, why don't you go talk to the kid in the bus? I'll start processing here,' Hunter said, breaking through Daniel's thoughts.

'I'll stay.'

'Nah, I changed my mind. Get the story from the other kid before he has more time to change it.'

Daniel tore his gaze from the frozen boy, and it landed on his brother. But Hunter wasn't studying the body or the scene. He was assessing Daniel.

Daniel flushed despite the cold. 'Sure,' he muttered and traveled alone back the way they'd come.

Josh had moved to the passenger seat of a small sedan, slouched so low in the seat he was barely visible. The same two women that were with him at the ambulance now waited near the front of the car.

'Ladies,' Daniel greeted. 'I'm Detective Daniel Wilder. I need to ask everyone a few questions.'

'Of course,' one woman responded, blinking rapidly. 'I'm Katelyn, Josh's social worker. This is Lily. We work together.' She gestured to the other woman. Wrapped in a long, pink coat, Lily reminded Daniel of an Easter egg against the snow.

'Which one of you found Josh?' Daniel asked.

'I did,' Katelyn replied. She wrapped her arms at her front, then rocked her weight from side to side in an uneven cadence. Maybe it was the cold or the situation or the dead child a football field from where they stood, but this woman's body language struck Daniel as edgy and nervous. He swung his gaze behind him and into the woods. There were half a dozen people back with the boy's body, and none of them could be heard or seen from here. Teenagers and drug dealers alike flocked to this end of the park because of how secluded it was from the outside world.

'How did you find him back there?' Daniel asked, refocusing on the woman.

'He comes to the park a lot, especially the basketball court.' Katelyn gestured with her chin down a crumbling strip of asphalt that once upon a time had been a road.

'Court's a half mile from here at least,' he said.

'There are walking trails all through these woods,' Lily spoke up. 'We make it a point to be pretty familiar with where our kids might be. As I'm sure you know, Brecken Park is a favorite.'

'So that spot in the woods in the middle of nowhere, that's a choice place for him to go?' Daniel pressed.

'I don't know how to explain it, I just . . . I pulled into this turn, headed for the court, and I had a feeling. I got out of my car, and I just followed it.'

'What, like a . . . maternal instinct?' Daniel reasoned.

'If that's what you want to call it.'

'What happened next?'

'I started calling his name over and over. I was about to turn around and go to the court, and . . .' Katelyn's voice cracked. 'And I heard a little boy's voice crying out for his mom. I just started running.'

Daniel paused, absorbing her story. His eyes flicked to the boy in the car. Josh hadn't moved a muscle since their conversation began.

'Why don't we all go to the station and get out of the cold. I'll interview him there,' Daniel suggested.

Katelyn shook her head. 'I don't think that's a good idea. Josh has been in the system since he was two years old. If we go down to the station, he won't say a word. He refused to go to the hospital. He's already worried he'll have to spend time in the detention center for running away.'

'I'll help make sure that doesn't happen,' Daniel offered on impulse, but he had no idea if he could save him from that.

Katelyn nodded, and her shoulders went slack. Beside her, Lily narrowed her eyes, considering him. Daniel had a feeling she had heard that party line before.

'If you take him in, he's not going to talk,' she said. 'If you want to get anything useful out of him, it'll be here.'

'We can start here. But depending on how the conversations progress, a trip to the station for everyone may become necessary,' Daniel countered.

'Of course,' Katelyn responded quickly.

'Katelyn should sit in the car with him,' Lily stated. 'He'll feel safer if she's there, and he'll be more likely to give you more information if he feels protected.'

'I'd rather speak with him alone,' Daniel said bluntly.

'That's not going to happen. He's a minor. He hasn't been charged with anything. If you speak with him, it's here, and it's with Katelyn or me present. But he's likely to say more with Katelyn there than me. Or we can bring in legal. Your call.'

'Fine,' Daniel acquiesced. To be the one seemingly in charge, Daniel felt wholly powerless. 'We can try your way. But if I don't get what I need, then we all go to the station. Understood?'

'Of course,' Katelyn said before shooting a warning look at her coworker.

Daniel and Katelyn climbed inside the car, Daniel in the driver's seat, Katelyn on the bench seat in the back. Josh focused straight ahead, his chin held high and rigid. A wet line ran the slope of his upper lip.

'Josh, I'm Daniel Wilder. I'm a detective. I need to ask you a few questions about what happened out here.'

'I don't know shit about what happened out here. You're the cop. You tell me.'

'I'm just worried about you right now. What were you doing out here last night?'

His jaw clenched. 'I needed some space.'

'I get that. Do you come out here a lot?'

'No.'

'Josh,' Katelyn interjected from the back seat, then she sighed. 'Most kids that live within walking distance are probably out here more days than they're not, including Josh. Forrest Hills High School is on the east side of the woods. They cut through going to or from school.'

'Do you go to school with that boy?' Daniel asked.

'I don't know where he goes. I don't even know him.'

'The officer first on scene said you did.'

'He's lying to you.'

'Josh, please,' Katelyn spoke up again, a stronger note of sternness in her voice. 'The detective is just trying to help. Tell him what you can. Help your friend. Help yourself.'

Daniel hesitated, considering her plea, her cooperation. She was pushing him to talk. That didn't speak to her being someone who would be nervous about what he might say.

'I think you know him, Josh,' Daniel said, conjuring the universal tone he'd heard from detectives, quiet and hard all at the same time. 'You sat beside him for hours in the cold and didn't call anyone. Why?'

'He was dead when I got to him! Are you going to leave a dead body in the woods?' Josh's eyes flashed at Daniel from their corners.

'How did you know he was dead?'

'I tried to wake him up, but he wouldn't. Then I saw that he wasn't breathing.'

'What did you do next?' Daniel asked.

'My phone wouldn't turn on. I think it was too cold. I came out to the road, but nobody was here.'

'So, you went back.' Daniel's voice lost some of the edge.

Josh looked out the window.

Daniel leaned into his space. 'You went back and what? Went through his pockets for anything worth taking?'

Josh whipped back to face him. 'It wasn't anything like that!'

'That's what it looks like to me,' Daniel lied. The body had shown no obvious signs of having been disturbed, a perfect, uniform layer of snow dusting his clothes. 'That's the way a DA is going to see it, too.' Out of his peripheral vision, he watched shock paint Katelyn's face.

'This is not at all what we agreed to,' she snapped, red touching her pale cheeks like his words had grabbed them and pinched. 'We're done here.' She cracked her door open, and urgency flooded Daniel's limbs.

'No one is leaving this car,' Daniel barked. 'There is a dead boy a football field from where we sit. You say you found him. If we're done here, I go get a warrant for your arrest, and you come into the station in handcuffs. Your social worker, too. Or you talk to me here and now. Your call. You came back from the road, and you what?'

'I just sat with him, OK?' Josh choked out. His eyes flashed with fear or desperation or both.

'You sat with him?'

'Yes! That's it!'

'Why?'

Josh crossed his arms at his front and pulled his legs into the seat, curling away from Daniel.

'Josh, why did you sit in the woods next to a dead body? You could've just left. You could've never told a soul. You were on the run. You found a dead boy. You stayed. Why?'

'He's scared of the dark,' Josh whispered.

'The boy in the woods?' Daniel asked.

Josh nodded.

'What's his name, Josh?' He paused. 'Please, I want to call him by his name.'

'Christian.' He blinked heavily. 'Christian Coleman.' Tears trickled from his eyes, then he doubled over, and his body shuddered with a gasping breath.

Daniel didn't know what to do with this breaking boy who was neither the day's victim nor suspect. This boy who he was responsible for tearing apart. His only solace was in knowing Hunter would have eviscerated Josh. His brother's customary interrogation tactics made Daniel's attempt at a hard-nosed interview look like a college application. And Hunter wouldn't have felt bad about it at all.

FOURTEEN

Lily – February 7, 2018

Lily sat with Katelyn and Josh at a fast-food restaurant, but they may as well have never left the car. Josh hadn't touched the cheeseburger Katelyn ordered for him. He hid his chin in the neck of his sweatshirt, and his hood cast a shadow over his vacant eyes. Lily hung her head. She felt every ounce of the weight he was carrying. She wondered how much he had witnessed in his young life, especially in the last twelve hours of it.

'Are you done?' Katelyn asked.

Josh removed a hand from his pocket long enough to push the uneaten food in her direction. 'Where are you going to take me?'

'He can stay with me,' Lily blurted. She wasn't sure which one of them was more surprised by her offer.

'That's not a solution,' Katelyn said.

'It can be for a night.' Lily looked Josh in the eyes and nodded at him. 'It will give everyone a little more time to find a more suitable long-term arrangement. I don't have a guest room, but I have a pullout sofa. It's comfortable, I promise.'

He watched her for a full two seconds, wringing his hands.

'It would be a temporary solution only,' Katelyn said to them both.

'I promise I won't make any trouble for you, Miss Lily,' Josh whispered.

'I know.'

The door to the restaurant swung open, and an army of teenage boys in identical black hoodies and matching gym shorts filed inside. Two chartered buses were visible in the parking lot, and more uniformed kids were heading for the door.

'If we're done here, we should free up the table,' Katelyn said. When no one responded, she began gathering the uneaten food on her tray.

'Can I use the restroom before we go?' Josh asked.

Katelyn nodded.

He slid from his seat and strode across the crowded restaurant. Lily and Katelyn watched him until he disappeared down the hall that led to the restrooms. The first wave of players to order food quickly filled every empty seat. Others opted to prop their meals on the dividing wall between the dining room and the ordering area near the counter instead of waiting for a table.

'I'm ready to be out of here,' Katelyn said, fatigue evident in her voice and on her face. She carried the tray to the trash can, Lily following behind, then they stood next to the exit.

'Where is he?' Katelyn cast her gaze down the hall.

'A ton of kids came in at once. There's probably a line in the bathroom, too,' Lily reasoned.

'Come on.' Katelyn shouldered her way to the restroom, where a line extended out of the propped door. Teenage boys gave them looks of surprise as they stepped into the men's room. Lily hung back by the doorway so she could keep an eye on the main exit and block Josh should he try to bolt past Katelyn.

'Josh?' Katelyn called. No one answered. 'Josh, come out. This is ridiculous.'

A few of the boys waiting in line laughed uneasily, but the note of panic in her voice acted like an emergency siren, and they were quick to move out of her way and allow her through.

'Josh? Don't make me look in these stalls!'

From her post by the doorway, Lily gnawed on her lip as Katelyn peered under each door. Josh had to be in there, didn't he? They hadn't let their guards completely down while they'd waited. She'd kept watch. She'd been vigilant.

At the last stall, Katelyn snapped upright, her expression frantic. 'He's gone.'

FIFTEEN

Daniel – February 7, 2018

Daniel watched the southside of Tula slide by the passenger window as Hunter turned on to the street listed as Christian's residential address. These few blocks always had a gray feel, regardless of the season. Today, kids dotted the sidewalks in splashes of color. They reminded Daniel of dandelions, determined to survive where they had landed.

Christian's final house was a gray box trimmed in white and was owned by his foster mother of record, Mona Howard. The small yard was a slick of mud, snow having been trampled by a thousand footprints. Hunter rang the doorbell, and inside, a small dog's yap began simultaneously as if he had somehow triggered both by pressing the button. The door cracked open only wide enough to peer through. A woman's face became visible in the gap. Her eyes were bloodshot, swollen, and brimming with more tears.

'Mona Howard?' Hunter greeted. 'I'm Detective Kepp, and this is Detective Wilder,' he continued as he presented his badge.

'Police just came by here.' Mona shifted her weight, which revealed a toddler clinging to her hip. 'If you don't mind, I have some very sad children to try to explain this to.'

'We're with homicide, ma'am,' Daniel said gently. 'We're trying to explain it, too.'

Mona stepped back and let the door swing open wider, then she gestured for them to follow her as she turned and moved deeper inside the house.

Children's artwork hung on every wall – from scribbles and glorified stick figures to a watercolor painting of the sun setting behind the city skyline. A small brown dog stood guard behind a baby gate, which separated the kitchen from the common area of the house. A potato, half chopped, was on a cutting board, the knife cast aside, and Daniel wondered if that's what she was doing when she had answered the door to the worst news imaginable.

Mona led them to the living room and gestured for them to sit on a tan microfiber couch. On the other side of the room, a boy, five or six years old, was building a tower of blocks. As soon as he noticed their arrival, he stood and ran to Mona. His fingers closed around her long skirt in two little fists.

'They need to ask me about your brother, baby,' she said softly. 'Why don't you go watch a little TV in my room.'

'It's not night-time,' he replied and pointed to the window, where weak, winter light shone through.

'It's all right. Just one show,' she replied, blinking rapidly. Then, in unspoken agreement, they watched the little boy scurry from the room before Mona turned back to face them. 'How can I help you?'

'What can you tell us about Christian?' Hunter asked, beating Daniel to the punch.

Mona sighed as she sat down, swinging the toddler from her hip to her lap, where she wrapped her arms around the little girl.

'Christian is a good boy, but he's a runner. He's run from every house he's been in, even his own family's home when he was put with his grandmother. She gave up trying to keep him. He's been in a detention center a couple times. He's got a record. Nothing bad, just enough that it colors a judge's opinion any time his file gets opened.'

'Where do you think he's been trying to get to?' Daniel asked.

'I'm not sure he even knows.' She squeezed her eyes shut, and the tears she'd been able to hold back before leaked out. The toddler in her lap looked up at her and patted her cheek.

'Did something happen specifically that may have set this into motion?' Hunter asked.

'I run this house with my brother, Calvin. He believes in firm boundaries, and he's not wrong. Kids need that. It's how they know that you care. Calvin found a good bit of money under Christian's mattress yesterday. He wanted to know where Christian got it. Christian wouldn't tell us where he'd come by it, so Calvin wouldn't give it back. Christian was upset, safe to say. So was Calvin. Broke trust on both sides. We were just trying to keep him safe. Most of the ways an underage kid can get fast money puts them in harm's way.'

'Do you remember how much money it was?' Daniel asked.

'Two hundred dollars. First thing I did when I noticed he was gone was check for the money. He had taken it.'

Nodding, Daniel made a note to ask the medical examiner if they'd found money in Christian's pockets.

'Did you expect he'd ever try to leave for good?' Hunter asked.

'When he first got here, he would disappear most evenings. That's why we started letting his brother watch one TV show after dinner, so he wouldn't worry too much about his brother being gone. But last week, I noticed that Christian was staying home more. He'd become more diligent about his homework, too. With his younger brother here, I figured he had a good reason to want to stay, to try. It's one of the reasons I didn't call it in when I went to wake him up and he wasn't there. Siblings do better together, and I didn't want to see them separated. I felt sure he was coming back. He's stormed out before, but he always comes back.'

'Can we see his room?' Daniel asked.

'Sure. I haven't touched anything other than the bed. Pulled the covers off looking for him. Even got down on my hands and knees and looked underneath. Doesn't matter how big they get; I've found boys near grown squeezed under a bed. But Christian wasn't here. I can't help wondering if somebody did something to him.'

Hunter leaned forward and clasped his hands together. 'There were no signs that he struggled in any way or was taken against his will. No obvious defensive wounds or bruising. This looks like an accident so far.'

'But how cold was he? How helpless and alone did he feel out there? And why did he sit down? Why didn't he keep trying to come home?'

'We are going to do everything in our power to figure out what happened and why. Until we get an ME report with results of a tox screen, we can't rule anything out,' Daniel stated.

Mona shifted her gaze to meet his. 'Is it wrong I hope someone caused this? Did this to him?'

'I think it hurts regardless,' Hunter answered.

'Which way to his room?' Daniel asked. He felt the first pull of ownership over the boy's ghost, and he wondered if that's what Hunter had meant the day before.

'Second door on the right.' Mona pointed down a yellow hall. She pushed herself off the couch, leaning to move the toddler back to her hip. Daniel doubted she would go a moment that day without carrying someone else's weight.

'You said Christian was home more than usual in the past couple weeks. How would he spend his time?' Hunter asked as they stood.

'He had a school project he was working on. It seemed like he was into it.'

'Did he tell you any specifics about it?' Daniel asked.

'He wouldn't talk much about it, but he asked for printer paper a couple times. He draws quite a bit. He writes poetry, too.'

'Does he have access to a computer here in the house?' Hunter asked.

'I have a computer for the kids to use, but I keep it in a separate room at the end of the hall. There's no door on it. I don't like them having the internet behind a closed door. Too many sickos getting access to kids that way.'

'If we need to, can we take the computer with us?' Hunter asked.

For the first time since letting them in, Mona hesitated. 'It's the only one we have for the kids,' she said. 'Can you look at it here?'

'We'll do a quick search here for today,' Hunter answered. 'But if we find anything suspect, we may need to take it in.'

'Whatever you need to do,' Mona said, then blotted fresh tears from her eyes.

'Thank you, Mona,' Daniel said, then followed Hunter down the short hall to Christian's open door.

The bed cover was in a wad on the floor. Daniel imagined Mona balling it against a sudden pit in her stomach, wondering what she would say to Christian's brother if he wasn't back by the time he woke up. Daniel looked at the second bed in the room, the train-pattern bed sheets, the sippy cup on the table beside it. The brothers shared a room. Would Christian have peered down at his brother before leaving and, if he had planned to stay gone, made a final gesture or left a note?

'We should interview the brother,' Hunter said, as if reading Daniel's mind. Then he pulled open the drawer in the bedside table and used the tip of his pen to leaf through the odds and ends, pausing when his phone rang. He glanced at the screen and turned his back to Daniel. 'Why don't you go get nosy with the computer the kids use?' he said over his shoulder.

'Sure.' Daniel walked out of the room, but he didn't go far, idling instead in the hall between the doors, waiting, listening, and feeling like a criminal.

'Kepp,' Hunter answered as he ducked inside Christian's room and eased the door mostly shut, but Daniel could still hear snippets of his end of the conversation. 'No, not that I know of . . . I don't think she'd be willing . . . Yeah, I know it was different back then.'

Daniel leaned against the wall, his gaze fixed through the sliver of space between him and Hunter, his mind split between wanting to dissect what Hunter had already said and not wanting to miss what he said next.

'Yeah, I know . . . That could be a major problem . . . If I see her, I'll take care of it.'

See who? Daniel's thoughts immediately jumped to Betty, but Hunter had said it regarding someone he hadn't seen. It was possible he was lying, but why would he need to? Unless someone else knew about Betty's 'pass' yesterday morning.

'Yeah, sounds good. Pull footage. I can be up there in twenty.'

Daniel pushed himself off the wall and darted to the computer room, then jiggled the mouse to awaken the screen so it looked like he'd been on task and entirely too preoccupied to eavesdrop. A Word document was open, the cursor blinking a few lines down on the blank page. Someone had written something and deleted it. The empty space was suddenly louder than Hunter's betrayal. Daniel prompted the undo option, but nothing came up.

'Martin got a hit on ballistics from the drug house shooting. He needs me back at the station pronto,' Hunter said.

Daniel spun round, then paused, studying his brother without responding. He knew Hunter was flat out lying to him, which took to his trust like sandpaper to silk.

'There's nothing here, anyway,' Hunter added before extracting himself from the door and slinking down the hall.

Daniel heaved a breath. He had no idea how to say no when it came to Hunter Kepp. Then he turned his back on the computer and his own instincts, leaving them both behind to follow his brother out.

SIXTEEN

Lily – February 7, 2018

Lily and Katelyn scoured the south end of the city from east to west, casting the light of attention down the shadowed alleys and vacant buildings Josh was known to haunt. He was nowhere to be found.

They drove around the outskirts of Brecken Park. The tree boughs painted shadows on the melting snow and swayed in the wind like mothers rocking fussing infants. At the turnoff for the access road to the court, the strip of yellow crime-scene tape became visible.

'I can't look,' Katelyn said, averting her gaze. But Lily couldn't bring herself to look away. She stared at the bleed of color in her side-view mirror as they made the turn until it faded from view.

A half mile up the crumbling road, they parked along the curb near the trail leading to the makeshift basketball court. Katelyn turned the car off and stole a glimpse in the direction where Christian and Josh were found hours before. It was no longer visible, but Lily could feel it all the same. Beside her, Katelyn leaned her head against the top of the wheel and gave herself over with a deep, choking sob, wresting Lily from her thoughts. She placed her hand on top of Katelyn's and waited.

'I can go look alone; you can stay here,' Lily whispered after the other woman's sorrow was spent.

'No. He's mine. I want to come.' Katelyn gathered herself with a few measured breaths then wiped her face dry, and they climbed out of the car.

Lily tailed Katelyn down the littered sidewalk until it ran out, unceremoniously ending at a line of trees and brush. They heard the court before they saw it, the pounding of a ball against asphalt, a clatter as it struck the backboard, and the cries of teammates announcing an opportunity or a warning.

The eroded corner of the wall came into view. Several kids sat on the edge in a cluster. Katelyn sped up, angling for them.

'Wait,' Lily hissed at her, barely loud enough to be heard above the noise from the court.

Katelyn paused.

'Let's just watch for a second from back here, see if we can spot him before anyone notices us,' Lily explained.

Katelyn nodded, then stepped over to conceal herself behind the trunk of a tree. Lily watched from where she stood on the trail, already shrouded from easy view. Most of the people watching were bundled in jackets and hooded sweatshirts, knit caps pulled down. Between their clothing and the fading light, it was nearly impossible to see their faces.

A girl stepped out of a messy line of onlookers and walked away from the others, her head down, hands shoved in her pockets, steps quick. It was Maya. Lily looked ahead of her, trying to guess where she was going. A woman stood behind a cluster of kids watching from the far corner of the court. She wore a black tracksuit, the hood pulled over her head far enough to hide the top half of her face, and the shadows cast from the trees at her back covering everything else. Maya angled for her, following the boundary between asphalt and earth until they were a breath apart. Then the woman withdrew a hand from her jacket and passed Maya something black and palm-size. As Maya turned away, a smile flickered across the woman's features, sad and gentle and fierce.

The hair on the back of Lily's neck stood up.

It was Rose's smile.

'I see Josh. He's not playing. He's just standing by himself, watching,' Katelyn whispered, but Lily couldn't tear her eyes away from where her sister stood enveloped in shadows at the far edge of the court. She blinked twice, waiting for her to vanish or turn into someone else.

That face, that smile, remained.

Lily stumbled forward, drawn to the furious, calculating flash of teeth like a moth to a flame. She would burn for the trade of one last touch.

'Dang it, there are two cops walking up to the court. I hope they don't spook him,' Katelyn said, but her voice sounded hollow and far away.

'Rose,' Lily whispered.

'Lily?' Katelyn called out to her.

'Rose!' Lily shouted.

On the other side of the court, the woman turned away.

'Rose! Wait!' Lily bolted forward, tripping over snow-covered roots and fallen limbs. The kids on the court scattered.

'Rose! Don't go!' she screamed, looking up. But the woman was gone.

The asphalt square cleared within seconds, except for two police officers who quickly approached Lily. Katelyn hurried to her side and waved them off.

'She's OK. We've had a long day. A traumatic day. I'll make sure she gets home,' Katelyn said, then guided Lily back to the car.

SEVENTEEN

Rose – February 7, 2018

I sit in my car, which is parked on the farthest row from the front door to Sirens in the last available spot, tapping a line of blow on the triangle of flesh between my throbbing thumb and pointer finger. Regret is there, too, but I need to be brave. I need to feel something other than cold, need to see something other than the silhouette of a shivering little girl in every shadow, need to hear something other than my song whistling through sleepy, seven-year-old lips.

It's just this one last time, I tell myself and snort it up my nose.

I gnaw on the torn corner of my thumb, trading the sting of raw pain for the dull ache of pressure until the cocaine makes short work of them both. After I'd scrubbed every trace of last night off my skin, I cut my nails to even out the ragged edges. Then I painted them dark blue to hide the bruising beneath the beds. I wish it was as easy to remember what happened with Easton as it was to cover up the evidence. But maybe it's best I don't remember. I'm not dead. At this point, that's what counts. Not everyone was so lucky last night.

Inside Sirens, customers pack both sides of the main stage. It's standing room only around the fish tank. Believe it or not, that warm salt water is a coveted spot among the working girls here. The tips are crap; most men won't pay for what they don't have a chance of touching. But it's quiet in there, and everything slows down.

I would kill for slow and quiet. But after Lily screamed my real name across the basketball court for everyone to hear, I'm on borrowed time. If she doesn't see me again, she might be able to tell herself that she imagined me, dreamed up my face on someone who looked like me. I know it's happened before over the years, no matter how hard I try to avoid it. But if she sees me again, she'll believe, and no matter how it goes after that, it would be cruel. If she's sure I am here and I leave her again, she'll know she wasn't why I came back. If she's sure I'm here and I stay, there will be no stopping her from seeing what I've become. Nor will there be a way to avoid answering for what I've done.

I haven't quit moving since I could walk and think in a straight line again this morning. I made a couple trades early to get the funds I'll need to stash Lyric somewhere out of town for the weekend if it comes to that. The first guy saw last night's souvenirs and was convinced I was a damsel in distress, which made him the hero who could heal me with his very average cock and a hundred dollars. The second saw the bruises and his eyes turned bright, his teeth peeking from his lips like kids peering at the dessert table.

Can I make more? he'd asked, already leaning forward, assessing the few remaining wound-free places on me for one to wreck.

Fifty bucks a bite, I'd said. I'd underestimated his budget, if not his appetite, but I can't complain. I only wish I'd scheduled them in reverse. I bet Mr Disney Prince would've just handed me his entire wallet if he'd seen the effects of the prick who'd come after him.

Then I went to the upscale mall at the north end of town to score a new look. Worst part of my day. I'd rather fuck for cash than endure the stares of store employees and uppity customers like they're just glad they're not me.

Tonight, I could be one of them.

I'm dressed in dark jeans, a fitted white blouse, red patent heels, and the white cashmere trench coat from the trash pile. Between the outfit, the 'fresh-look' cosmetics applied to my scarred, tired face by the sweet girl working the Revlon makeup counter at the mall, and a brown wig styled in a low ponytail, even men who've ogled every inch of me would probably swear they've never seen me before.

And that's exactly the point.

Men glance at me as I stride across the floor. Out of habit, I stare right back, flash a smirk or a wink, but every time, they look away when I return the eye contact. It's a strange feeling, even if it was planned, and it takes me a moment to realize that the gesture is a show of respect or of self-control. In its presence, I come face to face with how little I've seen either aimed at me before. I knew it would work – at least I'd hoped it would – but it is bewildering as fuck none the less.

The music shifts into something more frantic, and the girls on the clock come alive with a burst of movement. Some of the men holler. Cash is lifted in the air by the fistful. I am all but forgotten.

I stand still, gaze swinging from the entertainment area to the employee door. Easton rounds the floor once an hour on busy nights, usually spending about fifteen minutes socializing in the VIP section before retreating. Customers love to glad-hand him like he brought a circus to town and owns every rare beast in the ring. It won't be the end of the world if he spots me, but I want to know where he is before I move to the back of the house. There are more rooms, more walls, more doors, and more places to hide back there, but there's also no reason for me to be here at all.

Easton appears and cuts across the floor to the roped-off VIP area, smiling at no one in particular. As soon as he's engaged with a middle-aged man donning a bad comb-over and a navy sport coat, I check the time and slip through the door. My count-down starts now.

I head directly for his office. The door is locked, but I brought what I need to convince it otherwise. I slide inside, close the door, and engage the lock again. I start my search with the filing cabinets, expecting them to be locked, too. But every drawer pulls open, albeit loudly. They're stuffed with file folders and paperwork, receipts, permits, and page upon page of tiny print and legalese and signatures and dates. To read them would take all night, and I've got about twelve minutes left.

I move to his desk, where a laptop sits open in the center of the space. I strike a key, waking it up from hibernation. A box appears, requesting a password to go any farther, and I don't have it, nor would I have any idea what to guess. I'm tempted to unplug it and take it with me, but then what? All I know how to do with a computer is play solitaire.

I wish I was more tech savvy. Back when I used to procure identities and sell them up the chain, I got in the habit of logging the descriptions and information by my own little code – basic as fuck – changing one letter out for another like a kid writing secret notes to a best friend. More like math than words, which was always my strong suit, anyway. Believe it or not, crime goes high-tech faster than life above the proverbial table, but even as other girls took to encrypting the information they stole, I kept my own language. Any prepubescent hacker can take passworded or encrypted identities for themselves. The only one who can decode mine is me.

I leave the laptop alone and turn my attention to the drawers framing both sides of the space for a chair. They're all locked, but the shallow center drawer pulls open. It's mostly empty. He must regularly keep something rectangular in here, which has left an imprint on the blue liner.

There's a single key and a twenty-dollar bill resting in the bottom of an oversized coin dish tucked into the front corner. The key looks too big to open any of the drawers in the office. I tip the wooden dish over with an index finger. The bottom is hollowed out. An undersized thumb drive is taped along an inside edge.

It's a risk to take it.

It'd be fucking criminal not to.

I pluck it loose and drop it in my coat pocket, savoring a strange tingle of satisfaction like electric shock therapy. Then I slide out of Easton's office and strut to the exit like I own the whole building. It's a lie though. I know damn well these walls will always own me.

EIGHTEEN

Lily – February 7, 2018

They drove back to the restaurant parking lot in silence. Katelyn pulled alongside Lily's car and shifted into park.

'It's perfectly normal to think you saw your sister,' she began gently. 'With what happened today, the stress we're under, how close this all must hit home for you . . . It's normal.'

'She was there, Katelyn.'

'I know you think you saw her.' She rested her hand on Lily's. The sensation of touch and the look of pity on Katelyn's face made Lily want to put a fist through the passenger-side window. 'You need to find peace with what happened to you. Forgiveness isn't for the person who hurt you; it's giving yourself permission to heal, to let go.'

Lily tilted her head back against the back of the seat. 'I would probably tell someone else the same thing. It's also a load of crap.'

Katelyn frowned at her. 'Turn your nose up at it all you want. But you might want to ask yourself if obsessing over weather forecasts and chasing every missing kid in the department is working for you.'

Lily twisted in her seat to looked at Katelyn. 'That's rich coming from the person who asks for my help finding missing kids more than anyone else in the entire office.'

Katelyn lifted her chin and looked through the windshield, her silence egging Lily on worse than words ever could.

'You know, I never stopped looking for Natasha. Did you? Do you even think about her anymore?' Lily spat.

A child's cry escaped Katelyn. The pain in it washed over Lily, cooling her so quickly she felt brittle and thin as it passed. She shut her eyes, steadying her thoughts. Katelyn wasn't the only case worker who'd had a child in their care simply disappear.

When Lily finally brought herself to peer at Katelyn, tears were streaming down her colleague's young face.

'Katelyn, I'm sorry.' Lily's voice faltered. 'The choices these kids are making, they're not our fault. When someone doesn't want to be found, we can't blame ourselves for that. I'm sorry for what I said. It was me . . . me being mad at myself. I know I'm not healed. Not by a long shot. But I swear I'm trying.'

'I know you are. And I know you think I'm still a doe-eyed, goodie two-shoes, and maybe I am, but I care about these kids just as much as you do. But there's more than one way to care.'

'I completely agree. More than you know.'

'Then please understand that this is me caring, too.' Katelyn fished inside her coat pocket with her free hand and retrieved her phone. 'I'm calling in a new BOLO for Josh. We have searched everywhere I know to try. We can't be on every street in Tula at the same time. It's freezing outside, and it's going to start snowing again any minute. We are not enough to find him tonight, Lily.' Her voice was deeply tired and a little raw, as if every time she called Josh's name had worn a blister. 'Be mad at me if you want to.'

'I'm not mad at you.' Lily didn't know what to call the swirl of chill and heat becoming something reckless inside her chest.

'I didn't call it in soon enough when Natasha went missing,' Katelyn whimpered.

'Natasha was different. She was on the cusp of aging out when she ran. You weren't given much formal time to search. What I said before wasn't fair.'

'I don't want to lose another one.' Katelyn choked out the words.

'I'm not going to let you. Go home. Get some rest. I'll keep looking a little longer. I owe you that. If I don't find him in the next couple hours, I'll call it in myself, OK?' Lily offered. It was partly true. She was determined to continue the search, but she had no intention of renewing the BOLO. Josh had been through enough for one day.

'Are you going to your cabin tonight? If it's going to snow as bad as they say, you need to get on the road or you'll get stuck here again,' Katelyn reasoned.

Lily glanced at the snow-quiet sky. 'I am. Just for tonight, then again for the weekend. But I have time to look in a few more places on my way out of town.'

'I don't know, Lily. I don't want to wait. I have this feeling that if we don't bring in help and find him tonight, we might not ever find him.'

'Don't worry. Josh is tough as they come. That's what I like about him most. And the harder he thinks we're looking, the smarter he's going to be.'

'That's the truth.' Katelyn sighed. 'Will you call me on your way out of town and let me know any updates?'

'Of course.'

Lily climbed out of Katelyn's car and into hers, then watched her pull away. Her gaze drifted upward through her windshield. Even in the dark, the sky was thick and silver from horizon to horizon. A shiver gripped her core, and she clenched her teeth together to keep from gasping. No one should be left to spend a night like this alone.

NINETEEN

Rose – February 7, 2018

For the second time in my entire life, I stand outside the entrance to the Tula library. The first time happened three weeks after I'd left Lily in the woods. All I knew about a library at that point was that there was a card involved, which I didn't have, and that it was probably warm inside. The snow from the storm had long since melted, but I was still cold all the way through, and I'd yet to find a place I felt safe enough to sleep longer than an involuntary snatch or two. I'd turned my first trick for money overnight, hoping he'd take me somewhere dry and soft, but he'd led me down an alley and pinned me face first to a wet, grimy wall. To add insult to injury, he'd paid me five dollars when we'd agreed on fifty.

I'd passed through the library doors, wishing I was invisible, then tiptoed across the lobby, not knowing whether I was allowed to be there at all. After a half hour had passed with no one paying me any attention, I stopped hiding and started wandering the shelves. I'd peered at the covers the same way fancy people admire art in movies, pulled down a few that caught my interest where women in short skirts raised their swords or spears against monsters of all kinds. But when I opened them, the big words mocked me, and the small ones that I did know swam on the page.

I'd fled to the kiddie section and tucked myself into a corner, surrounded by stuffed animals and cartoons. I'd stayed there, back against the wall, then thumbed through board books with happy faces and simple problems until I fell asleep. I'd woken up to an old lady glaring at me, her hands shaking my shoulders.

You need to leave. You're scaring the young children, she'd said.

I've never tried my luck inside another library until right now.

According to the sign on the door, they closed fifteen minutes ago. I knock on the glass, glaring at it, then cup my hands to my face and peer in. All I see is darkness. I make two fists and pound against the door until it rattles in the frame. If no one answers, I'll make a way inside.

A woman walks into view. She's probably in her early twenties, dark hair pulled back, black-frame glasses taking up most of her face. From the other side of the glass, she sizes me up, and I've never been so glad to have suffered an afternoon at the mall.

'We're closed!' she calls from where she stands.

I press both palms to the glass. 'Please! It's an emergency!'

She rolls her eyes, then marches forward even though she makes it plainly obvious she doesn't want to. 'We're a library, not a hospital,' she snipes, but she unlocks the door and cracks it open. 'What do you need?'

'I just need a computer. Five minutes tops.' I dig into my purse and pull out a twenty-dollar-bill. 'Please.'

She heaves a sigh. 'Fine. Five minutes.'

I dash to the center of the library, where old-school computers sit on long, rectangular tables, and slam myself down into the nearest chair. My heart pounds in my chest. I tell myself it's because my cardiovascular health is trash and jogging from the door to the desk is the first time I've run in a decade, but it's been beating like a snare drummer on crack since I left Easton's office.

I plug the thumb drive into the computer. A box pops up, prompting a password. Fuck, I don't have time for this.

'Four minutes,' the girl calls from the door, as if I don't already know.

I type in SIRENS. The box flashes, denying access, and prompts me again.

ALIBI.

Access denied.

GIRLS.

Access denied.

Think, Rose. Think. I slam the heels of my hands into my forehead. Even though it's the second-to-last memory I want to revisit, I go back to the hallway in the casino and search for any words she'd said that would fit here and now.

She said they were talking about transferring her to another bar the guy owns in Miami. The dead girl's voice haunts my mind, echoes in my skull, vibrates in the roots of my teeth.

I swallow a sudden surge of bile and begin to type, the need to puke growing with every keystroke.

MIAMI.

Access denied.

I slap my hand on the desk. I'm so close and so far and I'm no good at this.

The rest of the girl's sentence comes roaring back: *a place called Palm Tree Express.*

Dread is a spider on my back, leaving a trail of goosebumps with every footfall.

PALMTREEEXPRESS.

The box vanishes, and several folder icons pop up.

The library falls away, the glowing screen like a tunnel in the dark. I click on the first folder. A plain text document appears. Short lines of pure gibberish are grouped into stanzas like someone closed their eyes and tried to type a poem with the keyboard upside down.

I stare harder, comparing lines, my brain calculating in the background the way it does when a bunch of numbers need adding up at the end of a shift. There's a pattern. Repeated fragments. I would bet Easton fucking Grimes covers his shit old-school style in his own language. Just like me.

I grab a fistful of money from my purse and run up to the girl. She's tapping her foot on the polished entryway and makes an ugly face when she sees me hauling ass toward her.

'I need more time,' I say, out of breath again, and shove the wad of cash at her. I'm tempted to ask if I can print everything out, which would give me all the time I need to decipher it. But if Easton found it on me, it might as well be a death certificate.

'Well, *I* need to go,' she snaps.

'The door auto locks, right? You can leave with a lot more money than you got paid to be here all day, and I can let myself out when I'm done. It's a win-win. I won't do anything stupid.

Please.' It takes everything I have for my vocabulary to match my outfit, to not just scream expletives until my lungs give out in hopes of scaring her away.

'Fuck. Fine. I hate this job anyway,' she says, then shoves the door open and stomps across the parking lot. While I wait for the door to click shut, I stare after her, mystified and on the brink of a crazy fit of laughter, then hurry back to the computer.

Two hours later, I've potentially deciphered a handful of letters, but I have my doubts. Having coded my own intel when I was gathering information for Hunter about Alibi and storing stolen IDs for myself seems to be both helping and hurting. Usually, I would solve the single-letter words first, which would help me plug them in elsewhere, but there aren't any. So I turn my attention to flagging groups of three or four letters that appear more than once. There's only a handful of those that have any common function, and once you can identify them, letters on either side can be narrowed down into words, too.

I study the shortest word I suspect has an ING buried in the middle: five letters, with the same letter on either side. 'S' is the letter that makes the most sense, which would make the word SINGS.

After what feels like even more hours, I have a series of words. A description. An age range and body build, with a note that these desired specifics are non-negotiable. Good teeth. Braces are deal breakers. Bonus points for sexually inexperienced. An extra grand on top of the listing price if she sings.

I'm right. I'm right. And fuck, I know exactly what that means.

But I was wrong about one thing. Easton hadn't stumbled upon Lyric. He'd hunted her down. This list isn't a catalog of who Easton has in his proverbial stable. It's an order sheet for what his customers want him to find. I would bet my soul the dead girl's sister is on this list, but even if I could stomach decoding the next description, I don't know what she looks like.

I snatch the thumb drive from the computer, every inch of me trembling, when a sudden thought sucker-punches me in the guts: when I left Easton's office, I hadn't locked the door. By now, he knows someone has been in there. I'd bet my life he already knows who.

Panic steals across my mind like a passing shadow and my

heart pulses too hard in my chest, making me gasp for air. I gasp and gasp and gasp, then I yank the thumb drive from the computer and bolt for the door.

I arrive at the south entrance to Brecken Park well past midnight with no memory of the drive. My phone is in my hand, and I know I made a phone call. I must have because before too long, another car pulls up close to mine. A kid rolls down his window. We make a trade, the movements as automatic and fluid as breathing, and they pull away.

I feed the darkness inside of me with cocaine, ketamine, and molly until it stops gnawing on my bones, then I reach into my coat pocket for the thumb drive. I need to feel it, to remember why I'm here, what I'm doing, why this has to be the last time I throw my brain down a hole just to make my mind stop screaming.

It isn't there. I spread my fingers wide inside both pockets, searching the seams. The frayed place I'd found before was hiding a hole.

'No.' I pat down the front of the coat, but I don't feel it anywhere. I turn on the interior lights and search the seat and the floor beneath it. Then I shove the door open so I can get better access to the narrow space between the seat and the frame.

There's nothing there.

I rip the coat from my back and spread it out on the hood of my car. The hole from the pocket feeds into the liner. There are more small holes all along the hem, but with any shred of luck, the thumb drive is trapped somewhere inside. Using my car key, I pull the thread out of the center seam and begin tearing away the fabric in strips so I can probe behind it. Along the hemline, I feel a lump and rip it out. But it's not the thumb drive. It's a rolled, torn piece of a white paper bag.

My phone rings on the dashboard with an incoming call from Lyric. I ignore her, pocket my phone, and move away from my car to the glow of a streetlight that spotlights the handicap parking place by the trailhead. My shoes sink in several inches of accumulated snow, which nearly pries them off my heels with every step, but I hardly register the chill. Once I'm standing inside the light, I unroll the paper. The writing is faint, shaky, loopy with youth, and made incredibly small to fit on the limited space:

> *Natasha was here.*
> *I don't want to be.*
> *Am I real? No one cares.*
> *No one's looking for me.*
> *If you're reading this,*
> *I guess I was real all along.*
> *But if you're reading this,*
> *I'm already gone.*

Tears come, hot and furious, blurring out the words. But Natasha's whole life is crystal clear, at least the chapter of it when she wore this coat and wrote this note before I found it in the trash bag at Sirens.

A mattress on the floor, if she was lucky.

A reaction to the sound of approaching footsteps like soldiers home from war probably feel about fireworks.

A numbness that settles at the very center of you, so thick and solid you can't even feel your heart beating when you press your palm to your chest.

This note is saying everything without saying nearly enough. The whole truth is found in the empty space, the gaps between the words and lines, filled in with whatever description she'd fit for the catalog on Easton's thumb drive.

If I take them both to the cops now, best-case scenario, they'd say they'll look into it, or that it doesn't mean anything. Even if they do understand what it's really saying, they'll say I wrote it, especially without proof this girl exists to be missing. But she exists everywhere.

Natasha has been a thousand girls. A hundred thousand. More.

I do not know her, but I can see her, feel her, hear her. Her words could've been mine, could still belong to Lyric, could've been written by the dead girl or her sister, could've been Lily's had that night leaving Everett's gone any other way than it did. This is the cost, over and over, of whoever I watch Easton destroy just so I can prove he's doing it. This was always going to be the cost. This is a truth that is never going to change.

My phone rings again with another incoming call from the phone I gave Lyric. I can barely form a sentence, let alone figure out how to keep this flesh-and-blood girl both safe and at arm's length. But if I don't answer, she might call Easton or go back to Sirens.

'What's up?' I say into the speaker.

'I'm here.'

'Where?'

'The park. Where we're supposed to meet.'

'You're too early. Like, days early, Lyric.' I press my fingertips into my eyeballs, which are throbbing like they've seen all they'd care to of this world and have activated a self-destruct button.

'Fuck you. This is a scam, isn't it? Either you come here, or I go to the police, and I'll tell them that you know Christian, I swear!'

'Christian's not coming,' I snap back at her, even though all I know is that he didn't answer the phone this morning, and he might still try to make the trip. I can only hope that thinking she's on her own will make her reconsider the whole deal.

'No shit. He's the only reason I'm getting out of here no matter what it takes.' She sounds deeply nervous, and I don't like it.

I can't afford to call her bluff. I'm high as a damn kite with more stashed in my car. What's worse, now that she seems like she's finally wising up to the situation, she thinks I'm in on it. I want to reach through the phone and throttle her, but stalling her is now my number-one priority. Everything else will have to wait.

'Chill, Lyric. I'm already here. Where are you?'

'The main path that goes from the Stop-N-Go to No Man's Land.'

'I'm on the south side. We have a bit of a walk between us. Tell you what. You head toward me, and I'll head toward you, and we'll meet in the middle.'

Meeting in the middle of the woods is suspect as fuck, and she should absolutely say no.

'Then what?' she asks.

I bare my teeth at the sky. 'I'll tell you when I see you. Start walking,' I say and hang up.

No matter what she decides or how this goes, I don't want an audience, and I won't be the only car to circle through this end tonight, so even though I'm in no shape for the walk, she sure as shit can't come all the way here. Hopefully talking to her face to face will lend me some credibility. If not, I'll have to figure out where to take her before I leave for good.

Ignoring a shuddering heart and a pang of nausea, I shoulder Natasha's coat back on. I can't shake the thought that I'm wearing her skin, but if I freeze to death, it won't help either of us. Then I make a fist around her note and head into the woods.

TWENTY

Rose – February 8, 2018

This isn't real.
          Lyric is slumped at the base of a tree.
          You are not allowed to be real.
Her hands dangle by her sides.
You are not fucking real!
Her forehead rests on swaying knees.
Please. Please don't be real.
I touch her neck. It's cold beneath my fingers, her pulse thready. I slap myself, needing it to hurt, needing to be sure. I barely feel it. The wind sounds like it's singing. The shadows are playing hide-and-seek with all my secrets.

I rip off my coat and wrap it around her shoulders, then scoop her off the ground. When I stand up and look ahead, the world is a black hole. There is no light, no trees, no paths. Only dark. A crowded, crushing nothingness. We're not alone out here.

The night throbs as if I'm inside the chambers of a thirsting heart. I try to run, but I stagger instead. I kick off my shoes. Wherever they land, I don't hear it. Beneath my bare feet, the ground feels spongy and unreliable, threatening to suck me under with one false step.

What have I done? The thought is darker than the night, heavier than the girl limp in my arms. Wind wails between the trees, sends a gust of snow sideways, slaps me across the face, and I swear I still hear that song – that godforsaken song – humming in the wild air. Or is it just my favorite narcotic trifecta playing tricks?

Something glows through the trees on the path ahead. I slow down and squint into the night. Warm light illuminates the underside of the same old railway trestle that I once stood on top of and thought long and hard about jumping off. Tonight, if my eyes are to be believed, an old man stokes a trash can fire beneath it, likely to escape the fresh snowfall. It should be a relief that I recognize where I am and know how to get out, but it's the opposite, because this is the exact wrong place for me to be. My car is parked on the south end of this trail, three times the distance I just barely survived carrying Lyric across.

I stagger to a stop and stare down at her, wondering how I'd gotten everything so wrong. In the scant cast-off light from the fire, her features look so close to mine at fourteen years old I nearly gasp. I sit there for longer than I want, longer than I should, dwindling snowflakes swirling down, casual and unaware.

Foam gathers in the corners of Lyric's mouth, spills out, makes a warm, wet place on my arm. I can feel it. Oh God. I can feel it. This is real. And she is overdosing.

I kneel to the ground, hugging her close. 'I'm so sorry,' I whisper over and over in her ear as I fish the syringe of naloxone out of my purse and stab her in the thigh. Then, keeping her pressed close to my chest, I slide my hand into her coat pockets. There's no phone, but she's carrying two hundred dollars exactly, and I would bet it's the same money that I gave her the day I met her. I can't be sure the Narcan is working, and she isn't coming around near as fast as she should. She needs more help, but for so many reasons, I can't risk getting caught with a dying girl in my arms. Especially this one.

I lift my wet gaze to the old man beneath the bridge. He is the only chance for both of us. I flick my gaze to the stack of cash and calculate a quick, messy plan that is full of holes and puts a lot of faith in someone I have never met and has no idea that this is coming. That he is a stranger is an odd source of comfort. Those who have hurt me most have always also been those who know me best.

I stand and gather Maya in my arms, making sure the cash will be visible as soon as we are, then mentally recite the instructions I plan to give him as I move toward his glow.

She's left me no other choice.

TWENTY-ONE

Rose – February 8, 2018

D awn breaks open the sky to the east, setting fire to the snow and shining platinum-tinted light on all my sins. Whatever happened last night, what I saw – the roots of it, the heart of it, empty and rotting, belong to me.

I stagger between the last stand of trees and spot my car. My blouse is soaked and see-through. My jeans are covered with mud. My wig is gone. The shoes. The coat, too . . . *her* coat.

I am the worst person I know.

I don't know how long I've been out in this winter hellscape effectively naked, but I deserve every fucking second of it. All night, I searched snow-covered trails for a little white piece of paper that I dropped while carrying Lyric. My skin is so numb and clammy I'd think I was already dead if not for a single image from the past ticking mercilessly in my brain like a clock with all its hands stuck in place while the gears run and run and run.

I have to kick my car door twice to break the ice before I can open it. I was so high last night that I left the keys on the dashboard and the doors unlocked. I probably have the snowstorm to thank for keeping this piece of shit from getting stolen.

After falling into the front seat, I slam the door, find my emergency stash in the glove box, and snort everything I've got. I lie back as a better numbness lays waste to the burn of thawing limbs. My body is a minefield of sensations, past and present, real and imagined. Voices echo inside of me, around me, through me.

But me, I'm not real. I'm just passing time. A place for other people – real people – to pass through. To feel.

I am the girl with the coat.

And I am the monster who cannot remember her name.

A little girl's cry escapes me. How many names have I been? How long has it been since someone called me Rose and I turned into the sound instead of fleeing? There has to be some kind of fucked-up psychology behind the sound of your own name triggering a fight-or-flight response.

Rose! I hear Lily's voice cry out in my head.

'Don't,' I whisper to us both, my mind clawing at the edge of consciousness. Even with my eyes closed, I can see the hole. 'Don't,' I repeat, then feel myself tipping forward, and I can't find anything solid to grab and hold.

I plummet upward and downward and nowhere at all. The darkness beyond is the only thing that knows all of me, where I've been, where I'm going. She catches me. She always catches me. She is the only safe place I have ever known.

TWENTY-TWO

Daniel – February 8, 2018

As Tula stirred to life under several inches of fresh snow, Daniel sat alone in the homicide wing of the station and peeled back the layers of Christian's history in an autopsy of his own. The ME confirmed that Christian's pockets were empty at his time of death – no cash, ID, or phone. Compiling a list of the homes and centers Christian had stayed in during his fourteen-year-long life took a solid hour and three printed pages. His rap sheet was equal in length. His foster mother hadn't lied about the nature of his charges – all of them petty and harmless.

He turned his focus to the CPS system, researching statistics on foster life for teenagers in Tennessee. A litany of history came up, from Georgia Tann and her black-market adoption schemes in the 1920s to current statistics about the future of foster children who aged out of the system. Nationwide, roughly 20,000 aged out each year, and almost half of those became homeless. Roughly a thousand kids a year aged out in Tennessee alone.

Another local news article noted that between 500 and 600 children were reported missing in Tennessee each month on average, with some missing for a matter of hours and other cases lasting days, weeks, or worse. It went on to detail the complicating factors of fragmented services, overburdened departments, a lack of centralized organization, and jurisdictional red tape, which lent themselves to subpar and slow communication for keeping track of when children were lost, found, and potentially lost again. Including all ages and demographics, there were currently more than 700 open missing person cases in their state, forty of them children. So many names. So many faces.

Farther down in the search results, a *Washington Post* article from two years prior caught Daniel's eye. Since 2000, more than 60,000 foster children had vanished nationwide, and subsequently those cases had been closed by state agencies. Not because they were found, but because they had formally stopped looking. Daniel blinked at the screen, disbelieving and a little nauseous. If, on average, the country was losing roughly 4,000 at-risk kids a year, 8,000 more had disappeared since the article published.

Daniel's phone rang. He lifted it to answer, his mind still swimming through the depths of those statistics. 'Tula Homicide, Detective Wilder speaking.'

'This is Lily. We met yesterday at Brecken Park,' a woman replied.

The mention of Brecken Park helped Daniel refocus, and he sought to place her voice. The Easter egg, he reminded himself.

'What can I do for you, Lily?'

'Josh is missing. We took him out for lunch, and he ran off. We spotted him at the park, but he got away from us, and we haven't seen him since.'

'Any idea what made him run?' Daniel's eyes returned to the numbers on his screen.

'Take your pick. You certainly gave him a reason. Josh doesn't have anything to do with Christian's death. He's a good kid. They were friends. You scared him to death.'

'I think he knows more than he's letting on. We'll get a BOLO out for him.'

'You've had BOLOs out for him more times than I can count. He's smart, he's quick on his feet, he knows how to blend in almost anywhere, and he'll see a cop coming from a hundred yards away.'

'What do you think we should do, then?' Daniel asked, growing impatient. He closed his eyes, centering himself. This woman was part of the statistics on his screen – but she was on the side of the solution, problematic though it may be, and he needed to remember that.

'I don't know.'

But she did know. He could hear it in her voice. What side of the statistics did she think he was on? He wasn't sure he knew how to answer that for himself.

'What aren't you telling me, ma'am?' Daniel glanced at Christian's picture, then to his note about 60,000-plus closed cases. Before she gave an answer, his cell phone buzzed against his face with a second incoming call. He pulled back to see Hunter's name flash on the screen. His brother hadn't been by the station yet that morning, and Daniel's sense of relief had been so strong he'd nearly felt guilty. 'I need to take another call. I'll get back to you with any updates,' he added, not sure he really meant it, then switched to Hunter's incoming call without waiting for her response.

'What's up?' Daniel asked Hunter as soon as the connection was made, determined to keep his voice neutral, something that sounded like he hadn't noticed whether Hunter had or hadn't been here, and nor did he care either way.

'Another kid was pulled out of the woods early this morning.'

Daniel's heart skipped a beat. 'At Brecken Park?'

'Technically. Other side though.'

'No Man's Land?' Daniel stood as he mentally mapped the most secluded area of the park, where a gravel lot stretched out from both sides of an out-of-service railroad bridge. The space had long served as a gathering place for teenagers, cheap beer, and illegal bonfires in the summer, then tent cities and transients in the winter.

'More or less. Homeless guy found her. He carried her out of the woods and flagged down a cop.'

'Did they hold him for questioning?' Daniel asked as he hurried for the exit.

'They tried. Guy was high as a kite. Said the Virgin Mary handed her to him and gave him two hundred dollars. Cops took the money in case it belongs to the girl. No way to know, I guess. He's heading to the sobering center now. Apparently he's a frequent flier.'

'Where are you?'

'Hospital. Kid's alive.'

'Alive?' Daniel broke into a run. 'Way to bury the lede.'

'Don't rush. Girl's unconscious. Body temp is eighty-five degrees. No telling how long she was out there. They're warming her up, but it's a slow process. I'll fill you in when you get here.'

A detail Hunter had mentioned ignited a flare in Daniel's recent memory. 'Wait, did you say two hundred dollars?' He paused mid stride and pressed the phone harder to his ear.

Silence answered. Hunter had already ended the call.

TWENTY-THREE

Daniel – February 8, 2018

Inside the emergency room at Tula Medical South, Daniel found Hunter leaning against a wall in the waiting area, his phone pressed to his ear. At the sight of Daniel, he ended the call and clipped his phone into its holder. Then the two of them stood across from each other in silence. Daniel had no idea how to be the first one to speak.

A woman in scrubs and a white coat approached them, and it was as if they had been cut from the invisible puppet strings holding them in their suspended, waiting positions.

'Officers, I'm Dr Cathy. I assume you're here for Jane Doe,' she greeted them. She slowed but didn't wait for them to answer. As they fell in step behind her, Daniel quickly got the impression she never stopped moving.

'I'm headed to her room now,' she continued. 'Her body is responding well. There's no sign of external physical injury. There's no way to know how long she was hypothermic or what kind of brain damage we may be looking at, if any, but the next twenty-four hours will tell us a lot. First, she needs to wake up.'

'Do we know anything about her yet?' Daniel asked.

'Not much. She looks to be fourteen, fifteen years old. EMS didn't find an ID or a phone on her person.'

No phone. It made for another similarity between Christian and this girl. Daniel kept the thought to himself.

They walked to the ICU and stepped inside the first room. It was as quiet and still as a morgue, with the exceptions of the steady beep of a machine monitoring Jane Doe's vitals and the barely audible footsteps of a nurse circling the foot of her bed. The girl was dwarfed by a pile of blankets. A pulse-ox monitor gloved her pointer finger, and an IV was taped to the back of her hand.

The pager hooked on the pocket of Dr Cathy's lab coat buzzed, and the unexpected sound of it was a needle prick to the ballooning tension in the room.

'I need to see to this,' she said, her eyes focused on the pager. 'I'll be back as soon as I can. Alert me if there's any remarkable change in the meantime,' she instructed the nurse, then she walked out of the room.

'Can we get a tox screen or draw blood, UA . . . anything?' Daniel asked.

Hunter arched a brow. 'You don't think they've already done that?'

'If they have, we need that information.'

'We have no right to that information.' Hunter's expression shifted from surprise to amusement. 'This girl is a patient, not a victim. At least not until she dies, or she wakes up and tells us otherwise.'

'Fine. I'll wait here. You can go,' Daniel said.

'Neither one of you is waiting in here,' the nurse said. 'Family only.'

'All due respect, you don't know who she is. How is her family supposed to visit?' Daniel argued.

Hunter turned for the door. 'Chill out, Danny. They'll call us with significant updates. There's nothing more we can do here.'

'How can you say that there's nothing to do? Two kids, two nights, same woods, two hundred dollars, no phones,' Daniel shot back.

Hunter held up his cell phone and took a picture of the girl's face. 'There. That's the whole reason I came. We can go run it through missing persons from the office.'

'I'm staying.' The frustration that had simmered inside of him for hours, days, years began to stir with the increase in heat.

Hunter stared at him, silent and unmoving. Daniel forced himself to stand still, too, preparing to defend the proverbial line he'd unintentionally drawn on the mica-flecked floor.

'Rookie,' Hunter muttered, and he walked out.

The nurse glanced at Daniel. He could tell she wanted to say something, that maybe she even felt bad for him now. Fixing discomfort was part of her job. Daniel wanted to tell her that there was no fixing what had broken between him and Hunter, that he couldn't tell her precisely where the wound was, or when or how it even started.

He forced a smile instead. 'Ignore us.' Then he took a picture of the girl with his own cell phone and left the room.

If she was in the local foster care system, Lily might be able to help identify her. It was a long shot, but it was the only shot he had from where he stood.

Daniel searched his call history for the number she'd called him with that morning, then prompted a new text message.

This is Detective Wilder. We found another teenager in Brecken Park. Identity unknown. I am sending her picture. Please do not share it outside the department until further notice. Do you recognize her, or is any child in your database who matches her description missing? Thanks in advance.

Daniel sent the message and the photo, then stowed his phone. As much as he hated to admit it, Hunter was right about how little Daniel could help Christian or this nameless girl from inside these walls.

Agitated, he pushed off the wall, eyes on the exit. The need to find something, anything useful before Hunter could drove him forward.

'Detective,' Dr Cathy called across the space.
Daniel whipped round.
'She's awake.'

TWENTY-FOUR

Rose – February 8, 2018

My eyelids crack open, and sunlight stabs through in white-hot blades. I grip the steering wheel with both hands and peel my face off the faux-leather cover, leaving a film of sweat, oil, and foundation. I glance in the rear-view mirror like the fucking masochist that I am, but I forget to prepare for who I will see looking back at me: my mother.

I curl my fingers to a fist and strike the glass over and over until there are more cracks than surface. When I'm done, I'm too full and too empty and heaving breaths like the one before it was hard up for oxygen. After all I've done, I can imagine the air itself assessing me for investment value and deciding no, not for her.

Weakness lays claim to every inch of me. My brain swims. I can't form a complete thought. I haven't eaten in two days. Maybe three. I can't remember. My memory is a hole.

Shaky and cramping, I drive back to Sirens where I can drink shitty coffee for free and eat a half-price meal on a box in the back of the building without people staring or whispering like they will if I go anywhere else.

I know what I look like to you. It's not your secret to keep from me, I want to say.

I park and walk toward the employee entrance. I'm having a hard time tracking a straight line, and I don't know if it's my heart or my brain that keeps begging me to turn around. I don't want to be here, I know that much. But if I want to eat, I don't have much of a choice.

Still, the closer I get to the door, the more like a traitor I feel. By the time my fingers are on the handle, I nearly can't stand myself. There are plenty of reasons to pick from, I'm sure, but they're all one big, loud scream, and I can't untangle the sounds into words.

'I've been looking for you.' A man steps through the pedestrian gate in the VIP privacy fence. He's heavyset and underdressed for our usual customer base, but as his face comes into focus, I recognize him immediately. My second day on the job, I led him to a cabana for an unwitting nap after I spotted role-play porn of a priest and a Catholic schoolgirl on his phone screen. He was my inspiration for leaving a card for the church in his wallet. Apparently, my attempt to scare him off is having the opposite effect, and in a second turn of events, I'm not actually in the mood for a fight.

I shake my head, hug my vibrating skeleton close so my bones don't rattle apart, and turn back for my car.

'I'm talking to you, bitch,' he growls at me, low and loud. His loafers scatter loose gravel as he lumbers closer. I keep walking, trying to speed up, but my legs threaten to buckle. The lot is checkered with a handful of cars, but we're the only two people out here. I should try to run past him and get inside the club, where coworkers and a bouncer and a bartender with a gun tucked under the register would be happy to intervene, but the man is between me and the door.

I am ten yards from my car, where I've stashed my .38 under the seat. I break into a jog, but in my current state, I'm stupidly slow. The sounds of his heavy breathing and uneven steps reach my ears too late, and a hand grips my elbow and spins me round so hard I nearly fall.

'Get your hands off me!' I snarl.

'I know what you did.' He jabs a finger at me, his wedding band winking in the sun.

'Does your wife know you fantasize about little girls in school uniforms?'

The back of his hand cracks across my face. I stagger sideways, my mouth flooding with the taste of iron as iridescent spots bloom across my vision. Adrenaline electrifies my blood, my brain, and memories grow like weeds, fast and unwanted. I cower, furious that the combination of ringing in my ears and the shaky feeling of early withdrawal is making it hard to think, hard to move, fight back.

'Hey!' someone else yells across the lot. I squeeze my eyes shut and open them again, desperate to focus.

'Mind your business,' the man barks. Then he sneers at me, lowering his arm, his knuckles still squeezed tight.

'I own this bar, and she is my business,' Easton's voice orders. His face appears over the man's shoulder. 'Get in your car and drive away, or did you forget who you're talking to?'

The man points at me again. 'This isn't over.'

'It's absolutely over,' Easton shoots back.

I glare at them both, blood boiling in my veins, frothing in the back of my mouth. I make a fist in my purse, sliding my fingers through my brass knuckles key chain, feeling the metal press into my skin, my tired fucking skin, and I clock the fat fuck right in the nose.

He staggers backward. His hands fly to his face.

'Now you can tell your wife you were mugged. You're welcome.' I yank open my car door, heart racing, head pounding, ears still ringing.

'Betty!' Easton calls at me. The genuine concern in his voice almost makes me hesitate. But then I remember the thumb drive, what I did to get it, what I found on it . . . that I lost it. Maybe not having it in my pocket would keep me alive here and now were I to stay, but I'm not interested in finding out.

Without responding, I crank the engine and peel out of the parking lot. I don't have an ounce of pretending left in me, and I don't think I'd survive a moment of truth.

TWENTY-FIVE

Lily – February 8, 2018

Lily arrived at Tula Medical South with a picture of a face she had recognized in a text message on her phone, a file that wasn't technically hers under her arm, and a storm of worry thundering in her heart.

Maya Summit was a fourteen-year-old girl who, with her younger brother, had called the system home since she was seven years old. Lily had shepherded Maya through her first cycles in and out of the system. More recently, and perhaps more importantly, Maya was who she thought she'd seen in the car with Rose and was undoubtedly the girl who she'd watched leave her pack of friends at Brecken Park to take something Rose had offered.

Rose and Maya had always reminded her so much of each other. She wondered if that was why she'd had a hard time reaching the girl, why she had let Maya call shots she would never normally allow, why she at last had to give Maya's case to Rachel to oversee. She couldn't trust herself. In a way, they were both calling the shots now, spurring Lily to sneak back into work and steal Maya's file from her case worker's desk.

Lily walked to the check-in area. Rose's fourteen-year-old voice gave instructions from within: *Just look like you belong – it's more than half the battle*, she'd once told Lily on her second day of first grade at a new school – the third one in as many months.

'Who are you here to see?' a nurse asked from behind the station desk.

'I'm here to identify a Jane Doe. An officer sent me her picture. I'm a case worker with DFACS, and they believe she's in the system.' Lily showed her Maya's file and pointed to the picture she'd printed of Maya, which she'd fastened to the outside of the file with a paperclip.

'That's her. Second floor. A nurse will have to buzz you into the ICU. Then follow the screaming. Can't miss her.'

The nurse hadn't been exaggerating. Lily could hear Maya the moment she swung open the stairwell door exiting to the second floor. She followed the string of profanities until she spied Maya through a window, the blinds down but half-open. Detective Wilder was standing beside her bed. He moved to sit.

'Back up, perv!' Maya practically spat at him.

'I just want to help you, Lyric,' he said, retreating a step, and Lily smiled despite the palpable tension.

'Get out of here or I'm calling security.'

'I am security.'

'You're a *cop*. I didn't do anything wrong.'

'You're a kid who spent the night in the woods in sub-freezing temperatures. You didn't do a whole lot right.'

'Get out!' she screamed.

Nurses approached, a doctor with them, and Lily faded against the wall.

The doctor motioned for the nurses to wait, then pushed open the door and stepped in. 'Detective, can we take a break? I need a word,' she said.

Detective Wilder appeared in the doorway, then he and the doctor moved together down the hall as the nurses dispersed.

'She's disoriented and combative. These are normal effects of someone possibly experiencing detox, plus just waking up from nearly freezing to death. I know you need your answers, and she hasn't earned a lot of leeway, but she does need time,' the doctor explained as they walked at a matched pace.

Lily slid Maya's file inside her coat and trailed behind. The two shook hands at the nurses' station before moving in opposite directions. Daniel headed for the exit.

Lily quickened her step. 'Detective Wilder,' she called out.

He stopped and glanced in the direction of her voice. There were bags under his eyes and two-day stubble on his face.

'Her name isn't Lyric,' Lily started. 'It's Maya Summit, and she's playing you.'

He rubbed his brow. 'Tell that to the doctor.'

'It won't do any good. Maya's only fourteen, but she's learned how to work anyone and everyone. She's been in the system half her life. You can't go in there and demand answers or act like you're on her side when we all know you're not. You have to be ready to offer something she wants, or she isn't going to hear anything you say.'

'Does she trust you?'

'She does.' Lily made her file visible. 'And I'm not going to jeopardize that by having a private conversation with her while you listen in from the doorway, especially when her friend just died.'

Daniel's brow shot for his forehead. 'Are you referring to Christian?'

'I am. My guess is she's going to have even more walls up than usual,' Lily said softly.

'How do I get her to talk to me?' he asked, leaning in.

'Tell her you know this is a third strike for going AWOL from a detention center, but that you can help keep her out of lockup.'

'How will I know if anything she says is the truth?'

'You won't.'

'Worth a shot, I guess,' he said. 'Any last words of wisdom?'

'She might seem tough, but she's all bark. I wouldn't bring up Christian yet, even though I'm sure you want to. Be patient. Even before this, she's been through horrors most people can't fathom. But that's not who she *is*. If you can find a way to talk about *her*, and not what *happened* to her, she might think you actually care.'

Guilt touched the detective's expression. 'Where should I start?'

'She loves music. She sings, plays the guitar. She's very talented. And she has a younger brother who adores her. She's run away more times than I can count, but this is the first time she's tried to leave Tula, at least that I know of.'

He nodded, lips pursed in thought, then walked swiftly back to Maya's room.

Lily followed him at a distance. She hadn't asked if she could stay and listen, but he also hadn't said that she couldn't.

Detective Wilder paused in the doorway. 'I'm sorry about before,' he began. 'It was my bad, a hundred percent. I'd like to start over. On your terms, this time. Can I come in?'

Maya must have nodded because he stepped into her room and disappeared from Lily's view. She eased closer to the open door, then leaned against the wall, pretending to scroll through her phone.

'I know you can get in trouble here,' his voice continued. 'This is your third strike for going AWOL, and I know what the punishment is. Maya, no one else knows you're here. Just me and you.'

'How do you know my name?' Maya asked, and Lily's heart skipped a beat. She hoped he had an answer ready.

'A friend,' he answered.

'Whatever. Why are you here? I didn't break a law.'

'We just want to understand what happened to you. Did you run away?' he asked.

'None-ya,' she replied.

Even though there was a wall between her and the conversation taking place, Lily could imagine Maya's Cheshire Cat smirk.

'I'm going to take that as a yes. If you help me at all here, if you can tell me why you ran away, where you were trying to go, if anyone was with you, what happened in those woods . . . anything, I can figure out how to get you out of a third strike. I can even see about finding a private foster home,' the detective said.

Lily winced. He was reaching, and she wondered if Maya heard it as plainly as she did.

'You can't do that,' Maya said flatly, confirming her suspicion.

'I know I can get you out of a third strike; I know I can keep you out of lockup and the detention center. The rest I don't know for sure, but I'll do everything I can.'

The conversation idled again. The room was so quiet that Lily could hear each time Maya shifted on her bed.

'What do you want to know?' she finally asked.

'Whatever you're willing to share. Start from the beginning.'

'I left right after lights out.'

'On your own?'

'Yes.'

'Why did you go to Brecken Park?'

'I like it there.'

'Did you get lost?'

'Clearly.'

'How long were you out there?'

'I don't remember. And that's the truth.'

'Was someone with you out there?'

'It's a park.'

Lily inched closer to the crack between the hinged side of the door and the frame.

'It was the middle of the night, and you know what I mean,' Detective Wilder countered.

'I'm not a snitch.'

He pounced, his hunger for a lead overriding his careful cadence. 'Does that mean you weren't alone?'

Lily imagined the shift in Maya's face, the realization that she had him on a hook and not the other way around.

'It means if someone else was out there, it's none-ya business.'

Lily fought the temptation to march in her room, take her by the shoulders, and shake some sense into her.

'Will you at least tell me where you were trying to go?' he asked.

'The beach.'

'In January?'

'Can you think of a better time to get out of here?'

'Did a friend encourage this? Or your family? Did they help you, in any way?' he continued.

'My only family is a seven-year-old kid.'

'Brother or sister?'

'Brother. His name is Tyler.'

'What's he like?'

'Better than me.'

Silence fell everywhere all at once, and even though the sound of her words had faded, the honesty in them lingered.

'Do you want me to call him?' Detective Wilder finally said. Lily could hear the emotion straining his throat from the hallway.

'Won't do any good. I haven't been able to see him in almost two years.'

'I'm sorry to hear that.'

'You say that like your feelings do something for me.'

'Fair. Were you going to leave him behind, or were you going to try to take him with you?' he asked.

Lily leaned back, feeling like they were all too close to the edge of something, the bottom too far a fall to see.

'I think I'd have caught real hell if I'd tried to take him with me. Don't you?'

'The guy who found you said the Virgin Mary gave you to him, along with some money,' Detective Wilder said quickly, and Lily suspected he was trying to throw the girl off her rhythm, make her mentally trip into admitting a piece of the truth. 'I'm wondering if it was yours.'

'Fuck, I don't know.' Genuine alarm drove her words to a higher octave, and Lily could hear her moving quickly on her bed.

'The doctor didn't mention finding any money on you, so if you had money, it's gone now.'

'Well, it was mine, then. And I need it. Every dollar,' she snapped.

'Prove it,' he countered.

'How?'

'Tell me how much it was, and in what kind of bills.'

'How am I supposed to know that? Can you tell me exactly what's in your wallet?'

'Nope. But I'm not trying to get my money back right now.'

As a few silent seconds passed between them, Lily rested her head against the wall, listening intently, strangely amused. If she didn't know better, she'd almost think they were father and daughter.

'Two hundred dollars. Mixed bills,' Maya muttered.

'How were you going to get to the beach for two hundred dollars with anything left over for when you actually got there?'

'You never heard of Greyhound?' she volleyed.

'So that's where you were walking? The bus station?'

'I sure as shit wasn't going to walk to the beach, genius.'

'Do you have a cell phone?' His voice followed hers immediately. They reminded Lily of two runners on the home stretch of a track, duking it out for the lead.

Maya scoffed. 'Hell no. Those things cause cancer, and the FBI uses them to track you.'

'You're full of shit,' he said.

'Prove it.'

'You're what, twelve?'

'Excuse you, fourteen.'

'Either way, too young for a work permit. Where'd you get the money?'

'I'll tell you once I'm in that private home you promised me.'

'Maybe you are a smart kid.'

'Maybe.'

'So, smart kid, why did you leave when you did? It was nineteen degrees outside.'

'No one would suspect it.'

'You must've been pretty lucky to get out without anyone hearing,' he countered.

'I'm just that good.'

'Nothing about what happened here is good, except that you woke up. Here's my card. If you need anything, remember anything, call me. OK? I'll be in touch.'

'You better make sure I don't get a third strike.'

'I'm going to do my best.' His shoes tracked several steps across the polished floor, then fell silent. 'One last question. Did anyone mess with you out there, give you a hard time? Someone that shouldn't have been there? Maybe someone you just met? Someone you wouldn't be snitching on?'

'Well, when I was falling asleep, I heard a lady singing close by. Real close. Kinda freaked me out, you know? But I figured I was already dreaming or maybe the hobos who live out there might be having a jam session.'

'Makes perfect sense,' he said wryly. 'What song was she singing?'

'Hell if I know.'

'That's too bad. A friend of mine said you were a real musician. I guess not.'

'What friend?'

'None-ya,' he replied.

Maya groaned.

'I could just start singing songs, see if something sounds familiar.'

'Please don't.'

Detective Wilder cleared his throat.

'Whisper,' she blurted. 'Maybe whisper mister? Whisper sister?'

Adrenaline ignited the length of Lily's spine. Instantly, every fiber of her being was aflame. When she gasped, she inhaled Rose's sour breath. How much did Maya remember? Was it this vivid and visceral for her? Did it threaten to swallow her, too?

'Something like that. It's probably some pathetic top-forty bullshit. That'd be a reason I didn't know it,' Maya added.

'That doesn't ring a bell with me either, and I like top-forty bullshit,' Detective Wilder answered.

'Too bad for you.'

'You don't remember anything else about it?' he asked.

Maya started humming, and the first four notes of the chorus of Rose's song rang out of the open door.

All around Lily, the bright hall blurred, white walls and white floors becoming a tunnel of snow. She could feel the ends of Rose's chilly hair feathering against her cheek like kisses of ice. Her knees buckled, and she surrendered to the floor.

Nurses' hands descended upon her, patted her face, held her under her arms, rubbed her back. Their voices arrived in her ears hollow and slow, as if they had traveled a great distance to reach her. Detective Wilder's face appeared. She reached out, grabbed his coat, and pulled herself into the present.

'She just collapsed,' one of the nurses said as he helped her to her feet.

Lily's face was hot. She wiped it with a finger and found it wet with tears.

'What's wrong?' Detective Wilder peered at her in earnest.

'I need to report a missing person,' Lily murmured.

'Just take it easy for a second. You already told me that Josh is missing.'

'Not Josh.' She squeezed his wrists and looked him in the eyes as her heart tipped to decision. 'My sister.'

TWENTY-SIX

Rose – February 8, 2018

The drive-through speaker box at Taco Bell is broken, but I'm too dizzy to make the drive to the next fast-food option. Between that and my budget, which is reduced to the change in my cupholders, I'm forced to order inside. At least this way I can get refills. Plus, the dining area has a small TV mounted in the corner, and it's about time for *The Price is Right*.

Only when I climb back out of my car do I remember that I'm barefoot. The ends of my toes look like angry cherries from too long in the damp cold. My shirt and jeans have dried, but they're stained with streaks of every brown in the big box of crayons I always envied on other kids' desks at school.

I shake the lingering sting out of my hand, and make a mental note to never buy a white shirt again. I'm just not the kind of girl that doesn't get dirty. I frown down at my shirt, my jeans, my blood-red toes. What the hell did I do this time?

I pull a pair of sandals from my satchel – the flimsy kind that they give you at cheap pedicure places – and coax them on my frozen feet. The 'no shoes, no shirt, no service' sign on the door to Taco Bell may very well add a qualifier once I've come and gone. Then again, I've been here straight after a shift with my butt cheeks as visible as my palms and no one said a thing. Still, even with most of my skin covered up, I've never felt quite this exposed.

I force myself out of the car and into the restaurant. It occurs to me that the state of my face might match the state of my clothes, but I busted my mirror before I saw myself. The big-eyed reaction of the kid at the register, though, is all but a reflection. Considering this is the closest cheap place to eat for people leaving Sirens, the staff here is sure to have seen plenty.

I must look like real hell.

Before I order, I give a cursory wipe of my face with my stained sleeve. Maybe I've made the situation better. Maybe I've made it worse. *That could be my tagline should my train wreck of a life ever become a movie.* I snort to myself, then prod my chest as the urges to laugh and to cry go to war beneath my ribs.

What the hell is wrong with me?

I grab my single taco from the tray they've placed it on like it deserves all that space. I pluck my kid-size cup from beside it and fill it with root beer, no ice, in case I'm kicked out of here before I have a chance to get a refill, then take a seat in the corner where I can see both doors and the TV.

The first bite of food conjures a full-body response that damn near feels like an electric shock. My body begins to buzz like someone flipped a tripped breaker back on. I close my eyes and allow relief to trickle in. Suddenly, the curtain of my eyelids is striped with the boughs of trees and their shadows, and I can hear the crunch of snow under racing feet. My eyes fly open. I gasp so hard and fast that I choke.

'Hey? Are you OK?' a girl calls from behind the register. I try to nod just to save face, but the room feels like it's spinning.

'Oh my God,' I hear her say. 'Scott, get out here.'

Another kid emerges from the kitchen to stand beside her, and I shove to my feet, nearly knocking my cup off the table.

'I'm leaving. I'm leaving,' I mumble between coughs, then cradle half a taco and my cup to my chest and move for the exit.

'Doesn't that kid do all that crazy mural art at the Boys and Girls Club?' the girl asks.

Out the corner of my eye, I see her point to where the TV is mounted on the wall.

'Yeah, that's Christian. Holy shit,' the boy says.

Everything around me slows down. The only thing I can hear is my pulse detonating in a chain of explosions. I lift my gaze to the television, where the news is running through top-of-the-hour headlines. A face I've only ever seen in my rearview mirror is now staring at me from the screen. My cup slips from my grasp, soda erupting upon impact, running across my raw feet in freezing currents. Colder still are the words captioned beneath his picture: Local Teen Found Dead at Brecken Park.

No. My knees threaten to buckle. *No, no, no.* I clutch at the door to keep from becoming a pile in front of it. My weight pushes the door outward, and a gust of winter bursts through the gap like an armed robber, slapping me in the face and snatching the air from my mouth.

I bow my head, so tempted to talk to other people's God that I wonder if I'm dying, too.

A girl's voice answers me from within. I almost want to smile, the idea of God being a teenage girl obscure enough to reach me even here.

But it is not God.

It's Lyric.

Pieces of last night hammer against my skull. I let go of the door and the rest of my meal to make two fists against my head. Bile and what I had managed to eat leave me, joining the root beer on the floor. The world around me moves in slow motion, the two kids at the counter gaping at me and starting in my direction, the TV going to commercial, someone hoping to use interest in a boy's death to drive business to their door. But everything is happening in silence, and all I can hear is Lyric.

She's not answering my wordless prayer.

She's singing my song.

TWENTY-SEVEN

Daniel – February 8, 2018

Daniel watched Lily in his rearview mirror as she followed him to the station in her own car, having insisted she was recovered enough to drive. Gone was the trembling, panicked woman who'd been reduced to a puddle on the floor of the ICU. Her expression was fierce, her eyes laser focused on the back of Daniel's car.

At the station, Daniel retrieved the paperwork they would need to file a missing person's report, then led Lily to the homicide wing, where he found Hunter sitting on top of his desk. He was flanked by a couple of fellow detectives, who clapped him on the shoulder as they passed. They looked to have had a breakthrough in the drug house shootout. Jealousy slid across the surface of Daniel's chest. As he ushered Lily into investigation room four, he mentally chased off the rush of emotion, then closed the door between his case and Hunter.

He took a seat opposite Lily at the small brown table nestled against the far wall of the square room. The woman sat upright in her chair, shoulders pulled back, chin slightly lifted. Daniel felt sloppy by way of comparison, and he caught himself correcting his posture.

'Thank you for doing this, Detective Wilder,' Lily said.

'Call me Daniel. I assume a missing person's report was filed at the time of her disappearance,' he added, tapping the paperwork on the table.

'I was seven, so I don't know for sure, but I would have to think so.'

'Have you personally filed a missing person's report for her before now?'

'Yes. The day I turned eighteen I filed for the first time, then again when I turned twenty-one. I didn't have much to go on,

and honestly, I still don't. But what's a sister supposed to do?'
She paused, sniffling, and shrugged. 'I've looked all over the
country on my own. I've had a few leads, but I've never actually
found her. Sometimes I swear I see her here. Driving down the
road. Walking in a crowd. Especially if snow is on the way. But
it's always there and gone in the blink of an eye. It makes me
feel . . . crazy.'

Her sorrow touched Daniel in his chest. In truth, there was
probably little point to filing a whole new report, and an update
would be much faster. But what he stood to gain here had little
to do with finding her sister and more to do with gaining credit.

He cleared his throat before continuing. 'OK, so you know
the drill. Let's start with what you know about her. Name, date
you last saw her, height, weight, and hair and eye color. The
basics.'

'Her name is Rose.'

'What's her last name?'

'I don't actually know. My mom called us different last names
every time she remarried or wanted a guy to think about marriage,
or if she crossed the wrong person and needed to disappear.
I can tell you that at one point we were the Sussex sisters. I
remember learning to write Ss in kindergarten.'

'But that's not your last name?'

'No. And even if it was mine, it isn't necessarily hers. Two
different dads,' she explained. 'I have no idea if my father's last
name is on my birth certificate, or if she even knew who my
father was. I never met him. I wouldn't be surprised if I wasn't
born in a hospital, to be honest.'

'Can you give me a physical description of Rose as you
remember her?'

'Her eyes are brown, and her hair was brown the night we left
home. I still have one picture of her.' She produced it from her
pocket. A girl sat sideways on the arm of a worn sofa, a guitar
across her lap, a curtain of hair covering everything but the tip
of her nose and the highest part of her forehead.

Daniel masked a sigh as he looked over the paperwork,
counting all the places they would no doubt have to leave blank.
'I'm going to help you in any way that I can, but that means
being honest with you, even when the news is bad. I don't know

how helpful this is really going to be. She's been missing a long time, and we have very little to go on.'

'We have everything to go on,' she countered, leaning forward. 'That song Maya remembers – that's my sister's song. There's just not a place for it on your form.'

'Your sister's song?'

'She wrote a song for me when I was little. She would sing it when we would move somewhere new or were living out of a car and I'd have trouble sleeping at night. She sang it to me the night she disappeared.'

Daniel stared across the table at this woman. She seemed well educated, well groomed, employed, social, and well adjusted. She had survived falling through so many cracks, beaten every statistic he had researched. It was sometimes easy to forget that someone who won a war didn't come through without scars.

'When I heard Maya say those words, hum a couple notes from the chorus, in that moment I was back in our woods. Rose is connected to this. If nothing else, I can't help seeing it as a sign that she's ready for me to find her, wherever she is.'

Daniel hesitated before continuing with his next question, but it had to be asked. 'You do realize you're connecting your sister to a potential attempted homicide. Do you expect to find your sister . . . or her body?'

'She couldn't be dead, or Maya wouldn't know the song. And I've seen her. I know I have.'

'OK, so why don't you walk me through the similarities that you see.' Daniel stood and moved to the whiteboard pinned to the wall beneath the clock. He wrote Christian and Maya's names along the top, then connected Josh to both of them with a line. On the right edge of the board, he wrote *Rose*.

'We ran away in what was supposed to be a snowstorm,' Lily began.

Daniel began a bullet list and jotted: *Snow*. 'OK.'

'We got lost, so we curled up at the base of a tree to wait for morning.'

He added the word: *Position*. 'OK, next.'

Lily didn't answer right away. Daniel glanced at her over his shoulder. Her gaze was cast to her lap, her cheeks sucked in, lips twisting in a bow.

'What don't you want to tell me?' he pressed.

'She got me drunk.'

Daniel rocked back on his heels.

'I don't think it was malicious,' Lily continued quickly. 'Looking back at that night now, I know she was already drunk when we left and three sheets to the wind by the time we gave up trying to find the car. She kept giving me a thermos and encouraged me to drink more. If I had to guess, based on memory, it was fruit punch and vodka.'

Daniel couldn't look at her. He didn't want her to see the judgement he felt claiming his face.

A knock sounded through the door, and Hunter's face appeared in the narrow frame of glass. He gestured for Daniel to join him outside. Daniel drew a question mark by Rose's name, excused himself, and stepped into the hall.

'Who did you bring in?' Hunter asked.

'One of the social workers we met at Brecken Park.'

'Is somebody else missing?'

'Kind of. Her sister.' Daniel proceeded to give Hunter the bare-bones rundown of the story Lily had told him.

Hunter folded his arms across his chest. 'I know this type. You need to be careful with her. She's going to attach her story to any kid found dead in the woods.'

'She's also my best source of information right now.'

'That's problematic, and you know it. She's not a reliable source. She has a personal interest in this case. She's going to put her spin on anything she tells you to help you solve it in a way that makes sense to her. You aren't going to be able to trust anything you get from her, knowing this history.'

'This coming from the guy who diverts from a murder investigation to answer a battery call and then pulls strings to get a stripper off the hook for identity theft?'

'Ouch.'

'There's no harm in filling out a renewed missing person's report and talking to her about what she might know about Maya, Josh, and Christian. She's the best resource I have on all three, and she doesn't even know her sister's last name. It won't distract from the case.'

'Danny, I'm telling you, the wrong direction in a case is a bigger hole to climb out of than no direction at all.'

'Oh, please. What in the hell would you even know about that?' Daniel snapped.

Hunter leveled a steely gaze at him, but didn't offer him a word. After two seconds spent in merciless silence, he turned his back on Daniel and walked off.

Daniel stared at him, speechless. Perhaps his brother had worked alone all these years because he was impossible to work with. They had been paired for training as a courtesy, a parting gift, a way the department could hold on to a sliver of Hunter's talent and process after his retirement. How was Daniel supposed to fill his shoes, to walk his walk, if Hunter left behind him not a trail but a canyon?

He took a moment to compartmentalize the conversation before returning to the incident room. Even if Hunter was right about Lily, she was more willing to help Daniel than Hunter ever would be, and that was enough for now.

'Why is there a question mark beside my sister's name?' Lily demanded the moment he swung open the door.

'Because I'm not sure she's involved in this case,' Daniel said carefully as he pulled the door shut behind him. 'You have my word that we'll open a formal search for her, but I can't in good faith link your sister's disappearance twenty-five years ago with what happened to Christian and Maya just because both incidents occurred in bad weather.'

'If you find my sister, you'll find what happened to them. I know it.'

Daniel hung his head and anchored his hands at his waist. Lily's expectations were already sky-high.

'We don't yet have any evidence that anything happened to Christian that wasn't by choice, and, in your own words, you have no idea what happened to your sister. There is no proof connecting these two tragedies.'

Lily looked away, chewing on her lip. Then she drew in a breath and began to sing. 'Whisper, sister, no matter how far. Whisper, sister, no matter how dark. Just whisper, sister, that's all you have to do. I'll come running home to you.'

'I assume that's part of Rose's song?' Daniel said gently.

Lily nodded. 'Will you at least put it on the board, please? It would mean a lot to me.'

'Why don't you write the words to the whole song down for me?' Daniel handed her a yellow pad of paper and a pen before jotting her note on the board.

'You see the connection, then?' She began writing the first line with a shaking hand.

'I'd like to have it in case there's a connection to be made. To be frank, Maya didn't sing *any* song. She hummed a few notes that all sounded more or less the same, then guessed at a few words. She admitted she wasn't sure what she heard.'

'She didn't trust you.'

'True. But I also don't think she would have a reason to hold that back.'

Lily's expression frosted. 'Well, if you can't guarantee she gets into that private home you promised her, you're never going to find out. I can do that for you. I can fudge the paperwork that she'll need to get moved into a private foster home instead of a detention center, which is where she's headed when she's discharged.'

'I only told her I could do that on *your* advice,' Daniel said, dismayed.

'And it worked when you needed it to. But if you want more from her, you're going to have to prove you're valuable to her for more than just promises, and you'll need me to make a crack and slip her through.'

'And what is it you think I'll be able to do for you?' he asked, the echo of Hunter's warning heavier upon return.

'Find my sister,' she said.

TWENTY-EIGHT

Rose – February 8, 2018

I open the door to my motel room. I'd forgotten the state I'd left it in. I'm not sure which one of us is the worse for wear. I rip off my sour clothes and throw them in the trash. I wriggle into a black tracksuit, then rinse my mouth with water from the sink and splash more on my face. My makeup runs in lines, and my tired eyes stare back at me. I have done terrible, inhumane things. But I have never felt more like a monster than I do right now.

I should never have come back here. It's my fault. All of it. I destroy things even when I'm actively trying not to. My mother was right about exactly one thing: the best way I can protect anything that matters to me is to leave it alone.

I have most of my stuff packed when my phone rings with a call from Hunter. I answer it while I toss the linens back on the bed, making sure I hadn't left something beneath them.

'You've got somebody on your tail.' His voice comes through quietly.

'In my line of work, you're going to have to be more specific.' I stuff the remainder of my clothes into a duffle bag.

'Someone just renewed your missing person's report.'

I shove the door open too hard. 'I don't know why that has anything to do with you, Hunter. If you're looking for something from me, just get to the fucking point,' I nearly shout, the phone pinched between my ear and my shoulder. I shut the door and turn around. Easton has parked his car beside mine and is standing between them.

'Stop being such a prick,' I bark into the receiver and end the call.

Easton cocks his head. 'Who was that?'

There's a good chance he heard the name, so I stick with the truth. 'Hunter.'

'Is Hunter a . . . boyfriend? No . . .' He brings a hand to his mouth. His eyes turn to slits. 'That's the name of that cop that came by Sirens the other morning.'

'He's both. Well, he thinks he's my boyfriend.'

'That stops now.'

I purse my lips. 'He pays well.'

'I don't care. I've had more cops in and around my building in the last three days than in the last three months, and I can't quite figure out why. There's only one other thing that I know of that's changed recently.' He levels his stare at me.

'Well, I can't help you with the cops, but you won't have to worry about me anymore. I quit,' I say, even though I doubt he'll let me leave that easy. 'And if you have something to say to me before I go, you should just say it,' I add, point-blank.

Either the response or the tone catches him off guard, and his eyes narrow. 'Someone was in my office yesterday, and I think it was you.'

'It was.'

His mouth drops open just a little.

'I'm a bad liar,' I lie.

'What were you doing in there?'

I chew on the inside of my cheek for a few seconds. 'Looking for your special mix. But I didn't find it,' I say, then let my gaze fall. 'I'm sorry.'

He lets out a long, slow breath, loud enough for me to hear. 'Just ask me next time, OK?'

I nod, then flick my eyes in his direction as I adjust the strap of the bag on my shoulder, baiting a switch in his attention.

'Where are you going?' he asks.

'I don't know yet.'

'Is this about what happened in the parking lot today?'

'What else would it be about?' In truth, that fat prick and his busted nose are the last thing on my mind and the least of my worries, but Easton doesn't need to know that.

'What happened to you was unacceptable. I'd like to put you up some place nicer for a few days.'

'What are you going to want for that?' I keep my face tense, but my mind takes off. Ten minutes ago, I'd talked myself into leaving town for good. Leaving this motel with Easton to go anywhere is a mind game I didn't see coming. Don't they tell would-be kidnap victims to fight like hell on the spot, to do whatever it takes to not go to a second location? Is that what this is – the beginning of a slow-motion abduction? It damn sure feels like it.

'For you to give me another chance and keep working. I told you that I run things differently, but I didn't show you that today.' He softens his gaze; strokes my cheek. A younger me would be eating this up and licking the damn plate.

'It's probably also a bad look for you if a working girl that's been around the block a time or twenty tells people she left Sirens because of too much violence at the workplace,' I reply.

'That's true.' He opens the passenger door to his car. 'Come on – I'll take you there. Stay just a night if you want. You can have a free hot breakfast in the morning, then go wherever. At least I'll feel better about it, and if you do tell people about how horrible it is to work at Sirens, well, I figure an honest girl like you wouldn't be able to leave this part out.'

I muster a smile. 'I'll follow you there.'

His fingers tap on the roof of the car. A word forms between his lips, but he keeps it to himself. Then he folds his proverbial hand of cards for this round and pushes the door shut.

I wonder why he's being so careful. He could've made more of a scene, dragged me to the car by my hair. My best guess is that Hunter's intervention the other morning has him more spooked than I've realized, especially with the snippet of our conversation that he was privy to when he arrived, which may have sounded like Hunter was pumping me for information that I wasn't willing to give up. He didn't come out and ask me about the thumb drive, which could mean he knows I'm lying and thinks I have it hidden somewhere, or it's something he doesn't want anyone to know exists. My money's on the former, and every move from here on out will be made with it in mind.

I follow behind his car to a Holiday Inn Express a couple blocks west of Sirens. Easton tells me to wait in my car while he secures a room for me. I spend the ten minutes while he's inside debating whether I should make a break for it. But with Easton having establishments in multiple states and likely trafficking between them, my guess is he's got just as many eyes looking out for any kind of trouble.

He reappears through the sliding doors and holds up a room key. I grab my purse and my bag, then climb out of my car. I reach for the key, but he swipes it behind his back.

'I'll see you to your room,' he says.

I knew he would, but it scares me all the same. When we get there, he follows me inside. I tell myself that if he was going to do anything to me, it would've been safer for him at the motel, where his name is not on the receipt.

'I've paid for the room through the weekend. I want you to stay here and lie low until we can make sure any customers who you may have offended understand that it's all settled now, OK?'

'Whatever you say, boss.' I meet his gaze and wait, trying to ignore surge after surge of adrenaline that is begging my body to do literally anything else.

He steps into me, grinning. His hands slide down my sides as his face grazes my neck. He's looking for a wire. I back to the bed and tug him with me by his shirt. Then I let him lie me down. He fishes a bag out of his pocket and puts a little molly on my tongue.

'What are you going to want for that?' I ask him after I've swallowed it down.

He parts my knees and thrusts himself inside. 'Tell me something no one knows about you. Not even that cop you've got wrapped around your finger.'

'He doesn't know me. He only thinks he does,' I say, buying myself time to think. It isn't exactly a lie, and the truth in it hurts more than I expect it to.

'You want him to know you, the *real* you, and want you anyway, don't you?' He pushes harder.

I arch my back; let out a gasp. 'Doesn't matter. He wouldn't.'

'What have you done that he would turn on you for?'

I look him in the eyes. He's hunting for leverage, and I'm going to give it to him. 'I killed someone.'

He goes stone still. 'You're not lying, are you?'

'No.'

'Good.' He grins the way a dog bares its teeth, then loses himself in me once more.

Pinned between his sweating body and the bed, I think of Hunter's phone call and shiver.

I can't leave town yet.

There's one thing I still haven't tried.

And there's more snow on the way.

TWENTY-NINE

Daniel – February 9, 2018

D aniel arrived for work two hours early. Even though he hated to admit it, Hunter's two-second read of Lily and her effect on this case had been spot on. He wanted to make heads or tails of how to proceed with the Rose component of the investigation before anyone else could add influence or bear witness. As an added buffer, he stole inside his investigation room. Rose's name claimed the outside edge of the board. He toyed with the idea of wiping her name away, imagining how satisfying it would be.

A furious voice flooded the department, startling him. He hadn't seen anyone else in the homicide wing when he'd passed through. Pricking an ear, he backed to the door to scope out the common area of the division. It was empty. The ruckus was coming from the adjacent wing, where financial crime detectives chased numbers and trails of dirty money from their better desk chairs and updated computers.

Daniel tossed the eraser on to the table and followed the yelling. A man was leaning over Detective Eric Ivey's desk. Ivey was the senior investigator in the financial crimes department. He was the one guy in the whole building who didn't think Hunter was a gift to the precinct. From the expression on Eric's face, he was also not a fan of the man crowding the other side of his desk.

'Wilder!' Eric called out upon spotting him in the door frame. Then he hopped up from his ergonomic chair and hustled toward him, pressing his loosened tie to his chest.

'Everything OK?' Daniel asked.

'This guy says a new dancer at Sirens drugged him and skimmed his credit cards.'

Daniel limited his initial response to a wry half-smile. For many reasons, he didn't want to expose the flashfire of curiosity that was already ripping through him.

'He won't formally file a report, and he has no actual proof that he's willing to give us. Doesn't want the wife to find out,' Eric added, lowering his voice. 'He was thinking he could report it as a financial crime and somehow keep his name out of it.'

'How can I help?' Daniel asked.

Eric threw a glance at the man, then down to his watch. 'Honestly, just ask him a few questions until he seems satisfied. I would, but I don't have time for this. I'm supposed to turn over a full analysis of seven years' worth of bank records to the DA by COB. Do you mind taking one for the team?'

'Sure. But you owe me one,' Daniel said, if only to cover up the fact that Eric had already given him plenty, and he waved for the man to follow him out.

'What's your name, sir?' Daniel asked as they took seats across from each other at Daniel's desk in the homicide wing.

'Mark . . . Smith.'

Daniel arched a brow. 'OK, Mark Smith, can you start from the beginning?' Daniel picked up his pen and flipped his notebook to a clean page.

'No. You can't write anything down.' He waved at the pen in Daniel's hand as if he was shooing away a fly.

'Sir, you came here on your own, so whatever happened must be important to you. I also have a rough idea what this is about, and there's no need to be embarrassed, but if you want me to help you, I need to make notes.'

'What if someone sees them?'

'I can promise you other people *will* see them. That's how we identify suspects and make arrests.' Daniel pushed up his sleeves and rested his elbows on his desk, then ripped a play straight out of Hunter's book. 'Detective Ivey asked me to help you because I'm a homicide detective.'

'Homicide?' Mark jumped as if he'd been electrocuted by the word. 'Did that bitch kill someone? I bet she did. She could have seen my driver's license. She might know where I live. I need to tell my wife, don't I?' Sweat bloomed on his forehead in a garden of panic.

'I wouldn't go that far yet. What I mean is that I'm good at keeping information quiet until I make the arrest. If you want her caught, you have to give me proof that I can use to do it.'

'OK.' Mark shifted in his chair. 'I went to Sirens with some friends from work last Friday. There's a new working girl. She already walks around like she owns the place even though she's not a headliner. She's pretty, but she's no spring chicken.'

'And this is the girl you believe skimmed your credit cards?'

'I know she messed with them.'

Daniel sat back. 'Do you have proof she actually recorded your information or took something?'

'I found a business card for a church mixed in with my cash. I know that wasn't there before.'

It seemed Hunter's favorite girl had a favorite signature. 'Do you think she took any money?'

'Maybe.'

'Do you know how much you had when you walked in the door?'

'About five hundred in cash, maybe a little more.'

'How much did you walk out with?'

'I tipped a few of the dancing girls. Broke some bigger bills at the bar. Paid for the first round of drinks for the whole table in cash.'

'So, you have no idea how much you spent,' Daniel summarized. 'Are you sure she had access to your wallet?'

'She invited me into one of the cabanas with her. Who was I to say no? It was fun at first. We were laughing, drinking . . . then I don't remember anything else until she walked me back to the table. Boys said I'd been gone over an hour. They figured I just had stamina.'

'But you don't?' Daniel asked wryly, subconsciously marking time on his desk with the end of his pen like he was counting down to the end.

Mark leaned forward. 'I gotta take those blue pills, you know? And I didn't take one. I wasn't going to take a girl into those private cabanas. I just go for the show. But she found out that

I'm a new VIP and started paying extra attention to me – asked *me* to come with her instead of any of the other guys. She even said she liked me so much that it was on the house and brought the first round of drinks for free.'

Daniel stopped tapping his pen. 'That didn't seem suspicious to you?'

'I thought it was my lucky day.' He shook his head.

Daniel almost felt bad for him.

'What happened next?'

'I had one of the guys drive me home. I still felt really dizzy; didn't want to risk getting pulled over. It's like I couldn't wake all the way up.'

Daniel's conversation with Lily stirred unbidden in his brain: how the drink her sister gave her made her so sleepy that she couldn't feel the snow. 'I'll look into this a little bit, dig around. I'll keep your name out of it for now. Can you give me a name or a description for this girl?'

'Curvy – naturally. You can tell. Real full lips, blue eyes, and I mean *blue*. Those were probably fake though. But I don't mind.'

'White, black, short, tall, young, old?' Daniel prompted.

'White. Average height. I don't know how old she is. She had shiny black hair, but I think it was a wig. I don't mind that, either. All the important things were real.'

'What about a name?'

'They call her Betty Fox,' he said, confirming what Daniel had assumed for most of the conversation. 'I'm sure it's just some bullshit stripper name. You know how they do. They think it makes them sound sexier or something.'

'Does it?'

'Helps it all seem like pretend, like we're all playing dress up for a little while, then we go back to our real lives, no harm, no foul. I can tell you she drives an old gray Saturn.'

'How do you know what she drives?'

'I saw her again.' Mark looked everywhere else but at Daniel.

'Where?'

'A parking lot somewhere.'

'You remember her vehicle make and color, but not what parking lot you were in?' Daniel narrowed his eyes. 'Any strip club worth its salt is going to have video cameras in the parking lot.'

'OK, I went back to ask her about the money. She punched me in the face! She had brass knuckles in her purse.'

Daniel stared openly at him, realizing the bags and darkness under his eyes weren't a product of fatigue, age, and shadows, but a very recent well-placed shot to the nose, the evidence masked by thick layers of cosmetics.

'Do us both a favor and don't go back to Sirens for a while,' Daniel advised.

'You couldn't pay me to go back there,' he said, but Daniel had a feeling it was just a matter of time. Then he watched the man fan his jacket and pry at his collar with his fingers as he made his way toward the exit, betting he'd sweated more bullets in a police station than he had at a strip club. He'd also been more useful than Daniel could've hoped. Betty had nothing to do with the Brecken Park case, but Ivey had asked Daniel for his help on a separate investigation. Who was he to deny a fellow detective his every effort, especially if he could talk to Betty without Hunter running interference?

Daniel drove to Sirens before he could talk himself out of it. Once he reached the parking lot, he rolled his shoulders, popped a Rolaid, and reminded himself that two men who had approached Betty in the last week had left the conversation with bloody noses, rifled wallets, and business cards for Jesus. He tried not to entertain the possibilities of what he'd face when Hunter inevitably found out.

Once inside the club, Daniel made a straight shot for the main bar at the center of the bright, crowded floor, where Easton Grimes was nursing a drink.

'Easton, right?' he called as he approached.

Easton looked up slowly, his gaze noncommitted until it landed on Daniel. Then his entire expression went to work.

'Surprised to see you here, Detective.'

'Working a case.' Daniel rounded the end of the bar and took the seat next to him. 'I got another complaint about Betty stealing credit-card numbers.'

'It wouldn't surprise me if that guy you met here a couple days ago has his buddies lodge similar complaints in the coming days. They're probably trying to scare her or get her fired. A man came by yesterday looking for her, then attacked her in the parking lot. She defended herself, but she's shook up and rightfully so. I've told her to take a few days off.'

'This guy said she slipped something in his drink. It seems another business card for a church was left behind in his wallet, so the accusation may have merit. I'm not saying I liked the guy, but he didn't strike me as a liar.'

'And I do because I own a strip club?' Easton said.

Daniel looked away, unsure of how to respond. Easton wasn't necessarily wrong, and that made him more uncomfortable than he wanted to admit.

'Sorry, that wasn't fair, and you're just doing your job,' Easton continued, filling the gap for him. 'We've had some real clowns in here lately. It worries me. Guys come in here and think they own a woman because they've seen her skin.'

'So why be a part of it?'

'I try to do it right. I pay them well, give them good security, and make sure they're OK mentally. This is a tough gig.' He paused, and they watched a waitress walk by, her lace belt stuffed with cash. 'It also earns a ridiculous amount of money. Girls come here with plans of using it as a stopgap between where they're at and where they dream of being. Then they realize whatever job they were aspiring to won't pay them near what they earn here, and whatever town they're trying to run to won't feel any freer than this.'

Daniel's thoughts turned to Maya, her cash, and her ill-fated plans. Could she have considered using Sirens or a place like it to fund her alleged trip to the beach? He brought up a picture of her on his cell phone. 'Have you ever seen this girl?'

Easton frowned at the screen. 'Looks a little young to be around here.'

'She would be.'

'Is this related to that kid I saw on the news? Boy who froze to death at Brecken Park?'

'Unrelated,' Daniel said, watching him closely. Easton's leap of a connection was more than a little suspect. Even though Lily had advised him against it, he wished he'd asked Maya about her relationship with Christian when he had the chance. If Easton had seen them together in any memorable capacity, the most likely place was here. But how would two high school kids get in here, and more importantly, why?

Easton's cell phone flashed on the bar top with an incoming call. He turned away to answer it, then hung up after only a few seconds. 'I have a meeting I need to get to, but if you need anything, call the club. They'll give you my cell if I'm not here.'

'Can I have a phone number for Betty?' Daniel asked.

'All due respect, absolutely not. That's her private information, and she can give it to you if she wants to or if you have a court order. That applies to her legal name as well, so I'll save you the question. I'll also consider your partner's favor from earlier this week repaid,' he added, then excused himself from the bar.

Daniel stayed long enough to watch the man stride toward the back of the space, sliding through customers like a shark through fish. He couldn't shake the feeling that Easton was still watching him even though he was the one walking away.

THIRTY

Rose – February 9, 2018

I fold the window drape in my fingers, then run the fabric between them, trying to force my mind to focus on the texture instead of the craving pulling at every vein in my body like a dragnet. It doesn't help that I've been watching the world pass by through the hotel-room window since Easton left, stewing in my own paranoia and the crash of coming down.

While Easton was inside me, glaring and furious, thrusting over and over just to make sure I knew he could, I had a vision of his face turning to red mush as it hovered above mine, dripping down and splattering my cheeks like ruby-colored snow. How to get it done seemed so clear, so simple in that earlier moment of pure rage.

Now, alone, crashing, and exhausted, that fury is still present, but it haunts the edges of me. My center, where it was born like a baby made of flame and spite, is cold, empty, and needing.

I glance over my shoulder at the little parting gift Easton left on the bedside table: a small, clear plastic bag containing a rainbow's assortment of pills. His special mix, just for me. The mix he didn't mention he had on him when I lied about looking for it in his office. I want to swallow them all, fast and dry, but I don't fucking dare. An old-ass stripper overdosing in a hotel room would make a mess for the staff but clean up a hell of a lot for him.

In case I had any doubt I was under surveillance, a black four-door has been circling the block every ten minutes for the last hour, swinging through the parking lot on every other interval, then passing behind my car. I can only hope whoever Easton has assigned to watch me is contented by the sight of the vehicle and won't come inside the hotel to check. Still, I feel the needling sensation of being stalked like prey all the same.

I have a working theory that men like strip clubs because they're the only public places willing to acknowledge that civilization is a smokescreen. It is without question the most dangerous lie we sell ourselves. Civility can swirl to nothing in a heartbeat for a million different reasons. We're predators, after all. Canine teeth. A stomach made for digesting meat. Nails protruding off our digits. Eyes set closer together. Maybe that's why men get off on the girls with big, wide-set eyes. It isn't just that it makes them appear younger. It also makes them look more like something they can chase down and eat. Beneath the vocabularies and the clothes and jewelry and cookie-cutter houses with tidy mowed lawns, we're still animals. Basic. Primal. Hungry.

The black car pulls down the row where I'm parked, slowing long enough to peer inside the back windows, then rolls on. I change my wig, pack my bag, then slip from the room. As I slink to the door to the stairs, I map out a plan in my writhing brain, if only to feel like I'm in control of something. I will watch the black car's next pass from the lobby, then I'll find a bus stop off this main road and ride it to Brecken Park, where the drugs available might not be pure but at least I'm sure those dealers are hoping I'll survive to buy again.

Like clockwork, the black car rolls through the lot, then merges back into traffic in the southbound lanes. As soon as he disappears, I walk through the main door like I have all the time in the world. The second I hit the sidewalk, it takes everything I have to not break into a run. I should get my hands on another car as soon as possible, if only temporarily. There are enough moving pieces in this end-game-puzzle-from-hell to not factor in a damn bus schedule. Not to mention, in the wide open, I am cornered as fuck.

I reach the bus stop and tuck myself into the corner of the shelter. The drone of passing cars has the same effect on me as that hippie music that crunchy, upper-middle-class ladies play in their hot yoga studios. As if they need help escaping the self-imposed stress of stability.

Shame on me. I shouldn't judge.

A cage is a cage is a cage.

The scene in front of me blurs. My mind travels where it wants, and that squishy, throbbing traitor takes me right back to the woods. But I can't get mad because there's an answer there, if not a million questions.

Lyric.

I can't prove in a matter of days what Easton is doing at Sirens, but maybe I don't have to.

I lean against the Plexiglass wall, the weight of all of it suddenly too much. Twenty years ago, this idea for a solution would not have felt like justice. I'm older now – if not wiser – and my bar is lower. We *dig* graves, after all, and if you want to bury someone, you have to be willing to lower yourself into that same pit of rotting earth first to get it done.

Hunter has known this truth – ugly as it is – all along. I think back to the hours we spent in his car two decades before, how grown I felt, how naïve I was, the secrets spilled in that small, stinking space, the promises we'd made in such dumb earnest. We'd met at The Alibi when I was seventeen, unbeknownst to him. He was twenty-eight and undercover at the time, unbeknownst to me.

Turns out, trust is built at the bottom of things, never at the top, and while we were there together, he saw me through the ugly side of getting clean the first time I really meant it, and he'd call me every time he felt like tracking down a pill or picking up a razor blade. When he found out my real age, he still kept coming around Sirens, if only because he had to. But he kept me at arm's length. And I kept his secrets.

Get grown, he'd say. *You get grown, and I'll wait on you till then.*

How old is grown enough? I once asked him, genuinely confused. I had felt like the adult in the room most of my life.

Twenty-five, he'd said.

I'd wrinkled my nose. *That's not grown. That's just old. You won't want me then.* I'd tried to talk him down to twenty, but the man would not be moved. Then I told him I loved him. The man I'd known as 'H' for nearly a year had looked at me long and hard, took my hand in his, and told me he was an undercover cop for a narcotics task force who suspected The Alibi was running drugs and laundering money.

My heart loved him even harder, this white knight in ripped-up jeans and a black T-shirt who I thought would help me save the girls I'd walked through the gates of that hellhole. And the first thing out of my dumb mouth was: *What about the girls?*

I told him about how underage girls moved through The Alibi's basement like water through a pipe.

How a few had disappeared the way puddles evaporate in the sun.

How four of Tula's finest had worn paths up and down those stairs, and how they were the customers all the working girls feared most.

For more than a year, I kept track of names and ages of almost everyone who walked in the door more than once, the schedule of basement customers who came and went on a regular basis, girls who came back the worse for wear, and girls who went and stayed gone. I witnessed things I'll never unsee, heard conversations that still echo across my worst nightmares, all to pass along as much information as I could to the only man I've ever loved.

Finally, a task force raided The Alibi on a Tuesday night. Hunter's coworkers – who'd been there every Tuesday for damn near a year – didn't show up.

The next time I saw Hunter, I begged him to turn them in, to tell the higher-ups what I knew, what I'd seen. How he had to do something to stop it, to act now, not wait for another girl to go missing to do the right thing. But they walked clean and free, and he couldn't tell me why. Just that he was lonely and scared and couldn't risk making enemies, and when those coworkers found me and beat me and left me for dead, the only word he had left for me was *go*.

I told him he didn't know the first thing about loneliness, about fear, about enemies. Then I told him about Lily.

He looked me dead in the eyes, and my mother's words echoed right out of his mouth: *It'll be safer for her if you're gone*, he said. He gave me his gun and his promise to watch over my baby sister, and even though in one fell swoop he'd broken every promise he'd made before it, I took his word and his revolver, and I swore I'd never look back.

I guess that does make me a liar.

I started coming back to Tula every time it snowed. Just long enough to *see* but never long enough to see it melt. In the last decade, I finally started counting. Nineteen times in the last ten years. But just like snow, unsettled dust keeps falling till it lands. And here the fuck we are.

There is no right thing. That's what I've learned. It's what Hunter already knew. He already understood the value of compromise: a forfeit of the right thing for the sure thing.

I get it now, H. That's the only thing I have left to say to him now, should I get the chance. But I'd just as soon keep it to myself.

I am on my own. I've always been on my own. At least I know it this time. I'd do well to remember that I'm just a summary of wounds – wounds I own, and wounds I've made.

THIRTY-ONE

Daniel – February 9, 2018

Daniel parked his car in the convenience-store parking lot across the street from the top end of Brecken Park and within sight of a common entry point. The 200-acre sprawl of green space had a half dozen official entrances and twice as many unofficial foot-worn ways in. No Man's Land was tucked in the northwest corner. There were no vehicle access points, parking lots, or marked trails in that quadrant of the park – just a couple footpaths and hand-me-down urban legends that kept the next generation's interest on life support.

He imagined the homeless man emerging from the trees, a girl half-dead in his arms and Bible verses fumbling from his lips. The man had been accidently released from the sobering tank before Daniel had arrived to talk to him. The only other place he knew to look for him was under the old train bridge.

As Daniel crossed the road on foot and scanned the underbrush for the telltale dent in the overgrowth, he couldn't help wondering what would've become of the man had Maya died, unable to clear him of blame. Then again, there was no way to be sure how long he'd waited to find her help, how close he'd come to too late. If she had died, where did culpability begin?

Casting the thoughts aside, he focused instead on the uptick of trash scattered along the ground. Ahead, a bush was decorated with beer cans and food wrappers like an unofficial trail marker, the footpath visible beyond. Daniel stole one last glimpse over his shoulder, then stepped into the woods. Peekaboo sunlight knifed through the canopy of naked limbs, speckled the ground, and warmed the back of his neck like a stare. Halfway to No Man's Land, the feeling became so strong he turned around, but all he found was an empty trail, a scrapbook of footprints.

The old train trestle came into view. Vines climbed up the pillars, nearly concealing the metal surface beneath. At the bottom, concrete feet were tagged with graffiti and rung with old cans and bottles. A shopping cart rested on its side with a wheel in the air like a dead deer gone stiff. Daniel walked past it and deeper into the shadow of the bridge. Soiled, threadbare blankets littered the ground. The temperature was well above freezing for the first time in four days, and what was left of the snow dripped like rain from the edges of the overpass.

Standing beneath the shelter, Daniel stared through the falling water. Something was moving between the trees in the direction from which he'd come. He quickly shifted for a better view, keeping himself concealed in the shadows.

Josh appeared on the trail. His gaze was cast downward. He hadn't seen Daniel yet, but if he stayed where he stood, the boy was sure to see him soon. Daniel eased in the direction of one of the pillars, trying to stay out of sight. He wasn't fast enough. Josh looked up. His eyes caught on Daniel, and he stopped walking mid-stride.

'It's cool, Josh.' Daniel stepped fully out from the cover of the pillar. 'I'm Detective Wilder, a friend of Lily's, remember?'

Without a word, Josh took off at a dead sprint, bolted across the open area in front of the bridge, and dashed into the woods on the other side.

Daniel chased behind him, but he was no match for Josh, who slipped through trees like water over rocks. His backpack thumped hard against him, and he increased his lead, unbothered by the weight, perhaps urged on by the pressure striking between his shoulder blades. Within seconds, he disappeared around a sharp turn. Daniel refused to give up, pushing himself faster, but Josh was too far ahead.

Sounds reached him through the trees: shouts and a dribbled ball, a violent rattle as a plane of metal was struck. The trail he was sprinting down would likely let out on the basketball courts. If he burst out of the woods, he would do nothing but send everyone scattering. Discouraged, Daniel slowed to a walk.

'Five-oh, five-oh,' he heard Josh announce to whoever was ahead of him, dashing any hope Daniel had of arriving without seeming like a threat.

He exited the woods with his hands open at his sides. Everyone who'd been playing moments before had already begun leaving in every direction, flipping up the hoods of their sweatshirts and slinging backpacks over shoulders. An orphaned ball rolled across the asphalt and bumped against a concrete wall, which was covered in graffiti.

'Josh,' Daniel called as he swung his gaze across the makeshift court. But he had faded into the traffic of moving bodies, and no one else looked in a pointed direction, giving him up.

'No one thinks they can take me in a little one-on-one?' Daniel said, louder this time, and he scooped up the ball. 'Come show a cop how it's done.' His quip elicited a laugh or two, but no one so much as turned around.

Movement in his peripheral vision drew his eye. A woman in a black tracksuit emerged from another trail. It was Betty. Her hair was blonde today, the wig cut at an angle along her chin. Her movements were fast and jerky, and her lips moved with silent words. She cut directly across the court, eyes straight ahead as if she was all alone on this crumbling patch of asphalt.

'Betty!' Daniel said.

She kept walking.

'Betty, it's Daniel. Can I ask you a question?'

She drew her arms tight across her chest, and her stride quickened. 'Tell your brother not to call me. It's over.'

'What's over?'

'All of it.'

'Are you OK?'

'Never better.'

'What are you doing out here?'

'What are *you* doing here?' She turned her glassy eyes upon Daniel. They were bright amber in color, bloodshot in the whites, and rimmed in red. But it was her pupils that gave her away, fixed and too large. Crack cocaine, if Daniel had to guess.

'I'm here for a kid who died out here a couple days ago,' Daniel said, deciding to throw her a bone.

'Sounds like you're a little late.'

'Seriously?'

'Cops are always too late.' She shifted from foot to foot. Every inch of her vibrated.

'Please, I could really use your help.'

'Sounds like it.'

'Do you know a boy named Josh Marsden?'

'Maybe. Probably. I don't know,' she muttered.

'What about Maya Summit or Christian Coleman?'

'Natasha,' she blurted, then she wheeled away from him and struck off again at a surprisingly quick pace, repeating the name.

'Who is that?' Daniel called at her back as he hurried to catch up.

'She wrote a note. I had her jacket. I had proof. I lost her. I lost them. All of it. I lost all of it . . .' she said rapid-fire, breaking into an uneven jog.

'Betty, please. Help me here, and maybe I can help you find the jacket.' Daniel's gaze swept ahead of them to the stretch of woods where she was pointed. If she took him up on it, they might be out there all day.

'I don't want your help,' she spat.

'I'm trying to keep you out of trouble. Another guy came into the station and said you drugged him and skimmed his cards. Maybe Hunter's OK with it, but I'm not OK with any part of whatever deal y'all have going on, and he's retiring in three months. I covered for you this time, but next time I can't promise that.'

'Three months from now, neither one of you will have to worry about me at all,' she said, then she left the asphalt and moved toward the trees.

'What does that mean, Betty? What are you doing out here?'

'I'm just out for a walk and being harassed by you,' she called without turning around.

'Yeah, I could say the same,' Daniel returned dryly, then slowed to a stop and watched her disappear into the woods, wholly frustrated with them both.

As soon as she was out of earshot, Daniel called Hunter.

'Your girlfriend is at Brecken Park and she's high as a kite,' Daniel said the moment his brother answered.

'Girlfriend?'

'Betty,' Daniel prompted. 'She's out of it pretty bad right now, Hunter. She refused to answer questions. She just rambled about a jacket and a note and someone named Natasha . . . and proof. What the hell is going on here?'

'You tell me. I heard another guy came into the station sporting a couple black eyes and beef with Sirens.'

'Tell me about Betty,' Daniel said evenly.

'I told you not to worry about it. That's all you need to know right now.'

'She's breaking the law, and you're letting her get away with it. What does she have on you?' Daniel demanded.

'Loyalty. That's what she has on me. Some of us still know what that means,' Hunter replied, then ended the call.

'Wow,' Daniel muttered to the emptiness around him.

The silver sky opened. Light rain pattered against the

pavement, filling the cracks and sliding in tiny rivets down the collar of his jacket. The walk back was going to feel a lot longer in the rain.

THIRTY-TWO

Lily – February 9, 2018

L ily pulled into the parking garage beneath her apartment and sat in her car with the engine idling and the heater on. An afternoon shower had ended, and rays of light were being coaxed through the darkening cloud. She felt lighter, too, practically made buoyant by Detective Wilder's interest in Rose. This new space gave rise to hunger, and she realized she hadn't eaten much in days.

From inside her car, Lily called in a takeout order at a barbeque hole-in-the-wall four blocks away, then checked the weather forecast on her phone to burn some time. The low would hover above freezing tonight. The cloud cover made the last traces of the afternoon feel dark. She smiled to herself as she turned off her car and climbed out, opting to walk the short distance to the restaurant to pick up her food, even in the mist.

Fifteen minutes later, she stood at the counter, exchanging five dollars for a double portion of pulled pork with extra sauce.

Don't mind me. Just eating my feelings, she thought, but it was Rose's voice in her head. She could see her sister at fourteen in a blue corner chair, her bare legs tucked beneath her, the handle of a spoon dangling from her mouth, and a tub of Everett's Rocky Road ice cream in her lap. The scene played on, and Lily could hear the snap of a belt pulling loose from jeans, the crack of dead skin against living. Rose had become a tumbleweed of limbs while their mother stood in the opposite corner, gaze averted, lips pressed in a traitorous line.

Lily left the restaurant on trembling legs. The memory followed her, and as she walked to her apartment, she fought the paranoia of being watched. She glanced back, but no one was behind her.

Ahead, a cross street intersected the main road. Lily had the light and hustled across. To her left, the road was lined with vacant buildings. A certainty spread through her: someone was in those shadows, watching her.

No one is there, Lily, she silently told herself, coaching her feet and eyes forward, and she repeated it to herself the rest of the way home.

At the walk-up for her apartment, she paused outside the door and stared at her third-floor window. She imagined herself standing on the other side of the glass, watching the street, testing each bite of barbeque for temperature against her lips before popping it in her mouth. All at once, she realized what she was longing for: she wished Rose was standing in this spot right now, checking in on her baby sister.

The darkened view into her apartment prodded at the loneliness in Lily, and she had the sudden urge to paint this scene, giving color and shape and texture to this feeling without a name. She withdrew her phone from her coat pocket, framed the shot in her viewfinder, and snapped a series of pictures to use for later.

A car approached, slowing as it drew near. The car would have passed within an arm's reach had Lily been standing on the curb instead of beneath the trees framing the walk-up, but Lily could still see the driver plain as day. The woman wore a hat pulled low, concealing half her face. Her shiny blonde hair was lopped off at her chin and shielded her profile. The car slowed down as it drew even with the stairs leading to Lily's apartment, and the driver turned to look full face at Lily's dark window.

Rose.

Lily leaped from beneath the tree and waved her arms, desperate to get her attention. 'Rose!'

The engine whined with a sudden demand, and the car jumped forward. Lily lifted her phone to snap a picture of the vehicle. The handle on the takeout bag ripped in protest of the sudden movement, and her meal became a murder scene on the sidewalk, splattering across the concrete and the tops of her feet. She hopped backward, mouth agape, gaze tumbling down. Then she swung her focus back to the road, all at once furious and terrified and unequivocally unsure, and took as many pictures as she could of the car as it accelerated through a red light and out of sight.

With a shaking finger, Lily scrolled through the photos she took, but the flash had been turned off, and for all her effort and sacrificed food, she had twelve frames of darkness and a blur of tail lights. Desperate, she dialed Daniel Wilder.

'Hello?' the detective's voice came through the phone, and for a moment Lily couldn't find the words to reply. 'Lily? Everything OK?'

'I just saw my sister.' Tears pricked the corners of her eyes. 'She just drove by my apartment.'

'Are you sure?'

'Yes, I'm sure. I saw her. She slowed down the car; she looked up at my window. I tried to flag her down, but she sped off.'

'Did you get a plate number? Even a partial?'

'No.'

'Did you get a picture?'

'I tried, but the flash was off. None of the pictures show anything. But I swear I saw her just now!'

Daniel exhaled audibly against the receiver. 'I know how bad you want to believe that you've seen her, but I find that reality hard to believe. From what it sounds like, she's done her best to avoid you for twenty-five years. Why would she suddenly be making herself known, driving by your apartment? If you want me to take this seriously, you need to take it seriously, too. Let me do my job. I'll call you if I find anything or if I have any questions. Until then, the best thing you can do for everyone is to give us time and space to get real work done.'

Lily's mouth fell open.

'Goodbye, Lily,' he said, then he hung up before she could respond.

Lily pocketed her phone, her mind reeling. She scraped up what she could of her meal back into the bag and threw it in the sidewalk trash can. Then she walked slowly up the stairs, into her apartment, and to the other side of the window. She peered down. From that height, it looked like her food had left a bloodstain on the concrete.

Lily knew she'd seen Rose in that car. And she knew what Rose would say if she were standing beside her here and now: *This is why you don't involve or trust the police.*

For once in her adult life, Lily felt like her sister would have been right.

Her thoughts turned to Maya and the bridge she had helped build between the girl and the detective – a bridge she might need to burn down. If Daniel wanted future access to Maya, he would have to go through her. And if Maya remembered more about the night in the woods than she was letting on, Lily would do herself a favor by offering a trade to Maya directly. Lily had more control over what happened next than Daniel did, and a reminder of who really held the cards here certainly wouldn't hurt anyone involved.

Lily retrieved Maya's file from her purse and found her case worker's cell phone number, then dialed.

'Hey, Rachel. It's Lily.'

'Hi, Lily. Is everything OK?' The words came a little slow, and Lily would bet she had caught her in the middle of her typical after-work bottle of wine.

'Everything's fine. I wanted to check on Maya. Any news?'

'She's going to be discharged tomorrow morning.'

'That's great to hear. Where's she heading?'

'I'm trying to get her into that group home near the Boys and Girls Club. The house leader is good with kids like Maya, and there's a decent after-school music curriculum at the club. I'm hoping it'll give her a sense of belonging.'

'Do you worry it's too much of a reward considering the choices she made? I heard her playing the detective that questioned her like a fiddle. You know how she does. I worry what she'll try next if she gets away with this, especially if she finds out about Tyler's adoption coming up,' Lily said carefully.

'I hadn't thought of it that way,' Rachel answered. Lily heard her swallow; felt her considering.

'I know we all care about her, especially with what she's been through, but if she were still my responsibility, I might help steer the judge toward a more secure decision, honestly. Make her face some consequences,' Lily added firmly.

Rachel swallowed again. 'You're right. God, I hate being the bad guy. But I guess sometimes the hard call is the right call.'

Relief spilled through Lily, cool and tingling, but guilt was there to meet it, burning like a flame. A single tear gathered and fell. She squeezed her eyes shut against the threat of more.

'They are one and the same,' she said.

THIRTY-THREE

Daniel – February 9, 2018

Daniel confronted his whiteboard. Rose's name, cast to the outside in red erasable ink, screamed at him in Lily's voice. Whatever string-pulling Lily might be able and willing to do on his behalf was seeming less worth the cost with every interaction.

His own older brother had – for all intents and purposes – been missing from his life, too, even when he was right in front of him. More than once, Daniel had wondered if Hunter literally vanishing would be a kinder absence than the vacancy of his presence. Then again, Daniel had the privilege of knowing where Hunter was. Maybe all Lily really needed was an answer, but he had no idea where to start searching for one. Rose would have been fourteen, no job, no money, no social network or safety net. How would a teenage girl survive?

His thoughts shifted to Betty. He didn't want to think about her when he should be focused on Christian and Maya, but his mind kept circling back. Why was she taking her clothes off and skimming credit cards at what looked like a hard-won forty years old? Was she a number belonging to the statistics he'd read about? Maybe Easton was right: somewhere along the way, the woman had turned to stripping as a means to an end, then decided the money was worth the cost of doing business.

'Who are you, Betty Fox?' Daniel murmured. 'What do you have on my brother, and what were you doing at Brecken Park this afternoon?'

The answer to his last question was probably the simplest explanation: the south end of Brecken Park was like a mobile mart for anything a person wanted to buy by the pill or ounce. He recalled how she'd presented herself when he'd first met her at Sirens – bold and self-possessed, her hungry, glittering eyes fixated on Hunter. But it had all been an act.

Daniel had a sinking feeling the Betty he'd seen today at Brecken Park was the real woman behind the mask: angry and desperate as hell, escaping reality temporarily by way of a choice drug. It wasn't a stretch to think that Rose could at one point have been in Betty's position, and that Maya, without intervention, stood a higher-than-average chance of one day dancing in those tall, clear heels.

A first wave of empathy for Betty washed over Daniel. Her hold on Hunter had nothing to do with him, nor the relationship he didn't have with his brother. She was a separate entity. He needed to remember that and treat her accordingly. He uncapped a marker and added Betty's name beneath Rose's as a reminder to himself, then he wiped the question mark from beside Rose's name. It was highly unlikely she was a piece of the Brecken Park case, but it went without question that someone should look for her, even if just for a little while.

By Lily's count, they weren't yet in the system when they'd run from home. Rose's disappearance had never tallied a mark on anyone's list. No one's but Lily's. Problematic though it may be, if Daniel wanted to find Rose, he needed to look at this board through Lily's eyes for a bit and pretend Maya had woken up with the sisters' song in her memory.

If that were the case, what else connected the two?

One: Rose was drunk, and Maya was likely overdosing. It was plausible that intoxication had led to Christian falling asleep in the snow, but Daniel needed evidence. Daniel wrote: *Tox screen results* beside his name.

The only other obvious commonality between the three was the snow. He wrote the question on the board, then shifted his focus to Betty's name. The footpaths at Brecken Park were clearly familiar to her, even as high as she was. The kids who frequented the court were a community all their own, a network they could count on.

Why did she go to Brecken Park? Daniel added the question to his growing list on the board. *Who is Natasha?* Daniel's assumption was that she was a coworker from Sirens. Had Betty expected to meet her out there? If so, why?

Daniel's thoughts moved from Betty to Easton, particularly his reaction to seeing the picture of Maya. Best-case scenario, Maya had come by Sirens looking for work, and Easton was spooked and played dumb, using the news story about Christian in an attempt to throw Daniel off. With Maya discovered alive and with no complaints of assault or coercion, Daniel had yet to define what worst-case scenario would be here. But she could have easily ended up in the morgue beside Christian. So why didn't she?

Daniel approached the board as if it had a secret.

Who was singing in the woods? Daniel wrote beneath Maya's name. Then he detailed all he knew: *A woman's voice.* The transient had mentioned the Virgin Mary carried Maya close to the fire where he was sitting beneath the bridge and told him what to do. Could the woman have been singing to Maya as she carried her out? And if this woman was somehow responsible for what happened to Christian, why did she carry Maya out of the woods instead of deeper in?

He stepped back to look at the board, which had been so empty less than an hour before. He didn't have any answers yet, but it felt like the right questions were finally taking shape.

THIRTY-FOUR

Lily – February 10, 2018

Even though it was barely nine a.m. on a Saturday, Lily was in the parking lot of the detention center in time to watch Rachel and an accompanying officer exit the building. She slid deeper into her seat, hiding herself from easy view until they climbed back into the car and pulled away. Then she drew a breath, steeling herself. Maya would be most likely to accept a visitor in that first hour after being checked into custody, when the door to the outside world still felt like it swung both ways.

An invisible clock she couldn't name was ticking; she'd felt the proverbial hand begin to move with every beat of her heart. She was desperate for one chance alone with Maya to see what else she might remember about the night she nearly froze to death and the song she woke up singing. It was a risk, coming here for her own gain. Selfish. Wrong. If Lartesha found out, she might even lose her job. But when it came to understanding Rose, she was willing to do anything.

Before she could talk herself out of it, Lily grabbed her purse and headed inside.

At the check-in desk, Lily caught herself fiddling with the strap of her purse, then clasped her hands at her front. 'I'm with DFACS. I'd like to see Maya Summit,' she said.

'Didn't y'all just bring her in here?' the officer, a heavyset older woman, asked her from behind the Plexiglass barrier.

'Yes. She was also just released from the hospital. The detective on her case asked me to check in with her to see if she's ready for a full interview,' Lily said, reciting the lie she'd mentally rehearsed in the car.

'The way she was carrying on, I don't think she's in a helpful frame of mind.'

'Will you just ask her. Please?'

'Sign in.' She slid the visitor log closer but not so close that Lily didn't have to stretch for it. 'And I'll need your driver's license.'

Lily handed over her ID before signing her name.

'Go ahead and take a seat,' the officer said, returning the license. 'I'll call you up when she's ready.'

Lily picked a chair with its back resting against the front wall of the building. A handful of other people were waiting, too. One by one, they were called into the visitation room. Lily scrolled through weather apps on her phone, dug aimlessly through her purse, then finally checked the time. Twenty minutes had passed.

She approached the check-in station again, wondering if she'd been forgotten, and cleared her throat.

'Can I help you?' the woman asked without looking up from her cell phone, where a game of Candy Crush had thrown up rainbow-colored blocks all over the screen.

Lily arched a brow. Three days' worth of frustrations reared their heads all at once. 'I've been here almost half an hour,' she said in a measured tone, determined to remain calm.

'Congratulations. I've been here since six a.m.'

'Maya Summit,' Lily said point-blank. 'Yes or no, and I'll be out of your way.'

The officer pursed her lips and glanced up at Lily, tipping her screen where Lily could better see that she'd lost the game. Lily stared back. She would sooner feed the woman her phone than offer her condolences. With a sigh, the officer pushed a button on the side of her radio receiver.

'Has Maya Summit been brought up for visitation?' the officer asked.

The radio crackled. 'She didn't want to come,' a voice on the other end responded, ending in a chirp.

New panic pushed out from an old place buried deep within Lily and fluttered its shriveled wings. 'Maybe she thinks I'm here with the detective. Does she know it's just me?'

The officer repeated Lily's question to her counterpart.

'I told her. She wouldn't come.'

The officer shrugged at Lily, softening for the first time. 'Look, they can be like that when they first arrive sometimes. Tell your detective to give her a minute to settle. She'll be itching for something to do before too long.'

Lily conjured a tight smile in place of a response, then turned on her heel and strode hastily for the exit.

'Lily? What are you doing here?' Katelyn's voice called from her left, where the doors Lily had been denied access beyond were now swinging shut behind her coworker. 'Aren't you supposed to be spending all weekend at your cabin?'

'I heard Maya was being transferred here. I knew she'd be upset. I couldn't leave town without checking on her. She's always been a special one for me.' Lily couldn't bring herself to admit out loud that Maya had refused to see her. 'What about you? Why are you here on a Saturday?' she asked as they moved together toward the exit.

'I have one going to court next week. I wanted to prepare him a little bit.'

'I'm sure he's grateful,' Lily managed to reply.

Katelyn winked at her. 'I learned from the best.'

A swell of emotion took Lily by surprise. 'Thank you. I . . .' Her voice faltered, and she had to clear her throat before she could continue. 'I don't feel like anyone worth learning from right now.'

Katelyn took Lily by the arm. 'Are you OK?'

Lily shook her head.

'Why don't we go get coffee and dessert somewhere? Talk about anything but work,' Katelyn said.

'I won't have anything to talk about.'

'Come on. One hour. We'll buy every piece of pie and cake on the menu.'

Katelyn's order sounded like something Rose would have wanted to do, and the thought stole Lily's breath. It was so much easier to keep Rose in a box – the memories, the longing, the hole her sister's absence left in every moment, every space, the hope that one day she would come back on her own to fill them all in.

Lily met Katelyn's gaze with brimming eyes.

'Let's get out of here,' Katelyn said, then took her by the elbow and ushered her to her car.

A half hour later, they sat at a table for two so covered in dessert plates they didn't have room to rest their hands.

'This was one of my best ideas ever,' Katelyn said as she sampled a lemon cake.

Lemon anything had been Rose's favorite. Their mother's, too. Lily smiled at Katelyn, then forced a small bite of coffee crumble down her throat if only to have an excuse to stay quiet.

Since they first sat down, she had been trying to come up with one whole sentence that didn't involve Josh, Christian, or Maya, and she knew she wouldn't be able to speak Rose's name without a fresh wave of grief flooding her chest. She spooned off a tiny bite of lemon meringue pie, and her mind wandered back to Anne. She wondered if this was what the old woman's world was like: so many thoughts and no way to communicate them. Lily took another bite and imagined the secrets she had locked up inside. Some of them Lily had put there for safekeeping.

'Looks like we have a winner,' Katelyn said, a pleased expression on her face.

Lily smiled back at her. 'Let's get a piece of this to go. There's someone I want you to meet.'

THIRTY-FIVE

Daniel – February 10, 2018

Hunter's rare, infectious laughter reached Daniel through the gap he'd left open in the door to investigation room four. He leaned back in his chair and watched his brother stand from his desk, grab another piece of pizza from the box near the front of the room, then fetch a beer from a blue cooler beside it. He cracked it open and guzzled it. From the look of things, the drug house case had cracked wide open, too.

It was an unspoken truth that department rules tended to relax for anyone who had come in to work on the weekend, but anybody else would have had their asses handed to them for bringing a case of beer into the station. While Hunter had long been an exception to most regulations, now that he was three months shy from retirement, he was practically untouchable. Daniel knew he should be grateful – it was typically against protocol for family to work together. But if the higher-ups were hoping the bent rule would result in Daniel becoming Hunter Kepp 2.0, they were going to be sorely disappointed.

Another round of laughter trespassed into his space. He righted his chair and turned his back on the door, then scrolled through the pictures he'd taken with his phone at Brecken Park over the past few days. Snow might be important, but, more likely, this location meant something to someone.

'Swear to me you didn't tell her,' Hunter said from behind him.

Daniel spun round. Hunter was flush with drink, but before Daniel's eyes, the color drained out of him.

'Tell who what?' Daniel looked from his brother to the board and back. Hunter was reading his notes on the Brecken Park case.

Hunter took a swig of his beer, then waved his hand. 'I'm just messing with you.'

'Bullshit. What did you see up there?'

'Come have a drink with us,' Hunter replied instead.

'It's barely noon,' Daniel muttered as he stole a glimpse at the board and immediately realized Hunter's reaction could only have to do with one name up there: Betty.

'What does Betty have to do with this, Hunter? Give me something, or I'm going to dig deeper on my own. I won't stop, Hunt. I love you, I do, no matter how you feel about me. But I won't stop.'

Hunter reached back for the door and pulled it shut, closing them inside the space. 'I need to tell you something, but it doesn't leave this room. It doesn't leave us. Swear to me,' he said, his face contorting with a frightening urgency.

'I swear.' Daniel didn't want to mean it, but he did. He'd never seen his brother this way before. 'You're scaring me, Hunt.'

'Betty Fox. You want to know who she is?' Hunter walked up to Daniel's board and touched her name. 'She's Rose. Swear to me you didn't tell Lily.'

Daniel blinked and shook his head. There was no way he'd heard him right. 'What do you mean "she's Rose"?'

'Betty Fox. Her name is Rose, and she's got a sister named Lily, who can never find out about her.'

Rage made a fist around Daniel's throat, denying space for words or breath for a long moment. 'You knew . . . all this time, you knew? How could you keep this from me?' he finally sputtered.

'I don't owe you Betty's story, and neither does she.'

'What the hell does she have on you?' Daniel hated how much he felt like crying.

'I met her during my undercover days. We spent a lot of time together. She used to watch my back. She let me know when something was going on in her circles that tipped her moral compass. Now that she's here, she might do it again. She already hinted that she suspects something. I have to protect that. You do, too.'

'Tipped her moral compass?' Daniel echoed, incredulous. 'She roofies men and skims their credit cards, and you make decisions based on her *moral compass*?'

'She knows what's important and what's not.'

Daniel wanted to punch him square in his mouth. 'And you think you're important to her, too? Is that it?'

'Be careful here, Danny.'

'You be careful! That woman has flown under the radar for two decades. What did she do, just come out and say: "My name is really Rose and there's a sister I left to die who might come looking for me one day, but we're going to pretend she doesn't exist," and you don't think she was using you somehow? Hell, maybe she's just now collecting.'

His brother's eyes met his, and they held each other's gaze. 'Betty's an old CI of mine. She caught wind of some bad shit going down at that strip club Easton Grimes owns now back when it was The Alibi. Kids were being run through there . . . worst-case scenario shit.'

'Jesus, Hunter.' Daniel made a fist and pressed it against the sudden pit in his stomach.

'You don't know the half of it.' His eyebrows lifted, but the rest of his face fell as if recalling the memory took more effort than he'd expected. 'She did some undercover work for us, helped us get intel we never would have been privy to without her. Two of the traffickers were also cops in this precinct, and one of them was a good friend of mine. A couple more cops here were customers. None of them were ever brought to the carpet for it. She was after me like I owed her money, wanted me to make a stink about it, and I wouldn't do it.'

'And that's why you think I'm wrong about her, why you protect her now,' Daniel concluded.

'It gets worse. She got jumped in an alley not long after it all went down. A cop stood watch to make sure they were able to take their time with her. They beat her within an inch of her life and left her to die.' Hunter hung his head. 'I thought she was dead when I found her. Once she was mended enough to walk, I gave her a gun and enough money to leave town, and I told her to go and never come back.'

'Why haven't I ever heard of any of this? Do people know?'

Daniel asked, his mind spinning, the very floor and foundation he was standing on suddenly both less reliable.

Hunter snorted, then sipped his beer. 'You think *Betty* has secrets? She's got nothing on this department.'

'Late is better than never, Hunter. You could say something now,' Daniel pleaded. He could hear how young he sounded, how painfully optimistic, but he didn't care.

'That was twenty years ago, and those guys are gone, cops in other towns. What good would come of blowing all that up now?'

Hunter touched his arms, drawing short lines on his shirt with his finger. Daniel wondered if he even knew he was doing it.

'Talk about a moral compass. You don't feel any responsibility to make it right?'

Hunter smiled at him. 'You sound just like her,' he said, then his expression lost all traces of playfulness. 'You can't run and tell Lily where her sister is, OK? I would bet she's only back in town for a little while. I know she wouldn't want her seeing her like that. She's never wanted Lily to know where she is, and she doesn't want to hurt her all over again when she leaves.'

'Rose needs treatment, Hunter,' Daniel said, changing tone and tactics, and he realized he was working his brother like he might a suspect. 'If you care about her, you'll get her into rehab.'

'Betty, Daniel. Call her Betty. And she's clean. I know what it looks like when she's not.'

'She was in the stratosphere when I saw her at the park.'

'Nerd,' Hunter replied, weakly grinning. 'I need you to keep this for me, OK? I'll help you on this, I will. I'm all in from here on. But if I help you, you keep Lily in the dark, and you keep Betty out of it. It's me or her, Danny. Your choice.'

'It's an investigation, not a trade-off. I can keep the details from Lily for now. But if Betty is involved in this, I can't keep her out of it. I won't.'

Hunter looked down at Daniel and rested a hand on his shoulder. 'Why can't you lie to me just once in your life?'

'Why won't you trust me just once in yours?'

Hunter held Daniel's gaze. 'Your girl Maya got checked in at juvie this morning. Thought you might want to know,' he said, and he walked out.

THIRTY-SIX

Lily – February 10, 2018

From the passenger seat, Lily directed Katelyn to Bright View, explaining Anne's history along the way. Katelyn grew quieter with every passing mile and detail. For the first time since Lily had met Katelyn, she didn't quite seem to know what to say.

Once there, Lily led the way into the lobby and up to the reception desk.

'Hi, Marlene,' she greeted the older woman behind the counter.

'Lily, it's always so good to see you! I know Anne will be pleased you've come by. She's seemed down since the last time you left. Go on back,' Marlene said and pressed the button allowing them through to the long-term unit. Katelyn followed behind her, carrying the to-go bag.

Anne was strapped into her wheelchair, facing a window. Her upper body rocked back and forth in quick, short motions. Her eyes and her face were pointed in two different places.

'Hi, Anne,' Lily said quietly. She moved a chair in front of Anne, and Katelyn found a perch on the foot of Anne's bed. Anne's fingers fluttered on the armrest. 'This is my friend, Katelyn. We brought you something.'

Katelyn handed Lily the bag. She pulled out a plastic spoon and coated it with a thin layer of pie so Anne could experience the flavor without risking a choke, then offered it gently to her mouth. Anne smacked her lips, and the drool began immediately, pooling in the downturned corner of her mouth, dribbling out as it overflowed. Lily fed Anne the slice of pie a sliver at a time, allowing silence and patience to settle the room.

'This is . . . beautiful,' Katelyn murmured.

'Don't talk like she can't hear you,' Lily cautioned. 'She hears everything we say, don't you, Anne?'

'I didn't mean it in a bad way,' Katelyn said.

Anne's light brown eyes were fixed on a point beyond Lily's left shoulder. They still held a spark of temper. Would she have screamed Katelyn right out of the room, batted the spoon from Lily's hand, if only she could?

But Katelyn was right, too. Something about it *was* beautiful in its own way. Anne's life, her stories, her secrets, her past – they were buried treasures now, locked up tight inside her mind where they wouldn't ever come out. Humanity tended to place more value in anything that had to be discovered or mined, from truth to sea glass to gold, and Anne had that in spades.

On the flipside, though, she was worthless. Those memories and secrets, wants and grievances were impossible to ever turn loose upon the world. She would take it all with her when she died. She had no choice in it.

Lily knew she was holding on to her own secrets as if she'd had no choice. She hadn't told Detective Wilder the whole truth. She had not yet shared with him that she thought she'd seen Rose in a car with Maya and another child. Nor had she told him that she'd seen Maya with Rose at Brecken Park the same day Christian was found dead. She knew it might shift his thoughts about Rose as a victim from the past to something worse in the present. But it didn't matter anymore. It couldn't. She had to be willing to pay any price to keep Rose from vanishing again.

THIRTY-SEVEN

Daniel – February 10, 2018

It took all Daniel's charm and twenty bucks to convince the desk clerk at the juvenile detention center to let him speak with Maya without telling her who had come to see her. Fifteen minutes later, the door to the private visiting room swung open, revealing Maya and a uniformed guard at her side.

'Take me back to my room,' Maya said to her guard the moment she set eyes on Daniel.

'Do you have something better to do?' the guard asked.

Daniel almost felt sorry for her.

Maya skulked to a chair, then dragged the legs across the floor and plunked down.

'I'm not the reason you're here,' Daniel started.

'Sure.'

'No, really. I'm a homicide detective. If you're not a suspect in a murder, I have no control over what happens to you.'

She crossed her arms at her front, guarding her chest. 'I'm not telling you anything else.'

'Is there anything left to tell?'

'No.'

They waited nearly a full minute in silence. She leaned back to rest her head on the top of the chair. It looked miserably uncomfortable.

'I don't do drugs,' she said to the ceiling. 'I smoked cigarettes a few times as a kid, but they're gross.'

'Yes, they are. And you're still a kid.'

'Only by the numbers.'

Daniel propped his elbows on the table between them and rubbed his closed eyes.

'You're missing the point,' she continued. 'I don't do drugs. I take Depakote for seizures. That's it. I've never done the hard stuff.'

'Maya, if I had a dime for—'

'Listen, asshole. I was seven years old when my parents over-dosed on heroin in the front seats of the car. I sat in the back seat for a day and a night before someone found us, my brother's diaper stinking and him squalling because he's hungry and babies aren't really impressed with juice boxes, plus they don't know how to drink out of a straw.' Her cheeks turned red, her eyes, too, her irises nearly violet against the spiderweb of veins, the wheels of her mind turning behind them.

'That's horrific, Maya, and I'm sorry you went through it, but I'm not sure why that's relevant,' Daniel replied, straining emotion from his voice.

'The drug test! Everybody keeps saying my piss test was positive! That's part of why I'm stuck in this shithole.'

'I doubt that's the reason. They suspected an overdose when they found you, and there was Narcan in your system. I don't think they can use an early failed drug test to put you in here. It can cause a false positive,' Daniel explained.

She bolted upright. 'Right? And wouldn't that mess up a drug test? I know that's why I'm in here. Can you tell them that? Vouch for me?'

'First, Narcan is only given when someone's overdosing. Second, if you weren't high, how do you explain falling asleep in the snow?'

Maya looked away from him. 'Someone was nearby, and I didn't want to get caught, so I hid in some trees, but they were slow to move on, and I got tired.'

'You didn't just go in the other direction?'

'Why the *hell* do you care?'

'I am a *homicide* detective,' Daniel repeated slowly. 'Another kid died in the woods not long before you were found, and it doesn't make a whole lot of sense to me that two kids would decide to take naps in the snow at Brecken Park in the middle of the night just because.'

'I don't know what you're talking about,' she said, but her body, tense and jumpy, told Daniel otherwise.

'I think you do. His name was Christian Coleman. He died at Brecken Park the other night' Daniel obliged anyway.

Her hands trembled for a split second. She dropped them out of view. 'I heard that was an accident or some shit.'

'Did you know him?'

'No.'

'Maya,' Daniel said softly.

'Stop acting like you know me!' She glared hard, and her eyes became two holes. 'You're just like the rest of them.'

Against his better judgement, Daniel laughed.

'That's funny to you?'

'I wish I was like the rest of them . . . that I felt even a little like I belonged,' Daniel said plainly.

'If this is where you try to say you understand what I'm going through, you can save it.'

'I have no idea what you're going through,' Daniel stated. 'I grew up with two parents who took great care of me and an older brother who hates my guts and always has. I have never been a ward of the state. I have never been arrested.'

'God, you're boring.'

Daniel shrugged. 'Maybe that's why he doesn't like me.'

'Who?'

'My brother. He's a cop, too. And my boss.'

'That sucks.'

'You're telling me.'

They fell quiet for a few seconds, but the tension ebbed like an outbound tide. The water was still present, but a little farther from shore, giving them more room to walk.

'It's not easy to be the younger sibling,' Daniel finally said.

'It's no picnic being the older one, either.'

Daniel leaned back. 'My brother just does what he wants. He gets his way all the time.'

'Bullshit.' She grunted in disgust. 'Trust me, older siblings get the shaft. We have to watch little-kid cartoons because the big-kid shows make you bored and crabby or scared. We're the ones who get blamed, who get punished worse, who have to watch you for days on end when your parents want to take a break from being functioning adults or sleep for three days straight. We are the ones who don't get fed if there's only enough food for one. *You* get to do whatever you want.'

Daniel's throat drew tight as his mind painted the picture of this girl's reality.

'I miss him, though,' she murmured.

'Your brother?'

'He's been with the same foster family for over a year now. They don't let me see him. They say it'd be too hard for him to say goodbye to me over and over. They say *I'm* too hard. Do you . . . do you think you could make them let me see him?'

'I don't want to promise you anything that's out of my control.'

'But you could try.'

Daniel's gaze traveled the room; regarded the walls. She might be the one in custody, but right now he felt absolutely cornered. 'Christian was an older brother.'

'Here you go.' She sank back against the chair and folded her arms. 'None of that was real, was it? Do you even have an older brother? Guard!'

'Maya, please. I think someone killed Christian. I don't know how to say that to you any other way. I can't prove it. He has a younger brother. So do you. Maybe one day you'll be able to see yours again. But Christian's little brother will grow up without him, and I don't think it was an accident. I am begging you here. Tell me something, anything, because no one else believes me. You and I are all Christian has on his side.'

Her guard stepped inside the doorway. Maya looked at her, then shook her head. 'Sorry, not yet,' she mumbled. She watched from her peripheral vision until the guard retreated from view. 'I really don't know what happened to Christian,' she continued quietly. 'We were going to try to leave together, but we weren't leaving that night. Whatever happened to him, it had nothing to do with me or our plan.'

'You're not telling me enough,' Daniel pleaded.

'You lied to me,' she shot back.

'I didn't lie to you, but I didn't deliver, either. I will own that. I'm going to try to get you moved out of here, OK?'

'To where?'

'I'd like to put you in protective custody, for now. It'll still be an institutional setting, but it'll be more like . . . a really boring camp, less like . . . this.'

'You mean prison for kids?' she retorted, her armor of wit returning. 'What's in it for you?'

'That you tell me more once I get you there.'

'I can do that.' She stood, preparing to leave.

'Hey, one last thing. What you said about the song, "Whisper Sister," was that true?'

'Yeah.'

'Who was singing?'

'I don't know.'

'I think you do.'

'I think I don't owe you shit while I'm still in here.'

'If I sang part of the song, would you know if it sounded familiar?'

'Please don't.' She rolled her eyes before covering her face with her hands.

'Well, now I have to.' Daniel made a dramatic show of clearing his throat, then flipped in his notebook to where he'd copied down the words of Lily's song. Then he hummed a few bars, hunting his memory for Lily's performance. Maya dropped her hands an inch and watched him over the tips of her fingers.

'Just whisper, sister, that's all you have to do,' Daniel sang.

'I'll come running home to you,' she finished the line, her voice raspy and low. 'Yeah. Fuck, that's weird. But if you're hoping to be a singer, don't quit your day job just yet.'

Daniel's response caught in his throat, having to push past a spell of shock before becoming sound. 'I . . . I don't plan to.'

'Good. Your singing is a crime against humanity.'

Daniel's pulse felt too fast and too slow at the same time. He wanted so badly to ask her who was singing, anything about the voice she might be willing to tell, but he knew if he pushed now, he might lose her for good. The questions would have to wait until he'd done something for her.

'I know you've heard this before, but you can trust me, Maya. I'm on your side.'

'Trust is a two-way street, Wildman,' Maya returned, then she was escorted from the room.

His thoughts stormed inside his head. The line of Lily's song was barely important sixty seconds prior, a few words steeped in uncertainty, residue from someone else's trauma. So how did they now belong to Maya, too?

The most likely option was that the song wasn't original: Lily's sister hadn't written it and had merely claimed it as her own. For a teenager willing to leave her drunk young sister in the snow, that possibility wasn't a stretch.

Daniel tapped open the internet on his phone and entered a full line of Lily's song into the search engine. The specified search yielded zero results; the song, aside from the sisters, did not appear to exist.

'What the hell is going on here?' Daniel asked the empty room.

Hunter might have been able to turn his back on the petty crimes of an old friend, but surely to God this new connection was solid enough to earn his interest now.

THIRTY-EIGHT

Rose – February 10, 2018

I can feel the approach of a winter storm in my bones. They ache in a quiet way, like babies who've been left alone long enough to learn that crying doesn't deliver, but they still can't help whimpering. I wonder if Lily feels me coming the same way I feel the snow.

There I go again – not knowing if I'm making something better or worse.

I'm sitting in the same car I brought across the country, parked in the back corner of the Big Lots parking lot, the heater limping even though it's on full blast. It's a terrible idea eight ways from Sunday. I should be sitting in a hospital parking lot, the safest square of asphalt a girl like me can find to set up camp. I should've kept the car I stole from Brecken Park, but after Lily caught me driving by her place to make sure she was alone, I ditched it as fast as I could.

I should be back in the room Easton paid for, waiting for him, naked and agreeable. But I do my best thinking in the driver's seat of a car, where a decision can become movement with the press of a foot. And I have a lot of decisions to make quickly if I'm going to pull this off with any chance of surviving it.

First order of business: I need an alibi for why I left and where I've been so when Easton catches up with me, which he will, I'll have an answer he'll believe.

Second: I need a way to bury him – that could be metaphorical or literal. It's going to have to be a game-time decision.

Third: I need money to get two people out of Tennessee – farther if possible.

And I'm going to need a lifetime's worth of luck. Considering the luck fairy has passed me over every chance she gets, that sparkly little bitch owes me.

And I need to stay sober.

A wave of shame rolls through me so strong I nearly reach into the glove box for a pill-sized life raft. I ball my throbbing hands into my lap and draw my knees beneath my chin, then rock myself calm in the driver's seat.

The only person I know who could talk me off this ledge of want is Hunter, but I'd be tempted to tell him everything. Some truths are too damn expensive.

I think back to my list once more, go over the things I need, feel in my gut how quickly and desperately I need them.

My thoughts land on Detective Daniel Wilder.

Birds and stones come to mind.

I smile to myself and start my car.

THIRTY-NINE

Daniel – February 10, 2018

Daniel could count on one hand the number of times he'd been inside a strip club before his first day in homicide, and now he was heading back for the third time this week. Sirens was the only place he could think to go next that might possibly have answers for him. He wasn't sure what exactly he was after, but he felt a pull to that building that he couldn't shake. If nothing else, he could ask about Natasha.

He had the impression that looks counted when it came to Easton Grimes and his willingness to spend time in someone's company, so he'd opted to go home long enough to change into slacks and a tailored shirt before coming here. Still, as he strode inside the main door to Sirens, he was without exception the most casual person in the building.

He made a quick scan for Rose, but if she was there, she wasn't readily visible. At the back of the main room, the curtains that had been closed during his first visit were now pulled open, revealing an inset section elevated on a platform. Teal and silver panels were suspended between the floor and the ceiling. A tapered staircase entryway was framed by two giant palm trees with a velvet silver rope strung between them, closing off the empty section.

The only crowd in the building was gathered around the swimming tank, where several women swam topless. Inside the glass, light refracted in the water. Bending, broken rays played against bare skin, giving the swimming girls the illusion of shimmering scales.

'Detective.' Easton's familiar voice came from behind Daniel's shoulder. 'You're becoming quite a regular.'

'Here on business,' Daniel replied.

Easton smirked. 'Of course you are. On a Saturday, no less. Betty's not here, so I'm afraid you're wasting your time.'

'I'm not here for her.'

'Who are you here for, then?' He crossed his arms at his front, which pulled the sleeves of his crisp, white button-down farther up his arms, revealing scratches on his hands and wrists.

'Well, I was going to ask you about Natasha, but right now I'm more interested in you,' Daniel replied and cast a pointed glance at the shallow, straight lines of scabs on Easton's skins. They looked to have been made by human fingernails or one hell of an angry cat.

Easton dropped his hands to his hips and lifted his chin. 'I am on the clock right now, Detective Wilder.'

'You're the owner. It's your clock. And it'll take less time to cooperate. Less of a scene, too. Or I can get loud and start barking words like "skimming credit cards," "aggravated battery," and "selling stolen identities." Your call.'

Easton lifted his chin. 'Where's your boss?'

'You mean my *partner*? He's pulling warrants,' Daniel lied. He had no idea where Hunter was. But he was immediately curious why Easton would rather deal with Hunter. Daniel was willing to admit that if Easton found Hunter the easier detective to hoodwink, one of the two of them was wholly snowed by his older brother.

'Warrants for what?'

'I'm not at liberty to say. But you can either answer questions for me here, or we can go to the station together and Hunter can tell you all about it after we're done,' Daniel bluffed.

Several customers had diverted their attention from the swimming women to the two of them.

'I would love to continue this conversation in my office, especially regarding the customer who attacked a valued employee. Right this way,' Easton said, raising his voice, then struck off toward the back of the building where an employee door was tucked behind another large palm tree.

As Daniel followed a step behind, he threw together a barebones strategy for this impromptu interview. First and foremost, he would leave Rose out of the conversation. She was a dead end until he had something irrefutable to leverage. But if he could get Easton to admit to having met *Maya*, he could tie Sirens and everyone who worked there to the Brecken Park investigation when it at last received the attention and resources it deserved. He put this goal center stage in his mind and stepped inside Easton's office.

The space was surprisingly small. For all the obvious upgrades in the public area, the wood paneling and the set of old metal filing cabinets lined up against the wall made Daniel feel like he'd stepped back in time about thirty years. A brown velour chair was positioned in the front corner beneath a tall, brass floor lamp, and several folding chairs were stacked in the opposite corner. The only thing that looked new in the room was a plush leather office chair, which was completely at odds with the laminate-topped, crescent-shaped desk it sat behind.

'Thanks for your cooperation,' Daniel said, opting to pull out a folding chair.

'All due respect, Detective, you didn't give me much of a choice,' Easton replied as he took his seat. 'Why do you keep coming back here?'

'Maya Summit.' Daniel pulled a picture of her from his folder and placed it on the desktop. 'She says she met you,' he lied.

'Well, she didn't.'

'She's in protective custody, which means we have a very good reason to believe what she's telling us.'

'What is she telling you?'

'That's confidential. But I'm interested in your version of events.'

'I'd like my lawyer present,' Easton stated.

Inwardly, Daniel panicked. Even though Easton wasn't detained, and their conversation wasn't being recorded, the lawyer bell couldn't be unrung.

'That's as far as we go, then.' Daniel stood as if he was unbothered by Easton's request and moved to put his chair away. 'It's not a good look, though. The harder I have to work for your version of events, the less likely I am to believe them.'

'Well, what did that girl say?' Easton asked again.

'It's a wild story, I won't lie to you. Maybe it's the truth, maybe it isn't. But right now, I have no reason to suspect that she's lying unless you give me one.' Daniel kept his expression open and earnest, as if he was handing Easton a lifeline instead of rope to hang himself with.

Easton raised his hands in forfeit. 'OK, yes, I have seen Maya before. She came by looking for a job. She had a boy with her, that Christian kid. I guess she thought he was her bodyguard or something. They both had fake IDs. She tried to convince me to hire her. I said we only hire adults – real adults – twenty-one and up, no exceptions. They left, end of story.'

'Is that why you mentioned Christian when I asked you about Maya before?' Daniel pressed, feeding out more proverbial rope.

'I saw what happened to him, and I remembered that they'd come here together. I worry about these kids!' He banged his fist on the table. 'They think they're grown, that nothing can touch them. I remember the stupid shit I did at their age. It's a wonder I survived. A teenager ballsy and desperate enough to walk in here like they can handle this, the pressure that comes with it, the risks . . . Kids like that get exploited.'

By the time Easton finished talking, he was flushed. But if he thought his theatrics were a good cover for his bullshit, he didn't realize how bad it stank. It also gave Daniel the link he'd been looking for. Even if most of what Easton had said was a lie, his admission that Maya and Christian were inside Sirens created the possibility that 'Betty' had seen them, too, and the woman seemed every bit as enterprising as her boss.

Daniel reached for the door. 'Thank you, Easton. That's all I need for now.'

Surprise moved across Easton's features like a flicker of light. 'Are you sure? I'm happy to answer more questions.'

'I may have more for you later, but this helped me make sense of a couple things.'

'If you tell me what you're trying to sort out, I can be of more assistance.' Easton stood up behind his desk.

'You've helped more than you know.' Daniel opened the door. Natasha's name briefly fluttered across his mind before being swept up in the storm of his thoughts. He had what he needed for now. He would not be distracted. Following up about Natasha later would also give him a reason to return. 'I'll be in touch. Don't leave town,' he said to Easton over his shoulder, then stepped out and pulled the door shut behind him.

Even though Daniel was entertaining a small sense of victory, he also felt worse for wear. Head down and a little dizzy, he strode to his car, which he'd parked on the far side of the dumpster, all but shielding his vehicle from traffic. He climbed in the driver's seat and started the engine, his thoughts crowding to fit inside the four-door sedan. Then he put the car in reverse and looked in the rearview mirror.

Rose was in the back seat, staring straight at his eyes in the mirror.

'Jesus Christ,' he said, whipping round, right hand feathering the holster on his service revolver.

'I heard you were looking for me.' Her eyes were green today and painted with heavy black eyeliner, giving them a catlike shape.

'I'm taking you to the station.' Daniel hated the tremble in his voice.

'Duh. I'm making this part easy for you, so when I say it's time for me to leave, you're going to make it easy for me, OK?'

'Are you armed?' he asked.

'Aren't you?'

'You're behind me.'

'Would you rather I drive?' She smirked at his reflection.

'No.'

'Relax. I know you and big brother aren't exactly besties, but you really think I'd hurt you?'

'I don't know what to think about you or what you'd do.'

'That's fair.'

He studied her in the rearview mirror. 'Who's Natasha?'

'Never met her.' She stared back, unblinking. 'And that's the truth.'

Daniel dropped his gaze and let out a long breath. The woman was either a psychopath or a walking contradiction. She'd also been out of her mind when he'd run into her at the park and had been talking out of her head.

'But you should ask Easton next time you drop by,' she added.

Daniel's eyes flashed back to the mirror. Was she just messing with him, or was she serious? Or had she somehow overheard the beginning of his conversation with Easton? His first instinct was to call Hunter and ask him how to handle the stick of dynamite in his back seat. But there was a reason Rose had come to him instead of Hunter. Even if she didn't offer him an honest word, there might be something to be gained by understanding why.

'What's your endgame here, Rose?'

'I don't know yet.' She looked out the window. 'But don't you ever call me that again.'

FORTY

Daniel – February 10, 2018

As Daniel walked Rose through the station and to an interview room, he realized he couldn't go into this conversation with any semblance of a plan. Rose was too quick, too slippery, too seasoned. She was someone he would have to learn to dance with instead of fight.

They took seats on opposite sides of a rectangular, brown table. She looked right at home in the metal folding chair, and it struck him that she might have more interview experience than he did.

'Do you have any idea why I've been looking for you?' Daniel asked.

'Could be any number of things.' She glanced at her watch.

'Why don't I save us both time and tell you what I know.'

'Sure.'

'You drug men and skim their cards.'

'Prove it.'

'I have two formal complaints.'

'That's not proof. That's just butt-hurt boys running their mouths. You should hear some of the shit that Hunter has said about you. Does that make it all true, just because he said it?'

It shouldn't hurt, biting words coming from a cornered suspect, but it did.

'You should hear what your sister says about you,' Daniel said quietly.

Rose lifted her chin but didn't respond.

'They're wonderful things. I've heard what kind of life she hopes you have, how she misses you. I've heard about what happened the morning Lily woke up drunk and alone in the snow. She loves you anyway. Do you know that?'

'It's not a crime to not want to be found.'

'That's true. But why put her through it at all?'

'I'd put her through more if I was in her life.'

'Like what?'

Rose leaned back, propped the back of her head on the back of the chair, angled her face to the fluorescent light, and closed her eyes as if she was lying in the sun. The clock on the wall marked time, filling the silence. She was refusing to confirm or admit to anything, and Daniel was all at once annoyed and impressed.

'Easton told me Maya and Christian came by Sirens,' Daniel said, changing tactics.

'Am I supposed to know these names?'

'I would think so. Easton said Maya came to see you, specifically,' Daniel lied.

Rose cocked her head and gave Daniel a pitying smile. 'Is this the best you can do?'

'Maya is a singer.' Daniel let the words hang in the air for a second. 'She sang a song for me. It was pretty, kind of folksy. Made me think of Stevie Nicks. They don't make music like they used to. She taught me part of the song. She said you'd written it and that you sang it to her in the woods,' he lied again.

She came forward and propped her elbows on the table. The sleeves of her jacket slipped down. Her arms were covered in scratches. 'Sing it to me,' Rose said, her eyes glittering.

'What happened there?' He pointed at her wrists, and his mind turned to Easton.

'Kink,' she replied without dropping her stare from his eyes.

'I don't believe you.'

'I don't care.'

A hard knock struck the outside of the door. Daniel peered over his shoulder. Hunter stared back at him through the narrow rectangular window, his frigid eyes damn near frosting the glass.

'Big brother's not happy with you. You should see the marks *he* likes to leave,' Rose said in a sing-song voice.

'I'll be right back,' Daniel said, struggling to keep his composure. 'We're not finished.'

'Want to bet on it?' she replied.

He ignored her as he left the room, then pulled the door shut behind him. Without a word in greeting, Hunter grabbed Daniel by the arm and towed him down the hall until they ran out of floor before the main area.

'What the hell is she doing here?' Hunter demanded.

'Maya and Christian were inside Sirens recently.'

'So? Half the town has been inside Sirens recently. What does that have to do with Betty?'

'Rose, Hunter. Call her by her name! It's Rose's song Maya knew. She was there that night. She had to be.'

'That's a leap and you know it.'

'Maya knows the song Rose sang to Lily, and Easton admitted Maya and Christian had come by there. It's not a leap. Rose also told me to ask him about someone named Natasha. Who is Natasha?'

'Hold on, you brought Easton in, too?' Hunter spat, nearly purple with rage.

'I interviewed him at the club.'

Hunter curled a finger in front of his mouth, and a vein on his forehead throbbed with his rising pulse. 'I know that you care about people and about your job. I know you will always do what you think is right. But sometimes . . .' He trailed off, stole a glance over his shoulder, then resettled his gaze on Daniel.

'I sold Betty out to tell you the truth, and look what you did with it. You probably just blew any trust she had left in this department all to hell.'

Daniel gaped at him, searching for words. He couldn't bring himself to admit to Hunter that Rose had let herself into the back seat of his car while he was questioning Easton. Saying it out loud would only make him hear how he'd been played by them both. If Rose's goal in coming here had been to blow him and his brother even farther apart, she'd just done it.

'We're supposed to be working on this together,' Daniel finally said.

'Are we? You've made it clear from the jump that you didn't want help with the Brecken Park kids, that *you* were the lead, *you* knew what was best. You don't tell me where you're going, who you've talked to, or why. You bring in Betty *and* question Easton without asking me what I think. I thought you'd understand why she didn't want little sister seeing her greased up at some strip joint, and you would leave her the hell alone. I didn't think you'd bring her back with you. I didn't think you'd be so damn *childish*. You're embarrassing yourself. You're embarrassing *me*. What if another department is helping higher-ups with an undercover operation going on at Sirens and you just took a shit all over it?'

The internal fire of self-righteousness that Daniel had been feeding since the moment Hunter interrupted his interview snuffed out in an instant. Had he taken this case about a frozen boy and a singing girl, and made it about himself? A sick feeling passed through him.

'Is that true? Is that what's happening here?' Daniel asked.

Hunter leaned into him so that their faces were inches apart. 'Of course that's what's happening here. There is an investigation already underway at Sirens that they do not want us fucking up. Federal white-collar shit that we're lucky they're still letting this department keep their hands in. Money laundering. Bribery. Extortion. Fraud. A network that spans the entire southeast. Why the hell do you think the number crunchers wanted you to interview the meathead that came in about Betty? Why do you think two unmarked cars have been sitting in the parking lot across the street, or did you not even notice them? Why do you think

I jumped on a battery call at a strip club? Think, Danny. Do you know me at all?'

'No, I don't know you! You set me up to look like an idiot every chance you get! If you want me to make smarter choices, then you need to fill me in, keep me in the loop. You've had me at arm's length my entire life. If you can't be my brother, at least be my partner.' Daniel was nearly yelling by the time he finished.

Hunter's gaze fell to the carpet. Around them, the department went quiet. When Hunter looked up, his face was furious.

'This is why they don't let family work together in here. You make everything too damn personal, Danny. This is not about you, and it's not about us. If you would get over those two things, you'd be doing a world of good for yourself, your cases, and the department. You're not ever going to be able to tell everyone in this precinct every detail about what you're working on or what you know. You won't always be able to collar every perp. Sometimes you have to pick the big fish over the school of smaller ones. Sometimes you have to trade up one for the other until you get who you want. You will let some criminals go. You will keep secrets. Lots of them. That's all part of the job. I've tried to cover your ass so that you don't make a fool of yourself to anyone but me, but I'm all done now. If you believe in justice and in good police work, stay away from Sirens, don't breathe a word about this to Lily, and cut Betty the fuck loose.'

'Christian matters, Hunter. Maya, too. Rose is a part of whatever happened to Maya. Maya sang her song. That means something. She's back here for a reason, and if you don't know what it is, then it isn't in a good way.'

'You have no idea what you're talking about.'

'I'll prove it to you. I'm going to take Rose's picture to Maya right now. If she looks me in the eye and tells me Rose isn't who sang to her at Brecken Park, then I'll let her go. But not a minute before. And if I'm right, you need to help me on this.'

Hunter held his gaze for a full second. 'You are no partner of mine.' He shoved both hands in his pockets, turned on his heel, and left Daniel standing in the shadowed end of the hall alone.

*

Thirty minutes later, Daniel arrived at Bright View, a long-term care facility where he'd been able to secure a protective-custody stay for Maya. Under his arm was a folder with Rose's picture mixed in among the photographs of eleven other women with similar features. In his heart was a tangle of hopes.

Maya's new room was dark. He found her sitting cross-legged on the floor in a rectangle of weak light filtering in through her window, which overlooked the parking lot.

'Are you doing OK in here?' he asked, lingering at the threshold as if to ask for silent permission to cross.

'The food's better.' She narrowed her eyes. 'Why are you here?'

'I need to ask you something. Did you ever go to Sirens looking for work?'

'The titty bar?' Her eyes found her chest. 'I think I'd need big implants first, don't you?'

'Beauty . . . beauty comes in all forms. Jesus, Maya,' Daniel sputtered, marveling at the instant peak of discomfort. Then he refocused and caught her grinning. 'Very funny,' he said.

She rested her chin on her knee. 'Yeah, I went in there.'

'When?'

'The other day.'

'Were you trying to get hired as a dancer?'

'I don't know what I was trying to do.'

'I'm going to need a little more.'

'You and everybody else.' Maya heaved a sigh. 'I asked if I could sing for tip money there or even in the parking lot, but I got shuttled out of there pretty quick.'

'And that's it?'

'That's it. Unless you count being told not to come back.'

'That's the best advice they could've given you.'

'Whatever.'

Daniel sat down next to her on the floor. 'I think I found the woman who sang that song you hate so much. I think she had something to do with what happened to you at Brecken Park. I think she might have told you she would help you get out of town.'

Maya averted her eyes, withdrawing.

'I think you told me about that song because you wanted me to find her, because deep down you know she did something wrong, and the song is the best way I could track her down without you giving up her name. I want to talk to her about what happened the night you ran off, but I need to confirm she's the right person. I'm going to show you a group of pictures. If the person who you met in the woods that night and sang to you is here in these pictures, all you have to do is point to her. You don't even have to say her name.'

'That woman is friendly with you cops. Even if I tell you who she is, you won't do shit. Y'all never do, and it only ever gets worse after that,' Maya whispered.

'Try me.'

Maya's expression became a knot. 'If I help you do this, *really* help, will you ask my brother's foster parents to let me see him?'

'I can make a phone call on your behalf as long as you tell me the truth. But it has to be the honest-to-goodness, swear-on-the-Bible kind of truth about who sang to you in those woods.'

'OK. I'll tell you if I see her. I swear. God's honest truth.' She took the pictures of twelve women and flipped through them one at a time. 'She's not there, Wildman.'

Daniel rocked back, more stunned than he'd been prepared to feel, coming face to face with how convinced he'd been that he was about to be proven right. 'Are you absolutely sure? You can look again. Take your time. Her hair or her makeup might be different here than when you saw her.'

'I'm sure. She is not in these pictures. You wanted the truth, and I gave it to you, I swear. Can you call about my brother right now? Maybe I can even talk to him on the phone. They have a nice visiting room for when kids come. He'll have more toys in there than he'll know what to do with.'

'Maya, are you positive she isn't here? The woman who sang that song at Brecken Park? That's all I need.' Even though he knew he shouldn't do it, Daniel shuffled Rose's picture to the top and put his finger near her face.

Maya glanced at the picture, then looked up at him with liquid eyes. 'I will point to whoever you want me to point to. I can say whatever you need me to say. Just call my brother. Please!'

Instantly, it was over. Nothing Maya said from that moment would hold any legal value. Daniel closed Rose's picture inside his notebook, knowing he would have to let her go the moment he returned to the station, and he left Maya crying in a patch of flickering light.

FORTY-ONE

Lily – February 10, 2018

Lily stood on the front porch of her cabin and clasped her hands around a scalding mug, barely feeling the burn. Tomorrow's forecast had turned for the worse, calling for a hundred-year winter storm, the likes of which she hadn't seen since the night Rose had led her into the woods. It had been a long, hard winter, and she'd learned how to cope with a lot, but she wasn't sure how to prepare for this.

A call came through on her phone, startling her so badly she nearly dropped it on the frost-covered deck. Katelyn's name flashed on the screen. Lily had to walk to the far edge of the porch before answering or she knew the call wouldn't hold the connection.

'What did you do?' Katelyn said as soon as Lily answered. There was an edge in her voice, sharpening the question into an accusation.

Lily froze. 'Excuse me?'

'I just got off the phone with Rachel. Maya's been transferred to Bright View.'

'What? Why?'

'Some kind of protective custody order from that detective. You didn't have anything to do with this?' Katelyn asked.

'Not at all. I wouldn't have the power to do that even if I wanted to,' Lily answered, keeping her own tone light and un-affected. She wouldn't want Katelyn to feel like she'd offended her, or else Katelyn would want to make amends in person, especially after their time bonding over dessert. Lily wasn't in the mood to play nice face to face.

'Did the detective give Rachel any explanation?' Lily asked.

'He told her that the precinct had an interest in maintaining Maya's safety, and that they wanted to give her access to a therapist.'

Lily stayed quiet, deep in thought. Maya moving to Bright View wasn't all bad. The staff there were kind, accommodating, and familiar, and the therapy services were exceptional. But it would be easy for an enterprising patient like Maya to find a way out. Over her years spent there in various capacities, Lily had learned of several paths patients had taken to escape with little to no detection.

'Lily? Are you still there? I'm so sorry if I offended you.'

'I don't have good phone service here. And you didn't offend me at all. It's never offensive to want the right things for the kids in your care.'

'Good, you made it to your cabin. You need a little space from all this.' The saccharin-coated relief seeping from Katelyn was so thick and sticky that Lily felt the need to wipe her cheek.

'It's where I find my peace when I need it most,' Lily murmured, but her thoughts were in upheaval.

Daniel may not have yet found her sister, but he had clearly found something big enough to warrant moving Maya without any help from her, and she wanted to know what it was. She'd been waiting to tell him about Rose and Maya when she thought there was information she might gain in trade. What if he'd found out another way? What if she was already too late?

'Thanks for calling,' Lily said, then hung up before Katelyn could reply.

Immediately, she dialed Daniel. After two rings, it went straight to voicemail. She looked at the screen to check for signal. Two bars. She should be fine. She redialed, and as it rang, she gnawed her lip until she tasted iron. She dabbed at her mouth with her fingertips. When she pulled them back, they were spotted with blood. In her ear, the detective's voicemail tripped again. Desperation set upon her soul like locust to a field.

'Answer, damn it!' she screamed into the night. She wiped the blood from her fingers, moved back to the one place on the porch that always seemed to deliver a call, then dialed a third time.

'Lily,' Daniel said in lieu of a greeting. His tone was agitated and telltale – this was not a call he wanted to answer. Had he watched her last two calls come through and simply chosen not to answer? Worry urged her heart to a galloping beat.

'Do you have any updates for me?' she asked.

'I don't or I would have called.'

Lily needled at her scalp with her fingernails. 'You don't think moving Maya to protected custody is an update?'

'I updated her case worker. That's got nothing to do with you.'

Lily's mouth fell open. 'But Maya has everything to do with Rose.'

'No, Lily.'

Lily could almost see him shaking his head, closing his eyes. Red seeped into the edges of her vision.

'Don't treat me like a child, Detective. Something has changed. I know it.'

'You're also not an officer of the law. You're not investigating a potential homicide or a cold-case missing person. I'm not going to treat you like you are. There are and will be pieces to this investigation you will not be privy to, and that's in the best interest of integrity and the outcome.'

'I haven't been completely honest with you.' She swelled with a deep inhale, feeling more childlike with every passing second. 'Maya met Rose at Brecken Park. I saw them together. Rose gave her something. It was the day before Maya was found in the woods. And earlier this week, I think I saw them together in Rose's car.'

On the other end, Daniel was silent.

'Did you hear what I said?' she demanded.

'I did. If it was Rose that you saw with her, what do you think that would mean?'

Grief pinched her everywhere at once, and she nearly gasped with pain. She knew this would be the potential cost of telling him what she saw, but she could feel him slipping away, and Rose with him. She stared out across the yard, tracing shadows.

'Lily, I don't know how to say this to you,' Daniel began, then he hesitated.

Lily didn't dare count. If she started, she wasn't sure she'd ever stop.

'It's fair to say that your sister has likely been a victim in her lifetime, according to statistics.' Regret was a lead weight in his voice. 'But *if* she's involved with what happened to Maya, it wouldn't be as a victim. Do you understand what I'm saying to you?'

'Daniel . . .' Her voice broke. She doubled over, then found the front wall of her cabin and sank to the porch. 'Please. I just want to see her.'

'I want to see where Rose left you,' he said firmly.

Lily's racing heart went still. 'Why?'

'Sometimes in an investigation, you need to go back to the beginning. If this is related, in whatever capacity, the woods you two ran through, the place she left you, that's the beginning. Show me. Walk me through those woods. Tell me everything you want to tell me. Then give me the time and space to do my job, and I'll give you answers as soon as I can. Does that sound fair?'

Lily lifted her gaze to woods she couldn't see and watched the past play itself out on the dark screen of the winter night before her. 'I can do that.'

'I imagine it's going to be incredibly hard to go back there, but we'll get through it together, OK?' Daniel soothed. 'If you need anything, call me. I'll pick up immediately. I swear. Text me the address, and I'll see you there tomorrow. I hope we'll get some answers for you soon.'

'I hope so, too,' Lily managed to say, then the phone slid through her fingers and tumbled to the raw wooden floor. She wrapped her arms around her legs, pressed her head into her knees, and let her heavy heart sink all the way down.

FORTY-TWO

Daniel – February 10, 2018

Daniel rested his head in his hands, succumbing to the weight of pressure, and stared blankly at his computer in front of him. A weather-forecast website was open on the split screen. On the left, the local area radar cycled through a forecast of the next few hours. Snow was coming, the purple edge of it bleeding down the top of the map. On the right was a historical database of Tennessee's missing people.

Using snowfall as his only guide, he'd done a deep dive to find if any other kids in the county system had left their home during the snow and had yet to be found. The upside was that snow was rare this far south, and he'd clocked right through nine years' worth of weather. In that span of time, there'd been nineteen snow days. He'd then begun working backward, checking the older report dates on missing children to see if any had occurred during the snow.

He'd expected to find at least a few, told himself less than half would have to be considered a coincidence, and that more than half still wouldn't prove much. But as he moved from date to date, he caught himself holding his breath. At the halfway point, he sat back and stared, disbelieving and light-headed. During every measurable snowfall event in greater Tula and the surrounding sprawl over the first five years of weather data, one kid would vanish for good.

As he studied his list, he realized the similarities didn't end there. Each child was a teenager and a ward of the state. It would be unwise to ignore the pattern, but it would be equally problematic to ignore that those two factors didn't lend themselves to make it easier and more likely to run. The two lines of Rose's song haunted the edges of his mind, slid themselves inside of every thought. On the way home from Bright View, he'd racked his brain for who else would know a song shared only between sisters, but he'd come up empty.

His gaze gravitated toward his notes, where he'd jotted down important pieces from his conversations with Easton. A surge of guilt drew his eye to his brother's desk, which Hunter had turned around so that they no longer faced each other. No one else in the department could get away with the things Hunter did. He was royalty around here. He might as well have traded his desk for a throne the day he solved his first case.

A memory of the first time they'd walked into Sirens struck Daniel – the throne floating above the water where Sirens' song-stresses gave striptease performances. It was possible Rose had sung their special song for an audience. The eerie tune was in keeping with what he'd heard when they were there, and the lyrics weren't hard to remember, especially the last two lines Lily had sung. Customers and coworkers could have them memorized in a single performance. His thoughts turned to Natasha. Rose had mentioned her twice, once while high and once sober. Whoever she was, it was likely she was real. And Rose had readily linked her to Sirens.

Whether that was a flat-out lie could be anyone's guess, but if nothing else, he could figure out who she was. He picked up his phone to call Easton. A text message alert popped up on his screen. Lily had sent the location of where they were to meet the following morning. The area was an extremely remote, unincorporated stretch of land a half hour north of Tula, which was unpatrolled by police other than responding state officers. It would be an ideal place to tuck away. A perfect place to hide a crime.

Hunter had once told him that the hardest part of his job was thinking like a killer, but it was also the best way to track them down. In this case, Daniel needed to stop thinking like someone who was digging for the truth and start thinking like someone who was trying to get away with hiding it.

Daniel glanced down at his paper, reconsidering his strategy, then dialed the main number for Sirens, deciding to ask whoever answered to speak to Natasha. It would be the best way to ascertain if she was connected to the business without Easton or Rose gatekeeping the link.

'Thank you for calling Sirens. How may I help you?' a woman purred through the phone.

Daniel felt himself flush. 'Is Natasha there?' he asked.

'Natasha?' Confusion touched her voice. 'I don't know . . .'

'She left her coat at my place,' Daniel lied, remembering what else Rose had said at the park. 'With the snow coming, I just want to get it back to her. She said she works there. I can drop it off if she's there.'

'Just a second,' the woman said. Murmurs sounded through the speaker, then were muffled, and he imagined she'd covered the receiver with her hand. 'Sorry, Natasha doesn't work here anymore. She lied to you, baby.'

'Figures,' Daniel muttered, feigning dejection. 'Did she ever even work there?' he fished.

'Another girl said a Natasha used to work here but got transferred to Miami. I've been here since the spring, and I've never met her. Might not be your girl. Come on by anyway. We'll make sure you forget all about her.'

Daniel cleared his throat to keep from laughing, then started to open his mouth, curious if they knew whether their Natasha had been a singer and might have known Rose's song, but he realized it wasn't likely. Even if it was the right Natasha, Rose had only recently returned to Sirens. She and Natasha wouldn't have been there at the same time.

'I'll do that,' Daniel said instead, then ended the call.

Across the room, Hunter stood at his desk, breaking Daniel's concentration. They hadn't exchanged a word since their blow-up in the hallway, that tension made worse when Daniel had come back to the precinct from Bright View and discovered Hunter had already released Rose.

Hunter plucked his keys from his desk and walked straight to Daniel. 'I need to talk to you about something. Outside.'

Daniel wanted to tell him to go to hell. But there was something undefinable he longed for more than that, so he stood and followed him out.

They walked to the parking lot and climbed in Hunter's car. Hunter cranked the heat, then stared through the windshield to the gray brick wall in front of him for a solid minute.

'What do you think you know about my first case?' he finally asked.

'You and your partner got the call on a double murder – wife with a secret lover . . .' Daniel started dutifully, his heart thrumming in his chest. 'Alice Bowman and her personal trainer were found murdered in her bed. You suspected the woman they used for their routine yard service even though all the evidence pointed to the husband, and she had a solid alibi and seemingly no motive.' He paused and glanced at Hunter as if he was a student looking at a teacher to make sure he was getting the answer right.

'Keep going,' Hunter said, but he only had eyes for the wall straight ahead.

Daniel faced forward, too, and told the rest of the story to the dashboard. 'Your partner was convinced it was the husband, who was a preacher with political aspirations, had a mistress of his own, and a weak alibi. She railroaded you and the entire investigation. Turned out the preacher wasn't the killer, and he accused the department of planting evidence. It almost sank the whole investigation and made the department plenty of enemies. Your partner was fired, and you solved the case on your own.'

'What was her name?' Hunter asked.

Daniel frowned, and his eyes flicked to their corners. 'Who?'

'My partner.'

'I don't know.'

'Her name was Patty Teft. She'd been in homicide four years when I came on. They put us together, said between the two of us, a woman and a rookie, we might make up one detective. Then they gave us a case they said would be straightforward, dots all in a line.'

Daniel stole a long look at his brother out of his peripheral vision. Hunter was staring at nothing as he spoke, digging his fingernails into his steering wheel hard enough to leave little half-moons in the leather.

'Patty suspected from the jump that the crime scene looked staged,' Hunter continued. 'I found evidence that pointed to the husband, but I knew it wasn't enough. So, I added a little to it to make it seem airtight, and then *I* railroaded *her*.'

'Hunter, stop,' Daniel interjected, twisting in his chair. He could barely believe what he was hearing, let alone comprehend it. All he had ever wanted was for his brother to let him in. But what if in sharing this truth, Hunter only pushed him farther away?

'No. Let me finish,' Hunter said. 'I found out I was dead wrong. We were both looking at being canned over it. The preacher wanted our heads on a pike. He was talking about suing the department, the city, anybody he could think of. Patty sat me down in her car, just like I'm doing to you now, and she said: "I'm telling you, it's the lawn care girl." She laid out her evidence, and then she said: "And *you* have to be the one to bring her down. They'll believe you over me. I'll say everything that happened earlier, everything *you* did, was all me. And you take this second chance, and you run with it."'

They sat in stunned silence for a moment. Hunter's secrets didn't begin and end with Rose. Was everything Daniel had ever believed about his brother built on lies?

'She was right, obviously.' Hunter paused again long enough to wipe his face. 'I climbed the ladder, and she became a cashier at Big Lots.'

'How . . .?' Daniel stopped himself before he could finish the question.

'How could I let that happen, keep letting it happen, not fix it?' Hunter finished for him.

Daniel looked away.

'She kept saying *she* was fine, that *it* was fine, and it was easier to believe her. She'd say: "Go catch enough bad for both of us." But I couldn't make a move without her. I would call her to get her read on a scene or a suspect. Then one day she said to me: "You need to be sure as you were on that first case even when you were dead wrong. I can't give that feeling back to you. You need to find it for yourself." But I never did. In all these years, I never have found it.'

'So you work alone,' Daniel summarized, stunned and devastated.

'Patty died six years ago. She was getting the shopping carts people left in the parking lot and saw a guy trying to rob a lady. She got in between them, and the guy fired a shot before running away. She bled out in the parking lot. She's in my head. Every case. Every *minute*. I can hear Patty on this, loud and clear. Your Rose is my preacher. So what if she's still skimming cards from whiny perverts? *We* are in *homicide* and *she* is not a killer, and that's all that matters. It's possible what happened to Christian really was an accident, and that there may not be a killer to find here at all.'

'But we do have a body, and we almost had two. You don't think the timing is at least a little suspect?' His growing list of other children who'd vanished in the snow resurfaced in his mind and weighted the front of his tongue. Had he discovered the connection his first day, hell, even yesterday, he would've run straight to Hunter with it. Tonight, this list felt like an ace of spades, and for now, he wanted to keep it hidden.

'Of course I do. But I also think kids do dumb shit, and they do even dumber shit when they have a friend to do it with. Those kids had bounced all over this city. Leaving and running is what they know. Sometimes it really is that simple.'

Daniel considered his next words carefully. Temptation to tell his brother everything still lingered, but so did the want to punch him square in the teeth. 'I'll keep Rose's secret for a little while longer, but none of this feels simple to me.'

Hunter nodded, but it felt more like a forfeit than an agreement. Between the exaggerated shadows and the toll of the conversation, his brother looked like he'd aged a decade in a matter of minutes.

Time was waging war inside Daniel, too. For one brief moment, the child within him wished he could go back to when Hunter existed to him only at a distance, lifted up and out of reach on his golden pedestal. But the man Daniel was still becoming had learned here and now that pain and truth often arrived holding hands. You either welcomed them both with open arms or not at all.

FORTY-THREE

Rose – February 10, 2018

My car idles beneath a lamp in the parking lot of a Big Lots. Easton's car appears opposite mine. We stare at each other in the orange glow of the lamp, both of our faces more shadows than shapes.

Easton's headlights go dark, making him instantly more visible. I haven't been this scared in a long time. If he decides I need to disappear, I don't know if he'll kill me himself or if he has people who do it for him. Maybe that sounds dramatic. But all I know is when I admitted to killing someone, he didn't pull away, wasn't horrified, didn't ask me who or how.

He hops out of his car, slams the door, and hustles over to the passenger-side door. I reach across the console and crack it open for him, knowing he'll wait for an invitation, still selling the notion that he believes in respect and permission.

The seat groans under his weight as he slips inside. Then he peers at me in earnest, his expression boyish and worried.

'Where have you been? I went by the hotel a couple times, but you haven't been there,' he asks.

'I got picked up by that detective. He kept me to the very last legal minute. Just got out. They didn't have enough to hold me.'

His expression hardens. 'You should've called. I would've had our attorney come for you.'

'No, they don't need a reason to start digging into you. Wilder said he had proof about the credit cards. I can't imagine what, and he wouldn't say. But it couldn't have been much because here I am.'

'Why does a homicide detective care about any of this?'

Panic slithers up from my belly and burrows into the base of my throat. A homicide detective wouldn't have brought me in about identity theft unless they were looking for a way through a bigger door. I have played this round loose and very, very wrong.

'I'm sure it's personal,' I start. 'I ended things with Hunter when you told me to. Maybe they're looking to settle a score. You know he's Hunter's half-brother,' I add, hoping this will be news.

He lifts a brow. 'You're shitting me.'

'I wish I was. I should get out of town, disappear for a while. I don't want this to make trouble for you. I think they're watching me. Maybe both of us,' I warn. The possibility of being the targets of a stakeout should make him a little more reluctant to do anything rash.

Easton pulls a leather glove off his hand and touches my face. I rest my head into his palm, a move that is trusting and vulnerable as fuck. Then I stare at the glove, the paper-thin leather, the thing he's never worn before.

'Let's get out of here. We can go anywhere you want,' he croons.

I shiver. 'Somewhere warm.' I look up at him. 'Can we leave soon?'

'Tomorrow. I'll clear my schedule. Do you have somewhere in mind?'

'No. Surprise me.'

'Be careful what you wish for.' He smiles back at me, but it doesn't touch his eyes. 'I'm going into work. Stay the night at the hotel. I'll leave you with some money to buy some clothes tomorrow. Then we'll head out of town, OK?'

'You're too good to me.'

'I know.' He steps out of my car and shuts the door, pressing a hand on the windowpane, leaving an imprint on the glass of the glove he will probably wear again when he drives me out of town to kill me.

FORTY-FOUR

Lily – February 11, 2018

Lily hurried to the front desk at Bright View, which had just opened for morning visitation hours. Maya was visible through a window in the common area. Her stare was fixed on the dreary parking lot beyond.

'How is she?' Lily whispered to Marlene as she signed the visitors' log.

'She's doing OK. Watches the road a lot,' Marlene answered. 'We've had to up her seizure meds. She's had some episodes. Panic attacks, too. A couple of them have been pretty severe.'

'Has she said anything about what happened to her?'

'Not yet. You might be able to connect with her, though.'

'I'll do my best.'

Lily walked quietly across the carpet, then bent down on her knees so she didn't tower above the girl.

'Maya,' she said gently. 'It's been a long time. Do you remember me?'

Maya turned to look at Lily's face. Lily wondered how far back Maya might recall. Lily had been who officers contacted when they first pulled Maya and her little brother out of their parents' car. Between the heat and the exposure to the sun, the bodies of her parents and the waste in her brother's diaper had spoiled rapidly. Lily could still conjure the smell, and she had no doubt it was etched in Maya's mind as well.

Lily smiled, directing warmth at her. Maya tilted her head, her eyes searching the depths of Lily's.

'I . . . I don't feel good,' Maya said, and clutched at her heart with one hand while she grabbed the front of Lily's shirt with the other.

'What's wrong?' Lily said and cupped Maya's cheeks in her hands. They were clammy with cold sweat, and her breathing came too quickly.

'Help me,' Maya gasped. Her eyes searched the room as if she didn't see Lily right in front of her. Lily cradled the girl to her chest. Maya clutched at Lily's coat. Her tears became a damp place over Lily's heart.

'Marlene!' Lily called out. The older woman barreled toward them. Two more orderlies came to their aid, and together, they carried Maya to her room. They laid her down on her bed and covered her with blankets. Still, she shivered. Lily's heart ached. She knew that cold, how it began on the inside so there was nowhere to run that it wouldn't already be.

A nurse filled a syringe with a sedative. Lily had to look away as she pierced Maya's arm. Every one of her muscles tensed with the memory of the needle and the panic that necessitated it. How, for just a split second, it got so much worse before it got better. At last, Maya's arms slid down from their hold on her ribs, and her eyes fluttered closed.

Maya slept for nearly an hour before her eyelids cracked open.

'Maya, it's just you and me now,' Lily whispered.

The girl didn't answer.

'You gave us quite a scare. What happened to you before, that shouldn't have happened. I'm sorry for everything you've been through. For all of it.'

'What happened exactly?' Maya asked, narrowing her eyes in an attempt to focus.

'You had a panic attack. They said it's happened a couple times before. What are you scared of, Maya?'

Her face crumpled, and she pitched forward, her entire body racking with sobs. 'I just want to see my brother again. Please. Just one more time. I'll do anything.'

'OK,' Lily said, overcome with shared grief. She would give anything for Rose to feel this way about her. 'I can do that on one condition.'

'What do you want?'

'I don't know what exactly happened to you in those woods, Maya. But if you do, if you remember, don't tell anyone yet, OK? Soon. But not yet.'

Maya stared at Lily, chin trembling. 'I keep quiet, and you'll let me see my brother?'

'I will take you there as soon as I can. I'll make his foster parents understand how important a big sister is. I'd do anything for mine.' Lily reached forward and gently tugged a lock of her hair. 'I need to ask you a couple questions, and it's important you tell me the truth, no matter what it is. Will you do that?'

Maya nodded, and fresh tears fell.

'I saw a woman give you a phone at Brecken Park the other day. It looked pretty secret. Was it to contact her?' Lily asked as gently as she could manage.

Maya wiped her face with her sleeve. 'Yeah,' she whispered to the floor.

'OK.' Lily drew a breath to steady herself against a flood of emotions. 'This last question might be even harder to answer, but I still need the truth. The real truth.' She paused again until Maya met her gaze, then continued: 'When you get out of here, are you going to try to leave Tula again?'

Maya parted her lips, then, without answering, turned her eyes once more in the direction of the window. Rose's desperation was written all over her profile, that same future no doubt etched in the stars.

FORTY-FIVE

Daniel – February 11, 2018

Daniel had been standing for twenty minutes on the shoulder of the curvy two-lane road forty minutes north of Tula where Lily had told him to meet her. In that entire span of time, only one other car had passed.

The map Lily had forwarded to Daniel indicated that the woods bordering the side they were on continued uninterrupted until they reached a shorter, parallel street that connected back to the main road on both ends and was designated as an unimproved road called New Hope Loop. Daniel checked the flag on the map again, then made sure he was still getting service. The strength of his cell signal shifted in and out of range with every step he took.

Headlights appeared at the top of the hill to the left and set the late morning fog aglow. He backed off the curb and watched the car approach. The headlights flashed, then turned off, and Lily's face appeared through the windshield.

She stepped out of the car. Her eyes were bloodshot and puffy. Guilt made a home in him, and he wasn't sure why. He'd come for her just as much as for himself. Maybe even more so.

'Are you OK?' Daniel asked.

'It was harder coming back here than I thought it would be.' Her voice turned to vapor in front of her face.

'We don't have to do this,' he said as a formality. He knew she'd walk in there. There was no way she could be in such proximity to where she'd been left alone and not want to show someone, if only to share the pain. He'd give anything to walk with someone down his memory lane and show them how hard he'd tried to be a brother Hunter would want.

'I can do it. I came this far.' She glanced at the sky, where a thick blanket of silver clouds was gathering on the north horizon. 'Maybe I'll finally find what I've been looking for,' she added.

'What's that?' Daniel asked.

'What would make a person leave,' she said, then she walked into the trees.

Wordlessly, Daniel followed close behind. The forest floor was a carpet of frosted needles and leaves. Pines grew straight and skinny out of the ground like bristles on a brush. Lily wound through them, tracing a path only she could see. Every couple of minutes, Daniel peered back the way they'd come, trying to commit something remarkable to memory should they get lost, but it all looked the same.

Lily cut between a triangular clump of oak trees, then stopped in her tracks. In front of her, a grove of older evergreens grew in a crescent shape. The boughs leaned over the inside of the arch, offering a natural shelter to the earth below.

She shook her hands out at her sides. 'We spent the night right here. When I woke up, Rose was gone.'

The scope of Lily's truth and trauma hit Daniel full force. 'I can't imagine what that felt like.'

Lily pressed her back to a tree, sank to the wet earth, and rested her head on her knees. The rhythmic shudder of her shoulders was the only way he knew she'd begun silently crying. Daniel dropped his chin to his chest. He'd suggested they come out here, he'd put her in this position without much thought to what he'd put her through while she was here, and all the while, he'd convinced himself he was doing it for Lily.

The whole truth was that he'd been expecting to find evidence of Rose – not twenty-five-year-old evidence, but something newer, proof she'd been here in the last few days, spent time out here during the recent snow. Yet the woods were utterly undisturbed as far as he could see.

If he came away from here with nothing, put Lily through reliving her grief for nothing, he wasn't sure he'd be able to forgive himself for being every bit the disappointment his brother was.

He crouched down and put his hand on her shoulder. 'How can I help?'

Lily lifted her head and smiled at him as fresh tears rolled out of her bloodshot eyes. 'This is cathartic. I didn't realize how much this place still haunts me. Maybe now, finally, I can let it go.'

Her words sent up a flare in Daniel's mind. This spot might only mean something to Lily, made significant to her by what could've been a random, impulsive choice. If Rose found this grove of trees by accident in the dark, she might not have the first clue where they were, what they looked like, or how to get back to them. The house they ran from might be a more significant location for her.

Daniel hooked a thumb over his shoulder. 'I'm just going to walk through to your old road, then I'll be right back, OK?'

'New Hope is the other way,' Lily rasped, gesturing in the opposite direction.

As Daniel moved away from her, he had to force his guilt aside and his focus ahead. He had to find something out here, or he wasn't sure he'd be able to face Hunter ever again.

On the map, the stretch of woods was a narrow swath, but it felt endless once inside its heart. The trees looked to be mostly types of pine, the boughs long and limbless until at least ten or fifteen feet up. Being surrounded by patterns of gray lines had the same effect as a house of mirrors, and he had to briefly close his eyes against a spell of dizziness. It would be easy to get lost out here during the day. It would've been a miracle for a kid to navigate these same woods at night in the rain.

The ground sloped downhill to a short, shallow gully, which was still flooded with old rainwater and snowmelt. He veered off the informal path, looking for an easier place to cross. A clearing appeared between the trees, the wide, dished patch of wet earth cloaked in morning mist.

Slowly and quietly, he stepped into the space, feeling like he was intruding even though he was alone. The shroud of fog pushed back as he moved deeper in, at last revealing the ground. At his feet, the toe of a boot protruded from the mud near the base of the closest tree. The rubber sole was still intact, but chunks of the upper material had been eaten away by time, moisture, and insects.

Through the holes, the bones of a foot were visible.

His heart, his breath, the air itself fell still. He lifted his gaze, disbelieving, and stared across the clearing. Little lumps of earth sat beneath the border of trees like a seven-year-old girl waiting for her big sister to come back, over and over and over, as far as the fog would let him see.

FORTY-SIX

Rose – February 11, 2018

Easton's skin is sticky, sucking at me wherever it touches, and the seatbelt buckle is digging into my hip. I remind myself that it was my idea to have sex in his car in the hotel parking lot. *Let's keep things interesting*, I'd said, when he'd balked at the idea at first. To get him in the trunk, I need him pliable, satiated, and in the back seat. Still, my hands itch with want to shove him away, fingers curling with the temptation to claw at him like a furious cat. I am so tired of pretending to like being petted.

In my mind, I travel back in time to the first boy who looked at me as if I was made of magic. I remember how timid he was as I shrugged off my hoodie and stood in front of him in a tattered sports bra. He couldn't make himself say a word. I remember how he touched me, his fingers light as whispers on my arms, and I could see in his gaze that he wasn't sure any of it was real.

The back seat of Easton's car disappears as I conjure the memory of the boy's bedroom, wood paneling on the walls, tan carpet under my feet, a plain bed in the corner, no headboard or footboard. Two pairs of sneakers lined up beneath. He was older than me but shorter, and I probably had twenty pounds on him. The room had smelled like a boy – body spray and earth, and when he took his glasses off and set them on the bedside table, I'd spied a nearly empty box of tissue paper and a key to his car.

I can give you the real thing, if you want it, I'd said.

He had been scared to pull off his shirt, scared I'd see his ribs, his skinny waist, his bird chest, and laugh at him. He'd covered himself with his arms, and I'd had to take him by his elbow and guide him to the bed, pull him down on top of me. He hadn't tried to kiss me, but he watched my face until he caught me looking back at him, and then he squeezed his eyes shut. He palmed my shoulders, sliding twice between my legs, and it was over.

I think I love you, he said, his voice so earnest, trembling with vulnerability.

You do? I asked.

He nodded, eyes wide and staring down at me.

Cool. I smiled. *Do you think I can borrow your car? Just for a night?*

Yeah . . . I mean, yeah. Can we do this again tomorrow?

Probably. I'd shrugged beneath him, then had suddenly felt too hot, too weighted down by his frame, no matter how much he looked like I could string sheets of tissue paper from the underside of his twiggy arms to his bumpy sides and fly him in the air like a kite.

Easton grunts as he finishes. My mind crashes back to the present, trading one weight for another. I long to climb out from under him, out of this car, find a shower, turn it as hot as it will go, and stand in the spray until my skin sloughs off and swirls down the drain.

'Take the edge off for you?' Easton regards me, his pupils yo-yoing as he tries to focus.

'Yeah.' I manage a smile. 'You want a drink? I'll drive.' I eye a flask tucked in the front pocket of my weekender bag, where I've mixed a tequila sunrise laced with GHB. I envy Easton's nearing future, should I manage to get it down his throat. What I wouldn't give to forget.

'I changed my mind.' He climbs off me and pulls his pants up. Then he settles back against the seat; rakes a hand through his hair.

'About what?'

'We're not leaving tonight.' Impatience creeps over him, and I watch his skin itself become antsy. He's not a large man, but he is strong, a braid of lean muscle and bone. He taps his fingers on the window ledge, unlocks the door, then locks it again. Up, down. Up, down. The sound is maddening.

I don't disagree with him. I want this trip to be off more than I want to never have sex again. But more than that, I need this over with so I can go pick up a girl that may or may not come willingly, then get the fuck gone. I can't sit around and wait for him to iron any wrinkles out of his plan. I have a plan, too.

'Why not?' I pout.

'The weather's already bad. I'm not trying to get stuck in the road and need to call for help. More cops are the last thing we need. Let's leave tomorrow.' He pulls the lock up one more time and moves to open the door. Everything inside me feels too fast – my blood, my breaths, my mind, and in the centrifuge effect, desperation solidifies. I fling myself across him and slam the lock down.

'What the hell are you doing?' he demands.

'Just wait a second.' My voice quivers. I force my entire being to relax, praying to whatever might hover above that I appear too submissive or too enamored to attempt tricking him, and that the gun I stowed under the passenger seat will not be too far out of reach if I need it. 'I know what you're doing, Easton. What you're really doing.'

His eyes travel me the same way the skinny boy's did that afternoon in his room, but Easton, I know, isn't looking for magic. He's looking for a wire again.

I slide my shirt above my bra so my skin is covered in nothing but pale light and shadows. 'You don't need to say a word,' I say. 'I just want you to know that I know, and I want in. Really in. Fifty-fifty split on anybody I bring you. I've done it before. Back when the building you're in was The Alibi. And I'm good at it. Really good. Yes or no? You can even nod or shake your head if you want to. No hard feelings either way. But we're still going on a trip. So stay in the fucking car.'

'Damn, Betty.' A smirk appears on his face, and my blood runs cold despite my racing heart. With my offer, I've built a box around me and a bear. 'You're feeling gutsy tonight. This is what keeps a relationship . . . interesting.' He places his palm on my chest. There is no doubt that he can feel my heart drumming against my ribs.

'You can think about it as long as you want. You don't have to answer now,' I say, attempting to back off slowly, casually.

'I do, though. Don't I?' He regards me for a full five seconds. I catch myself marking time in my head, wondering if I'm counting down to my own execution.

'Look, lover. I'm not an idiot, and neither are you. With that VIP section getting fuller by the day, I would bet you already have more demand than you can manage. If young is what you need, you need a woman to make them feel safe. You know it, and I know it, and I'm good at it. Let me show you how good I can be,' I whisper in his ear, leaning over him, ignoring how exposed I've made myself in this position. 'I know about Natasha.' It's a gamble, and I'm borrowing from the proverbial house to make it, but my pockets are empty.

'Then you know more than I do.' He sits back and regards me with new uncertainty. 'Business partners should trust each other,' he says, ignoring what I've said. He fishes in his pocket and plucks out a bag of white powder.

'I found her note. Tell me what happened to her,' I persist.

'Your guess is as good as mine. She was a favorite. I made her a great offer. One day she left after her shift, and she never came back. That's the truth.' He dips his finger in the bag, then he reaches for me instead of giving it to himself first, waiting for me to take it. 'Do you trust me yet?'

'No.' I open my mouth, and he slips his finger under my tongue. The taste of it saturates my mouth in an instant, and panic hits me full force as I feel how much he's deposited under my tongue.

'What's interesting to me is that someone else just asked about her, too. That detective. Your boyfriend's little brother,' he says, holding my gaze. A tiny, slow movement draws my eye, Easton's hand gliding down his leg and to his overnight bag like a bead of water down a spout. His gaze flicks to me and away again in a blink. I don't know what he's reaching for, but I get the distinct impression only one of us will leave this back seat under our own power.

I spill forward, spitting out everything I can, and sprawl across his lap. My hair blankets his view of his hands while mine slide beneath the seat, fumbling for my bag. But it's just out of reach, and my trembling, sweaty fingers keep slipping.

He shoves me off him. I fall to the floor of the car in a twist, and my limbs tangle themselves under the seats. Adrenaline and helplessness and whatever Easton put in my mouth fight for space in my veins. Every inch of me flounders and strikes out like these are the last movements I'll ever make.

Beneath the passenger seat, my fingertips bump against something cold, hard, and cylindrical. It's a metal flashlight. I flick it on with my thumb. A glow floods the space. Easton throws himself backward. I sit up fast, squeezing one hand around the flashlight while the other claws at his shirt, hissing through my teeth with effort and terror and rage. Then I swing the flashlight at the side of his head, connecting with his temple so hard the lightbulb goes dark, and Easton slumps against the door.

With shaking hands, I pluck a syringe filled with GHB from my bag and slip it into the corner of his mouth, then hold his jaw shut for a full minute to let it absorb. I tie his wrists and ankles together, fish the car keys out of his pants pocket, drop down the back seat, and shove him over and over until he's most of the way in the trunk. Sweating and panting, I push the seat back up until it clicks, then rest my ear against the seatback and wait to see if he begins stirring or banging, but I only hear my own breathing, which is loud as a freight train.

Snow speckles the windshield. Within seconds, the air turns chilly inside the vehicle, two bodies no longer throwing off the heat of exertion. I climb through the front seats and crank the engine. Then I turn on the windshield wipers and watch spellbound as the only way out of Tula becomes clear.

FORTY-SEVEN

Daniel – February 11, 2018

The temperature had begun to plummet. If he was being honest with himself, Daniel couldn't decide if the chill belonged to the weather or to him.

The recovery team had exposed two bodies so far. The remains were positioned identically: curled up on their sides, hands folded across their chests, skeletons desperate to keep warm. Even with his eyes closed, he saw the high-contrast, crescent-shaped outline of bone against dark earth. If he ever slept again, he had no doubt they'd visit him there, too.

Similarly, Daniel could still hear the choking sounds of Lily's grief. She had left for home once the yellow tape went up an hour before, effectively excluding her from her sister's woods. In haunted silence, Daniel watched his brother radio the station and request an APB for Rose.

You were wrong again, Hunter, he wanted to say, but he couldn't bring himself to do it. Instead, he turned his back on him and walked away.

Daniel strode deeper into a quiet, empty stretch of woods, his insides churning with regret. He realized he was hunting for a place to disappear. A stiff wind rifled through the fallen leaves.

They somersaulted between trees like kids playing tag. Daniel followed them, the wind at his back. They skittered ahead of him into a small, oval-shaped clearing. Then the current of air dropped instantaneously. The sudden stillness was eerie, once again leaving him with the feeling of something watching the back of his neck. At the far edge of the clearing, a familiar pattern emerged from the pallet of decay: depressions of earth in two even rows. Eight in all.

'Hunter,' Daniel said into his radio. The device squealed, feedback from the recipient being too close. Daniel whirled round, and Hunter appeared between the trees.

'I think we've got more bodies,' Daniel said, nodding at what he'd found. It wasn't lost on him that of all the things he needed to say to his brother, this news was the easiest to deliver.

'We've got a bigger problem. Just got an APB. Maya's missing.'

Daniel stared at him, furious and terrified, and in the space between them, snow began to fall.

FORTY-EIGHT

Lily – February 11, 2018

Little snowflakes dotted her windshield. Her hands gripped the steering wheel, knuckles blanched. The steep, gravel driveway to her cabin was already slick, and the yard was turning pebble gray. Between the weather and the graveyard, she hadn't been sure she was going to be able to make the drive. At least no one could find her here unless she wanted them to.

Her tires briefly slipped traction in the mud. She pulled on to dead grass, gaining purchase on more solid ground, then left her car in the shadow of a steep bank where it would be better protected than parked on the open ground closer to the house.

Lily unpacked her car, eternally prepared to spend an unscheduled night in the snow. These patterns were her safety net and her safe space, and Rose had once again found a way to unravel both. Tears fell fast and uncontrolled. There was no turning back now.

Rose's number was in Lily's pocket. Her face was in Lily's head, her sister's fourteen-year-old voice in her ear.

The world around her was turning whiter with every blink. Fear yawned inside her and stretched its limbs. Lily couldn't imagine spending the night alone. But she also couldn't lose Rose to Daniel, not without giving her one more chance to do the right thing.

Before she could talk herself out of it, she dialed Rose's number.

'Who is this?' Rose's gravelly voice came through the speaker.

Lily's heart jumped into her throat, and for a solid second, she couldn't speak.

'Rose,' she finally choked out. 'It's me.'

'Lily?' her sister responded softly, and it was as if each snow-flake was suspended in the air, as if the world, all at once, had shuddered to a stop.

'Yeah,' Lily whimpered, and fresh tears came.

'Where are you?'

Lily's heart cracked wide open. All she had ever wanted was for Rose to care where she was, for her to come find her baby sister on her own. She closed her eyes and gathered her thoughts. Even though they hadn't spoken in twenty-five years, Lily knew how quickly her sister could cut and run. But the truth was all she could think to give her.

'Do you remember the neighbor's yard we ran across, the little farmhouse on the other side of the old hay field?' Lily asked.

'Yes.'

'I'm there, at that house. But the snow is really coming down and sticking to the road, and now I can't leave.'

'What are you doing there?' Rose's tone was so harsh it nearly felt like a slap through the speaker, and Lily caught herself touching her cheek.

'I've been looking for you,' she said. Fury and love and grief strangled her from the inside out, and she had to fight for every breath. 'I know you said not to, but I can't help it, Rose. I filed a new missing person's report with the police. I'm working with a detective. He asked me to show him the place where you . . . where we . . . the woods. He wanted to see the woods. He found something, and I . . . I . . . It started to snow. I didn't know what to do. I just came here. I'm sorry. I didn't know what else to do.'

'No, that's good, Lily. I know right where you are. Stay there. Don't leave. I'll come to you.'

Fear bubbled out of Lily and ran unchecked down her face. She'd heard this before; felt this same desperate hope.

'Please don't leave me here again,' she whimpered.

'Lily, listen to me. Don't call anyone else, OK? Everything that's happened, it's my fault, and I know that. I'll come pick you up. I'll answer all your questions. I'm going to take you with me like I should have when we were kids, OK?'

'Where are we going to go?' Lily's hope sank with every new promise Rose made, quiet fury building as she realized Rose had yet to promise that she wasn't going to leave again. Still, she couldn't believe how bad she wanted this to be real.

'Somewhere warm. I'll pack for us both, and I'll be there as soon as I can. A couple hours. Three at the most. You promise me you won't leave, and you won't call anyone, especially the detective,' Rose said more than asked.

'What if you don't come?' Lily whispered.

'I will, Lily. I know you don't have any reason to trust me. I know that. I've earned that. But I need you to know that everything I've done, I did for you.'

Lily clutched her phone hard as a little girl's heart thundered in her chest. 'Promise me.'

'I have to go now, but I'm coming to you. OK?'

Even though everything of her was screaming at her to hang up and call Daniel, the magic of Rose's voice in her ear was the only thing she could hear.

'OK.'

FORTY-NINE

Daniel – February 11, 2018

By the time Daniel arrived back at the precinct, the station was a storm of sound and movement. Officers spoke urgently into phones. Footsteps rushed in and out of the room; others shuffled back and forth to mark off cleared locations on a posted map of the city.

Patrolling officers were stationed near every known entrance to Brecken Park. Several more searched the nearby streets. The taskforce tracking Easton's money manned the wire established on his phone, but either he'd ditched the tapped line for a new one, or he wasn't answering calls.

Hunter dropped the phone in its cradle, and his hands traveled to his eyes and pressed against them. 'Maya walked out on her own. They have it on video surveillance. She knew where she was going. Walked right out of the scope of the camera angle. They think she had help.'

'Why?' Daniel asked.

'They noticed she was gone not ten minutes after she left. They sent cars down both directions of the road. Nothing. She either met someone with a car or hitchhiked on the spot.'

Daniel shook his head. How could she have trusted anyone to help her run away again?

An officer called to confirm that neither Rose nor Easton was at Sirens or any of the local addresses Hunter had provided where Rose was known to go. Daniel called Rose and Lily's phones once more. Neither woman answered. Next, he gathered all the information he'd found on Lily, Rose, Christian, and Maya, and headed to an empty incident room where he could spread everything out on the table, with the goal of connecting just one piece to another.

Daniel ordered the pictures and notes chronologically: the photos from Christian's death, then Maya's photograph. Next to her, he placed the interview with the homeless man from beneath the bridge, then circled where he'd said the Virgin Mary told him to save the girl, and Maya's medical chart, which had just come through on email, and noted that her only external physical injury at the time of admission was a bullseye bruise in her thigh from a suspected administration of injectable Narcan. Daniel flipped back through the first responders' notes, but only a single nasal spray administration of the drug was mentioned. She must have been given the first dose by someone else before she'd been found.

Not a homeless guy half out of his head.

Not whoever might have intended to kill her.

What if someone else knew to be there? Someone who knew to watch out for a girl walking into the woods in the snow to meet someone promising a better life.

FIFTY

Rose – February 11, 2018

I pick the lock on Lily's apartment door then close it behind me. My view of her home has been limited to a window's worth of space from the street while on the move. Now, I can see everything, and it's overwhelming.

On the far wall hangs floral wallpaper and a rose-shaped clock. The area rug beneath her couch is bordered with vines, the corner of telltale petals peeking from underneath a coffee table. I move across the room to the open kitchen, which, from a decoration standpoint, is an island of neutrals and raw woods among a sea of floral. For the next five minutes, I play a silent game with her, guessing where she puts her cups, her bowls, her spoons, then opening a cabinet door or drawer to see if I'm right. But I'm wrong. Every time, I am wrong. She doesn't even keep kitchen shit in here. Story of my life. I don't have time for this, but I can't stop. Not until I've peeked inside every closed place.

Two minutes later, I begin a new game: find Lily's money.
I'm better at this one. Two grand taped in a plastic bag behind
the toilet. Another thousand folded inside a shadowbox picture
frame. A thousand taped on the backside of a bedside-table
drawer. Four sets of a thousand dollars rolled tight and slid inside
a hole she'd drilled in each of the wooden legs of her bed.

Never the mattress, girls, Mom once said, the one piece of
advice she gave that I have followed consciously and intention-
ally. *Everyone knows to look for money in a mattress. So look
there. Every time, look there. But if I catch you hiding so much
as a piece of candy in or under your mattress, I will wear your
ass out.*

It's not lost on me that I haven't searched Lily's mattress, even
though she was probably too young to remember the night Mom
first gave us the pearls of wisdom, liquor on her breath, a change
of clothes stuffed in her purse, a new wig on her head, and
another woman's diamond ring on her finger.

I travel back to the kitchen, every cabinet door and drawer
left pulled open, and close them one by one. Of course we would
organize kitchens differently. For one, I've never owned a kitchen.
More importantly, though, our mother never cooked or cleaned
or unpacked dishes into an empty house. We always moved into
another man's home and learned where he liked his things.

I wander back into Lily's room and pack a bag for her. While
I stuff her money inside her socks, I have to square with how
alike Mom and I still are. Maybe chasing and running away are
really the same thing, more the same coin than the fact that
they're opposite sides.

Now there's really nothing left to do but leave. I'm usually so
good at it. But walking out of her apartment is somehow harder
than it was to walk in – and I'd had to come through a locked
door to do it. Maybe it's because I don't know how this next step
is going to go. All roads forward are covered in snow – literally
and metaphorically, or whatever. Not to mention the I-have-a-
bound-and-unconscious-man-in-my-trunk situation. He's also not
the only person I might have to move by force tonight.

Thankfully, extra cargo space seems to be a selling point for
Easton's bougie ride. I don't want to think about how he's probably put it to use any more than I want to acknowledge that I

might be testing its capacity here shortly. The truth, whether I like it or not, is that Easton makes more sense to me than my own sister. I would bet I could find his silverware drawer on the first try.

The thoughts herd me to Lily's door, her bag rolling behind me like a good dog, and I reach for the handle. My gaze catches on a series of paintings hung beside the door frame in a grid so evenly spaced it's certifiable. The whole installation would be hidden by the open door. The frame closest to me marks the bottom corner. On first inspection it's just a bunch of brown and white smears with a thicker gray line running top to bottom. I step back, wondering if every picture is a piece of a larger image, but it still doesn't make much sense. There is repetition there, though: that thick, gray line repeated in a pattern inside every frame.

And then I see it.

I really see it.

In the opposite corner, the first picture; a girl is curled over her own knees at the base of a tree in the snow. Brown hair curtains her shins in wet, knotty clumps. There is a gap of space between the curve of her back and the bough of the tree, a space I should have filled, a space that probably felt bigger than the entire world when Lily first noticed it was there instead of me.

Of all the things I've considered, blamed myself for, and punished myself for, I never considered this part: the moment that she woke up and still thought I was behind her.

How it must have felt when that moment ended.

That part – the leaving part – was already done by the time I realized she was awake. There was no way to undo it by reappearing. The wound had been made. I only realize now that it's been bleeding ever since.

My eyes travel the path of her paintings where the girl disappears one frame at a time until all that's left is a smatter of white and brown slashes in the last image. But the indentation is plain to be seen with no little girl to block it: the place I should have been. I glance out the window to a world turned white, and suddenly I am ice cold. Slowly, my gaze slides back to Lily's paintings, to the place in each frame where she should be. Understanding dawns like sunlight on snow, and I bolt out of the apartment.

FIFTY-ONE

Daniel – February 11, 2018

D aniel coasted down the snow-covered rural road that led to Rose's woods. The open dark loomed in every direction. Somewhere in it, a runaway kid was unequivocally out of reach.

He glanced at his phone and scrolled in search of Lily's contact. He'd tried calling her twice since leaving the station to return to the recovery site, but both times had gone to voicemail. He couldn't imagine what she might be thinking, how she might be coping. He should've insisted she stay at the station, but after discovering dead bodies in the woods where she'd been left as a kid, all he could do was nod when she said she wanted to go home.

Ahead of him, a glow illuminated the night in a dome shape and turned the falling snow silver. It reminded him of a winter wonderland snow globe. But there was no magic there – only spotlights and recovery teams searching for more bodies.

Someone had tipped off the media. News trucks, reporters, and camera crews covered every inch of the new yellow tape strung across the road and along Rose's woods. Daniel eased his car on to the shoulder. Reporters descended upon his door even before he opened it, jamming microphones in his face the moment he emerged. They followed him as he walked toward the woods, hurling questions like stones. For all their efforts, Daniel gave them nothing but silence, his eyes on the tape, his mind already in the woods. At last, he ducked beneath the tape, marveling how a ribbon's worth of a barrier elicited more respect than the dead.

Just inside the trees, tents covered a narrow swath of ground. Beneath them, people kneeled to take pictures, brush debris from bone, and flag any articles of evidence with numbered markers. Hunter stood beside a state trooper, shoulders sagging, a clipboard pinned at his side.

'Any updates?' Daniel asked him.

'Just that between the growing number of bodies and a hundred-year snowstorm, the county units have too much to do and not enough manpower to do it. I put a call into the county sheriff and they're going to extend jurisdiction for us here during recovery until we can make heads or tails of what the hell we've got,' Hunter said.

'Thanks for coming out,' the trooper interjected and extended a hand in greeting to Daniel.

'How many bodies have they found?' Daniel asked as they shook hands.

'Five so far, all curled in the fetal position, all found about three feet deep, lying on their sides with faces and limbs pointing to the right,' the trooper answered.

'There's another forensic team beginning readings on the second area you found. They're speculating those remains will be older,' Hunter said.

'Why?' Daniel asked.

'The ground is dished instead of mounded, and the radar has them deeper. It's going to be harder going, more roots to cut through. Looks like our killer got more confident as time went on. Stopped taking quite so many precautions.' Hunter glanced at the row of bones.

Beyond the exposed graves, the woods were a maze of light and shadow. Daniel couldn't shake the gnawing feeling that Maya was already lost within it.

FIFTY-TWO

Lily – February 11, 2018

Through the front window of the old cabin, Lily watched an unfamiliar car roll down the snow-covered driveway and pull behind the house. She pressed her face and fingertips to the glass pane and stared into the night. From the shadowed far corner of the lot, her sister emerged and came across the snow like a ghost. True to form, she left no footprints marking proof of her weight, her path.

Panic gripped Lily's throat. She should've handled this differently, at least called Daniel the moment Rose had agreed to meet with her. She could still call him. There was still a locked door between her and Rose. There was still time.

The wooden boards of the front porch steps creaked beneath Rose's weight. The sound of her moving only a few feet from where Lily stood dispelled all thoughts of Daniel and of what Rose might have done between when she last walked away from her and right now. Lily rested her fingers on the doorknob. She would've sworn on her life that she felt Rose touching the other side, the hum of her sister's presence sliding through the metal and stirring inside her own heart.

Lily unlocked the deadbolt. From the other side, Rose pulled open the door. Snow stretched out behind her in a blank canvas, her form like ink spilled in the shape of a woman. She was somehow backlit by the night, silver at her edges, and Lily's breath caught in her throat.

'You came,' Lily whispered. Her eyes, dry from an evening spent in cold air, began to burn with a slick of tears. She reached out for her sister, watching as the lines of age and circumstances vanished from her face, and she became fourteen and blameless all over again.

Rose smiled briefly, teeth flashing in the dark, then leaned away and crossed her arms at her chest, denying Lily access to her hands, her heart.

Lily choked on a breath as if she'd been punched. She'd dreamed of this moment a thousand times, Rose appearing in the dark and snow, but she had never been able to picture what might happen next. They weren't kids. They had nothing to run away from but the past.

'Let's go. We need to leave while we still can, Lily,' Rose said and backed up a step.

Lily's gaze lifted above her head to the woods beyond, where law enforcement crawled like ants between the trees and over the ground. If they found Rose now, she would lose her forever. 'No.'

'Yes.' Rose reached out for her with a movement sudden and strong, her hand striking like a snake, hungry to grab and hold.

Lily moved faster, pivoting to the side. 'You said you would answer my questions, Rose. We're going to do that here. Then we'll figure out who's going where.' She slid a hand into the pocket of her coat and touched her cell phone and a small plastic bag to make sure both were still there.

'We don't have time for this, Lily. Let's get on the road.'

'No.' Lily glared, then backed a step inside the house, leaving one hand on her phone and the other on the door handle. Her heart pounded in her chest, carrying twenty-five-year-old rage from limb to limb. 'Do you know how long I've waited for you, and now you want to tell me that you don't have time? How dare you! You can come in and sit down and give me the conversation you owe me, or you can leave. I've managed just fine on my own. I don't need you. I don't need you!' By the end, she was screaming, words tearing loose from her like a kite in the wind. She knew she was lying. She wanted to beg her sister to stay, to plead with her to honor the promise she made to a little girl, but she was desperate for Rose to *want* to. And there was no forcing that.

'I know you're mad at me. That you've been mad at me. And you should be, OK? But we need to go. I'll tell you everything you want to know once we're in the car. The roads are getting worse by the minute.'

'No. I'm not leaving with you. Stay with me and we'll leave in the morning.' Lily tried to blink her eyes clear, but the tears fell faster. 'What happened that night that made you leave me? I've asked myself that thousands of times. I've tried to understand it. You wouldn't believe the things I've done to try to understand it. What did I do to deserve being left?' She doubled over as the truth left her body and reached her from the outside, hitting her everywhere at once. A wail erupted from deep within her and swelled in the night.

'I'm sorry, OK? I'm sorry. I fuck everything up. It's a real talent, OK? And it's one of the reasons I left and stayed gone. You're right. Let's go inside. We can wait out the storm and talk here.' Rose's hand found her arm, and they stood still for a full second, at last connected over miles and years and lifetimes, but all Lily could feel in her sister's touch was the same haunting indecision. Still, Lily couldn't stop herself from turning into the house, and she led her sister inside.

Rose let go as they moved into the common area. The only visible signs of life in the room were a wooden kitchen table with two chairs, a mug set at each place, and a tea kettle, which was white with little yellow flowers budding from a vine painted down the spout. Lily had spent twice as long as necessary just arranging the tea set, wanting everything to be perfect if her sister actually showed up. It was possible she'd put more effort into positioning two cups and spoons than her sister had put into what she should say. Lily hadn't realized how badly she'd wanted an apology until she didn't get it. Already, nothing had gone like it should have.

Rose walked to the window that looked out from behind the kitchen sink. She peered into the distance, where Everett's old house had nearly collapsed from age and elements.

'How could you ever come back here?' Rose whispered.

Lily moved closer to her until they stood side by side. 'How could you not?'

Rose didn't so much as glance in her direction. 'I need to ask you a question, and I need you to be honest with me.'

'OK.'

'Are we alone?'

Alarm bit down on Lily's bones; chewed on the marrow. She threw a glance through every visible window, but the night outside was still. 'I don't know. Are we?' When Lily's gaze landed back on Rose, she was staring right at her.

Rose studied her for several seconds, then motioned to the table. 'Can we sit?'

'Sure.' Lily picked a chair and stood behind it, then watched Rose walk back and forth first, uncommitted even though she was the one who'd suggested sitting down.

'It's so damn cold in here, Lily.'

'We can put on some tea. I set the table when you said you were coming. I put water in the kettle before the power went out, but you'll have to use a lighter for the burner.' It felt insane to be talking about water and power and lighters when all Lily wanted to talk about was one night twenty-five years before and every winter since. But Lily still knew Rose well enough to see when the pressure was becoming too much, when a battle would be won at the expense of the war, and she wasn't in the frame of mind to lose.

'Who lives here now?' Rose asked.

'No one.'

'Are you sure?' Rose asked, every inch of her tense and wound up like a coiled spring.

'I'm sure.' Lily watched her, waiting for her to soften. Wanting her to thaw. To crack open. 'What about you, Rose?'

'What about me?'

'Where did you go? Where have you been? Where have you lived?' Lily whispered.

'Everywhere. Nowhere. You think you want to know, but I promise you that you don't.'

'I do.'

'Look, I'll tell you whatever you want to know. You don't have to believe anything I say. I probably wouldn't if I was you,' Rose said as she rolled her thumb over her lighter, sparking flame. 'But if you only believe one piece of it, believe this: I never left you. Not really. And never on purpose.'

She paused to ignite the gas burner. Lily didn't say a word, not daring to interrupt whatever train of confession Rose had boarded.

'I mean I did walk away from you. Obviously I did. But I didn't . . . I didn't mean to stay gone. I was just looking for a car. But when I came back . . .' Rose trailed off again and leaned against the cabinets, staring at the floor. 'Anyway, I made it to Tula after a couple days. Figured out how to not die. That first summer, I saw you by chance. You were playing tag in a field next to the Baptist church. I just . . . stared. Even though I'd imagined finding you a thousand times, I didn't know how to walk up to you, where to start, what to say. You left before I could figure it out, so I followed you home to see where you lived. I was ready to break you out if something looked wrong, I swear, but you'd found good people, and I wasn't about to mess that up for you.'

'I would've given anything for you to have walked up to me in that field,' Lily choked out.

Rose sat down and folded her arms on the table. 'That's because you don't know me. Everything I touch, then and now, it all goes to shit. I'm just like Mom. I stayed away from you because of that, to keep you safe, to give you a chance at a real family, and that's the God's honest truth.'

'A real family,' Lily echoed her, nodding uncontrollably. A new blade of anger wedged itself in her throat. '*You* are my family, Rose. You're all I've ever had. When I was twelve, my foster parents asked me if I wanted to be adopted, to become a *real* family. I said no. Broke their hearts. Broke what was left of mine. And honestly, things were different with them after that. I couldn't blame them. In a way, I understood how they felt.'

'Do you know what I would've given for someone to say something like that to me? That's the whole reason I—' Rose went still. Her eyes turned dark. 'Who the fuck are you to say no to an offer like that?'

'Who am *I*? I was seven years old when you left me in the snow, seven years old with a con artist for a mother who gave us new last names any time she changed jobs or towns or boyfriends or whenever someone was looking for her. I don't even know what my given last name really is, do you know that?' Lily let out an angry laugh. 'But I thought *you* did, and if I was adopted, if I changed my name, belonged to new people, claimed them as my *real* family, you might never find me. When they told me that I had to have a last name, I was hysterical. I screamed at them, "I'm Lily! Just Lily!" And my poor foster mother, bless her heart, she said, *That's beautiful, Lily. Why don't we call you Lily Just*? I kept that name for you, so that you could find me. Now, at thirty-two years old, every time I write my name, I still think of you and the fact that you haven't found me yet. Somewhere along the way, I realized you didn't even care enough to try.'

'Of course I cared! I cared enough to not get in your way. I didn't want to do to you what Mom did to us. I didn't want to ruin all the good.'

'But you ruined everything anyway! Do you have any idea how it felt to wait for you to come back, to wonder if you weren't claiming me because I wasn't good enough? All I have ever tried to do is be the good sister, the obedient sister, who was still waiting for you to be the one to find me, just like you asked me to. Even when I knew you were coming back to Tula every winter. Every time it snowed, I'd see your face. Do you know how crazy that made me feel? How much worse that was than if you'd just stayed gone?'

'If that's how you see it,' Rose said, and there was a sudden chill to her voice.

Lily slid a hand in her coat pocket and checked an opened packet of sugar with her fingertips to make sure it hadn't spilled. Then she stole a glimpse of the blue flame bringing the water to a boil in the kettle.

'I thought you had more than this to say to me,' Lily said without looking at her.

'I have plenty to say to you, and I'll tell you what happened the night I left you, but on one condition.'

'What's that?'

'When this conversation is over, no matter what is said, no matter how much you hate me, you and I are going to leave this place together, like we should have, and we are never going to come back. Everything that's happened between then and now, it's over. We will leave all this behind, and we will be sisters,' Rose said.

Lily couldn't deny how badly she wanted Rose's words to be the truth. Nor could she deny how little she believed in them.

Rose reached across the table, extending an open hand. Desperation shone on the surfaces of her eyes. Lily studied her face, wondering how many lies Rose had told since walking in the door, wondering how much it mattered either way, and even though she hated her more than she ever thought possible, she placed her hand in Rose's open palm.

FIFTY-THREE

Rose – February 11, 2018

've already lied to my sister twice since walking in her door. I have no intention of answering all her questions here, and I did not come alone.

Lily watches me expectantly, her fingers still anchored on the rising edge of my palm, and even though a grown woman sits across from me, I still see the child version of her peering through her face, looking to me as if I have all the answers, as if I *am* an answer. I reach into my pocket with my free hand and toggle the little plastic bag I've brought along as a last resort.

'You wouldn't wake up,' I say, and the honest words fall between us like stones. 'We'd been asleep for a while. When I'd woken up, there was so much snow on the ground, my legs were buried, and it was still coming down hard. I knew we needed to move. I tried to wake you up, but you were out. I was going to try to carry you, but I was sick and hung-over and stiff. And scared.'

'So you left me?'

'I never meant to leave you. Not like that. I covered you up with my jacket, tried to build a nest around you with anything I could find to keep you warm, and I was going to come right back.'

'Where did you go?'

'I wanted to try one more time to find the car. I'd told a kid from school that I just needed to borrow it for the night. I had parked it in the woods on a flat place close to the main road. It was a perfect spot. But the reason we couldn't find it is because it wasn't there. I guess he'd found it and taken it back. I didn't know what to do. All I knew is that we needed a car, and I went to find one.'

I hesitate, then glance at what I can see of the old house through the window. 'Everett's car was the only car I could think of. I knew where the keys were. I'd snuck it out for a drive before. I figured we could dump it once we got to the city, or take off the plate, sell it to someone for a couple hundred bucks.'

Lily's eyes cut to slits. 'You honestly think someone would buy a car from a kid?'

'Don't you? I know what I've seen in my line of work. I can't imagine what you've seen in yours.'

She settles against the chair, considering, working her lower lip between her teeth. Then bolts upright as if the back of the chair has become electrified. 'Are *you* what happened to Everett?'

'Yeah. I'm what happened to him.' I run my tongue over my teeth. I still taste exhaust whenever I think about it. 'I got to the edge of the yard and noticed the car was running in the garage. Everett had passed out drunk in the driver's seat. I should've turned around, gone back to you, but I walked toward him instead.

I closed the garage, slow and quiet so the door wouldn't screech too much on the tracks. Then I hid behind some bushes, waited to hear the car turn off or for someone to know what I'd done and come save him; stop me. I waited and waited, but no one came. Around dawn, smoke started seeping out from cracks in the garage door. I guess the engine had overheated. I was sure it was about to blow up. Then the car went quiet, and the morning felt so still, like the world was frozen in time. I don't know how long I stood there, just waiting to feel . . . something. But it never came. Then I heard a siren, and I thought they knew what I'd done. I thought they were coming for me.'

'But they were coming for me?' Lily murmurs.

I nod. 'I ran back through the woods, went right back to where I'd left you. You were gone, but your backpack was still there. I thought someone had taken you. I found your footprints and chased every step you'd taken. When I finally saw you, you were on the hip of a police officer who was talking to a woman. I guess you'd come out of the trees while she was walking her dog, and she'd called the police. I hid behind a tree and watched them talk about you; look up and down the road. The officer walked right by me – didn't even see me. Neither did you. You stuck your head under his chin, had your thumb in your mouth like you were two years old. Then you reached out for the lady, and she took you and held you like you *mattered*. I watched them put you in the back of that police car, then watched it drive up that road until it disappeared. I never left you, Lily. I let you leave me.'

FIFTY-FOUR

Lily – February 11, 2018

Emotion coated Lily's eyes and bent her vision. In front of her, for a split second, Rose was fourteen years old. Then she blinked, and the real Rose came into focus. Her face was a patchwork of lines, scars, and too much makeup.

'That's the same thing,' Lily said, recovering. 'I was seven years old. All you had to do was make a sound, wave a hand, tell them who I was, claim me!' She brought her fist down on the table, and their empty mugs rattled. 'But no, you had just killed a man and wanted to save your own skin. God, Rose. Have you ever thought about anyone else for one second in your entire life?'

'All I wanted was to do for you what Mom could never do for us. What I would never have been able to do for you.' Rose's gaze fell, and Lily realized she was crying. She wondered at the rage she felt at the sight of her tears and the desire to slap her sister instead of wiping her face dry.

'And what's that?'

'A home. A *real* home . . . A chance to *live* . . . not just survive. Do you have any idea how many times my choices have damn near gotten me killed? How could you still think for one second that being with me would've been better than the life you had? Even on the night we ran I knew you deserved so much more than I could possibly have given you. I have never chosen myself over you, Lily. Over and over, every choice I've made, I have been choosing you, saving *you*. And I'd do it again. All of it. Even that night. Every step,' Rose whispered.

The words were akin to a knife in Lily's chest, and she gasped at the pain, which struck her everywhere at once.

'You'd do it *all* again?' Lily asked, her voice in tatters. 'You'd leave me again?'

'No, that's not what I mean, and you know it. I've taken bullets of all kinds for you, shots you didn't even know were aimed in your direction. And I'd take them all again. I'd kill for you again. I'd cover your tracks again. And I am not going anywhere without you ever again.'

But for Lily, her sister's words weren't enough. All she'd ever wanted was right in front of her: Rose, her truth, and her company through a winter's night, and yet Lily still felt deeply, irreparably alone.

FIFTY-FIVE

Rose – February 11, 2018

The tea kettle shrieks. Lily stands before I can and moves to the stove, seemingly abated, at least for the moment. She pins her long hair on top of her head and begins pouring water into two mugs.

'I don't know if that's what you always wanted to hear from me, but it's the truth,' I say.

'Well, I don't know if you want to hear *this*, but you look a lot like Mom,' she says.

'I wouldn't know. I haven't seen her in years.'

'I saw her the other day. I took a coworker to meet her and brought her a slice of lemon meringue pie,' she replies, glancing back at me. Then she tears open a couple sugar packets and upturns them into the tea. 'I'm sure she'd love to see you, too, you know. Though she's not one for words these days. I think she has a lot of regrets.'

'I bet she does.' I look away from Lily and press my fingertips against the old wooden tabletop. I imagine it's been here since the day we darted across the front yard of this house. I wonder if the man saw us, if he hoped we'd make it, if that's why, all these years later, his family opened this home to the girl who saw his property as an ocean to cross to freedom.

She sets the mugs down and lowers herself back into her chair. I take a sip, wanting her to see I'm grateful, even if I'm full of shit. She's made it too sweet, and it nearly makes me pucker.

'She showed up at my door about ten years ago,' Lily starts. 'She seemed so happy to see me. She invited me out to dinner at this incredible Italian place. She talked about all the work she'd done on herself, the goals she had, how she wanted to help me find you. Then the bill came, and she couldn't find her wallet. I paid it, of course, then invited her home with me. It had become pretty clear that she had nowhere else to go. She drank an entire handle of vodka and fell asleep at my kitchen table.'

Lily reaches up and uncoils her hair, and I see she'd fastened it to her head with the world's skinniest screwdriver. 'She hadn't changed, Rose. Not a bit. But she wanted to. I could see that. She just needed my help.' She spins the screwdriver in her fingers. Then she looks me square in the face. 'You're a lot like her, aren't you?'

'I don't want to be,' I whisper.

'Why did you really come here tonight?'

In the bright glare of her steadfast gaze, I can think of nothing to give her but the truth. 'Because of what happened at Brecken Park.'

'*You* are what happened at Brecken Park. So eager to lead another kid through the snow to a brand-new life, weren't you? For all that talk about how you staying away is for the better, you sure couldn't leave her alone. Maya has a little brother. I couldn't let that happen.'

Adrenaline shoots through my chest. 'It wasn't my idea,' I say. 'I found out Maya had been lured into a weekend trip to Nashville by the new owner of a strip club where I just started working. His name is Easton Grimes. He'd all but promised to hook her up with a development deal, but I thought it was just bait for trafficking.'

'And you couldn't just tell her that?'

'I tried to tell her in so many words, but she couldn't see it for what it was, and I needed proof to expose what Easton is doing, so I pretended I was in on it. Then I gave her two hundred dollars and every reason and every excuse to bail, but it didn't work. She called me and said she was in Brecken Park, ready to go to Nashville, and that if I didn't show up, she was going to the cops instead. So I went to meet her just to shut her up. I was high. Too high. And I had no idea where I was going to take her.'

'God, you haven't changed at all, have you?' Lily interrupts, laughing bitterly.

'I am trying! I wanted to be different, for it to turn out different. But when I saw her in the woods, *you* were there, too, sitting behind her, singing to her. I couldn't believe what I was seeing.

I thought I was hallucinating. Then you left, and she didn't get up. She was just curled in a ball at the base of a tree. I still wasn't convinced she was real until I touched her. She barely had a pulse, and her skin was like ice. I had Narcan in my purse. I punched it in her leg, and I carried her as far as I could.'

'You could carry her, but not me.'

I hide behind the mug, take another drink, my mouth cotton dry. 'You didn't leave me any other choice! That's why I gave Maya to a homeless man and told him what to do instead of calling an ambulance. I was terrified that if I brought her to the hospital, she'd wake up, see me, and remember you. I *chose* you.'

'Is that what you tell yourself? It couldn't possibly be that *you* didn't want to be arrested,' she taunts.

'No. That wasn't it at all. I was just trying to keep all of you safe!' I snap back at her, a wave of dizziness knocking my filter flat.

'I've known Christian and Maya a long time. Both of them have little brothers, but they run away, Rose. Just like you. I have helped keep them safe for years. Then *you* find them, and look what happens. Just look.'

'How . . . how did you . . .' The first words come out in heaves, but I can't wrap my mind around the rest of the question tightly enough to make it leave my mouth. What the hell is wrong with me?

'How did I find out about your little plan?' A pitying smile transforms her face. 'You.' She takes a sip, letting the word hang in the room like a noose, then sets down her mug to stare at me. 'You ran a red light and almost hit me, and I saw them in your car. I figured you might be headed to Brecken Park, so I drove there, too. I didn't see you there, but I found them. You already had Maya wrapped around your finger. She barely told me anything. Christian was a different story.'

Even though it's just the two of us in this cold cabin, I hear the newscast announcing his death, see the headline run across the screen in my mind. 'What happened to him?' I gasp out.

Lily grins, and her teeth glint in the dark. 'You,' she says again.

'No. I didn't . . . I didn't touch him.'

Lily puts a hand to her chest. 'I didn't either,' she replies. 'But you'd made him so nervous. He told me about the Nashville trip. He told me he didn't want to go, but he knew someone who might want to go in his place. I told him to meet me at the park again later that night, and that we'd figure it out. But it was snowing, Rose. I can't be alone in the snow, and I was so afraid Christian's change of heart would scare *you* off or he'd tell someone about you and your plan before you ever got the chance to come find me, and I needed you to know that I knew you were here. We both know you wouldn't be here with me right now otherwise.'

'What did you do to them? What did you do?' These are the only words I can force out. My brain feels like it's tilting inside my skull, and my eyelids want so badly to close.

'Every time it snows, I see it as another opportunity to understand what might have made you get up and walk away from me. I find someone just like you who's desperate to leave their life behind, even though it would mean abandoning a little brother or sister, and I bring them to our woods. I teach them our song, and I give them something to make sure they're not scared, just like you did for me, and I sit all night with them. I never leave until their last breath. I only walked away from Maya when I saw you coming. It was the perfect opportunity to see what you would do with a girl freezing to death in the snow. I told her I could arrange regular visits with her brother, but I needed a favor first. Nothing much. Just a phone call. I wanted to watch you leave her all alone the way you left me so maybe I could understand why. But you didn't.'

'I'm sorry,' I sputter. A vortex of nausea opens in my gut and begins swirling faster and faster. I push my fist against it, wondering if there's any way to stop it from pulling the rest of me in. 'I'm scared, Lily.'

'It'll pass,' she says. 'I put a little something in your tea that should help with that.'

Before my eyes, Lily's face slides apart in two halves. The room behind her blurs out of focus, and I spill on to the floor. Darkness claims my vision, but I can still hear Lily talking, recalling how ten years ago, after our mother had passed out on the kitchen table, she took that long, skinny screwdriver she'd just used to pin up her hair and hammered it through the corners of our mother's eyes. She'd taken her time, thrashed it around in her brain, then dropped her in an alley near the hospital. How she did that for all of us.

Then she begins to sing.

FIFTY-SIX

Rose – February 11, 2018

My skin is wet. I rub my fingers together and find them slick between, but I can't separate my hands. My arms tingle with numbness. My seat and thighs are cold and damp, and for a moment I wonder if I've fallen asleep drunk and pissed myself.

My head swims slowly toward the clear, and my eyes flutter open, but the dark lifts only a little. The front of me is warmer, and it takes me longer than it should to realize there's a person between my legs, a head resting on my thigh.

'Just whisper, sister, that's all you have to do,' my sister's voice sings quietly, and I jerk to attention as she finishes the song. Wind moans overhead and slaps me in the face.

'Where are we?' I slur.

'How does it feel to wake up in the woods, not knowing where you are or what might happen next?' Lily crouches in front of me, and her face becomes visible.

'Terrifying.' I look down at the head in my lap, a girl's smooth profile, eyes closed, hair spilling over my leg. My hands are bound to hers with pantyhose. 'Maya?' I ask as I recognize her. 'Maya! Wake up! Maya, can you hear me?' I jiggle my arms, trying to rouse her.

'She's asleep,' Lily says. 'I didn't want her to be scared. You understand.'

'*I* left you. *I* hurt you. She has nothing to do with it!'

'She has everything to do with it!' Lily stands, towering over me. 'You chose her, you did for her what you wouldn't do for me.'

'She can help us start over. That's what I want for us. I have a plan. Everything is going to be OK. But I lied to you. I didn't come alone.'

Lily swings her gaze toward the house. 'Who did you bring with you?'

'Easton Grimes. I know he's trafficking kids. I just can't prove it yet to anyone who matters.'

'And you brought him *here*?'

'He's tied up in the trunk of the car.'

'What is *wrong* with you?' Fury pulls its strings on her face and her voice.

'No, it's OK. It's good. We can take what we've both done, and we can turn it into good.'

'If you can't prove it, how do you know it's actually happening?' she spits out at me.

'I took a thumb drive from his desk. I decoded some of the words. There are more folders on it with probably all kinds of other information, too, but I lost it the night you had Maya in the woods. But it's happening, Lily. There's no question about that.'

Hesitation settles on Lily, quieting everything about her, reminding me of a snow-sky, unapologetic and silent and inevitable. Then she lifts her chin and hurls her gaze down her nose at me.

'Even if it's happening, how can you possibly think abducting a business owner and bringing him here leads to anything good for either of us, especially without proof?' she asks.

My head is still spinning, and the plan I'd come up with that seemed at least a little likely to work now sounds insane when said back to me. But I keep going because this is it. Easton taking the fall for Lily's crimes is the only road out for both of us.

'I'm still figuring it out! I was playing him, but he was playing me, too. He tried to kill me, and I just beat him to the punch. I'm making it up as I go.'

'That's just your MO, isn't it? I thought you were the smart one of the two of us. Wasn't that you? Smart as a fox? Tell me you didn't know exactly what you were doing the night you left me.'

'I've already told you my reasons. I was also fourteen years old and scared out of my mind!' I breathe hard. I'm deeply exhausted even though I'm sitting still. 'But I'm not scared now. This plan will work, if you would just listen.'

'And what is it?'

'What happened to Christian and Maya, Easton can go down for all of it. We'll tell Maya that Easton drugged Christian in the woods to keep him quiet about Maya's trip to Nashville. Then he spiked a drink meant for you, that you shared with Maya. You and her both nearly died in those woods, but you managed to call me. I came and I got you both out. It didn't go according to plan, but it was all part of setting him up. We give Maya a bunch of money and tell her that she's an undercover hero. And me and you, we'll get the hell out of here, and we'll never look back.' I glance at Maya again, desperate to feel her warm breath on my leg, but it's numb from cold.

Disappointment drips all over Lily's features. 'How are you going to pin a murder, an attempted murder, and an abduction on a man tied up in the trunk of a car?'

'We can kill him and make it look like Maya did it in self-defense. We'll tell Maya exactly what to say. She's good, Lily. She can do this. We can figure this out. Please, Lily.'

She kneels in front of me, her eyes soft and searching, and she wipes my tears away with her fingers. 'All of this was for you, Rose. All I ever wanted was to understand what made you leave, what I could have done differently to make you stay.'

'You didn't do anything wrong, Lily. I'm so sorry.'

'Will you sing for me?'

'Of course – of course I'll sing for you.'

Lily curls up beside us and drapes her arm across Maya and me; rests her head beneath my chin. I stare at Maya, keep my eyes on her face, and sing our song. My voice is steady by the end, nausea giving way to a new resolve.

I will get us out of this.

I will see us through.

I left Lily in those woods. I created the hole she fills, and even if the way she's chosen to fill it isn't my fault, I made that hole, dug it out all around her.

Lily pulls away from me. 'Why are you looking at Maya?'

'I wasn't looking at anyone. I was just thinking . . . trying to figure this out.'

A tiny laugh escapes her, rocking her back. She retrieves something from her pocket. 'I wanted to save Maya, too, you know. But she knows too much. I tried to visit her at the detention center, and she refused to see me. Then even the sight of me at Bright View scared her so bad that she had a panic attack. A stack of money won't change her memories.' She extends her palm, where a little white pill sits in the middle. 'You can't be totally sure she won't rat me out. And I can't just take you on your word. Show me that you choose me.'

'What is that?'

'The only way out. Don't play dumb. It's not a good look for you.'

'Lily, no.'

'She's already asleep. She won't feel a thing. One of you is taking it. The police think you did this, Rose. That you killed Christian and tried to kill Maya. They think you put all those children in the ground.'

I pin my elbow against my side, feeling for the handle of my gun, wondering how I can shift it into my hands, but it's gone.

'Looking for this?' She pulls my revolver out of her coat pocket. 'You never meant to leave here with me, did you? You didn't come running for me. You came for Maya.'

'I came for you! Lily, I swear to you. I thought if I came for you and we left town together, I would fix what I broke in you, and you'd be OK. You wouldn't have to do what you did in the park ever again. I was going to force you to come with me if you didn't want to come willingly. I didn't even know Maya was here. Just let her go, and then we can leave. You don't have to do this.'

'*You* did this. *You* have to fix it.' She puts the pill in my fingers.

I glance down at Maya. She hasn't stirred since I woke up. Whatever Lily gave her, she may be half-dead already. If I die and Lily lives, what's to say Lily won't kill her as soon as I stop breathing? Could I say yes, could I kill this girl, if it means saving others from my sister?

FIFTY-SEVEN

Daniel – February 11, 2018

From the passenger seat of Hunter's car, Daniel pointed at the turn for New Hope Loop. If Rose was holding Maya at her childhood house and Daniel didn't check it, he'd never forgive himself. The only surprise so far was how easy Hunter had been to convince it was worth looking into.

Wind rattled the car frame as they banked a wide turn and coasted downhill. New Hope Loop felt a world away from the recovery operation. The lights and voices from the woods between the two roads were wholly trapped within the trees.

An old farmhouse came into view, sitting at the back of a large field. Daniel wouldn't have seen it at all had he not known to look. The yard was lumpy, and the dark house was frozen in layers of ice and time.

Daniel's gaze swung across the road and caught on faint, parallel indentations in the snow.

'Stop,' he barked.

Hunter punched the brakes, and the car fishtailed, nearly spinning around before coming to a stop. 'Jesus, Danny. A little warning next time.'

'Someone's been here.' Daniel pointed down the driveway, where the pair of grooves veered off to the right and ended at a vehicle parked in a low spot that hugged the bank. It had been there long enough to be covered in six inches of snow.

'Could be the owner,' Hunter reasoned.

'Maybe. I don't want to leave without checking. Stay in the car if you want.'

Hunter pulled to the curb to let him out. Daniel's feet sank into the snow up to his calves.

'Go side to side walking down the driveway. I'd hate to see you bust your ass,' Hunter said, a wry smile playing on his lips.

'Sure you would,' Daniel muttered to himself, but he took his advice and made a zigzag pattern down the hill.

At the bottom, he glanced back at Hunter's car. Hunter watched him from on top of the hill. His eyes were focused on the house like a huntsman in a blind. His attention was both reassuring and altogether something opposite.

Daniel knocked on the front door and announced his presence. No one answered. He peered through the lone square window on the front of the house. The edge of a table was visible, as was a wooden chair with spindly legs. Daniel tested the handle and found the door locked. He had no imminent-danger cause to force the door, although he doubted Hunter would say much if one good kick managed to get it open.

Instead, he walked off the porch and around the side of the house. There was one window on the adjacent side, but it was too high for him to see through without gripping the sill with his fingertips and scrabbling up the planked wall with his feet. He glanced back at the car, wondering if Hunter was watching and having himself a good chuckle at his expense, but the car was empty.

A thumping sound drew Daniel's ear.

'Hunter?' He drew his gun and positioned it at his front, then swung it in unison with his gaze.

'Tell me you didn't see that,' Hunter said, wiping snow from the back of his pants as he came into view.

'Shh,' Daniel ordered, and they both froze. The banging began again. It was coming from behind the building. They exchanged a glance before sprinting around the house.

A car was parked close to the back wall, invisible from both sides of the home. It was topped with several inches of snow. Someone was inside and, from the sound of things, not happy about it.

'Tula PD!' Daniel announced as they rushed to the vehicle.

The sounds stopped. The windows were too tinted to see through, but the windshield was a lighter shade. The front seats were empty, as was the visible section of the back of the car. They each took a side and tried the doors. All of them were locked.

Hunter circled the back of the vehicle, then went still.

'Someone's in the trunk,' he mouthed. 'I'll handle the car. You still feel like kicking in that front door?' he asked, and Daniel took off across the snow.

FIFTY-EIGHT

Lily – February 11, 2018

The pill was white as snow against Rose's fingers. Panic climbed Lily's spine. What Rose had in her hand could be absorbed through the skin. If she held the pill too long, she would kill herself either way. All Rose had to do was tip her wrist half an inch, and the solution to everything would fall right in Maya's slack mouth.

Lily peered at Rose, mystified by how many obvious things she was missing. Her sister, *smart as a fox*, had a dead girl in her lap and hadn't noticed it yet.

Earlier today, she'd given Maya a step-by-step plan for how to slip out of Bright View undetected, including the perfect window to run, then picked her up in the employee lot behind the dumpster. She'd half expected her to refuse to get in her car, but Lily had shown Maya a recent picture of her brother and she'd climbed right in.

Already tonight, Lily had waited with Maya through a grand mal seizure, stroked her hair until the knots of taut muscles at last released, and the last bit of life sank from her like the sun dipping below the horizon, beautiful and quiet.

'We don't have to do this,' Rose whispered, breaking the spell. 'I'll give this to Easton instead. We can lock Maya somewhere in the house, leave a letter about what Easton's doing, and get the hell out of here. It doesn't matter what Maya tells them. Even if I fuck up everything else, you can't deny that I know how to hide.'

New grief pricked Lily's heart. 'You can't save Maya,' she tried to explain. 'This is your last chance to save me.'

Lily wanted this to work so badly, but she'd known to prepare for the reality that Rose might let her down again. She thought about those steps now and found a measure of solace in knowing she would control what would happen next, regardless of Rose's choice.

The preparations had begun years ago when she wrote Rose's name in place of her own on the hand-printed rental agreement she'd signed with the man who owned the old farmhouse. It had been so easy to convince him which sister she was, and he mercifully understood that she didn't want anyone to know where she was living.

That piece of paper was tucked inside a shoebox in the cabinet by the stove, along with Lily's personal cell phone, the phones she'd taken from Christian and Maya, the pictures she'd captured of Christian and Maya at Brecken Park, Christian sitting on the front steps of his house, and Maya at the coffee shop, tuning her guitar before her last open mic night, where Lily had followed her to so she could make sure Maya wouldn't accompany Christian to the woods. She'd even printed out the photo she'd taken of her own apartment window. After Rose had blacked out from the tea that she'd spiked with more than double the fentanyl she usually used, Lily had brought every piece from the box she needed her to touch, wrapping Rose's limp fingers around them one by one as she lay face down on the floor.

'Lily,' Rose said quietly, and Lily dropped her gaze from the direction of the house to her sister's pale face. 'I don't think you would kill me. I think this is a test.'

'This is not a test. This is a choice. *Your* choice.' She had made it so easy for Rose, maybe too easy. And Rose was going to screw it up all the same.

'Exactly.' Her sister smiled weakly. 'If this pill can kill me, you'd never let me take it. You want to know if I trust you. That's what this is really about.'

'No, Rose. You're wrong. This isn't about trust. I don't trust you. I will never trust you. This is me seeing if you will choose me, if you would do whatever it takes to save me this time.'

'I love you, and I know you love me. And I have to believe that if this would really kill me, you'd never let me do it. You don't trust me, and I earned that. But this is me trusting you.

Please remember, above everything else, above all the mistakes and the bullshit, please remember that I came back. When you called me, I came back for you,' she said, choking on the last word.

Their eyes met for a full second, neither of them moving. Then Rose slapped the pill into her own mouth.

FIFTY-NINE

Rose – February 11, 2018

The bitter taste of the pill coats every inch of my mouth within a single second, and even if I wanted to spit it out, it's already too late. I could spit and spit and spit and die before my tongue went dry. Within seconds there's a plummeting feeling in my middle and a weightlessness at the ends of my limbs, and I know whatever she gave me wasn't just for show.

Rage turns Lily's eyes into holes. 'Maya's already dead, and you didn't care enough about me to even check first. You leave me every chance you get.'

My gaze slides down to where Maya rests in my lap, her face too still, her cheek unmoving, eyelids resting a sliver apart. It's the same face the other girl was wearing when I left her on the hotel bed and ran.

I want to clutch her to my heart and rock her, to tell her I'm sorry. I'm sorry about so many things. I'm too late. Not just hours late but years.

Guilt is a fire in my belly, bringing my stomach to a boil, and the acid turns into foam in my throat, climbing higher with every breath. I fight to swallow it down, refusing to vomit on this dead girl in my lap, but it travels out of my nose. All I can do is rock backward so it slides down my front instead of dripping on Maya's face.

The sensation of falling faster by the second devours me from the legs up. I gasp for air, my chest igniting, the oxygen burning into nothing upon entry. The edges of my vision blur, and the center focal point becomes too sharp as if I'm staring down a telescope. I can only hope that what they say about your life flashing before your eyes as you die doesn't happen to me. In all my nearly forty years, I can't think of one single moment I want to see again.

Lily reaches inside her coat and pulls my gun from the waist of her pants, holding it upside down by the barrel.

'You're not leaving without me this time.' She fits the handle of the gun inside my palms, pulls the pantyhose tighter. My body cannot hear my brain's commands to yank my arms away even though it's screaming.

She leans close, holds the end of the barrel of the gun inches from her chest. 'You don't get to leave this world feeling like a hero, like you gave *anyone* a second chance. Maya's dead in your lap, and you're about to shoot me with your gun. *This* is what you do, Rose! This is who you are.'

Her hands clutch around mine in a vice-like grip, her finger guiding mine through the trigger. With every ounce of fight left in my being, I resist the pressure of her finger on mine, pushing down.

'Your last name is Carter.' My words slur in a pool of foam. But it does what I want it to, and Lily goes still. 'Your name is Lily Mae Carter.'

As my body starts to convulse, I close my eyes, focus everything I have left on my thumb, and slide it through the backside of the trigger as far as it will go, pushing my knuckle up against the thin piece of metal. I feel the coil condensing, reaching that suspended place between what is and what will be. Then she gives one last squeeze.

Black curtains crash against both sides of my vision, meeting in the middle, and the sound of her scream chases what is left of me into the dark.

SIXTY

Daniel – February 11, 2018

The interior of the house was silent and still. Two mugs sat on the kitchen table, half drunk, their sides gone cold. The chairs were pulled out at odd angles. Daniel's eyes roamed over the sparse room, searching for other signs of recent activity, but his mind was on Hunter. He sent a bullet of a prayer skyward that Maya was in the trunk of that car. It would stand to reason that she had stopped banging on the inside of the trunk when she heard them because she didn't want to be found by cops and sent to lockup.

Daniel moved down a short hallway to a single bedroom. A twin-size bed was positioned perpendicular to the door, an antique vanity beside it, and a pair of narrow, slatted closet doors was tucked into the corner. Wind beat against the warbled pane of a small, square window. The skinny doors flexed nearly imperceptibly, but the edge of the thin, floral skirt that covered the legs of the bed danced in an invisible breeze. Daniel held a hand to the bottom of the window, but no air was coming through. The draft was coming from inside the closet.

Daniel flipped one door open with his fingertips. Several jackets hung on a rack, shoved to one side, bottoms swaying. He reached through the clothes and pushed, and the back wall split into a second pair of doors. He crept through the new exit and found himself on a platform, empty but for a basic, older-model wheelchair. A handicap ramp ran down in the exterior wall in a long, slow hill and ended at a square, flat area behind the house.

'Danny?' Hunter called, then swept the beam of his light in Daniel's direction.

'House is empty,' Daniel answered. 'What did you find in the car?'

'Easton fucking Grimes. Tied up and pissed off. Back-up's on the way, but we're spread thin. A couple uniforms are coming from the recovery site. Grimes says the last thing he remembers is Betty hitting him in the head in the back seat of his car.'

'And she brought him here,' Daniel muttered to himself. He swung his flashlight from one corner of the yard to the other and back again. There was a nearly invisible line crossing the yard on a diagonal track. He leaned against the porch railing, squinting into the dark as he followed the path with his light. A woman's scream erupted from the woods beyond.

Daniel hopped the railing, landed on his feet in the snow, and started across the yard.

'Daniel, wait for back-up!'

Daniel knew his brother was right. Hunter shouldn't leave Easton unattended, and he shouldn't chase a scream into the night by himself.

He hesitated, his eyes on Hunter's face, when another scream bleated from the trees.

'Danny!' Hunter barked, but Daniel was already running.

SIXTY-ONE

Lily – February 11, 2018

Lily stared at her chest where a hole should be, the same place she'd felt a void since she was seven years old. But there was only the same intangible wound. Her fingers were still wrapped around Rose's, squeezing down on the trigger, but it wouldn't budge.

She glared at Rose, furious and stunned. Her sister's eyes stared out at nothing. Her lips hung slack, suspended in the middle of a breath. Lily released her grip on Rose's hands, took her by the shoulders, and shook her. Rose's head snapped back, and her jaw fell open.

It was over. It was *over*.

'No!' Lily shook her harder. 'Rose!' She reached a hand back and slapped her across the cheek. Rose's chin swung to her shoulder from the force of the blow. Foam dribbled out of the corner of her mouth. Lily covered her face with her hands and screamed through her fingers.

'Tula PD! Announce yourself!' Daniel's voice called out, and a flashlight illuminated the black.

Panic erupted from her quaking heart. She drew a quick breath to steady her nerves and the tremors in her hands. Then she untied the pantyhose from Rose's wrist and looped it over Maya's hands.

'Daniel! Help me!' Lily belted the words into the night. Then she fell forward into Rose's lap and clung to her sister as if without her to hold on to, she might at last sink beneath the snow.

SIXTY-TWO

Daniel – February 11, 2018

Lily was bent over Rose, her hair spilled across Rose's lap, her shoulders shaking.

'Lily, get back!' Daniel trained the beam of his flashlight between them, and it glinted on the barrel of a gun. Rose's fingers clasped around the handle, her pointer finger on the trigger.

He leaped for Lily, hooked his arms around her waist, and dragged her away. She howled and slapped at his hands, knocking the flashlight to the snow. But he barely felt the impact. His eyes and every thought were fixated on the gun in Rose's folded hands.

'Rose just took something. A . . . a pill. She started choking right after. I . . . I don't think she's breathing,' Lily stammered. 'Do something!'

'Stay here,' Daniel ordered, then he drew his own gun and moved closer. Without his flashlight, Rose was nothing but a shadow, an entity of darkness like a wraith in the woods. The ends of her hair twisted in a gust of wind, but the rest of her remained utterly unmoving.

Keeping his gun aimed in the middle of her form, he leaned down, studying her face. Her eyes were half-open. Stray light from unknown sources refracted in pinpoints on their surfaces, reminding him of stars. Foam had erupted from her nose and mouth. He holstered his gun, pulled off his gloves, and wiped her airways clean. Not daring to hope, he held his bare fingers in front of her face, testing for breath, then waited for five seconds, ten. Nothing. He moved his fingers from her face to the side of her neck to feel for a pulse and found none.

His chin fell to his chest. 'She's gone.'

'Rose! Don't leave me! Come back!' Lily screamed, as if Daniel's arrival had given her a grain of hope her sister might survive. She sank to her knees, gasping and moaning, but he barely registered her or the outpouring of her shock and grief.

His eyes had finally adjusted to the dark, and there was a body in Rose's lap, face obscured by hair and position, wrists bound with pantyhose. He leaned closer and swiped the hair away.

Maya.

'No.' The word seeped from him like blood from a wound. Daniel dropped to his knees and put a finger under her nose but felt no stir in the air around her face. She was alabaster, her lips tinged unnaturally dark against her frozen skin.

'Maya,' he rasped, her name squeezing up his throat where grief had already made a burning home.

He patted her cheek, each interval of contact striking harder than the last. He gripped both sides of her face and stared openly at her. He bowed his head alongside hers. 'Please,' he whispered in her ear, his cheek pressed firmly against hers.

Beneath the surface chill of her skin, the ghost of warmth still lingered. He moved his fingers to the side of her neck.

'She's dead,' Lily blubbered. 'I checked her first . . . as soon as I could . . . as soon as Rose . . . I swear I checked her . . .' Lily's voice dissolved into moaning.

Daniel tuned her out, then closed off every sense to everything else but this girl in his arms. He steadied his other hand on her throat, forced his mind to idle, and waited.

Beneath his fingertips, Maya's pulse fluttered.

'Hunter!' Daniel screamed into the dark. 'Hunter! I need a bus! Now! Hunter! Bus!'

Warm. I need to get her warm. He pulled his beanie off his head and covered her head, then ripped his coat off his body and wrapped it around Maya's torso. His heart pounded. Even though he was kneeling in snow, every inch of him felt like it had caught fire. Trembling with adrenaline, he scooped her into his arms and held her fast against his chest. He thought back to Josh, still lost somewhere, who'd sat with his dead friend in a frozen world.

I know now, Josh, he would tell him if he ever saw him again.

'Hunter!' he screamed, then he whipped his gaze to Lily. 'Why are you here? What happened out here?'

Lily's face was liquid, and her mouth hung open. She reached out for them. Daniel twisted away, then curled over Maya, desperate to trap as much heat as possible between them.

'What the hell happened, Lily?' he shouted at her.

'Rose called me,' she whispered. 'She said she wanted to apologize in person for everything she'd done to me. She said it had to be tonight, that . . . that she had done some terrible things, and that she wanted to kill herself, that it was the only way she knew she'd never hurt anyone again, but that she owed me a conversation first.'

'But you already knew what she'd done, didn't you?'

'No! I had no idea Maya was with her.'

'Why didn't you call me the second she contacted you?' Daniel practically snarled at her. He knew he was treating her like a criminal, and it wasn't entirely fair. Then again, Lily may not have done this, but she could've stopped it. She could have tried.

'The way she was talking, it felt like if I didn't come meet her tonight, I'd never get a chance, and I knew you'd never let me come see her. I swear I didn't know Maya was with her when I talked to her. When I got to the house, I heard her call out for me. I followed her voice. She made me walk through trees alone, and I found them here. She had a gun. She was waving it all around. She said she wanted to show me what she should've done to herself the night we ran instead of leaving me. Then she put a pill in her mouth. She'd been holding Maya up, but then she got too weak, and I saw her eyes, how they weren't really open or shut and she— God, it happened so fast.' Her voice broke, and she covered her face in her hands.

'Did Rose give something to her, too?' Daniel demanded.

'I don't know,' Lily choked out between sobs.

'Damn it, Lily. What *do* you know?' But he realized it didn't matter – that Maya didn't have time for it to matter. 'Do you have more Narcan?'

'Why would I have that?' Lily's eyes were wide and wild, tears pouring from them like rain.

Daniel leveled his stare at her. The theory he'd begun piecing together earlier in the station, if it was true, might save Maya a second time. 'I know what you did at Brecken Park. I need you to do it again. *Maya* needs you to do it again.'

Lily's expression became the portrait of peace, of pity. 'She's dead, Detective.'

Daniel's entire being went still. He sank back on his heels, the weight of Lily's certainty too much to carry in the same arms as the girl he'd failed. He peered down at Maya, grief gathering in his eyes, and cradled her face to his heart.

'What's going on? Bus is going to take a minute. Volunteer unit,' Hunter said, jogging up from behind them.

Daniel turned in time to watch recognition wash over his brother.

'Oh my God. Rose.' His voice broke over her name. He fell to his knees beside her and checked for breath and pulse. Daniel knew he wouldn't find either. Still, Hunter began compressions immediately and furiously, pushing two beats a second into her chest.

Daniel's own heart broke open. His brother had been wrong about so many things, but here and now, the advice he'd given him in the car came roaring back: *Be sure*. Hunter had never once told him to be right. At last, he understood the difference, and Maya's only chance of surviving was for him to be damn sure about what he'd sensed beneath his fingertips when he'd touched her throat.

Careful to keep his coat around her, he laid her flat on the snow, tilted her chin back, pinched her nose, and breathed his air into her lungs. Then with the heels of his hands and a silent prayer to anything that might be listening, he urged her heart to keep beating.

SIXTY-THREE

Lily – February 11, 2018

More officers filed into the woods, beams from their lights sweeping through the trees, voices and footsteps and squeals from their radio as loud as rush-hour traffic. Despite the chaos, Daniel didn't flinch, didn't stop, his small shoulders pulsing his hands against Maya's chest in an unrelenting rhythm, and Lily wondered if he was aware of anything but the corpse under his hands.

Lily gasped and gasped, training her gaze on Detective Kepp's hands as he became Rose's heart, forcing blood through cooling veins.

Gasp.

Gasp.

She was drawing the breath she wished Rose would take.

Lily sank to her knees and moaned.

'Get her out of here!' Detective Kepp sat back from Rose long enough to growl, jerking his chin in her direction without slackening the beat in his hands.

A pair of officers crouched on either side of Lily and tried to take her by her elbows, but she twisted like a fish on a hook, ripping herself from their grasps.

'Get her in a squad car. Easton Grimes, too,' he ordered.

'I'm not leaving my sister!' Lily cried out and crawled toward her, hands sinking beneath the white.

For the first time, the detective looked straight at her. 'I know your sister. She'd want you out of the snow. Don't you think?'

Shock hit Lily everywhere at once. 'Yes,' she whimpered.

The two officers approached her again and lifted her to her feet, then she let them lead her from the woods.

She'd always thought she'd feel vindicated should she ever be

in the position to leave Rose behind, but walking away from her
evoked a physical pain, like her skin was being torn from the
connective tissue beneath, her very bones drawn to her sister's
body through her flesh like metal to a magnet. More than once,
she fell to her knees on her last walk out of these woods.

They approached the back of her cabin, where a pair of paramedics were sliding a backboard and a couple bags out of the
back of their ambulance and a police officer was standing with
a well-dressed man. He had a black eye, and his stylish clothes
were wrinkled, two indications this was the bar owner Rose had
stuffed in the trunk of a car.

'Kepp wants Mr Grimes and the sister secured in cars until
transport gets settled,' the officer to her left announced to the
other uniforms as they neared each other.

'He just radioed for a ten-seventy-nine. Shouldn't take long.
Pretty sure half the county staff is on the other side of those
trees,' another officer answered.

'What's a ten-seventy-nine?' Lily asked.

The officers on either side of her shared a glance above her
head but gave no answer to her.

Nervousness nipped at Lily's skin from the inside out. Did the
detectives already suspect what really happened out there? Were
they coming for her? If all the evidence she'd planted still failed
to point the detectives to Rose instead of her, she would need a
lawyer, and a good one, just in case.

'It's been a long night, gentlemen. My car is here, and I'd
really like to be heading home now,' Easton said.

'Your car isn't going anywhere. It's part of an active crime
scene,' the officer who seemed to be in charge told Easton
point-blank.

'That seems excessive. Betty's certainly fired, but I don't even
know that I'll press charges. It's not worth the hassle, and I'm
fine.'

Betty? Lily frowned at Easton, her sister's real name weighting
the front of her tongue. Then she swallowed it down, keeping it
to herself.

'I'm glad to hear it. Not everyone is so lucky tonight,' the
officer responded.

Easton stood taller, as if an inch difference in height would give him a better vantage point through the black woods. 'What do you mean by that?'

'Our detectives will be filling you in. They've asked that both of you wait until the scene is secured, then you'll be going to the station for interviews. I realize it's not convenient, but I would recommend cooperating.'

Easton's expression turned to stone. 'I'd like to call my lawyer so he can meet us there.'

'You can do that in the car,' the officer answered.

'I don't have my phone. I think Betty took it.'

'You can make the call once we get there.' He gestured for Easton to follow him up the hill to where several patrol cars were parked. Lily trailed them up the driveway, fiddling with the last thing of Rose's she had in her pocket.

Shouts erupted at the top of the hill. Several reporters and camera crews were perched along the curb and began descending the driveway the moment their group came into view. The two escorting officers gestured for Lily and Easton to wait, then surged ahead of them to force the media back. Silently, Lily drew even with Easton, then took his wrist in her fingers. He gaped at her in a flash of surprise and tried to pull away, but she held fast and pressed the thumb drive she'd found in Rose's car four nights ago into his palm.

After she'd left Rose with Maya in the snow, she'd gone back to where Rose had told Maya she'd parked and found her car along the side of the road at the south end of the park. The interior lights were still on. The keys were on the dashboard. The driver's seat had been flung back on its track.

Lily had climbed inside and put her hands on the steering wheel, feeling the grooves where her sister most often held it when she drove. In that moment, hope had filled her that Rose looked for signs of Lily, too. Maybe she'd saved a photograph of the two of them or written her a letter, even on a postcard.

Nearly rabid with desperation, Lily had searched every inch of Rose's car. The only interesting thing she'd found was a thumb drive stuck between the driver's seat and the console, wedged beneath the column where the seatbelt connected to the floor. All the way home that night, she'd held out hope that Rose had been secretly writing to her or about her or even journaling, and that she'd saved it on the thumb drive.

The next morning, she'd paid a hacker kid she knew from the Boys and Girls Club to find a way past the password. He'd figured it out, but the contents were nonsense. She'd only learned what was on it when Rose had told her in the moments before she died.

Lily had been so disappointed.

She flicked her eyes at Easton. 'My sister took this from you.'

'What do you want for it?' he whispered in her ear.

'Your lawyer.'

A look passed between them, sharp and cold, two edges of a blade.

'How do I know there aren't copies?' he asked.

'You don't,' she replied. Of course she'd made a copy.

From the road, the officers called out for them. Easton held her gaze a second longer, then pocketed the thumb drive and started up the hill. Lily lingered, falling far enough behind to watch Easton secured in the back of Hunter's car while she considered what to do with him. Lily had seen men like Easton Grimes before, watched them slide through loopholes in the justice system like water through a crack. When it came time to sit for her interview with the detectives, she could repeat what Rose had told her about him, but who was going to believe that Rose was a killer and honest in one fell swoop?

She allowed herself to be helped into the second car. Then they shut her door, turned away, and ambled back down the driveway, leaving her alone.

A flash of movement near the bottom of the driveway caught her eye. The paramedics were returning from the woods carrying the backboard between them. An officer hurried alongside, one arm raised, his hand suspending a bag of fluids for an IV.

Lily pressed her face and both hands against her window, not daring to hope.

But what if . . . *what if*?

Her heart swelled with a sudden storm, thunder and lightning, rage and awe, fire and rain.

Her sister wasn't as clever as she'd liked to have believed, but she was a survivor. Rose could beat anything. Could she have beaten death itself to come back to her?

Lily's breaths fogged the glass. She wiped furiously at the vapor, creating a clearer space on the window. Someone was on the backboard, a mound of life beneath a pile of blankets.

Rose.

She leaped for the door and yanked on the handle, but it didn't open. She'd been locked in.

Helpless, Lily pressed both palms to the glass and stared hard at the survivor being led from the woods. The backboard passed in front of headlights. At the top, Daniel's tan coat was spread, sleeves spread wide like open arms, his hope for Maya an armor made of wool.

SIXTY-FOUR

Daniel – February 12, 2018

D aniel's limbs ached as he changed positions again in the bare-bones hospital chair. There weren't many ways to sit, and he was pretty sure he'd tried all of them in the countless hours since Maya had been fully resuscitated and admitted into the ICU. But he wouldn't trade it. Not for food or a bed or to be with Hunter interviewing Lily and Easton.

This was where he wanted to be – in the corner of Maya's room, keeping watch. She was a child, and should she wake up, she should not have to open her eyes to an empty room.

He'd fallen asleep a handful of times, but when his mind courted silence, all he could hear was the short, guttural noise that had come from the deepest place inside his brother as the coroner loaded Rose's lifeless body into their van.

His phone buzzed at his hip, and Hunter's name flashed on the screen. Daniel eased himself out of the chair to keep it from squeaking, then moved on soft feet to the hallway.

'How's it going?' Daniel asked, keeping his voice low.

Hunter let out a hard, long breath before answering. 'Neither Easton nor Lily is changing their stories, and for two people that

have allegedly never met, their versions of events line up pretty
damn well. With the laundering investigation at stake, we can't
risk showing our hand just yet. Easton's attorney just walked
them both out of here. Get this – he's representing Lily now, at
Easton's request.'

'Why would he do that?'

'No idea. Seemed like it was a surprise to Lily, too.'

For a few seconds, neither one of them spoke, thoughts filling
the quiet space between them, and Daniel was acutely aware that
this moment was a first.

'I'm sorry about Rose,' Daniel finally said. 'No matter what
she did or didn't do, I know she meant something to you. I wish
it hadn't gone that way.'

'Yeah.' The little word was thick with emotion.

'How are you holding up?' Daniel asked.

'I don't know. None of this makes sense. I know Rose. I *know*
her. But everything we found in that cabin is pointing straight
to her. I can't pretend I don't see that.'

Daniel carefully considered how to answer. 'Evidence isn't
always black and white. You told me once that this job is gray.
Evidence can be gray, too.'

'It's not just what we found at the cabin. Lily's got Rose on
her security video. Rose broke into her apartment, packed a bag,
and stole a bunch of money. Then she freaks out and just bolts.
It was weird.'

'We can do a follow-up at Lily's in a day or two. Look around.'

'Yeah. I'll show you the video when you get back. Maybe
you'll see something I don't. How's Maya?'

Daniel leaned to peer through Maya's door, where she slept
under several blankets. An IV bag with warm fluids hung from
a pole, and a fan blew constant warm air across her.

'No change. She's been on seizure meds, which gave her a
fighting chance against the opioid overdose, but the MRI was
positive for signs of a stroke.'

'Jesus.' In the background, Daniel could hear Hunter light a
cigarette and pull a drag. A second spell of quiet was cast between
them, but this one drew Daniel's deepest fears to the surface.

'Did I make this better or worse?' Daniel asked quietly.

'What do you mean?'

'What if I'd never pushed? What if I'd let it go, focused on the drug-house shoot-out with you? This could've all gone so differently . . . for everyone.'

'I don't know that it would've gone differently, Danny. I just think no one would've known it had happened. Call me if there's any change.'

'Will do.' Daniel hung up, returned his phone to the clip on his belt, and leaned against the wall. With every passing second, he felt less sure than he had the moment before, like he was being buried alive under layer upon layer of the unknown.

Down the hall, the doors to the ICU swung open. A man and woman stepped through, escorted by Dr Cathy. Their tension was palpable even from the ten yards separating them.

Daniel straightened and moved to the side of Maya's door. From the new angle, a boy became visible trailing behind them, one hand clutching the woman's hand and the other hugging a floppy-eared rabbit to his front. The boy glanced up and met Daniel's gaze. Maya's amber eyes were staring right at him.

The rest of the world dropped away. This little boy was the one thing Maya had left in the world that no one should've been able to take from her. Wonder and fury fought for space in Daniel's chest. He took a step to the right, filling the doorway.

'This is the detective I was telling you about,' Dr Cathy said, smiling warmly. 'Detective Wilder, this is Maya's brother, Tyler.'

'I'm glad he's here. She will be, too,' Daniel said, trying and failing to keep his tone neutral. 'These two will need to wait out here with me.' He gestured to the man and woman. 'They've made it formally known that they are not her family, and I have questions for them, anyway,' Daniel said, but it was Hunter's voice and his *I-dare-you* implication coming out of his mouth.

Dr Cathy's expression was a question mark. 'Do I need to remind you that you are also not family, yet we've let you set up camp in her room?'

'Please don't defend us. He's not wrong,' the woman inter-jected. She glanced at the man with her and moved closer to him. 'It's probably for the best if we don't go in there. If Lily finds out that we all went to see Maya . . . with the adoption hearing next week . . . I don't know. Maybe this was a mistake.'

Daniel's blood ran cold. 'What do you mean, "if Lily finds out"?'

Discomfort passed over her like a shiver, then she blinked rapidly and turned her attention to Dr Cathy. 'Would you take Tyler to see his sister?'

Dr Cathy nodded, took the boy by the hand, and walked him in.

Daniel's mind and heart picked different directions. His mind was now fixated on this woman and why Lily's name was in her mouth. But his heart wished he could watch Tyler touch Maya and listen in on whatever the little boy had to say to his big sister. He would give anything to be able to relay every moment, every detail to her when she at last woke up.

'I'm Gretchen,' she started. 'This is my husband, Steve. We're Tyler's foster parents, but I guess you already knew that.' Gretchen's eyelids fluttered, and she swallowed hard. 'Dr Cathy said you're a big reason Maya's still alive. I want to personally thank you for that.'

'What happened with Lily?' Daniel asked point-blank.

Her entire being sank where she stood, and she looked at her husband again. 'I can't do this.'

Steve grabbed Gretchen's hand and held it, then he began talking. 'When we accepted Tyler as a foster placement, we all fell in love with each other pretty much right away. Lily could tell. She had concerns. She told us that she'd had to move him several times because he had an older sister who was dangerous, who had the potential to hurt him, who had hurt him before. She said she couldn't let him stay with us if we let them see each other, that we had to promise to keep her out of his life, or she wouldn't be able to recommend adoption. If we agreed, she promised to write a letter of recommendation for us but said she'd bring it to the hearing herself,' Steve explained.

'I know how selfish it is to keep them apart,' Gretchen blurted out, her voice breaking. 'But I couldn't lose him. He's my *son*. And we thought we were doing the right thing. Then Maya came to Bright View. I don't work on her floor, but I heard the nurses talking about her – about how she was funny and smart, about how much she loved her brother, about how hard it was to see someone so young be so *sad*.'

Daniel hung his head, remembering how he'd left Maya weeping and alone in her room. He was in no place to judge these people. 'That sounds like the Maya I've been getting to know,' he murmured.

'I kept wanting to go by and see her, but I talked myself out of it every time. Then yesterday, Maya's social worker Rachel called us and told us what had happened, that she might not wake up, and asked if we wanted to bring Tyler by to see her, just in case. We'd never communicated directly with her before, only through Lily. Rachel seemed surprised when we brought up our concerns about Maya. I realized that it didn't matter who she was. She's a *child*, a *sister*, and if I denied Tyler a last chance to see her, I didn't deserve to be his mother, no matter how bad I want to be.'

By the time Gretchen was finished talking, what had remained of Daniel's certainty lay in ruin. What Lily had demanded of these people couldn't possibly be legal and was, at the very least, completely at odds with who he thought she was. In talking about Lily and Maya, it was as if these people were describing strangers.

Daniel's mind returned to the dark woods where all three of them had been together for the last time. When Maya needed Lily most, she hadn't tried to save her. She hadn't even seemed interested in trying. Her face flashed before his eyes – the expression she'd given him when he'd asked her to get Narcan. Her features had been obscured by shadows, but confusion was plain to be seen there, even in the black of night. She'd had no idea what he was talking about.

The pieces to everything he thought he'd known flipped unequivocally on their heads and fit back together, painting a horrible picture. The floor tilted beneath his feet. He grabbed his phone, heart pounding, when Dr Cathy rushed out of Maya's room.

'I need to make a call. I'll be right back,' Daniel managed to spit out.

'Wait, Detective,' Dr Cathy called after him. 'Maya's awake.'

Daniel turned around, pressing his palm against his pounding heart, disbelief coursing through his veins.

Dr Cathy met his gaze. 'She's asking for you.'

SIXTY-FIVE

Daniel – February 13, 2018

D aniel reached the intersection adjacent to Lily's apartment and pulled around to the back of the building. It was early, barely sunrise. Hopefully, they would catch her unaware.

Hunter pulled his car close to Daniel's back bumper, and a line of squad cars and two SWAT vans moved around them, making a proverbial net on both sides of the corner in case Lily tried to run.

'How do you want to proceed, Wilder?' Hunter's voice came through the speaker on his hand-held radio.

Daniel glanced in his rearview mirror and took stock of his brother's face. Hunter met his gaze and nodded. Beside him, the unit leader brought his radio to his mouth, ready to relay any decisions or information to his team.

'I'll go up alone, but I'll keep my receiver engaged so you can hear if I run into trouble. Otherwise, let me talk her out of the house and secure her in a vehicle. Then we'll proceed with the search,' Daniel said.

'Copy that,' Hunter replied.

Daniel exited his car and crossed the alley. The windows to Lily's unit were visible. The lights inside were on. One window was propped wide open. Floral-print curtains danced on the exterior brick in time to the faint music whispering through the gap. As Daniel entered the stairwell, the voice faded, and the pregnant quiet chased him from landing to landing.

Daniel reached her door and knocked. 'Lily, it's Daniel.'

No one answered.

He knocked again. 'Lily, I need to ask you a couple questions about Rose.'

When she didn't answer, he tested the handle and found it

unlocked. He pressed an ear against the wood, straining for sound. Nothing stirred on the other side.

'Lily, I need to come in and check on you, OK. Your door is unlocked. I'm opening it now.'

Only silence answered.

Daniel unholstered his gun, turned the handle, and eased the door open with his shoulder. Before entering, he evaluated what he could see. The main area of the apartment was empty, and the singing he'd heard earlier had stopped. He leaned for a better view around the closer corner, where a short hall led to a closed door. Behind it, someone was whispering.

'Lily!' he called, louder this time, and nearly started toward the sound, when he realized he was in the same position Rose had been in when she'd gotten spooked on the security video.

Daniel swung around. On the wall to the left of the door, pictures hung in simple wood frames arranged in a checkerboard. The pictures closest to him looked like a tornado of white and brown lines. His gaze moved to the top-left corner, where he discerned an outline of a girl curled up in a ball. Familiarity washed over him; her position was a replica of how they'd found Christian. And the shaky brown line at her back was the trunk of a tree.

He stepped closer, horrified and transfixed, then shifted to the next picture to the right. The outline was more filled in. The girls' arms had slipped down, the backs of her wrists dangling in mud, flesh curled back and peeling from her forearms as she began to rot. One hand moved to his mouth and the other to his gun as his stare traveled the grid left to right, top to bottom, where frame by frame, the girl in the snow decayed to bone at the base of a tree.

The whispers at the back of the apartment grew louder.

Daniel bolted down the hall and shoved himself through the door, expecting resistance but finding none. The bed was made, the floor swept. The voices were coming from a CD player that was plugged into the wall, track eight flashing on the front. Their hushed conversation was so quiet, Daniel could hardly discern words. He could tell one voice belonged to Lily, but the other, a boy, was unfamiliar.

A vase of rose stems sat on the sill of the open window. All the blooms were cut off. A piece of paper was trapped beneath the vase, and a small silver gift box was tucked into the corner of the window frame.

Daniel lifted the piece of paper first. It was a numbered list of twenty-two names with dates beside them, beginning a decade before and moving forward to early this year. A name near the bottom of the list caught his eye: Natasha Edgewood – the nineteenth name, which belonged to the only confirmed identity of the nineteen bodies in the woods off New Hope Loop, a name Rose had tried to give him, and a name yet to be publicly released. The paper shook in his hands. He now knew how Natasha had died, but he would make it his life's work to figure out why Rose had told him to ask Easton about her. He owed Rose that and so much more.

Christian, Maya, and Rose were the last three names on the list. The date beside Maya's name had been erased. He touched the place, felt the indentation, and imagined Maya buried and forgotten under the ground instead of sleeping in Gretchen and Steve's home. As the meaning of the list became crystal clear, his stomach became an empty pit, his throat squeezing too tight to swallow.

A long pause in the whispering drew his ear. He snatched a glimpse of the CD player, confirming that the eighth track was still playing, then reached for the box. It was tied shut with a white ribbon and was tagged with a label: *To Hunter, From Rose.* Inside was a red thumb drive. Before he could radio his brother, Lily's voice filled the room.

'Can you sing for me now?' she asked.

Daniel whipped round, but he was still alone.

'I can't remember the words, Miss Lily. I . . . I don't feel good. I'm sorry.'

'It's OK, Adam. Here, drink a little more. You'll feel better soon.'

The voices fell silent, and Daniel's blood ran cold, goosebumps rising all over his skin.

'There,' Lily started again. 'Are you ready now? I'll sing with you if it'll help.'

'Then you'll take me to the bus station?'

'Just sing with me, Adam. Then we'll figure out the rest.'

'OK,' he said through chattering teeth.

Daniel's focus leaped from the CD player to the eighth name on the list: Adam Crawley. It wasn't just a record of bodies. It was so much worse. Lily had recorded every child buried in those woods, and she'd made herself a playlist.

She'd played him the whole time, too. Every minute, every word, every interaction had been a chance to see who she was and what she was doing, and he'd missed it.

Daniel didn't know he was crying until he started tasting the salt from his own tears.

'Danny? What's going on? Are you OK?' Hunter's voice crackled on the radio.

Before he could respond, Adam and Lily began to sing.

'This is all my fault,' Daniel whispered, dizziness and guilt claiming him the way waves claim a beach.

'Stay right there,' Hunter said. 'I'm coming.'

SIXTY-SIX

Lily – February 27, 2018

Lily sat in her new car, parked along the curb in the angular shade of a palm tree. Easton's new rental house was a modest beachfront bungalow three doors down. Through the hedges lining his tiny front yard, Lily could see his front door well enough to tell when it opened. She could also see the water bottles from his running belt on the windowsill he consistently left to air-dry after his nightly runs. A lesser person might steal them. But she was generous. She'd left something inside.

She glanced in her rearview mirror. Her hair was now a pallet of silvers and grays, chopped into a pixie cut suited for a movie star. With the additions of red lipstick, designer sunglasses, and tight clothing, she barely recognized her own reflection. Considering her real face was all over the news, she could only hope no one else would, either. She would never be able to return to Tula. People wouldn't forget about her the way they'd forgotten to keep looking for Josh Marsden, slow and quiet, little by little.

Over the last year, most people had forgotten to keep looking for Natasha, too. But not Lily. Last January, she'd spotted her sitting at the bus stop near Sirens, taking shelter from a scant flurry of snow. She was shivering, legs bare except for knee-high boots, not even wearing a coat. In the car, Natasha had given her a sob story about how scared she was to keep working there, how they wanted to send her to Florida to keep a wealthy man warm through the winter, how she'd loved to sing until she learned she'd been picked for the job in part by her voice, how she was desperate for a way out of the life she'd made for herself.

Lily was nothing if not helpful.

She'd caught so much flak from Lartesha over the years for being behind on paperwork, when in reality she was way ahead. Never go to bed with work undone, and always make two copies of everything – those were her rules. She just didn't file hers where everyone else did. She imagined Easton knew something about the benefit to that, too.

He was someone they'd never stop looking for. Not with the copy of his thumb drive that she'd left as a parting gift from Rose for Detective Kepp, anyway, including a sweet little note explaining what it all meant. He and Detective Wilder would have no choice but to prioritize verifying the identities of the bodies against the list she'd left and to decode the information on Easton's thumb drive, which should keep them plenty busy while she took care of one last thing.

It had been easier to procure a solid fake ID and buy black-market fentanyl than it was to find an affordable rental in the coastal southern Georgia town with a landlord who was willing to take a lump-sum cash payment and not ask too many questions. But now she had all three.

Easton's door opened, and he emerged to collect his water bottles, then retreated inside, leaving the door ajar. Last night, Lily had lain awake in her new bed, listening to the ocean whisper its secrets to the sand, and thought about her sister – her choices, her lies. Even though Lily finally had answers, none of them made sense. She always thought she'd be healed by the truth, that the hole within her would at last stitch shut enough to scar.

But now there was no hole; it had become something bigger – an emptiness that knew no edges, no bottom.

Rose's death had effectively handed Lily a life sentence. Her sister had left her with no choice but to live as she had, trading town for town, name for name, face for face, with nothing real to call her own. At last, Lily knew her real name, and she would never be able to use it.

Easton came back out, shut the door behind him, then jogged down the length of hedges and into the road, those bright yellow water bottles hooked to his back. For the first time in weeks, Lily smiled. The man carried water for every run, but she'd yet to see him drink a drop before the last half mile home, when he routinely slowed his pace to cool down.

In the four days since she had started watching him, Easton's evening runs were the one thing about his daily pattern that rarely changed. He crisscrossed through neighborhoods of beach bungalows, then picked up his pace down a rolling two-lane road until he reached the entrance to a fishing pier. From there, he ran home on the beach, following the border where the water lapped the sand.

The first time she'd watched him, she'd wondered if he was doing it on purpose, his footprints filling in within minutes of his passing.

Disappearing.

You're playing my sister's game, Easton Grimes, she'd thought. *Of all people, why did she come back to Tula and stay for you when in twenty-five years she never stayed for me?*

She parked and climbed out. Cloaked in twilight, she picked her way down the dunes, tucked herself in a spot among the tall, dead grass, and waited. Some piece of her had hoped that after Rose died, her ghost might haunt her, lurk in the shadows, sit down next to her here and now. But even in death, Rose had let her down. The question about Easton followed her, though, nestling beside her in the chilly sand. She stared at the empty space and glared, but she couldn't scare it away.

Easton ran by, and Lily let him pass. Then she strode after him, putting her feet where his shoes had left marks.

As she walked, she imagined how he would slow down, start to stagger. How she would catch up to him, and he would stare

at her once they were face to face, trying to place her. How his
confusion would be made worse by how uncomfortably warm
he felt despite his guzzling water. At some point, he'd drop to
his knees and reach a hand up for her. Of course, she'd crouch
down with him to show him he wasn't alone. She would bear
witness in those final moments when even the worst people are
tempted to confess their sins, but foam would fill his mouth,
making it too difficult to speak. *It's OK. Rose already told me,*
she would say.

A cold wind came off the water, and the moon slid from behind
a cloud, illuminating the beach. She shivered and pulled her pink
coat tight. Bathed in silver light, the sand turned white as snow.